Darkness Comes

He turned, looked up at the wall above the door. Two radiant silver eyes glared at him from the duct opening. That was all he could see of the creatures. Eyes without any division between whites and irises and pupils. Eyes that shimmered and flickered as if they were composed of fire. Eyes without any trace of mercy . . .

The ravenous intruders swarmed up his chest, up his back and on to his shoulders, all of them the size of rats but not rats, all of them clawing and biting. They were all over him, pulling him down. He went to his knees. He let go of the beast he was holding, and he pounded at the others with his fists. One of them bit off part of his ear. Wickedly pointed little teeth sank into his chin. Then the darkness grew deeper and an eternal silence settled over him.

Darkness Comes

Dean R. Koontz

A STAR BOOK
published by
the Paperback Division of
W. H. ALLEN & Co. PLC

A Star Book
Published in 1984
by the Paperback Division of
W. H. Allen & Co. PLC
44 Hill Street, London W1X 8LB

First published in Great Britain
by W. H. Allen & Co. PLC, 1984

Printed and bound in Great Britain by
Anchor Brendon Ltd, Tiptree, Essex

ISBN 0 352 31479 6

Because the original door prize was
too hard to accomplish, this book is
dedicated to some good neighbours –
Oliviero and Becky Migneco,
Jeff and Bonnie Paymar
– with the sincere hope that a mere
dedication is an acceptable substitute.

(At least, this way, there's much less
chance of a law suit!)

I owe special thanks to Mr Owen West
for giving me the opportunity to publish
this variation on a theme under my by-line.

PROLOGUE

Penny Dawson woke and heard something moving furtively in the dark bedroom.

At first she thought she was hearing a sound left over from her dream. She had been dreaming about horses and about going for long rides in the country, and it had been the most wonderful, special, thrilling dream she'd ever had in all of her eleven and a half dream-filled years. When she began to wake up, she struggled against consciousness, tried to hold on to sleep and prevent the lovely fantasy from fading. But she heard an odd sound, and it scared her. She told herself it was only a horse sound or just the rustle of straw in the stable in her dream. Nothing to be alarmed about. But she couldn't convince herself; she couldn't tie the strange sound to her dream, and she woke up all the way.

The peculiar noise was coming from the other side of the room, from Davey's bed. But it wasn't ordinary, middle-of-the-night, seven-year-old-boy, pizza-and-ice-cream-for-dinner noise. It was a sneaky sound. Definitely sneaky.

What was he doing? What trick was he planning this time?

Penny sat up in bed. She squinted into the impenetrable shadows, saw nothing, cocked her head, and listened intently.

A rustling, sighing sound disturbed the stillness.

Then silence.

She held her breath and listened even harder.

Hissing. Then a vague, shuffling, scraping noise.

The room was virtually pitch-black. There was one window, and it was beside her bed; however, the drape was drawn shut, and the alleyway outside was especially dark tonight, so the window provided no relief from the gloom.

The door was ajar. They always slept with it open a couple of inches, so Daddy could hear them more easily if they called for him in the night. But there were no lights on in the rest of the apartment, and no light came through the partly open door.

Penny spoke softly: 'Davey?'

He didn't answer.

'Davey, is that you?'

Rustle-rustle-rustle.

'Davey, stop it.'

No response.

Seven-year-old boys were a trial sometimes. A truly monumental pain.

She said, 'If you're playing some stupid game, you're going to be real sorry.'

A dry sound. Like an old, withered leaf crunching crisply under someone's foot.

It was nearer now than it had been.

'Davey, don't be weird.'

Nearer. Something was coming across the room toward the bed.

It wasn't Davey. He was a giggler; he would have broken up by now and would have given himself away.

Penny's heart began to hammer, and she thought: Maybe this is just another dream, like the horses, only a bad one this time.

But she knew she was wide awake.

Her eyes watered with the effort she was making to peer through the darkness. She reached for the switch

8

on the cone-shaped reading lamp that was fixed to the headboard of her bed. For a terribly long while, she couldn't find it. She fumbled desperately in the dark.

The stealthy sounds now issued from the blackness beside her bed. The thing had reached her.

Suddenly her groping fingers found the metal lampshade, then the switch. A cone of light fell across the bed and onto the floor.

Nothing frightening was crouched nearby. The reading lamp didn't cast enough light to dispel all the shadows, but Penny could see there wasn't anything dangerous, menacing, or even the least bit out of place.

Davey was in his bed, on the other side of the room, tangled in his covers, sleeping beneath large posters of Chewbacca the Wookie, from *Star Wars*, and E.T.

Penny didn't hear the strange noise any more. She knew she hadn't been imagining it, and she wasn't the kind of girl who could just turn off the lights and pull the covers over her head and forget about the whole thing. Daddy said she had enough curiosity to kill about a thousand cats. She threw back the covers, got out of bed, stood very still in her pyjamas and bare feet, listening.

Not a sound.

Finally she went over to Davey and looked at him more closely. Her bedside light didn't reach this far; he lay mostly in shadows, but he seemed to be sound asleep. She leaned real close, watching his eyelids, and at last she decided he wasn't faking it.

The noise began again. Behind her.

She whirled around.

It was under the bed now. A hissing, scraping, softly rattling sound, not particularly loud, but no longer stealthy, either.

The thing under the bed knew she was aware of it. It was making noise on purpose, teasing her, trying to scare her.

No! she thought. That's silly.

9

Besides, it wasn't a *thing*, wasn't a boogeyman. She was too old for boogeymen. That was more Davey's speed.

This was just a . . . a mouse. Yes! That was it. Just a mouse, more scared than she was.

She felt somewhat relieved. She didn't like mice, didn't want them under her bed, for sure, but at least there was nothing *too* frightening about a lowly mouse. It was grody, creepy, but it wasn't big enough to bite her head off or anything major like that.

She stood with her small hands fisted at her sides, trying to decide what to do next.

She looked up at Scott Baio, who smiled down at her from a poster that hung on the wall behind her bed, and she wished he were here to take charge of the situation. Scott Baio wouldn't be scared of a mouse; not in a million years. Scott Baio would crawl right under the bed and grab that miserable rodent by its tail and carry it outside and release it, unharmed, in the alley behind the apartment building, because Scott Baio wasn't just brave – he was good and sensitive and gentle, too.

But Scott wasn't here. He was out there in Hollywood, making his TV show.

Which left Daddy.

Penny didn't want to wake her father until she was absolutely, positively, one hundred per cent sure there actually was a mouse. If Daddy came looking for a mouse and turned the room upside-down and then didn't find one, he'd treat her as if she were a *child*, for God's sake. She was only two months short of her twelfth birthday, and there was nothing she loathed more than being treated like a child.

She couldn't see under the bed because it was very dark under there and because the covers had fallen over the side; they were hanging almost to the floor, blocking the view.

The thing under the bed – the *mouse* under the bed! – hissed and made a gurgling-scraping noise. It was almost like a voice. A raspy, cold, nasty little voice that was telling her something in a foreign language.

Could a mouse make a sound like that?

She glanced at Davey. He was still sleeping.

A plastic baseball bat leaned against the wall beside her brother's bed. She grabbed it by the handle.

Under her own bed, the peculiar, unpleasant hissing-scratching-scrabbling continued.

She took a few steps toward her bed and got down on the floor, on her hands and knees. Holding the plastic bat in her right hand, she extended it, pushed the other end under the drooping blankets, lifted them out of the way, and pushed them back onto the bed where they belonged.

She still couldn't see anything under there. That low space was cave-black.

The noises had stopped.

Penny had the spooky feeling that something was peering at her from those oily black shadows . . . something more than just a mouse . . . worse than just a mouse . . . something that knew she was only a weak little girl, something smart, not just a dumb animal, something at least as smart as she was, something that knew it could rush out and gobble her up alive if it really wanted to.

Cripes. No. Kid stuff. Silliness.

Biting her lip, determined not to behave like a helpless child, she thrust the fat end of the baseball bat under the bed. She probed with it, trying to make the mouse squeal or run out into the open.

The other end of the plastic club was suddenly seized, held. Penny tried to pull it loose. She couldn't. She jerked and twisted it. But the bat was held fast.

Then it was torn out of her grip. The bat vanished under the bed with a thump and a rattle.

Penny exploded backwards across the floor – until she bumped into Davey's bed. She didn't even remember moving. One instant she was on her hands and knees beside her own bed; the next instant she banged her head against the side of Davey's mattress.

Her little brother groaned, snorted, blew out a wet breath, and went right on sleeping.

Nothing moved under Penny's bed.

She was ready to scream for her father now, ready to risk being treated like a child, more than ready, and she did scream, but the word reverberated only in her mind: *Daddy, Daddy, Daddy!* No sound issued from her mouth. She had been stricken temporarily dumb.

The light flickered. The cord trailed down to an electrical outlet in the wall behind the bed. The thing under the bed was trying to unplug the lamp.

'*Daddy!*'

She made some noise this time, though not much; the word came out as a hoarse whisper.

And the lamp winked off.

In the lightless room she heard movement. Something came out from under the bed and started across the floor.

'*Daddy!*'

She could still only manage a whisper. She swallowed, found it difficult, swallowed again, trying to regain control of her half-paralysed throat.

A creaking sound.

Peering into the blackness, Penny shuddered, whimpered.

Then she realized it was a familiar creaking sound. The door to their bedroom. The hinges needed oiling.

In the gloom, she detected the door swinging open, sensed more than saw it: a slab of darkness moving through more darkness. It had been ajar. Now, almost certainly, it was standing wide open. The hinges stopped creaking.

The eerie rasping-hissing sound moved steadily away from her. The thing wasn't going to attack, after all. It was going away.

Now it was in the doorway, at the threshold.

Now it was in the hall.

Now at least ten feet from the door.

Now . . . gone.

Seconds ticked by, slow as minutes.

What had it been?

Not a mouse. Not a dream.

Then what?

Eventually, Penny got up. Her legs were rubbery.

She groped blindly, located the lamp on Davey's headboard. The switch clicked, and light poured over the sleeping boy. She quickly turned the cone-shaped shade away from him.

She went to the door, stood on the threshold, listened to the rest of the apartment. Silence. Still shaky, she closed the door. The latch clicked softly.

Her palms were damp. She blotted them on her pyjamas.

Now that sufficient light fell on her bed, she returned and looked beneath it. Nothing threatening crouched under there.

She retrieved the plastic baseball bat, which was hollow, very lightweight, meant to be used with a plastic Whiffle Ball. The fat end, seized when she'd shoved it under the bed, was dented in three places where it had been gripped and squeezed. Two of the dents were centred around small holes. The plastic had been punctured. But . . . by what? Claws?

Penny squirmed under the bed far enough to plug in her lamp. Then she crossed the room and switched off Davey's lamp.

Sitting on the edge of her own bed, she looked at the closed hall door for a while and finally said, 'Well.'

What had it been?

The longer she thought about it, the less real the encounter seemed. Maybe the baseball bat had merely been caught in the bed's frame somehow; maybe the holes in it had been made by bolts or screws protruding

13

from the frame. Maybe the hall door had been opened by nothing more sinister than a draught.

Maybe . . .

At last, itchy with curiosity, she got up, went into the hall, snapped on the light, saw that she was alone, and carefully closed the bedroom door behind her.

Silence.

The door to her father's room was ajar, as usual. She stood beside it, ear to the crack, listening. He was snoring. She couldn't hear anything else in there, no strange rustling noises.

Again, she considered waking Daddy. He was a police detective. Lieutenant Jack Dawson. He had a gun. If something *was* in the apartment, he could blast it to smithereens. On the other hand, if she woke him and then if they found nothing, he would tease her and speak to her as if she were a child, Jeez, even worse than that, as if she were an *infant*. She hesitated, then sighed. No. It just wasn't worth the risk of being humiliated.

Heart pounding, she crept along the hall to the front door and tried it. It was still securely locked.

A coat rack was fixed to the wall beside the door. She took a tightly rolled umbrella from one of the hooks. The metal tip was pointed enough to serve as a reasonably good weapon.

With the umbrella thrust out in front of her, she went into the living room, turned on all the lights, looked everywhere. She searched the dining alcove and the small L-shaped kitchen, as well.

Nothing.

Except the window.

Above the sink, the kitchen window was open. Cold December air streamed through the ten-inch gap.

Penny was sure it hadn't been open when she'd gone to bed. And if Daddy had opened it to get a breath of fresh air, he'd have closed it later; he was conscientious about such things because he was always setting an

14

example for Davey, who needed an example because he wasn't conscientious about much of anything.

She carried the kitchen stool to the sink, climbed onto it, and pushed the window up farther, far enough to lean out and take a look. She winced as the cold air stung her face and sent icy fingers down the neck of her pyjamas. There was very little light. Four storeys beneath her, the alleyway was blacker than black at its darkest, ash-grey at its brightest. The only sound was the soughing of the wind in the concrete canyon. It blew a few twisted scraps of paper along the pavement below and made Penny's brown hair flap like a banner; it tore the frosty plumes of her breath into gossamer rags. Otherwise, nothing moved.

Farther along the building, near the bedroom window, an iron fire escape led down to the alley. But here at the kitchen, there was no fire escape, no ledge, no way that a would-be burglar could have reached the window, no place for him to stand or hold on while he pried his way inside.

Anyway, it hadn't been a burglar. Burglars weren't small enough to hide under a young lady's bed.

She closed the window and put the stool back where she'd got it from. She returned the umbrella to the coat rack in the hall, although she was somewhat reluctant to give up the weapon. Switching off the lights as she went, refusing to glance behind into the darkness that she left in her wake, she returned to her room and got back into bed and pulled up the covers.

Davey was still sleeping soundly.

Night wind pressed at the window.

Far off, across the city, an ambulance or police siren made a mournful song.

For a while, Penny sat up in bed, leaning against the pillows, the reading lamp casting a protective circle of light around her. She was sleepy, and she wanted to sleep, but she was afraid to turn out the light. Her fear made her angry. Wasn't she almost twelve years old?

And wasn't twelve too old to fear the dark? Wasn't she the woman of the house now, and hadn't she *been* the woman of the house for more than a year and a half, ever since her mother had died. After about ten minutes, she managed to shame herself into switching off the lamp and lying down.

She couldn't switch her mind off as easily.

What had it been?

Nothing. A remnant of a dream. Or a vagrant draught. Just that and nothing more.

Darkness.

She listened.

Silence.

She waited.

Nothing.

She slept.

WEDNESDAY, 1:34 A.M.

Vince Vastagliano was halfway down the stairs when he heard a shout, then a hoarse scream. It wasn't shrill. It wasn't a piercing scream. It was a startled, guttural cry that he might not even have heard if he'd been upstairs; nevertheless, it managed to convey stark terror. Vince paused with one hand on the stair railing, standing very still, head cocked, listening intently, heart suddenly hammering, momentarily frozen by indecision.

Another scream.

Ross Morrant, Vince's bodyguard, was in the kitchen, making a late-night snack for both of them, and it was Morrant who had screamed. No mistaking the voice.

There were sounds of struggle, too. A crash and clatter

as something was knocked over. A hard thump. The brittle, unmelodic music of breaking glass.

Ross Morrant's breathless, fear-twisted voice echoed along the downstairs hallway from the kitchen, and between grunts and gasps and unnerving squeals of pain, there were words: 'No . . . no . . . please . . . Jesus, no . . . help . . . someone help me . . . oh, my God, my God, please . . . *no!*'

Sweat broke out on Vince's face.

Morrant was a big, strong, mean son of a bitch. As a kid he'd been an ardent street fighter. By the time he was eighteen, he was taking contracts, doing murder for hire, having fun and being paid for it. Over the years he gained a reputation for taking any job, regardless of how dangerous or difficult it was, regardless of how well protected the target was, and he always got his man. For the past fourteen months, he had been working for Vince as an enforcer, collector, and bodyguard; during that time, Vince had never seen him scared. He couldn't imagine Morrant being frightened of anyone or anything. And Morrant begging for mercy . . . well, that was simply inconceivable; even now, hearing the bodyguard whimper and plead, Vince *still* couldn't conceive of it; it just didn't seem real.

Something screeched. Not Morrant. It was an ungodly, inhuman sound. It was a sharp, penetrating eruption of rage and hatred and alien need that belonged in a science fiction movie, the hideous cry of some creature from another world.

Until this moment, Vince had assumed that Morrant was being beaten and tortured by other *people*, competitors in the drug business, who had come to waste Vince himself in order to increase their market share. But now, as he listened to the bizarre, ululating wail that came from the kitchen, Vince wondered if he had just stepped into the Twilight Zone. He felt cold all the way to his bones, queasy, disturbingly fragile, and alone.

He quickly descended two more steps and looked

along the hall toward the front door. The way was clear. He could probably leap down the last of the stairs, race along the hallway, unlock the front door, and get out of the house before the intruders came out of the kitchen and saw him. Probably. But he harboured a small measure of doubt, and because of that doubt he hesitated a couple of seconds too long.

In the kitchen Morrant shrieked more horribly than ever, a final cry of bleak despair and agony that was abruptly cut off.

Vince knew what Morrant's sudden silence meant. The bodyguard was dead.

Then the lights went out from one end of the house to the other. Apparently someone had thrown the master breaker switch in the fuse box, down in the basement.

Not daring to hesitate any longer, Vince started down the stairs in the dark, but he heard movement in the unlighted hallway, back toward the kitchen, coming this direction, and he halted again. He wasn't hearing anything as ordinary as approaching footsteps; instead, it was a strange, eerie hissing-rustling-rattling-grumbling that chilled him and made his skin crawl. He sensed that something monstrous, something with pale dead eyes and cold clammy hands was coming toward him. Such a fantastic notion was wildly out of character for Vince Vastagliano, who had the imagination of a tree stump, but he couldn't dispel the superstitious dread that had come over him.

Fear brought a watery looseness to his joints.

His heart, already beating fast, now thundered.

He would never make it to the front door alive.

He turned and clambered up the steps. He stumbled once in the blackness, almost fell, regained his balance. By the time he reached the master bedroom, the noises behind him were more savage, closer, louder – and hungrier.

Vague shafts of weak light came through the bedroom windows, errant beams from the streetlamps outside,

18

lightly frosting the 18th century Italian canopy bed and the other antiques, gleaming on the bevelled edges of the crystal paperweights that were displayed along the top of the writing desk that stood between the two windows. If Vince had turned and looked back, he would have been able to see at least the bare outline of his pursuer. But he didn't look. He was afraid to look.

He got a whiff of a foul odour. Sulphur? Not quite, but something like it.

On a deep, instinctual level, he knew what was coming after him. His conscious mind could not – or would not – put a name to it, but his subconscious knew what it was, and that was why he fled from it in blind panic, and wide-eyed and spooked as a dumb animal reacting to a bolt of lightning.

He hurried through the shadows to the master bath, which opened off the bedroom. In the cloying darkness he collided hard with the half-closed bathroom door. It crashed all the way open. Slightly stunned by the impact, he stumbled into the large bathroom, groped for the door, slammed and locked it behind him.

In that last moment of vulnerability, as the door swung shut, he had seen nightmarish, silvery eyes glowing in the darkness. Not just two eyes. A dozen of them. Maybe more.

Now, something struck the other side of the door. Struck it again. And again. There were several of them out there, not just one. The door shook, and the lock rattled, but it held.

The creatures in the bedroom screeched and hissed considerably louder than before. Although their icy cries were utterly alien, like nothing Vince had ever heard before, the meaning was clear; these were obviously bleats of anger and disappointment. The things pursuing him had been certain that he was within their grasp, and they had chosen not to take his escape in a spirit of good sportsmanship.

19

The *things*. Odd as it was, that was the best word for them, the only word: *things*.

He felt as if he were losing his mind, yet he could not deny the primitive perceptions and instinctive understanding that had raised his hackles. *Things*. Not attack dogs. Not any animal he'd ever seen or heard about. This was something out of a nightmare; only something from a nightmare could have reduced Ross Morrant to a defenceless, whimpering victim.

The creatures scratched at the other side of the door, gouged and scraped and splintered the wood. Judging from the sound, their claws were sharp. Damned sharp.

What the hell *were* they?

Vince was always prepared for violence because violence was an integral part of the world in which he moved. You couldn't expect to be a drug dealer and lead a life as quiet as that of a schoolteacher. But he had never anticipated an attack like this. A man with a gun – yes. A man with a knife – he could handle that, too. A bomb wired to the ignition of his car – that was certainly within the realm of possibility. But this was madness.

As the things outside tried to chew and claw and batter their way through the door, Vince fumbled in the darkness until he found the toilet. He put the lid down on the seat, sat there, and reached for the telephone. When he'd been twelve years old, he had seen, for the first time, the telephone in his uncle Gennaro Carramazza's bathroom, and from that moment it had seemed to him that having a phone in the can was the ultimate symbol of a man's importance, proof that he was indispensable and wealthy. As soon as he'd been old enough to get an apartment of his own, Vince had had a phone installed in every room, including the toilet, and he'd had one in every master bath in every apartment and house since then. In terms of self-esteem, the bathroom phone meant as much to him as his white Mercedes

Benz. Now, he was glad he had the phone right here because he could use it to call for help.

But there was no dial tone.

In the dark he rattled the disconnect lever, trying to command service.

The line had been cut.

The unknown things in the bedroom continued to scratch and pry and pound on the door.

Vince looked up at the only window. It was much too small to provide an escape route. The glass was opaque, admitting almost no light at all.

They won't be able to get through the door, he told himself desperately. They'll eventually get tired of trying, and they'll go away. Sure they will. Of course.

A metallic screech and clank startled him. The noise came from within the bathroom. From this side of the door.

He got up, stood with his hands fisted at his sides, tense, looking left and right into the deep gloom.

A metal object of some kind crashed to the tile floor, and Vince jumped and cried out in surprise.

The doorknob. Oh, Jesus. They had somehow dislodged the knob and the lock!

He threw himself at the door, determined to hold it shut, but he found it was still secure; the knob was still in place; the lock was firmly engaged. With shaking hands, he groped frantically in the darkness, searching for the hinges, but they were also in place and undamaged.

Then what had clattered to the floor?

Panting, he turned around, putting his back to the door, and he blinked at the featureless black room, trying to make sense of what he'd heard.

He sensed that he was no longer safely alone in the bathroom. A many-legged quiver of fear slithered up his back.

The grille that covered the outlet from the heating duct – *that* was what had fallen to the floor.

He turned, looked up at the wall above the door. Two radiant silver eyes glared at him from the duct opening. That was all he could see of the creature. Eyes without any division between whites and irises and pupils. Eyes that shimmered and flickered as if they were composed of fire. Eyes without any trace of mercy.

A rat?

No. A rat couldn't have dislodged the grille. Besides, rats had red eyes – didn't they?

It hissed at him.

'*No*,' Vince said softly.

There was nowhere to run.

The thing launched itself out of the wall, sailing down at him. It struck his face. Claws pierced his cheeks, sank all the way through, into his mouth, scraped and dug at his teeth and gums. The pain was instant and intense.

He gagged and nearly vomited in terror and revulsion, but he knew he would strangle on his own vomit, so he choked it down.

Fangs tore at his scalp.

He lumbered backward, flailing at the darkness. The edge of the sink slammed painfully into the small of his back, but it was nothing compared to the white-hot blaze of pain that consumed his face.

This couldn't be happening. But it was. He hadn't just stepped into the Twilight Zone; he had taken a giant leap into Hell.

His scream was muffled by the unnameable thing that clung to his head, and he couldn't get his breath. He grabbed hold of the beast. It was cold and greasy, like some denizen of the sea that had risen up from watery depths. He pried it off his face and held it at arm's length. It screeched and hissed and chattered word-lessly, wriggled and twisted, writhed and jerked, bit his hand, but he held on to it, afraid to let go, afraid that it would fly straight back at him and go for his throat or for his eyes this time.

What *was* it? Where did it come from?

22

Part of him wanted to see it, had to see it, needed to know what in God's name it was. But another part of him, sensing the extreme monstrousness of it, was grateful for darkness.

Something bit his left ankle.

Something else started climbing his right leg, ripping his trousers as it went.

Other creatures had come out of the wall duct. As blood ran down his forehead from his scalp wounds and clouded his vision, he realized that there were many pairs of silvery eyes in the room. Dozens of them.

This had to be a dream. A nightmare.

But this pain was real.

The ravenous intruders swarmed up his chest, up his back and onto his shoulders, all of them the size of rats but not rats, all of them clawing and biting. They were all over him, pulling him down. He went to his knees. He let go of the beast he was holding, and he pounded at the others with his fists.

One of them bit off part of his ear.

Wickedly pointed little teeth sank into his chin.

He heard himself mouthing the same pathetic pleas that he had heard from Ross Morrant. Then the darkness grew deeper and an eternal silence settled over him.

PART ONE

Holy men tell us life is a mystery.
They embrace that concept happily.
But some mysteries bite and bark
and come to get you in the dark.

—The Book of Counted Sorrows

CHAPTER ONE

1

The next morning, the first thing Rebecca said to Jack Dawson was, 'We have two stiffs.'

'Huh?'

'Two corpses.'

'I know what stiffs are,' he said.

'The call just came in.'

'Did you order two stiffs?'

'Be serious.'

'*I* didn't order two stiffs.'

'Uniforms are already on the scene,' she said.

'Our shift doesn't start for seven minutes.'

'You want me to say we won't be going out there because it was thoughtless of them to die this early in the morning?'

'Isn't there at least time for polite chit-chat?' he asked.

'No.'

'See, the way it should be . . . You're supposed to say, "Good morning, Detective Dawson." And then I say, "Good morning, Detective Chandler." Then you say, "How're you this morning?" And then I wink and say'—

She frowned. 'It's the same as the other two, Jack. Bloody and strange. Just like the one Sunday and the one yesterday. But this time it's *two* men. Both with crime family connections from the sound of it.'

Standing in the grubby police squad room, half out of

27

his heavy grey overcoat, a smile incompletely formed, Jack Dawson stared at her in disbelief. He wasn't surprised that there had been another murder or two. He was a homicide detective; there was *always* another murder. Or two. He wasn't even surprised that there was another *strange* murder; after all, this was New York City. What he couldn't believe was her attitude, the way she was treating him – this morning of all mornings.

'Better put your coat back on,' she said.

'Rebecca—'

'They're expecting us.'

'Rebecca, last night—'

'Another weird one,' she said, snatching up her purse from the top of a battered desk.

'Didn't we—'

'We've sure got a sick one on our hands this time,' she said, heading for the door. 'Really sick.'

'Rebecca—'

She stopped in the doorway and shook her head. 'You know what I wish sometimes?'

He stared at her.

She said, 'Sometimes I wish I'd married Tiny Taylor. Right now, I'd be up there in Connecticut, snug in my all-electric kitchen, having coffee and Danish, the kids off to school for the day, the twice-a-week maid taking care of the housework, looking forward to lunch at the country club with the girls . . .'

Why is she doing this to me? he wondered.

She noticed that he was still half out of his coat, and she said, 'Didn't you hear me, Jack? We've got a call to answer.'

'Yeah. I—'

'We've got two more stiffs.'

She left the squad room, which was colder and shabbier for her departure.

He sighed.

He shrugged back into his coat.

He followed her.

Jack felt grey and washed out partly because Rebecca was being so strange, but also because the day itself was grey, and he was always sensitive to the weather. The sky was flat and hard and grey. Manhattan's piles of stone, steel, and concrete were all grey and stark. The bare-limbed trees were ash-coloured, as if they had been severely scorched by a long-extinguished fire.

He got out of the unmarked sedan, half a block off Park Avenue, and a raw gust of wind hit him in the face. The December air had a faint tomb-dank smell. He jammed his hands into the deep pockets of his overcoat.

Rebecca Chandler got out of the driver's side and slammed the door. Her long blonde hair streamed behind her in the wind. Her coat was unbuttoned; it flapped around her legs. She didn't seem bothered by the chill or by the omnipresent greyness that had settled like soot over the entire city.

Viking woman, Jack thought. Stoical. Resolute. And just look at that profile!

Hers was the noble, classic, feminine face that sea-farers had once carved on the prows of their ships, ages ago, when such beauty was thought to have sufficient power to ward off the evils of the sea and the more vicious whims of fate.

Reluctantly, he took his eyes from Rebecca and looked at the three patrol cars that were angled in at the kerb. On one of them, the red emergency beacons were flashing, the only spot of vivid colour in this drab day.

Harry Ulbeck, a uniformed officer of Jack's acquaintance, was standing on the steps in front of the handsome, Georgian-style, brick townhouse where the murders had occurred. He was wearing a dark blue regulation greatcoat, a woollen scarf, and gloves, but he was still shivering.

From the look on Harry's face, Jack could see it wasn't the cold weather bothering him. Harry Ulbeck was chilled by what he had seen inside the townhouse.

'Bad one?' Rebecca asked.

Harry nodded. 'The worst, Lieutenant.'

He was only twenty-three or twenty-four, but at the moment he appeared years older; his face was drawn, pinched.

'Who're the deceased?' Jack asked.

'Guy named Vincent Vastagliano and his bodyguard, Ross Morrant.'

Jack drew his shoulders up and tucked his head down as a vicious gust of wind blasted through the street. 'Rich neighbourhood,' he said.

'Wait till you see inside,' Harry said. 'It's like a Fifth Avenue antique shop in there.'

'Who found the bodies?' Rebecca asked.

'A woman named Shelly Parker. She's a real looker. Vastagliano's girlfriend, I think.'

'She here now?'

'Inside. But I doubt she'll be much help. You'll probably get more out of Nevetski and Blaine.'

Standing tall in the shifting wind, her coat still unbuttoned, Rebecca said, 'Nevetski and Blaine? Who're they?'

'Narcotics,' Harry said. 'They were running a stakeout on this Vastagliano.'

'And he got killed right under their noses?'

'Better not put it quite like that when you talk to them,' Harry warned. 'They're touchy as hell about it. I mean, it wasn't just the two of them. They were in charge of a six-man team, watching all the entrances to the house. Had the place sealed tight. But somehow somebody got in anyway, killed Vastagliano *and* his bodyguard, and got out again without being seen. Makes poor Nevetski and Blaine look like they were sleeping.'

Jack felt sorry for them.

Rebecca didn't. She said, 'Well, damnit, they won't get any sympathy from me. It sounds as if they *were* screwing around.'

'I don't think so,' Harry Ulbeck said. 'They were really shocked. They swear they had the house covered.'

'What else would you expect them to say?' Rebecca asked sourly.

'Always give a fellow officer the benefit of the doubt,' Jack admonished her.

'Oh, yeah?' she said. 'Like hell. I don't believe in blind loyalty. I don't expect it; don't give it. I've known good cops, more than a few, and if I *know* they're good, I'll do anything to help them. But I've also known some real jerks who couldn't be trusted to put their pants on with the fly in front.'

Harry blinked at her.

She said, 'I won't be surprised if Nevetski and Blaine are two of those types, the ones who walk around with zippers up their butts.'

Jack sighed.

Harry stared at Rebecca, astonished.

A dark, unmarked van pulled to the kerb. Three men got out, one with a camera case, the other two with small suitcases.

'Lab men're here,' Harry said.

The new arrivals hurried along the sidewalk, toward the townhouse. Something about their sharp faces and squinted eyes made them seem like a trio of stilt-legged birds eagerly rushing toward a new piece of carrion.

Jack Dawson shivered.

The wind shook the day again. Along the street, the stark branches of the leafless trees rattled against one another. That sound brought to mind a Halloween-like image of animated skeletons engaged in a macabre dance.

3

The assistant medical examiner and two other men from the pathology lab were in the kitchen, where Ross Morrant, the bodyguard, was sprawled in a mess of blood, mayonnaise, mustard, and salami. He had been attacked and killed while preparing a midnight snack.

On the second floor of the townhouse, in the master bathroom, blood patterned every surface, decorated every corner: sprays of blood, streaks of it, smears and drops; bloody handprints on the walls and on the edge of the tub.

Jack and Rebecca stood at the doorway, peering in, touching nothing. Everything must remain undisturbed until the lab men were finished.

Vincent Vastagliano, fully clothed, lay jammed between the tub and sink, his head resting against the base of the toilet. He had been a big man, somewhat flabby, with dark hair and bushy eyebrows. His slacks and shirt were blood-soaked. One eye had been torn from its socket. The other was open wide, staring sightlessly. One hand was clenched; the other was open, relaxed. His face, neck, and hands were marked by dozens of small wounds. His clothes had been ripped in at least fifty or sixty places, and through those narrow rents in the fabric, other dark and bloody injuries could be seen.

'Worse than the other three,' Rebecca said.

'Much.'

This was the fourth hideously disfigured corpse they'd seen in the past four days. Rebecca was probably right: there was a psychopath on the loose.

But this wasn't merely a crazed killer who slaughtered while in the grip of a psychotic rage or fugue. This lunatic was more formidable than that, for he seemed to be a psychopath with a purpose, perhaps even a holy crusade: All four of his victims had been in one way or another involved in the illegal drug trade.

Rumours were circulating to the effect that a gang war was getting underway, a dispute over territories, but Jack didn't put much faith in that explanation. For one thing, the rumours were . . . strange. Besides, these didn't look like gangland killings. They certainly weren't the work of a professional assassin; there was nothing clean, efficient, or professional about them. They were savage killings, the product of a badly, darkly twisted personality.

Actually, Jack would have preferred tracking down an ordinary hit man. This was going to be tougher. Few criminals were as cunning, clever, bold, or as difficult to catch as a maniac with a mission.

'The number of wounds fits the pattern,' Jack said.

'But they're not the same kind of wounds we've seen before. Those were stabbings. These definitely aren't punctures. They're too ragged for that. So maybe this one isn't by the same hand.'

'It is,' he said.

'Too soon to say.'

'It's the same case,' he insisted.

'You sound so certain.'

'I *feel* it.'

'Don't get mystical on me like you did yesterday.'

'I never.'

'Oh, yes, you did.'

'We were only following up viable leads yesterday.'

'In a voodoo shop that sells goat's blood and magic amulets.'

'So? It was still a viable lead,' he said.

They studied the corpse in silence.

Then Rebecca said, 'It almost looks as if something bit him about a hundred times. He looks . . . *chewed*.'

'Yeah. Something small,' he said.

'Rats?'

'This is really a nice neighbourhood.'

'Yeah, sure, but it's also just one big happy city, Jack. The good and the bad neighbourhoods share the same streets, the same sewers, the same rats. It's democracy in action.'

'If those're rat bites, then the damned things came along and nibbled at him after he was already dead; they must've been drawn by the scent of blood. Rats are basically scavengers. They aren't bold. They aren't aggressive. People don't get attacked by packs of rats in their own homes. You ever heard of such a thing?'

'No,' she admitted. 'So the rats came along after he was dead, and they gnawed on him. But it was only rats. Don't try to make it anything mystical.'

'Did I *say* anything?'

'You really bothered me yesterday.'

'We were only following viable leads.'

'Talking to a sorcerer,' she said disdainfully.

'The man wasn't a sorcerer. He was—'

'Nuts. That's what he was. Nuts. And you stood there listening for more than half an hour.'

Jack sighed.

'These are rat bites,' she said, 'and they've disguised the real wounds. We'll have to wait for the autopsy to learn the cause of death.'

'I'm already sure it'll be like the others. A lot of small stab wounds under those bites.'

'You're probably right,' she said.

Queasy, Jack turned away from the dead man.

Rebecca continued to look.

The bathroom door frame was splintered, and the lock on the door was broken.

As Jack examined the damage, he spoke to a beefy, ruddy-faced patrolman who was standing nearby. 'You found the door like this?'

'No, no, Lieutenant. It was locked tight when we got here.'

Surprised, Jack looked up from the ruined door. 'Say *what*?'

Rebecca turned to face the patrolman. 'Locked?'

The officer said, 'See, this Parker broad . . . uh, I mean, this Miss Parker . . . she had a key. She let herself into the house, called for Vastagliano, figured he was still sleeping, and came upstairs to wake him. She found the bathroom door locked, couldn't get an answer, and got worried he might've had a heart attack. She looked

34

under the door, saw his hand, sort of outstretched, and all that blood. She phoned it in to 911 right away. Me and Tony – my partner – were the first here, and we broke down the door in case the guy might still be alive, but one look told us he wasn't. Then we found the other guy in the kitchen.'

'The bathroom door was locked from inside?' Jack asked.

The patrolman scratched his square, dimpled chin. 'Well, sure. Sure, it was locked from inside. Otherwise, we wouldn't have had to break it down, would we? And see here? See the way it works? It's what the locksmiths call a "privacy set". It can't be locked from outside the bathroom.'

Rebecca scowled. 'So the killer couldn't possibly have locked it after he was finished with Vastagliano?'

'No,' Jack said, examining the broken lock more closely. 'Looks like the victim locked himself in to avoid whoever was after him.'

'But he was wasted anyway,' Rebecca said.

'Yeah.'

'In a locked room.'

'Yeah.'

'Where the biggest window is only a narrow slit.'

'Yeah.'

'Too narrow for the killer to escape that way.'

'Much too narrow.'

'So how was it done?'

'Damned if I know,' Jack said.

She scowled at him.

She said, 'Don't go mystical on me again.'

He said, 'I never.'

'There's an explanation.'

'I'm sure there is.'

'And we'll find it.'

'I'm sure we will.'

'A *logical* explanation.'

'Of course.'

That morning, something bad happened to Penny Dawson when she went to school.

The Wellton School, a private institution, was in a large, converted, four-storey brownstone on a clean, tree-lined street in a quite respectable neighbourhood. The bottom floor had been remodelled to provide an accoustically perfect music room and a small gymnasium. The second floor was given over to classrooms for grades one through three, while grades four through six received their instruction on the third level. The business offices and records room were on the fourth floor.

Being a sixth grader, Penny attended class on the third floor. It was there, in the bustling and somewhat overheated cloakroom that the bad thing happened.

At that hour, shortly before the start of school, the cloakroom was filled with chattering kids struggling out of heavy coats and boots and galoshes. Although snow hadn't been falling this morning, the weather forecast called for precipitation by mid-afternoon, and everyone was dressed accordingly.

Snow! The first snow of the year. Even though city kids didn't have fields and country hills and woods in which to enjoy winter's games, the first snow of the season was nevertheless a magic event. Anticipation of the storm put an edge on the usual morning excitement. There was much giggling, name-calling, teasing, talk about television shows and homework, joke-telling, riddle-making, exaggerations about just how much snow they were supposed to be in for, and whispered conspiracy, the rustle of coats being shed, the slap of books on benches, the clank and rattle of metal lunchboxes.

Standing with her back to the whirl of activity, stripping off her gloves and then pulling off her long woollen scarf, Penny noticed that the door of her tall, narrow, metal locker was dented at the bottom and bent out slightly along one edge, as if someone had been prying at it. On closer inspection, she saw the combination lock was broken, too.

Frowning, she opened the door – and jumped back in surprise as an avalanche of paper spilled out at her feet. She had left the contents of her locker in a neat, orderly arrangement. Now, everything was jumbled together in one big mess. Worse than that, every one of her books had been torn apart, the pages ripped free of the bindings; some pages were shredded, too, and some were crumpled. Her yellow, lined tablet had been reduced to a pile of confetti. Her pencils had been broken into small pieces. Her pocket calculator was smashed.

Several other kids were near enough to see what had tumbled out of her locker. The sight of all that destruction startled and silenced them.

Numb, Penny crouched, reached into the lower section of the locker, pulled out some of the rubbish, until she uncovered her clarinet case. She hadn't taken the instrument home last night because she'd had a long report to write and hadn't had time to practise. The latches on the black case were busted.

She was afraid to look inside.

Sally Wrather, Penny's best friend, stooped beside her. 'What happened?'

'I don't know.'

'You didn't do it?'

'Of course not. I . . . I'm afraid my clarinet's broken.'

'Who'd do something like that? That's downright *mean.*'

Chris Howe, a sixth-grade boy who was always clowning around and who could, at times, be childish and obnoxious and utterly impossible – but who could *also* be cute because he looked a little like Scott Baio – crouched next to Penny. He didn't seem to be aware that something was wrong. He said, 'Jeez, Dawson, I never knew you were such a *slob.*'

Sally said, 'She didn't—'

But Chris said, 'I'll bet you got a family of big, grody cockroaches in there, Dawson.'

And Sally said, 'Oh, blow it out your ears, Chris.'

He gaped at her in surprise because Sally was a petite, almost fragile-looking redhead who was usually very soft-spoken. When it came to standing up for her friends, however, Sally could be a tiger. Chris blinked at her and said, 'Huh? *What* did you say?'

'Go stick your head in the toilet and flush twice,' Sally said. 'We don't need your stupid jokes. Somebody trashed Penny's locker. It isn't funny.'

Chris looked at the rubble more closely. 'Oh. Hey, I didn't realize. Sorry, Penny.'

Reluctantly, Penny opened the damaged clarinet case. The silver keys had been snapped off. The instrument had also been broken.

Sally put a hand on Penny's shoulder.

'Who did it?' Chris asked.

'We don't know,' Sally said.

Penny stared at the clarinet, wanting to cry, not because it was broken (although that was bad enough), but because she wondered if someone had smashed it as a way of telling her she wasn't wanted here.

At Wellton School, she and Davey were the only kids who could boast a policeman for a father. The other children were the offspring of attorneys, doctors, businessmen, dentists, stockbrokers, and advertising executives. Having absorbed certain snobbish attitudes from their parents, there were those in the student body who thought a cop's kids didn't really *belong* at an expensive private school like Wellton. Fortunately, there weren't many of that kind. Most of the kids didn't care what Jack Dawson did for a living, and there were even a few who thought it was special and exciting and better to be a cop's kid than to have a banker or an accountant for a father.

By now, everyone in the cloakroom realized something big had happened, and everyone had fallen silent.

Penny stood, turned, and surveyed them.

Had one of the snobs trashed her locker?

She spotted two of the worst offenders – a pair of sixth-grade girls, Sissy Johansen and Cara Wallace – and suddenly she wanted to grab hold of them, shake them, scream in their faces, tell them how it was with her, make them understand.

I didn't ask to come to your damned school. The only reason my dad can afford it is because there was my mother's insurance money and the out-of-court settlement with the hospital that killed her. You think I wanted my mother dead just so I could come to Wellton? Cripes. Holy cripes! You think I wouldn't give up Wellton in a snap if I could only have my mother back? You creepy, snot-eating nerds! Do you think I'm glad my mother's dead, for God's sake? You stupid creeps! What's wrong with you?

But she didn't scream at them.

She didn't cry, either.

She swallowed the lump in her throat. She bit her lip. She kept control of herself, for she was determined not to act like a child.

After a few seconds, she was relieved she hadn't snapped at them, for she began to realize that even Sissy and Cara, snotty as they could be sometimes, were not capable of anything as bold and as vicious as the trashing of her locker and the destruction of her clarinet. No. It hadn't been Sissy or Cara or any of the other snobs.

But if not them . . . who?

Chris Howe had remained crouched in front of Penny's locker, pawing through the debris. Now he stood up, holding a fistful of mangled pages from her textbooks. He said, 'Hey, look at this. This stuff hasn't just been torn up. A lot of it looks like it's been *chewed*.'

'Chewed?' Sally Wrather said.

'See the little teeth marks?' Chris asked.

Penny saw them.

'Who would chew up a bunch of books?' Sally asked.

Teeth marks, Penny thought.

39

'Rats,' Chris said.

Like the punctures in Davey's plastic baseball bat.

'Rats?' Sally said, grimacing. 'Oh, yuck.'

Last night. The thing under the bed.

'Rats . . .'

' . . . rats . . .'

' . . . rats.'

The word swept around the room.

A couple of girls squealed.

Several kids slipped out of the cloakroom to tell the teachers what had happened.

Rats.

But Penny knew it hadn't been a rat that tore the baseball bat out of her hand. It had been . . . something else.

Likewise, it hadn't been a rat that had broken her clarinet. Something else.

Something else.

But what?

5

Jack and Rebecca found Nevetski and Blaine downstairs, in Vincent Vastagliano's study. They were going through the drawers and compartments of a Sheraton desk and a wall of beautifully crafted oak cabinets.

Roy Nevetski looked like a high school English teacher, circa 1955. White shirt. Clip-on bow tie. Grey vee-neck sweater.

By contrast, Nevetski's partner, Carl Blaine, looked like a thug. Nevetski was on the slender side, but Blaine was stocky, barrel-chested, slab-shouldered, bull-necked. Intelligence and sensitivity seemed to glow in Roy Nevetski's face, but Blaine appeared about as sensitive as a gorilla.

Judging from Nevetski's appearance, Jack expected him to conduct a neat search, leaving no marks of his passage; likewise, he figured Blaine to be a slob, scattering debris behind, leaving dirty pawprints in his wake. In reality, it was the other way around. When Roy Nevetski finished poring over the contents of a drawer, the floor at his feet was littered with discarded papers, while Carl Blaine inspected every item with care and then returned them all to their original resting places, exactly as he had found them.

'Just stay the hell out of our way,' Nevetski said irritably. 'We're going to pry into every crack and crevice in this fuckin' joint. We aren't leaving until we find what we're after.' He had a surprisingly hard voice, all low notes and rough edges and jarring metallic tones, like a piece of broken machinery. 'So just step back.'

'Actually,' Rebecca said, 'now that Vastagliano's dead, this is pretty much out of your hands.'

Jack winced at her directness and all-too-familiar coolness.

'It's a case for Homicide now,' Rebecca said. 'It's not so much a matter for Narcotics any more.'

'Haven't you ever heard of inter-departmental cooperation, for Christ's sake?' Nevetski demanded.

'Haven't *you* ever heard of common courtesy?' Rebecca asked.

'Wait, wait, wait,' Jack said quickly, placatingly. 'There's room for all of us. Of course there is.'

Rebecca shot a malevolent look at him.

He pretended not to see it. He was very good at pretending not to see the looks she gave him. He'd had a lot of practice at it.

To Nevetski, Rebecca said, 'There's no reason to leave the place like a pig sty.'

'Vastagliano's too dead to care,' Nevetski said.

'You're just making it harder for Jack and me when we have to go through all this stuff ourselves.'

'Listen,' Nevetski said, 'I'm in a hurry. Besides, when I run a search like this, there's no fuckin' reason for anyone else to double-check me. I never miss anything.'

'You'll have to excuse Roy,' Carl Blaine said, borrowing Jack's placating tone and gestures.

'Like hell,' Nevetski said.

'He doesn't mean anything by it,' Blaine said.

'Like hell,' Nevetski said.

'He's extraordinarily tense this morning,' Blaine said. In spite of his brutal face, his voice was soft, cultured, mellifluous. 'Extraordinarily tense.'

'From the way he's acting,' Rebecca said, 'I thought maybe it was his time of the month.'

Nevetski glowered at her.

There's nothing so inspiring as police camaraderie, Jack thought.

Blaine said, 'It's just that we were conducting a tight surveillance on Vastagliano when he was killed.'

'Couldn't have been *too* tight,' Rebecca said.

'Happens to the best of us,' Jack said, wishing she'd shut up.

'Somehow,' Blaine said, 'the killer got past us, both going in and coming out. We didn't get a glimpse of him.'

'Doesn't make any goddamned sense,' Nevetski said, and he slammed a desk drawer with savage force.

'We saw the Parker woman come in here around twenty past seven,' Blaine said. 'Fifteen minutes later, the first black-and-white pulled up. That was the first we knew anything about Vastagliano being snuffed. It was embarrassing. The captain won't be easy on us.'

'Hell, the old man'll have our balls for Christmas decorations.'

Blaine nodded agreement. 'It'd help if we could find Vastagliano's business records, turn up the names of his associates, customers, maybe collect enough evidence to make an important arrest.'

'We might even wind up heroes,' Nevetski said, 'although right now I'd settle for just getting my head above the shit line before I drown.'

Rebecca's face was lined with disapproval of Nevetski's incessant use of obscenity.

Jack prayed she wouldn't chastise Nevetski for his foul mouth.

She leaned against the wall beside what appeared to be (at least to Jack's unschooled eye) an original Andrew Wyeth oil painting. It was a farm scene rendered in intricate and exquisite detail.

Apparently oblivious of the exceptional beauty of the painting, Rebecca said, 'So this Vincent Vastagliano was in the dope trade?'

'Does McDonald's sell hamburgers?' Nevetski asked.

'He was a blood member of the Carramazza family,' Blaine said.

Of the five mafia families that controlled gambling, prostitution, and other rackets in New York, the Carramazzas were the most powerful.

'In fact,' Blaine said, 'Vastagliano was the nephew of Gennaro Carramazza himself. His uncle Gennaro gave him the Gucci route.'

'The what?' Jack asked.

'The uppercrust clientele in the dope business,' Blaine said. 'The kind of people who have twenty pairs of Gucci shoes in their closet.'

Nevetski said, 'Vastagliano didn't sell shit to school kids. His uncle wouldn't have let him do anything *that* seamy. Vince dealt strictly with show business and society types. Highbrow muckety-mucks.'

'Not that Vince Vastagliano was one of them,' Blaine quickly added. 'He was just a cheap hood who moved in the right circles only because he could provide the nose candy some of those limousine types were looking for.'

'He was a scumbag,' Nevetski said. 'This house, all those antiques – this wasn't *him*. This was just an image he thought he should project if he was going to be the candyman to the jet set.'

'He didn't know the difference between an antique and a K-Mart coffee table,' Blaine said. 'All these books. Take a closer look. They're old textbooks, incomplete

43

sets of out-dated encyclopedias, odds and ends, bought by the yard from a used-book dealer, never meant to be read, just dressing for the shelves.'

Jack took Blaine's word for it, but Rebecca, being Rebecca, went to the bookcases to see for herself.

'We've been after Vastagliano for a long time,' Nevetski said. 'We've had a hunch about him. He seemed like a weak link. The rest of the Carramazza family is as disciplined as the fuckin' Marine Corps. But Vince drank too much, whored around too much, smoked too much pot, even used cocaine once in a while.'

Blaine said, 'We figured if we could get the goods on him, get enough evidence to guarantee him a prison term, he'd crack and cooperate rather than do hard time. Through him, we figured to finally lay our hands on some of the wiseguys at the heart of the Carramazza organization.'

Nevetski said, 'We got a tip that Vastagliano would be contacting a South American cocaine wholesaler named Rene Oblido.'

'Our informant said they were meeting to discuss new sources of supply. The meeting was supposed to be yesterday or today. It wasn't yesterday—'

'And for damned sure, it won't happen today, not now that Vastagliano is nothing but a pile of bloody garbage.' Nevetski looked as if he would spit on the carpet in disgust.

'You're right. It's screwed up,' Rebecca said, turning away from the bookshelves. 'It's over. So why not split and let us handle it?'

Nevetski gave her his patented glare of anger.

Even Blaine looked as if he were finally about to snap at her.

Jack said, 'Take your time. Find whatever you need. You won't be in our way. We've got a lot of other things to do here. Come on, Rebecca. Let's see what the ME's people can tell us.'

He didn't even glance at Rebecca because he knew she was giving him a look pretty much like the one Blaine and Nevetski were giving her.

Reluctantly, Rebecca went into the hall.

Before following her, Jack paused at the door, looking back at Nevetski and Blaine. 'You notice anything odd about this one?'

'Such as?' Nevetski asked.

'Anything,' Jack said. 'Anything out of the ordinary, strange, weird, unexplainable.'

'I can't explain how the hell the killer got in here,' Nevetski said irritably. '*That's* damned strange.'

'Anything else?' Jack asked. 'Anything that would make you think this is more than just your ordinary drug-related homicide?'

They looked at him blankly.

He said, 'Okay, what about this woman, Vastagliano's girlfriend or whatever she is . . .'

'Shelly Parker,' Blaine said. 'She's waiting in the living room if you want to talk to her.'

'Have you spoken with her yet?' Jack asked.

'A little,' Blaine said. 'She's not much of a talker.'

'A real sleazebag is what she is,' Nevetski said.

'Reticent,' Blaine said.

'An uncooperative sleazebag.'

'Self-contained, very composed,' Blaine said.

'A two-dollar pump. A bitch. A scuz. But gorgeous.'

Jack said, 'Did she mention anything about a Haitian?'

'A what?'

'You mean . . . someone from Haiti? The island?'

'The island,' Jack confirmed.

'No,' Blaine said. 'Didn't say anything about a Haitian.'

'What fuckin' Haitian are we talking about?' Nevetski demanded.

Jack said, 'A guy named Lavelle. Baba Lavelle?'

'Baba?' Blaine said.

'Sounds like a clown,' Nevetski said.

'Did Shelly Parker mention him?'

'No.'

'How's this Lavelle fit in?'

Jack didn't answer that. Instead, he said, 'Listen, did Miss Parker say anything to you about . . . well . . . did she say anything at all that seemed *strange*?'

Nevetski and Blaine frowned at him.

'What do you mean?' Blaine said.

Yesterday, they'd found the second victim: a black man named Freeman Coleson, a middle-level dope dealer. He distributed to seventy or eighty street pushers in a section of lower Manhattan that had been conferred upon him by the Carramazza family, which had become an equal opportunity employer in order to avoid ill-feeling and racial strife in the New York underworld. Coleson had turned up dead, leaking from more than a hundred small stab wounds, just like the first victim on Sunday night. His brother, Darl Coleson, had been panicky, so nervous he was pouring sweat. He had told Jack and Rebecca a story about a Haitian who was trying to take over the cocaine and heroin trade. It was the weirdest story Jack had ever heard, but it was obvious that Darl Coleson believed every word of it.

If Shelly Parker had told a similar tale to Nevetski and Blaine, they wouldn't have forgotten it. They wouldn't have needed to ask what sort of 'strange' he was talking about.

Jack hesitated, then shook his head. 'Never mind. It's not really important.'

If it's not important, why did you bring it up?

That would be Nevetski's next question. Jack turned away from them before Nevetski could speak, kept moving, through the door, into the hall, where Rebecca was waiting for him.

She looked angry.

6

Last week, on Thursday evening, at the twice-a-month

poker game he'd been attending for more than eight years, Jack had found himself defending Rebecca. During a pause in the game, the other players – three detectives: Al Dufresne, Witt Yardman, and Phil Abrahams – had spoken against her.

'I don't see how you put up with her, Jack,' Witt said.

'She's a cold one,' Al said.

'A regular ice maiden,' Phil said.

As the cards snapped and clicked and softly hissed in Al's busy hands, the three men dealt out insults:

'She's colder than a witch's tit.'

'About as friendly as a Doberman with one fierce damned toothache and a bad case of constipation.'

'Acts like she don't ever have to breathe or take a piss like the rest of humanity.'

'A real ball-buster,' Al Dufresne said.

Finally Jack said, 'Ah, she's not so bad once you know her.'

'A ball-buster,' Al repeated.

'Listen,' Jack said, 'if she was a guy, you'd say she was just a hard-nosed cop, and you'd sort of admire her for it. But 'cause she's a hard-nosed *female* cop, you say she's just a cold bitch.'

'I know a ball-buster when I see one,' Al said.

'A ball-*crusher*,' Witt said.

'She's got her good qualities,' Jack said.

'Yeah?' Phil Abrahams said. 'Name one.'

'She's observant.'

'So's a vulture.'

'She's smart. She's efficient,' Jack said.

'So was Mussolini. He made the trains run on time.'

Jack said, 'And she'd never fail to back up her partner if things got hairy out there on the street.'

'Hell's bells, *no* cop would fail to back up a partner,' Al said.

'Some would,' Jack said.

'Damned few. And if they did, they wouldn't be cops for long.'

'She's a hard worker,' Jack said. 'Carries her weight.'

'Okay, okay,' Witt said, 'so maybe she can do the job well enough. But why can't she be a human being, too?'

'I don't think I ever heard her laugh,' Phil said.

Al said, 'Where's her heart? Doesn't she have a heart?'

'Sure she does,' Witt said. 'A little stone heart.'

'Well,' Jack said, 'I suppose I'd rather have Rebecca for a partner than any of you brass-plated monkeys.'

'Is that so?'

'Yeah. She's more sensitive than you give her credit for.'

'Oh, ho! *Sensitive!*'

'Now it comes out!'

'He's not just being chivalrous.'

'He's *sweet* on her.'

'She'll have your balls for a necklace, old buddy.'

'From the look of him, I'd say she's already had 'em.'

'Any day now, she'll be wearing a brooch made out of his—'

Jack said, 'Listen, you guys, there's nothing between me and Rebecca except—'

'Does she go in for whips and chains, Jack?'

'Hey, I'll bet she does! Boots and dog collars.'

'Take off your shirt and show us your bruises, Jack.'

'Neanderthals,' Jack said.

'Does she wear a leather bra?'

'Leather? Man, that broad must wear *steel*.'

'Cretins,' Jack said.

'I *thought* you've been looking poorly the last couple months,' Al said. 'Now I know what it is. You're pussy-whipped, Jack.'

'Definitely pussy-whipped,' Phil said.

Jack knew there was no point in resisting them. His protestations would only amuse and encourage them. He smiled and let the wave of good-natured abuse wash over him, until they were at last tired of the game.

Eventually, he said, 'Alright, you guys have had your fun. But I don't want any stupid rumours starting from

48

this. I want you to understand there's nothing between Rebecca and me. I think she *is* a sensitive person under all those callouses. Beneath that cold-as-an-alligator pose she works so hard at, there's some warmth, tenderness. That's what I think, but I don't know from personal experience. Understand?'

'Maybe there's nothing between you two,' Phil said, 'but judging by the way your tongue hangs out when you talk about her, it's obvious you wish there *was*.'

'Yeah,' Al said, 'when you talk about her, you drool.'

The taunting started all over again, but this time they were much closer to the truth than they had been before. Jack didn't know from personal experience that Rebecca was sensitive and special, but he sensed it, and he wanted to be closer to her. He would have given just about anything to be with her – not merely *near* her; he'd been near her five or six days a week, for almost ten months – but really with her, sharing her innermost thoughts, which she always guarded jealously.

The biological pull was strong, the stirring in the gonads; no denying it. After all, she was quite beautiful. But it wasn't her beauty that most intrigued him.

Her coolness, the distance she put between herself and everyone else, made her a challenge that no male could resist. But that wasn't the thing that most intrigued him, either.

Now and then, rarely, no more than once a week, there was an unguarded moment, a few seconds, never longer than a minute, when her hard shell slipped slightly, giving him a glimpse of another and very different Rebecca beyond the familiar cold exterior, someone vulnerable and unique, someone worth knowing and perhaps worth holding on to. *That* was what fascinated Jack Dawson: that brief glimpse of warmth and tenderness, the dazzling radiance she always cut off the instance she realized she had allowed it to escape through her mask of austerity.

Last Thursday, at the poker game, he had felt that

getting past Rebecca's elaborate psychological defences would always be, for him, nothing more than a fantasy, a dream forever unattainable. After ten months as her partner, ten months of working together, trusting each other, and putting their lives in each other's hands, he felt she was, if anything, more of a mystery than ever.

Now, less than a week later, Jack knew what lay under her mask. He knew from personal experience. *Very* personal experience. And what he had found was even better, more appealing, more special than what he had hoped to find. She was wonderful.

But this morning there was absolutely no sign of the inner Rebecca, no slightest hint that she was anything more than the cold and forbidding Amazon that she assiduously impersonated.

It was as if last night had never happened.

In the hall, outside the study where Nevetski and Blaine were still looking for evidence, she said, 'I heard what you asked them – about the Haitian.'

'So?'

'Oh, for God's sake, Jack!'

'Well, Baba Lavelle *is* our only suspect so far.'

'It doesn't bother me that you asked about him,' she said. 'It's the *way* you asked about him.'

'I used English, didn't I?'

'Jack—'

'Wasn't I polite enough?'

'Jack—'

'It's just that I don't understand what you mean.'

'Yes, you do.' She mimicked him, pretending she was talking to Nevetski and Blaine: '"Has either of you noticed anything *odd* about this one? Anything out of the ordinary? Anything *strange*? Anything *weird*?"'

'I was just pursuing a lead,' he said defensively.

'Like you pursued it yesterday, wasting half the afternoon in the library, reading about voodoo.'

'We were at the library less than an hour.'

'And then running up there to Harlem to talk to that sorcerer.'

'He's not a sorcerer.'

'That *nut*.'

'Carver Hampton isn't a nut,' Jack said.

'A real nut case,' she insisted.

'There was an article about him in that book.'

'Being written about in a book doesn't automatically make him respectable.'

'He's a priest.'

'He's not. He's a fraud.'

'He's a voodoo priest who practises only white magic, good magic. A Houngon. That's what he calls himself.'

'I can call myself a fruit tree, but don't expect me to grow any apples on my ears,' she said. 'Hampton's a charlatan. Taking money from the gullible.'

'His religion may seem exotic—'

'It's foolish. That shop he runs. Jesus. Selling herbs and bottles of goat's blood, charms and spells, all that other nonsense—'

'It's not nonsense to him.'

'Sure it is.'

'He believes in it.'

'Because he's a nut.'

'Make up your mind, Rebecca. Is Carver Hampton a nut or a fraud? I don't see how you can have it both ways.'

'Okay, okay. Maybe this Baba Lavelle *did* kill all four of the victims.'

'He's our only suspect so far.'

'But he didn't use voodoo. There's no such thing as black magic. He stabbed them, Jack. He got blood on his hands, just like any other murderer.'

Her eyes were intensely, fiercely green, always a shade greener and clearer when she was angry or impatient.

'I never said he killed them with magic,' Jack told her.

'I didn't say I believe in voodoo. But you saw the bodies. You saw how strange—'

'Stabbed,' she said firmly. 'Mutilated, yes. Savagely and horribly disfigured, yes. Stabbed a hundred times or more, yes. But *stabbed*. With a knife. A real knife. An ordinary knife.'

'The medical examiner says the weapon used in those first two murders would've had to've been no bigger than a penknife.'

'Okay. So it was a penknife.'

'Rebecca, that doesn't make sense.'

'Murder never makes sense.'

'What kind of killer goes after his victims with a penknife, for God's sake?'

'A lunatic.'

'Psychotic killers usually favour dramatic weapons – butchers knives, hatchets, shotguns . . .'

'In the movies, maybe.'

'In reality, too.'

'This is just another psycho like all the psychos who're crawling out of the walls these days,' she insisted. 'There's nothing special or strange about him.'

'But how does he overpower them? If he's only wielding a penknife, why can't his victims fight him off or escape?'

'There's an explanation,' she said doggedly. 'We'll find it.'

The house was warm, getting warmer; Jack took off his overcoat.

Rebecca left her coat on. The heat didn't seem to bother her any more than the cold.

'And in every case,' Jack said, 'the victim has fought his assailant. There are always signs of a big struggle. Yet none of the victims seems to have managed to wound his attacker; there's never any blood but the victim's own. That's damned strange. And what about Vastagliano – murdered in a locked bathroom?'

She stared at him sullenly but didn't respond.

'Look, Rebecca, I'm not saying it's voodoo or anything the least bit supernatural. I'm not a particularly superstitious man. My point is that these murders might be the work of someone who *does* believe in voodoo, that there might be something ritualistic about them. The condition of the corpses certainly points in that direction. I didn't say voodoo works. I'm only suggesting that the killer might *think* it works, and his belief in voodoo might lead us to him and give us some of the evidence we need to convict him.'

She shook her head. 'Jack, I know there's a certain streak in you . . .'

'What certain streak is that?'

'Call it an excessive degree of open-mindedness.'

'How is it possible to be excessively open-minded? That's like being *too* honest.'

'When Darl Coleson said this Baba Lavelle was taking over the drug trade by using voodoo curses to kill his competition, you listened . . . well . . . you listened as if you were a child, enraptured.'

'I didn't.'

'You did. Then the next thing I know, we're off to Harlem to a voodoo shop!'

'If this Baba Lavelle really is interested in voodoo, then it makes sense to assume that someone like Carver Hampton might know him or be able to find out something about him for us.'

'A nut like Hampton won't be any help at all. You remember the Holderbeck case?'

'What's that got to do with—'

'The old lady who was murdered during the seance?'

'Emily Holderbeck. I remember.'

'You were *fascinated* with that one,' she said.

'I never claimed there was anything supernatural about it.'

'Absolutely fascinated.'

'Well, it was an incredible murder. The killer was so

53

bold. The room was dark, sure, but there were eight people present when the shot was fired.'

'But it wasn't the facts of the case that fascinated you the most,' Rebecca said. 'It was the medium that interested you. That Mrs Donatella with her crystal ball. You couldn't get enough of her ghost stories, her so-called psychic experiences.'

'So?'

'Do you believe in ghosts, Jack?'

'You mean, do I believe in an afterlife?'

'Ghosts.'

'I don't know. Maybe. Maybe not. Who can say?'

'*I* can say. I don't believe in ghosts. But your equivocation proves my point.'

'Rebecca, there are millions of perfectly sane, respectable, intelligent, level-headed people who believe in life after death.'

'A detective's a lot like a scientist,' she said. 'He's got to be logical.'

'He doesn't have to be an *atheist*, for God's sake!'

Ignoring him, she said, 'Logic is the best tool we have.'

'All I'm saying is that we're onto something strange. And since the brother of one of the victims thinks voodoo is involved—'

'A good detective has to be reasonable, methodical.'

'—we should follow it up even if it seems ridiculous.'

'A good detective has to be tough-minded, realistic.'

'A good detective also has to be imaginative, flexible,' he countered. Then, abruptly changing the subject, he said, 'Rebecca, what about last night?'

Her face reddened. She said, 'Let's go have a talk with the Parker woman,' and she started to turn away from him.

He took hold of her arm, stopped her. 'I thought something very special happened last night.'

She said nothing.

'Did I just imagine it?' he asked.

'Let's not talk about it now.'

'Was it really awful for you?'

'Later,' she said.

'Why're you treating me like this?'

She wouldn't meet his eyes; that was unusual for her. 'It's complicated, Jack.'

'I think we've got to talk about it.'

'Later,' she said. 'Please.'

'When?'

'When we have the time.'

'When will that be?' he persisted.

'If we have time for lunch, we can talk about it then.'

'We'll make time.'

'We'll see.'

'Yes, we will.'

'Now, we've got work to do,' she said, pulling away from him.

He let her go this time.

She headed toward the living room, where Shelly Parker waited.

He followed her, wondering what he'd gotten himself into when he'd become intimately involved with this exasperating woman. Maybe she was a nut case herself. Maybe she wasn't worth all the aggravation she caused him. Maybe she would bring him nothing but pain, and maybe he would come to regret the day he'd met her. At times, she certainly seemed neurotic. Better to stay away from her. The smartest thing he could do was call it quits right now. He could ask for a new partner, perhaps even transfer out of the Homicide Division; he was tired of dealing with death all the time, anyway. He and Rebecca should split, go their separate ways both personally and professionally, before they got too tangled up with each other. Yes, that was for the best. That was what he should do.

But as Nevetski would say: *Like hell.*

He wasn't going to put in a request for a new partner.

He wasn't a quitter.

Besides, he thought maybe he was in love.

At fifty-eight, Nayva Rooney looked like a grandmother but moved like a dockworker. She kept her grey hair in tight curls. Her round, pink, friendly face had bold rather than delicate features, and her merry blue eyes were never evasive, always warm. She was a stocky woman but not fat. Her hands weren't smooth, soft, grandmotherly hands; they were strong, quick, efficient, with no trace of either the pampered life or arthritis, but with a few callouses. When Nayva walked, she looked as if nothing could stand in her way, not other people and not even brick walls; there was nothing dainty or graceful or even particularly feminine about her walk; she strode from place to place in the manner of a no-nonsense army sergeant.

Nayva had been cleaning the apartment for Jack Dawson since shortly after Linda Dawson's death. She came in once a week, every Wednesday. She also did some babysitting for him; in fact, she'd been here last evening, watching over Penny and Davey, while Jack had been out on a date.

This morning, she let herself in with the key that Jack had given her, and she went straight to the kitchen. She brewed a pot of coffee and poured a cup for herself and drank half of it before she took off her coat. It was a bitter day, indeed, and even though the apartment was warm, she found it difficult to rid herself of the chill that had seeped deep into her bones during the six-block walk from her own apartment.

She started cleaning in the kitchen. Nothing was actually dirty. Jack and his two young ones were clean and reasonably orderly, not at all like *some* for whom Nayva worked. Nonetheless, she laboured diligently, scrubbing and polishing with the same vigour and determination that she brought to really grimy jobs, for she prided herself on the fact that a place positively *gleamed* when she was finished with it. Her father – dead these many years and God rest his soul – had been a uniformed policeman, a foot patrolman, who took no graft whatsoever, and who strived to make his beat a safe one for all who lived or toiled within its boundaries. He had taken considerable pride in his job, and he'd taught Nayva (among other things) two valuable lessons about work: first, there is always satisfaction and esteem in a piece of work well done, regardless of how menial it might be; second, if you cannot do a job well, then there's not much use in doing it at all.

Initially, other than the noises Nayva made as she cleaned, the only sounds in the apartment were the periodic humming of the refrigerator motor, occasional thumps and creaks as someone rearranged the furniture in the apartment above, and the moaning of the brisk winter wind as it pressed at the windows.

Then, as she paused to pour a little more coffee for herself, an odd sound came from the living room. A sharp, short squeal. An animal sound. She put down the coffee pot.

Cat? Dog?

It hadn't seemed like either of those; like nothing familiar. Besides, the Dawsons had no pets.

She started across the kitchen, toward the door to the dining alcove and the living room beyond.

The squeal came again, and it brought her to a halt, froze her, and suddenly she was uneasy. It was an ugly, angry, brittle cry, again of short duration but piercing and somehow menacing. This time it didn't sound as much like an animal as it had before.

It didn't sound particularly human, either, but she said, 'Is someone there?'

The apartment was silent. Almost too silent, now. As if someone were listening, waiting for her to make a move.

Nayva wasn't a woman given to fits of nerves and

certainly not to hysteria. And she had always been confident that she could take care of herself just fine, thank you. But suddenly she was stricken by an uncharacteristic twinge of fear.

Silence.

'Who's there?' she demanded.

The shrill, angry shriek came again. It was a hateful sound.

Nayva shuddered.

A rat? Rats squealed. But not like this.

Feeling slightly foolish, she picked up a broom and held it as if it were a weapon.

The shriek came again, from the living room, as if taunting her to come see what it was.

Broom in hand, she crossed the kitchen and hesitated at the doorway.

Something was moving around in the living room. She couldn't see it, but she could hear an odd, dry-paper, dry-leaf rustling and a scratching-hissing noise that sometimes sounded like whispered words in a foreign language.

With a boldness she had inherited from her father, Nayva stepped through the doorway. She edged past the tables and chairs, looking beyond them at the living room, which was visible through the wide archway that separated it from the dining alcove. She stopped beneath the arch and listened, trying to get a better fix on the noise.

From the corner of her eye, she saw movement. The pale yellow drapes fluttered, but not from a draft. She wasn't in a position to see the lower half of the drapes, but it was clear that something was scurrying along the floor, brushing them as it went.

Nayva moved quickly into the living room, past the first sofa, so that she could see the bottom of the drapes. Whatever had disturbed them was nowhere in sight. The drapes became still again.

Then, behind her, she heard a sharp little squeal of anger.

She whirled around, bringing up the broom, ready to strike.

Nothing.

She circled the second sofa. Nothing behind it. Looked in back of the armchair, too. Nothing. Under the end tables. Nothing. Around the bookcase, on both sides of the television set, under the sideboard, behind the drapes. Nothing, nothing.

Then the squeal came from the hallway.

By the time she got to the hall, there wasn't anything to be seen. She hadn't flicked on the hall light when she'd come into the apartment, and there weren't any windows in there, so the only illumination was what spilled in from the kitchen and living room. However, it was a short passageway, and there was absolutely no doubt that it was deserted.

She waited, head cocked.

The cry came again. From the kids' bedroom this time.

Nayva went down the hall. The bedroom was more than half dark. There was no overhead light; you had to go into the room and snap on one of the lamps in order to dispel the gloom. She paused for a moment on the threshold, peering into the shadows.

Not a sound. Even the furniture movers upstairs had stopped dragging and heaving things around. The wind had slacked off and wasn't pressing at the windows right now. Nayva held her breath and listened. If there was anything here, anything *alive*, it was being as still and alert as she was.

Finally, she stepped cautiously into the room, went to Penny's bed, and clicked on the lamp. That didn't burn away all the shadows, so she turned toward Davey's bed, intending to switch on that lamp, as well.

Something hissed, moved.

She gasped in surprise.

The thing darted out of the open closet, through

59

shadows, under Davey's bed. It didn't enter the light, and she wasn't able to see it clearly. In fact, she had only a vague impression of it: something small, about the size of a large rat; sleek and streamlined and slithery like a rat.

But it sure didn't sound like a rodent of any kind. It wasn't squeaking or squealing now. It hissed and . . . *gabbled* as if it were whispering urgently to itself.

Nayva backed away from Davey's bed. She glanced at the broom in her hands and wondered if she should poke it under the bed and rattle it around until she drove the intruder out in the open where she could see exactly what it was.

Even as she was deciding on a course of action, the thing scurried out from the foot of the bed, through the dark end of the room, into the shadowy hallway; it moved *fast*. Again, Nayva failed to get a good look at it.

'Damn,' she said.

She had the unsettling feeling that the critter – whatever in God's name it might be – was just toying with her, playing games, teasing.

But that didn't make sense. Whatever it was, it was still only a dumb animal, one kind of dumb animal or another, and it wouldn't have either the wit or the desire to lead her on a merry chase merely for the fun of it.

Elsewhere in the apartment, the thing shrieked, as if calling to her.

Okay, Nayva thought. Okay, you nasty little beast, whatever you may be, look out because here I come. You may be fast, and you may be clever, but I'll track you down and have a look at you even if it's the last thing I do in this life.

Chapter Two

1

They had been questioning Vince Vastagliano's girl-friend for fifteen minutes. Nevetski was right. She was an uncooperative bitch.

Perched on the edge of a Queen Anne chair, Jack Dawson leaned forward and finally mentioned the name that Darl Coleson had given him yesterday. 'Do you know a man named Baba Lavelle?'

Shelly Parker glanced at him, then quickly looked down at her hands, which were folded around a glass of Scotch, but in that unguarded instant, he saw the answer in her eyes.

'I don't know anyone named Lavelle,' she lied.

Rebecca was sitting in another Queen Anne chair, legs crossed, arms on the chair arms, looking relaxed and confident and infinitely more self-possessed then Shelly Parker. She said, 'Maybe you don't *know* Lavelle, but maybe you've heard of him. Is that possible?'

'No,' Shelly said.

Jack said, 'Look, Ms Parker, we know Vince was dealing dope, and maybe we could hang a related charge on you—'

'I had nothing to do with that!'

'—but we don't intend to charge you with anything—'

'You can't!'

'—if you cooperate.'

'You have nothing on me,' she said.

'We can make life very difficult for you.'

'So can the Carramazzas. I'm not talking about them.'

'We aren't asking you to talk about them,' Rebecca said. 'Just tell us about this Lavelle.'

Shelly said nothing. She chewed thoughtfully on her lower lip.

'He's a Haitian,' Jack said, encouraging her.

Shelly stopped biting her lip and settled back on the white sofa, trying to look nonchalant, failing. 'What kind of neese is he?'

Jack blinked at her. 'Huh?'

'What kind of neese is this Lavelle?' she repeated. 'Japanese, Chinese, Vietnamese . . . ? You said he was Asian.'

'*Haitian*. He's from Haiti.'

'Oh. Then he's no kind of neese at all.'

'No kind of neese at all,' Rebecca agreed.

Shelly apparently detected the scorn in Rebecca's voice, for she shifted nervously, although she didn't seem to understand exactly what had elicited that scorn. 'Is he a black dude?'

'Yes,' Jack said, 'as you know perfectly well.'

'I don't hang around with black dudes,' Shelly said, lifting her head and squaring her shoulders, and assuming an affronted air.

Rebecca said, 'We heard Lavelle wants to take over the drug trade.'

'I wouldn't know anything about that.'

Jack said, 'Do you believe in voodoo, Ms Parker?'

Rebecca sighed wearily.

Jack looked at her and said, 'Bear with me.'

'This is pointless.'

'I promise not to be excessivly open-minded,' Jack said, smiling. To Shelly Parker, he said, 'Do you believe in the power of voodoo?'

'Of course not.'

'I thought maybe that's why you won't talk about Lavelle – because you're afraid he'll get you with the evil eye or something.'

'That's all a bunch of crap.'

62

'Is it?'

'All that voodoo stuff – crap.'

'But you *have* heard of Baba Lavelle?' Jack said.

'No, I just told you—'

'If you didn't know anything about Lavelle,' Jack said, 'you would've been surprised when I mentioned something as off-the-wall as voodoo. You would've asked me what the hell voodoo had to do with anything. But you weren't surprised, which means you know about Lavelle.'

Shelly raised one hand to her mouth, put a fingernail between her teeth, almost began to chew on it, caught herself, decided the relief provided by biting them was not worth ruining a forty-dollar nail job.

She said, 'All right, all right. I know about Lavelle.'

Jack winked at Rebecca. 'See?'

'Not bad,' Rebecca admitted.

'Clever interrogational technique,' Jack said. '*Imagination*.'

Shelly said, 'Can I have more Scotch?'

'Wait till we've finished questioning you,' Rebecca said.

'I'm not *drunk*,' Shelly said.

'I didn't say you were,' Rebecca told her.

'I never get potted,' Shelly said. 'I'm not a lush.'

She got up from the sofa, went to the bar, picked up a Waterford decanter, and poured more Scotch for herself.

Rebecca looked at Jack, raised her eyebrows.

Shelly returned, sat down. She put the glass of Scotch on the coffee table without taking a sip of it, determined to prove that she had all the will power she needed.

Jack saw the look Shelly gave Rebecca, and he almost winced. She was like a cat with her back up, spoiling for a fight.

The antagonism in the air wasn't really Rebecca's fault this time. She hadn't been as cold and sharp with Shelly as it was in her power to be. In fact, she had been almost pleasant until Shelly had started the 'neese' stuff. Apparently, however, Shelly had been comparing herself with Rebecca and had begun to feel that she came off second-best. *That* was what had generated the antagonism.

Like Rebecca, Shelly Parker was a good-looking blonde. But there the resemblance ended. Rebecca's exquisitely shaped and harmoniously related features bespoke sensitivity, refinement, breeding. Shelly, on the other hand, was a parody of seductiveness. Her hair had been elaborately cut and styled to achieve a carefree, abandoned look. She had flat wide cheekbones, a short upper lip, a pouting mouth. She wore too much make-up. Her eyes were blue, although slightly muddy, dreamy; they were not as forthright as Rebecca's eyes. Her figure was *too* well developed; she was rather like a wonderful French pastry made with far too much butter, too many eggs, mounds of whipped cream and sugar; too rich, soft. But in tight black slacks and a purple sweater, she was definitely an eye-catcher.

She was wearing a lot of jewellery: an expensive watch, two bracelets; two rings; two small pendants on gold chains, one with a diamond, the other with what seemed to be an emerald the size of a large pea. She was only twenty-two, and although she had not been gently used, it would be quite a few years before men stopped buying jewellery for her.

Jack thought he knew why she had taken an instant disliking to Rebecca. Shelly was the kind of woman a lot of men wanted, fantasized about. Rebecca, on the other hand, was the kind of woman men wanted, fantasized about, *and married*.

He could imagine spending a torrid week in the Bahamas with Shelly Parker; oh, yes. But only a week. At the end of a week, in spite of her sexual energy and undoubted sexual proficiency, he would most certainly be bored with her. At the end of a week, conversation with Shelly would probably be less rewarding than conversation with a stone wall. Rebecca, however, would never be boring; she was a woman of infinite layers and endless revelations. After twenty years of marriage, he would surely still find Rebecca intriguing.

Marriage? Twenty years?

God, just listen to me! he thought, astonished. Have I been bitten, or have I been *bitten*?

To Shelly, he said, 'So what *do* you know about Baba Lavelle?'

She sighed. 'I'm not telling you anything about the Carramazzas.'

'We're not asking for anything about them. Just Lavelle.'

'And then forget about me. I walk out of here. No phony detention as a material witness.'

'You weren't a witness to the killings. Just tell us what you know about Lavelle, and you can go.'

'All right. He came from nowhere a couple months ago and started dealing coke and smack. I don't mean penny ante stuff, either. In a month, he'd organized about twenty street dealers, supplied them, and made it clear he expected to expand. At least that's what Vince told me. I don't know first-hand 'cause I've never been involved with drugs.'

'Of course not.'

'Now, nobody but nobody deals in this city without an arrangement with Vince's uncle. At least that's what I've heard.'

'That's what I've heard, too,' Jack said dryly.

'So some of Carramazza's people passed word to Lavelle to stop dealing until he'd made arrangements with the family. Friendly advice.'

'Like Dear Abby,' Jack said.

'Yeah,' Shelly said. She didn't even smile. 'But he didn't stop like he was told. Instead, the crazy nigger sent word to Carramazza, offering to split the New York business down the middle, half for each of them, even though Carramazza already has *all* of it.'

'Rather audacious of Mr Lavelle,' Rebecca said.

'No, it was smartass is what it was,' Shelly said. 'I mean, Lavelle is a nobody. Who ever heard of him before this? According to Vince, old man Carramazza figured Lavelle just hadn't understood the first message, so he sent a couple of guys around to make it plainer.'

'They were going to break Lavelle's legs?' Jack asked.

'Or worse,' Shelly said.

'There's always worse.'

'But something happened to the messengers,' Shelly said.

'Dead?'

'I'm not sure. Vince seemed to think they just never came back again.'

'That's dead,' Jack said.

'Probably. Anyway, Lavelle warned Carramazza that he was some sort of voodoo witch doctor and that not even the family could fight him. Of course, everyone laughed about that. And Carramazza sent five of his best, five big mean bastards who know how to watch and wait and pick the right moment.'

'And something happened to them, too?' Rebecca asked.

'Yeah. Four of them never came back.'

'What about the fifth man?' Jack asked.

'He was dumped on the sidewalk in front of Gennaro Carramazza's house in Brooklyn Heights. Alive. Badly bruised, scraped, cut up – but alive. Trouble was, he might as well have been dead.'

'Why's that?'

'He was ape-shit.'

'What?'

'Crazy. Stark, raving mad,' Shelly said, turning the Scotch glass around and around in her long-fingered hands. 'The way Vince heard it, this guy must've seen what happened to the other four, and whatever it was it drove him clear out of his skull, absolutely ape-shit.'

'What was his name?'

'Vince didn't say.'

'Where is he now?'

'I guess Don Carramazza's got him somewhere.'

'And he's still . . . crazy?'

'I guess so.'

'Did Carramazza send a third hit squad?'

'Not that I heard of. I guess, after that, this Lavelle sent a message to the old man Carramazza: "If you want war, then it's war." And he warned the family not to underestimate the power of voodoo.'

'No one laughed this time,' Jack said.

'No one,' Shelly confirmed.

They were silent for a moment.

Jack looked at Shelly Parker's downcast eyes. They weren't red. The skin around them wasn't puffy. There was no indication that she had wept for Vince Vastagliano, her lover.

He could hear the wind outside.

He looked at the windows. Snowflakes tapped the glass.

He said, 'Ms Parker, do you believe that all of this *has* been done through . . . voodoo curses or something like that?'

'No. Maybe. Hell, I don't know. After what's happened these last few days, who can say? One thing I believe in for sure: I believe this Baba Lavelle is one smart, creepy, badass dude.'

Rebecca said, 'We heard a little of this story yesterday, from another victim's brother. Not so much detail as you've given us. He didn't seem to know where we could find Lavelle. Do you?'

'He used to have a place in the Village,' Shelly said. 'But he's not there any more. Since all this started going down, nobody can find him. His street dealers are still working for him, still getting supplies, or so Vince said, but no one knows where Lavelle has gone.'

'The place in the Village where he used to be,' Jack said. 'You happen to know the address?'

'No. I told you, I'm not really involved in this drug business. Honest, I don't know. I only know what Vince told me.'

Jack glanced at Rebecca. 'Anything more?'

'Nope.'

To Shelly, he said, 'You can go.'

At last she swallowed some Scotch, then put the glass down, got to her feet, and straightened her sweater. 'Christ, I swear, I've had it with wops. No more wops. It always turns out bad with them.'

Rebecca gaped at her, and Jack saw a flicker of anger in her eyes, and then she said, 'I hear some of the neese are pretty nice guys.'

Shelly screwed up her face and shook her head. 'Neese? Not for me. They're all little guys, aren't they?'

'Well,' Rebecca said sarcastically, 'so far you've ruled out blacks, wops and neese of all descriptions. You're a very choosy girl.'

Jack watched the sarcasm sail right over Shelly's head.

She smiled tentatively at Rebecca, misapprehending, imagining that she saw a spark of sisterhood. She said, 'Oh, yeah. Hey, look even if I say so myself, I'm not exactly your average girl. I've got a lot of fine points. I can afford to be choosy.'

Rebecca said, 'Better watch out for spics, too.'

'Yeah?' Shelly said. 'I never had a spic for a boyfriend. Bad?'

'Sherpas are worst,' Rebecca said.

Jack coughed into his hand to stifle his laughter.

Picking up her coat, Shelly frowned. 'Sherpas? Who're they?'

'From Nepal,' Rebecca said.

'Where's that?'

'The Himalayas.'

Shelly paused halfway into her coat. 'Those mountains?'

'Those mountains,' Rebecca confirmed.

'That's the other side of the world, isn't it?'

'The other side of the world.'

Shelly's eyes were wide. She finished putting on her coat. She said, 'Have you travelled a lot?'

Jack was afraid he'd draw blood if he bit his tongue any harder.

'I've been around a little,' Rebecca said.

Shelly sighed, working on her buttons. 'I haven't travelled much myself. Haven't been anywhere but Miami and Vegas, once. I've never even seen a Sherpa let alone slept with one.'

'Well,' Rebecca said, 'if you happen to meet up with one, better walk away from him fast. No one'll break your heart faster or into more pieces than a Sherpa will. And by the way, I guess you know not to leave the city without checking with us first.'

'I'm not going anywhere,' Shelly assured them.

She took a long, white, knit scarf from a coat pocket and wrapped it around her neck as she started out of the room. At the doorway, she looked back at Rebecca. 'Hey . . . uh . . . Lieutenant Chandler, I'm sorry if maybe I was a little snappy with you.'

'Don't worry about it.'

'And thanks for the advice.'

'Us girls gotta stick together,' Rebecca said.

'Isn't that the truth!' Shelly said.

She left the room.

They listened to her footsteps along the hallway.

Rebecca said, 'Jesus, what a dumb, egotistical, racist bitch!'

Jack burst out laughing and plopped down on the Queen Anne chair again. 'You sound like Nevetski.'

Imitating Shelly Parker's voice, Rebecca said, '"Even if I say so myself, I'm not exactly your average girl. I've got a lot of fine points." *Jesus*, Jack! The only fine points I saw on that broad were the two on her chest!'

Jack fell back in the chair, laughing harder.

Rebecca stood over him, looking down, grinning. 'I *saw* the way you were drooling over her.'

'Not me,' he managed between gales of laughter.

'Yes, you. Positively drooling. But you might as well forget about her, Jack. She wouldn't have you.'

'Oh?'

'Well, you've got a bit of Irish blood in you. Isn't that right? Your grandmother was Irish, right?' Imitating Shelly Parker's voice again, she said, '"Oh, there's nothing worse than those damned, Pope-kissing, potato-sucking Irish."'

Jack howled.

Rebecca sat on the sofa. She was laughing, too. 'And you've got some British blood, too, if I remember right.'

'Oh, yes,' he said, gasping. 'I'm a tea-swilling limey, too.'

'Not as bad as a Sherpa,' she said.

They were convulsed with laughter when one of the uniformed cops looked in from the hallway. 'What's going on?' he asked.

Neither of them were able to stop laughing and tell him.

'Well, show some respect, huh?' he said. 'We have two dead men here.'

Perversely, that admonition made everything seem even funnier.

The patrolman scowled at them, shook his head, and went away.

Jack knew it was precisely *because* of the presence of death that Shelly Parker's conversations with Rebecca had seemed so uproariously funny. After having encountered four hideously mutilated bodies in as many days, they were desperately in need of a good laugh.

Gradually, they regained their composure and wiped the tears from their eyes. Rebecca got up and went to the windows and stared out at the snow flurries. For a couple of minutes, they shared a most companionable silence, enjoying the temporary but nonetheless welcome release from tension that the laughter had provided.

This moment was the sort of thing Jack couldn't have explained to the guys at the poker game last week, when they'd been putting Rebecca down. At times like this, when the other Rebecca revealed herself – the Rebecca who had a sly sense of humour and a gimlet eye for life's absurdities – Jack felt a special kinship with her. Rare as those moments were, they made the partnership workable and worthwhile – and he hoped that eventually this secret Rebecca would come into the open more often. Perhaps, someday, if he had enough patience, the other Rebecca might even replace the ice maiden altogether.

As usual, however, the change in her was short-lived. She turned away from the window and said, 'Better go talk with the ME and see what he's found.'

'Yeah,' Jack said. 'And let's try to stay glum-faced from now on, Chandler. Let's show them we really *do* have the proper respect for death.'

She smiled at him, but it was only a vague smile now.

She left the room.

He followed.

2

As Nayva Rooney stepped into the hall, she closed the door to the kids' bedroom behind her, so that the rat – or whatever it was – couldn't scurry back in there.

She searched for the intruder in Jack Dawson's bedroom, found nothing, and closed the door on that one, too.

She carefully inspected the kitchen, even looked in cupboards. No rat. There were two doors in the kitchen; one led to the hall, the other to the dining alcove. She closed them both, sealing the critter out of that room, as well.

Now, it simply had to be hiding in the dining alcove or the living room.

But it wasn't.

Nayva looked everywhere. She couldn't find it.

71

Several times she stopped searching just so she could hold her breath and listen. Listen . . . Not a sound.

Throughout the search, in all the rooms, she hadn't merely looked for the elusive little beast itself but also for a hole in a partition or in the baseboard, a breach big enough to admit a largish rat. She discovered nothing of that sort.

At last, she stood in the archway between the living room and the hall. Every lamp and ceiling light was blazing. She looked around, frowning, baffled.

Where had it gone? It still had to be here – didn't it?

Yes. She was sure of it. The thing was still here.

She had the eerie feeling that she was being watched.

3

The assistant medical examiner on the case was Ira Gold-bloom, who looked more Swedish than Jewish. He was tall, fair-skinned, with hair so blond it was almost white; his eyes were blue with a lot of grey speckled through them.

Jack and Rebecca found him on the second floor, in the master bedroom. He had completed his examination of the bodyguard's corpse in the kitchen, had taken a look at Vince Vastagliano, and was getting several instruments out of his black leather case.

'For a man with a weak stomach,' he said, 'I'm in the wrong line of work.'

Jack saw that Goldbloom did appear paler than usual.

Rebecca said, 'We figure these two are connected with the Charlie Novello homicide on Sunday and the Coleson murder yesterday. Can you make the link for us?'

'Maybe.'

'Only maybe?'

'Well, yeah, there's a chance we can tie them together,' Goldbloom said. 'The number of wounds . . . the mutilation factor . . . there are several similarities. But let's wait for the autopsy report.'

Jack was surprised. 'But what about the wounds? Don't they establish a link?'

'The number, yes. Not the type. Have you looked at these wounds?'

'At a glance,' Jack said, 'they appear to be bites of some kind. Rat bites, we thought.'

'But we figured they were just obscuring the *real* wounds, the stab wounds,' Rebecca said.

Jack said, 'Obviously, the rats came along after the men were already dead. Right?'

'Wrong,' Goldbloom said. 'So far as I can tell from a preliminary examination, there aren't any stab wounds in either victim. Maybe tissue bisections will reveal wounds of that nature underneath some of the bites, but I doubt it. Vastagliano and his bodyguard were savagely bitten. They bled to death from those bites. The bodyguard suffered at least three torn arteries, major vessels: the external carotid, the left brachial, and the femoral artery in the left thigh. Vastagliano looks like he was chewed up even worse.'

Jack said, 'But rats aren't that aggressive, damn it. You just don't get attacked by packs of rats in your own home.'

'I don't think these were rats,' Goldbloom said. 'I mean, I've seen rat bites before. Every now and then, a wino will be drinking in an alley, have a heart attack or a stroke, right there behind the garbage bin, where nobody finds him for maybe two days. Meanwhile, the rats get at him. So I know what a rat bite looks like, and this just doesn't seem to match up on a number of points.'

'Could it have been . . . dogs?' Rebecca asked.

'No. For one thing, the bites are too small. I think we can rule out cats, too.'

'Any ideas?' Jack asked.

'No. It's weird. Maybe the autopsy will pin it down for us.'

Rebecca said, 'Did you know the bathroom door was

locked when the uniforms got here? They had to break it down.'

'So I heard. A locked room mystery,' Goldbloom said.

'Maybe there's not much of a mystery to it,' Rebecca said thoughtfully. 'If Vastagliano was killed by some kind of animal, then maybe the thing was small enough to get under the door.'

Goldbloom shook his head. 'It would've had to've been *real* small to manage that. No. It was bigger. A good deal bigger than the crack under the door.'

'About what size would you say?'

'As big as a large rat.'

Rebecca thought for a moment. Then: 'There's an outlet from a heating duct in there. Maybe the thing came through the duct.'

'But there's a grille over the duct,' Jack said. 'And the vents in the grille are narrower then the space under the door.'

Rebecca took two steps to the bathroom, leaned through the doorway, looked around, craning her neck. She came back and said, 'You're right. And the grille's firmly in place.'

'And the little window is closed,' Jack said.

'And locked,' Goldbloom said.

Rebecca brushed a shining strand of hair from her forehead. 'What about drains? Could a rat come up through the tub drain?'

'No,' Goldbloom said. 'Not in modern plumbing.'

'The toilet?'

'Unlikely'

'But possible?'

'Conceivable, I suppose. But, you see, I'm sure it wasn't just one animal.'

'How many?' Rebecca asked.

'There's no way I can give you an exact count. But . . . I would think, whatever they were, there had to be at least . . . a dozen of them.'

'Good Heavens,' Jack said.

'Maybe two dozen. Maybe more.'

'How do you figure?'

'Well,' Goldbloom said, 'Vastagliano was a big man, a strong man. He'd be able to handle one, two, three rat-sized animals, no matter what sort of things they were. In fact, he'd most likely be able to deal with half a dozen of them. Oh, sure, he'd get bitten a few times, but he'd be able to take care of himself. He might not be able to kill all of them, but he'd kill a few and keep the rest at bay. So it looks to me as if there were so many of these things, such a horde of them that they simply overwhelmed him.'

With insect-quick feet, a chill skittered the length of Jack's spine. He thought of Vastagliano being borne down onto the bathroom floor under a tide of screeching rats – or perhaps something even worse than rats. He thought of the man harried at every flank, bitten and torn and ripped and scratched, attacked from all directions, so that he hadn't the presence of mind to strike back effectively, his arms weighed down by the sheer numbers of his adversaries, his reaction time affected by a numbing horror. A painful, bloody, lonely death. Jack shuddered.

'And Ross, the bodyguard,' Rebecca said. 'You figure he was attacked by a lot of them, too?'

'Yes,' Goldbloom said. 'Same reasoning applies.'

Rebecca blew the air out through clenched teeth in an expression of her frustration. 'This just makes the locked bathroom even more difficult to figure. From what I've seen, it looks as if Vastagliano and his bodyguard were both in the kitchen, making a late-night snack. The attack started there, evidently. Ross was quickly overwhelmed. Vastagliano ran. He was chased, couldn't get to the front door because they cut him off, so he ran upstairs and locked himself in the bathroom. Now, the rats – or whatever – weren't in there when he locked the door, so how did they *get* in there?'

'And out again,' Goldbloom reminded her.

'It almost has to be plumbing, the toilet.'

'I rejected that because of the numbers involved,' Goldbloom said. 'Even if there weren't any plumbing traps designed to stop a rat, and even if it held its breath and swam through whatever water barriers there were, I just don't buy that explanation. Because what we're talking about here is a whole pack of creatures slithering in that way, one behind the other, like a commando team, for God's sake. Rats just aren't that smart or that . . . determined. *No* animal is. It doesn't make sense.'

The thought of Vastagliano wrapped in a clock of swarming, biting rats had caused Jack's mouth to go dry and sour. He had to work up some saliva to unstick his tongue.

He said, 'Another thing. Even if Vastagliano and his bodyguard were overwhelmed by scores of these . . . these *things*, they'd still have killed a couple – wouldn't they? But we haven't found a single dead rat or a single dead anything else – except, of course, dead people.'

'And no droppings,' Goldbloom said.

'No what?'

'Droppings. Faeces. If there were dozens of animals involved, you'd find droppings, at least a few, probably piles of droppings.'

'If you find animal hairs—'

'We'll definitely be looking for them,' Goldbloom said. 'We'll vacuum the floor around each body, of course, and analyse the sweepings. If we could find a few hairs, that would clear up a lot of the mystery.' The assistant medical examiner wiped one hand across his face, as if he could pull off and cast away his tension, his disgust. He wiped so hard that spots of colour actually did rise in his cheeks, but the haunted look was still in his eyes. 'There's something else that disturbs me, too. The victims weren't . . . eaten. Bitten, ripped, gouged . . . all of that . . . but so far as I can see, not an ounce of flesh was consumed. Rats would've eaten the tender parts: eyes, nose, ear lobes, testicles . . . They'd have torn open the body cavities in order to get to the soft organs. So would any other predator or scavenger. But there was nothing like that in this case. These things killed purposefully, efficiently, methodically . . . and then just went away without devouring a scrap of their prey. It's unnatural. Uncanny. What motive or force was driving them? And *why*?'

4

After talking with Ira Goldbloom, Jack and Rebecca decided to question the neighbours. Perhaps one of them had heard or seen something important last night.

Outside Vastagliano's house, they stood on the sidewalk for a moment, hands in their coat pockets.

The sky was lower than it had been an hour ago. Darker, too. The grey clouds were smeared with others that were soot-dark.

Snowflakes drifted down; not many; they descended lazily, except when the wind gusted, and they seemed like fragments of burnt sky, cold bits of ash.

Rebecca said, 'I'm afraid we'll be pulled off this case.'

'You mean . . . off these two murders or off the whole business?'

'Just these two. They're going to say there's no connection.'

'There's a connection,' Jack said.

'I know. But they're going to say Vastagliano and Ross are unrelated to the Novello and Coleson cases.'

'I think Goldbloom will tie them together for us.'

She looked sour. 'I hate to be pulled off a case, damn it. I like to finish what I start.'

'We won't be pulled off.'

'But don't you see? If some sort of animal did it . . .'

'Yes?'

'Then how can they possibly classify it as murder?'

'It's murder,' he said emphatically.

'But you can't charge an animal with homicide.'

He nodded. 'I see what you're driving at.'

'Damn.'

'Listen, if these were animals that were trained to kill, then it's still homicide; the trainer is the murderer.'

'If these were dog bites that Vastagliano and Ross died from,' Rebecca said, 'then maybe you might just be able to sell that theory. But what animal – what animal as small as these apparently were – can be trained to kill, to obey all commands? Rats? No. Cats? No. Gerbils, for God's sake?'

'Well, they train ferrets,' Jack said. 'They use them for hunting sometimes. Not game hunting where they're going after the meat, but just for sport, 'cause the prey is generally a ragged mess when the ferrets gets done with it.'

'Ferrets, huh? I'd like to see you convince Captain Gresham that someone's prowling the city with a pack of killer ferrets to do his dirty work for him.'

'Does sound far-fetched,' Jack admitted.

'To say the least.'

'So what does that leave us with?'

She shrugged.

Jack thought about Baba Lavelle.

Voodoo?

No. Surely not. It was one thing to propose that Lavelle was making the murders look strange in order to frighten his adversaries with the threat of voodoo curses, but it was quite something else to imagine that the curses actually worked.

Then again . . . What about the locked bathroom? What about the fact that Vastagliano and Ross hadn't been able to kill even one of their attackers? What about the lack of animal droppings?

Rebecca must have known what he was thinking, for she scowled and said, 'Come on. Let's talk to the neighbours.'

The wind suddenly woke, breathed, raged. Spitting flecks of snow, it came along the street as if it were a living beast, a very cold and angry wind.

Mrs Quillen, Penny's teacher at Wellton School, was unable to understand why a vandal would have wrecked only one locker.

'Perhaps he intended to ruin them all but had second thoughts. Or maybe he started with yours, Penny dear, then heard a sound he couldn't place, thought someone was coming, got frightened, and ran. But we keep the school locked up tight as a drum at night, of course, and there's the alarm system, too. However did he get in and out?'

Penny knew it wasn't a vandal. She knew it was something a whole lot stranger than that. She knew the trashing of her locker was somehow connected with the eerie experience she'd had last night in her room. But she didn't know how to express this knowledge without sounding like a child afraid of the boogeymen, so she didn't try to explain to Mrs Quillen those things which, in truth, she couldn't even explain to herself.

After some discussion, much sympathy, and even more bafflement, Mrs Quillen sent Penny to the basement where the supplies and spare textbooks were kept on well-ordered storage shelves.

'Get replacements for everything that was destroyed, Penny. All the books, new pencils, a three-ring notebook with a pack of filler, and a new tablet. And don't dawdle, please.'

Penny went down the front stairs to the ground floor, paused at the main doors to look through the bevelled glass windows at the swirling puffs of snow, then hurried back the hall to the rear of the building, past the deserted gymnasium, past the music room where a class was about to begin.

The cellar door was at the very end of the hallway. She opened it and found the light switch. A long, narrow flight of stairs led down.

The ground-floor hallway, through which she'd just

passed, had smelled of chalk dust that had escaped from classrooms, pine-scented floor wax, and the dry heat of the forced-air furnace. But as she descended the narrow steps, she noticed that the smells of the cellar were different from those upstairs. She detected the mild lime-rich odour of concrete dust. Insecticide lent a pungent note to the air; she knew they sprayed every month to discourage silverfish from making a meal of the books stored here. And, underlying everything else, there was a slightly damp smell, a vague but nonetheless unpleasant mustiness.

She reached the bottom of the stairs. Her footsteps rang sharply, crisply on the concrete floor and echoed hollowly in a far corner.

The basement extended under the entire building and was divided into two chambers. At the opposite end from the stairs lay the furnace room, beyond a heavy metal fire door that was always kept closed. The largest of the two rooms was on this side of the door. A work table occupied the centre, and free-standing metal storage shelves were lined up along the walls, all crammed full of books and supplies.

Penny took a folding carry-all basket from a rack, opened it, and collected the items she needed. She had just located the last of the textbooks when she heard a strange sound behind her. *That* sound. The hissing-scrabbling-muttering noise that she had heard last night in her bedroom.

She whirled.

As far as she could see, she was alone.

The problem was that she couldn't see everywhere. Deep shadows coiled under the stairs. In one corner of the room, over by the fire door, a ceiling light was burned out. Shadows had claimed that area. Furthermore, each unit of metal shelving stood on six-inch legs, and the gap between the lowest shelf and the floor was untouched by light. There were a lot of places where something small and quick could hide.

She waited, frozen, listening, and ten long seconds elapsed, then fifteen, twenty, and the sound didn't come again, so she wondered if she'd really heard it or only imagined it, and another few seconds ticked away as slowly as minutes, but then something thumped overhead at the top of the stairs: the cellar door.

She had left the door standing open.

Someone or something had just pulled it shut.

With the basket of books and supplies in one hand, Penny started toward the foot of the stairs but stopped abruptly when she heard other noises up there on the landing. Hissing. Growling. Murmuring. The tick and scrape of movement.

Last night, she had tried to convince herself that the thing in her room hadn't actually been there, that it had been only a remnant of a dream. Now she knew it was more than that. But just what was it? A ghost? Whose ghost? Not her mother's ghost. She maybe wouldn't have minded if her mother had been hanging around, sort of watching over her. Yeah, that would have been okay. But, at best, this was a malicious spirit; at worst, a dangerous spirit. Her mother's ghost would never be malicious like this, not in a million years. Besides, a ghost didn't follow you around from place to place. No, that wasn't how it worked. *People* weren't haunted. *Houses* were haunted, and the ghosts doing the haunting were bound to one place until their souls were finally at rest; they couldn't leave that special place they haunted, couldn't just roam all over the city, following one particular young girl.

Yet the cellar door had been drawn shut.

Maybe a draught had closed it.

Maybe. But something was moving around on the landing up there where she couldn't see it. Not a draft. Something strange.

Imagination.

Oh, yeah?

She stood by the stairs, looking up, trying to figure

it out, trying to calm herself, carrying on an urgent conversation with herself: —*Well, if it's not a ghost, what is it?*

—*Something bad.*

—*Not necessarily.*

—*Something very, very bad.*

—*Stop it! Stop scaring yourself. It didn't try to hurt you last night, did it?*

—*No.*

—*So there. You're safe.*

—*But now it's back.*

A new sound jolted her out of her interior dialogue. Another thump. But this was different from the sound the door had made when it had been pushed shut. And again: *thump!* Again. It sounded as if something was throwing itself against the wall at the head of the stairs, bumping mindlessly like a summer moth battering against a window.

Thump!

The lights went out.

Penny gasped.

The thumping stopped.

In the sudden darkness, the weird and unsettlingly eager animal sounds rose on all sides of Penny, not just from the landing overhead, and she detected movement in the claustrophobic blackness. There wasn't merely one unseen, unknown creature in the cellar with her; there were many of them.

But what *were* they?

Something brushed her foot, then darted away into the subterranean gloom.

She screamed. She was loud but not loud enough. Her cry hadn't carried beyond the cellar.

At the same moment, Mrs March, the music teacher, began pounding on the piano in the music room directly overhead. Kids began to sing up there. *Frosty the Snowman*. They were rehearsing for a Christmas show which the entire school would perform for parents just prior to the start of the holiday vacation.

Now, even if Penny could manage a louder scream, no one would hear her, anyway.

Likewise, because of the music and singing, she could no longer hear the things moving in the darkness around her. But they were still there. She had no doubt that they were there.

She took a deep breath. She was determined not to lose her head. She wasn't a *child*.

They won't hurt me, she thought.

But she couldn't convince herself.

She shuffled cautiously to the foot of the stairs, the carry-all in one hand, her other hand out in front of her, feeling her way as if she were blind, which she might as well have been.

The cellar had two windows, but there were small rectangles set high in the wall, at street level, with no more than one square foot of glass in each of them. Besides, they were dirty on the outside; even on a bright day, those grimy panes did little to illuminate the basement. On a cloudy day like today, with a storm brewing, the windows gave forth only a thin, milky light that travelled no more than a few inches into the cellar before expiring.

She reached the foot of the stairs and looked up. Deep, deep blackness.

Mrs March was still hammering on the piano, and the kids were still singing about the snowman that had come to life.

Penny raised one foot, found the first step.

Overhead, at the top of the stairs, a pair of eyes appeared only a few inches above the landing floor, as if disembodied, as if floating in the air, although they must have been attached to an animal about the size of a cat. It wasn't a cat, of course. She wished it were. The eyes were as large as a cat's eyes, too, and very bright, not merely reflective like the eyes of a cat, but so unnaturally bright that they glowed like two tiny lanterns. The colour was odd, too: white, moon-pale, with the faintest trace of silvery blue. Those cold eyes glared down at her.

She took her foot off the first step.

The creature above slipped off the landing, onto the highest step, edging closer.

Penny retreated.

The thing descended two more steps, its advance betrayed only by its unblinking eyes. Darkness cloaked its form.

Breathing hard, her heart pounding louder than the music above, she backed up until she collided with a metal storage shelf. There was nowhere to turn, nowhere to hide.

The thing was now a third of the way down the stairs and still coming.

Penny felt the urge to pee. She pressed back against the shelves and squeezed her thighs together.

The thing was halfway down the stairs. Moving faster.

Overhead, in the music room, they had really got into the spirit of *Frosty the Snowman*, a lilt in their voices, belting it out with what Mrs March always called 'gusto'.

From the corner of her eye, Penny saw something in the cellar, off to the right: a wink of soft light, a flash, a glow, movement. Daring to look away from the creature that was descending the stairs in front of her, she glanced into the unlighted room – and immediately wished she hadn't.

Eyes.

Silver-white eyes.

The darkness was full of them. Two eyes shone up at her from the floor, hardly more than a yard away, regarding her with a cold hunger. Two more eyes were little farther than a foot behind the first pair. Another four eyes gleamed frostily from a point at least three feet above the floor, in the centre of the room, and for a moment, she thought she had misjudged the height of these creatures, but then she realized two of them had climbed onto the worktable. Two, four, six *pair* of eyes peered malevolently at her from various shelves along the far wall. Three more pair were at floor level near the fire door that led to the furnace room. Some were perfectly still; some were moving restlessly back and forth; some were creeping slowly toward her. None of them blinked. Others were moving out from the space under the stairs. There were about twenty of the things: forty brightly glowing, vicious, unearthly eyes.

Shaking, whimpering, Penny tore her own gaze away from the demonic horde in the cellar and looked at the stairs again.

The lone beast that had started slinking down from the landing no more than a minute ago had now reached the bottom. It was on the last step.

6

Both to the east and to the west of Vincent Vastagliano's house, the neighbours were established in equally large, comfortable, elegantly furnished homes that might as well have been isolated country manors instead of town-houses. The city did not intrude into these stately places, and none of the occupants had seen or heard anything unusual during the night of blood and murder.

In less than half an hour, Jack and Rebecca had exhausted that line of inquiry and had returned to the side-walk. They kept their heads tucked down to present as small a target as possible to the wind, which had grown steadily more powerful. It was now a wicked, icy, lashing whip that snatched litter out of the gutters and flung it through the air, shook the bare trees with almost enough violence to crack the brittle limbs, snapped coat-tails with sharp reports, and stung exposed flesh.

The snow flurries were falling in greater numbers now. In a few minutes, they would be coming down too thick to be called flurries any more. The street was still bare black macadam, but soon it would boast a fresh white skin.

Jack and Rebecca headed back toward Vastagliano's place and were almost there when someone called to them. Jack turned and saw Harry Ulbeck, the young officer who had earlier been on watch at the top of Vastagliano's front steps; Harry was leaning out of one of the three black-and-whites that were parked at the kerb. He said something, but the wind ripped his words into meaningless sounds. Jack went to the car, bent down to the open window, and said, 'Sorry, Harry, I didn't hear what you said,' and his breath smoked out of him in cold white plumes.

'Just came over the radio,' Harry said. 'They want you right away. You and Detective Chandler.'

'Want us for what?'

'Looks as if it's part of this case you're working on. There's been more killing. More like this here. Maybe even worse . . . even bloodier.'

7

Their eyes weren't at all like eyes should be. They looked, instead, like slots in a furnace grate, providing glimpses of the fire beyond. A silver-white fire. These eyes contained no irises, no pupils, as did human and animal eyes. There was just that fierce glow, the white light from within them, pulsing and flickering.

The creature on the stairs moved down from the last step, onto the cellar floor. It edged toward Penny, then stopped, stared up at her.

She couldn't move back even one more inch. Already, one of the metal shelves pressed painfully across her shoulderblades.

Suddenly she realized the music had stopped. The cellar was silent. Had been silent for some time. Perhaps for as long as half a minute. Frozen by terror, she hadn't reacted immediately when *Frosty the Snowman* was concluded.

Belatedly she opened her mouth to scream for help, but the piano started up again. This time the tune was *Rudolph the Red-Nosed Reindeer*, which was even louder than the first song.

The thing at the foot of the stairs continued to glare at her, and although its eyes were utterly different from the eyes of a tiger, she was nevertheless reminded of a picture of a tiger that she'd seen in a magazine. The eyes in that photograph and these strange eyes looked absolutely nothing alike, yet they had something in common: They were the eyes of predators.

Even though her vision was beginning to adjust somewhat to the darkness, Penny still couldn't see what the creatures looked like, couldn't tell whether they were well-armed with teeth and claws. There were only the menacing, unblinking eyes, adance with white flame.

In the cellar to her right, the other creatures began to move, almost as one, with a single purpose.

She swung toward them, her heart racing faster than ever, her breath caught in her throat.

From the gleam of silvery eyes, she could tell they were leaping down from the shelves where they'd perched.

They're coming for me.

The two on the worktable jumped to the floor.

Penny screamed as loud as she could.

The music didn't stop. Didn't even miss a beat.

No one had heard her.

Except for the one at the foot of the stairs, all the creatures had gathered into a pack. Their blazing eyes looked like a cache of diamonds spread on black velvet.

None of them advanced on her. They waited.

After a moment she turned to the stairs again.

Now, the beast at the bottom of the stairs moved, too. But it didn't come toward her. It darted into the cellar and joined the others of its kind.

The stairs were clear, though dark.

It's a trick.

As far as she could see, there was nothing to prevent her from climbing the stairs as fast as she could.

It's a trap.

But there was no need for them to set a trap. She was *already* trapped. They could have rushed her at any time. They could have killed her if they'd wanted to kill her.

The flickering ice-white eyes watched her.

Mrs March pounded on the piano.

The kids sang.

Penny bolted away from the shelves, dashed to the stairs, and clambered upward. Step by step she expected the things to bite her heels, latch onto her, and drag her down. She stumbled once, almost fell back to the bottom, grabbed the railing with her free hand, and kept going. The top step. The landing. Fumbling in the dark for the doorknob, finding it. The hallway. Light, safety. She slammed the door behind her. Leaned on it. Gasping.

In the music room, they were still singing *Rudolph the Red-Nosed Reindeer*.

The corridor was deserted.

Dizzy, weak in the legs, Penny slid down and sat on the floor, her back against the door. She let go of the carry-all. She had been gripping it so tightly that the handle had left its mark across her palm. Her hand ached.

The song ended.

Another song began. *Silver Bells.*

Gradually, Penny regained her strength, calmed herself, and was able to think clearly. What *were* those hideous little things? Where did they come from? What did they want from her?

Thinking clearly wasn't any help. She couldn't come up with a single acceptable answer.

A lot of really dumb answers kept occurring to her, however: goblins, gremlins, ogres . . . Cripes. It couldn't be anything like that. This was real life, not a fairytale.

How could she ever tell anyone about her experience

in the cellar without seeming childish or, worse, even slightly crazy? Of course, grown-ups didn't like to use the term 'crazy' with children. You could be as nuts as a walnut tree, babble like a loon, chew on furniture, set fire to cats, and talk to brick walls, and as long as you were still a kid, the worst they'd say about you – in public, at least – was that you were 'emotionally disturbed', although what they meant by that was 'crazy'. If she told Mrs Quillen or her father or any other adult about the things she had seen in the school basement, everyone would think she was looking for attention and pity; they'd figure she hadn't yet adjusted to her mother's death. For a few months after her mother passed away, Penny *had* been in bad shape, confused, angry, frightened, a problem to her father and to herself. She had needed help for a while. Now, if she told them about the things in the basement, they would think she needed help again. They would send her to a 'counsellor', who would actually be a psychologist or some other kind of head doctor, and they'd do their best for her, give her all sorts of attention and sympathy and treatment, but they simply wouldn't *believe* her – until, with their own eyes, they saw such things as she had seen.

Or until it was too late for her.

Yes, they'd all believe *then* – when she was dead.

She had no doubt whatsoever that the fiery-eyed things would try to kill her, sooner or later. She didn't know *why* they wanted to take her life, but she sensed their evil intent, their hatred. They hadn't harmed her yet, true, but they were growing bolder. Last night, the one in her bedroom hadn't damaged anything except the plastic baseball bat she'd poked at it, but by this morning, they had grown bold enough to destroy the contents of her locker. And now, bolder still, they had revealed themselves and had threatened her.

What next?

Something worse.

They enjoyed her terror; they fed on it. But like a cat with a mouse, they would eventually grow tired of the game. And then . . .

She shuddered.

What am I going to do? she wondered miserably. *What am I going to do?*

8

The hotel, one of the best in the city, overlooked Central Park. It was the same hotel at which Jack and Linda had spent their honeymoon, thirteen years ago. They hadn't been able to afford the Bahamas or Florida or even the Catskills. Instead, they had remained in the city and had settled for three days at this fine old landmark, and even *that* had been an extravagance. They'd had a memorable honeymoon, nevertheless, three days filled with laughter and good conversation and talk of their future and lots of loving. They'd promised themselves a trip to the Bahamas on their tenth anniversary, something to look forward to. But by the time that milestone rolled around, they had two kids to think about and a new apartment to get in order, and they renegotiated the promise, rescheduling the Bahamas for their fifteenth anniversary. Little more than a year later, Linda was dead. In the eighteen months since her funeral, Jack had often thought about the Bahamas, which were now forever spoiled for him, and about this hotel.

The murders had been committed on the sixteenth floor, where there were now two uniformed officers – Yeager and Tufton – stationed at the elevator alcove. They weren't letting anyone through except those with police ID and those who could prove they were registered guests with lodgings on that level.

'Who were the victims?' Rebecca asked Yeager. 'Civilians?'

'Nope,' Yeager said. He was a lanky man with enormous yellow teeth. Every time he paused, he probed at his teeth with his tongue, licked and pried at them. 'Two of them were pretty obviously professional muscle.'

'You know the type,' Tufton said as Yeager paused to probe again at his teeth. 'Tall, big hands, big arms; you could break axe handles across their necks, and they'd think it was just a sudden breeze.'

'The third one,' Yeager said, 'was one of the Carramazzas.' He paused; his tongue curled out, over his upper teeth, swept back and forth. 'One of the immediate family, too.' He scrubbed his tongue over his lowers. 'In fact—' Probe, probe. '—it's Dominick Carramazza.'

'Oh, shit!' Jack said. 'Gennaro's *brother*?'

'Yeah, the godfather's little brother, his favourite brother, his right hand,' Tufton said quickly, before Yeager started to answer. Tufton was a fast-spoken man with a sharp face, and angular body, and quick movements, brisk and efficient gestures. Yeager's slowness must be a constant irritation to him. 'And they didn't just kill him. They tore him up bad. There isn't any mortician alive who can put Dominick back together well enough for an open-casket funeral, and you know how important funerals are to these Sicilians.'

'There'll be blood in the streets now,' Jack said wearily.

'Gang war like we haven't seen in years,' Tufton agreed.

Rebecca said, 'Dominick . . . ? Wasn't he the one who was in the news all summer?'

'Yeah,' Yeager said. 'The DA thought he had him nailed for—'

When Yeager paused to swab his yellowed teeth with his big pink tongue, Tufton quickly said, 'Trafficking in narcotics. He's in charge of the entire Carramazza narcotics operation. They've been trying to put him in the stir for twenty years, maybe longer, but he's a fox. He always walks out of the courtroom a free man.'

'What was he doing here in the hotel?' Jack wondered.

'I think he was hiding out,' Tufton said.

'Registered under a phony name,' Yeager said.

Tufton said, 'Holed up here with those two apes to protect him. They must've known he was targeted, but he was hit anyway.'

'Hit?' Yeager said scornfully. He paused to tend to his teeth and made an unpleasant sucking sound. Then: 'Hell, this was more than just a hit. This was total devastation. This was crazy, totally off the wall; that's what *this* was. Christ, if I didn't know better, I'd say these three here had been *chewed*, just chewed to pieces.'

The scene of the crime was a two-room suite. The door had been broken down by the first officers to arrive. An assistant medical examiner, a police photographer, and a couple of lab technicians were at work in both rooms.

The parlour, decorated entirely in beige and royal blue, was elegantly appointed with a stylish mixture of French provincial and understated contemporary furniture. The room would have been warm and welcoming if it hadn't been thoroughly splattered with blood.

The first body was sprawled on the parlour floor, on its back, beside an overturned, oval-shaped coffee table. A man in his thirties. Tall, husky. His dark slacks were torn. His white shirt was torn, too, and much of it was stained crimson. He was in the same condition as Vastagliano and Ross: savagely bitten, mutilated.

The carpet around the corpse was saturated with blood, but the battle hadn't been confined to that small portion of the room. A trail of blood, weaving and erratic, led from one end of the parlour to the other, then back again; it was the route the panicked victim had taken in a futile attempt to escape from and slough off his attackers.

Jack felt sick.

'It's a damned slaughterhouse,' Rebecca said.

The dead man had been packing a gun. His shoulder holster was empty. A silencer-equipped .38 pistol was at his side.

Jack interrupted one of the lab technicians who was moving slowly around the parlour, collecting blood samples from various stains. 'You didn't touch the gun?'

'Of course not,' the technician said. 'We'll take it back to the lab in a plastic bag, see if we can work up any prints.'

'I was wondering if it'd been fired,' Jack said.

'Well, that's almost a sure thing. We've found four expended shell casings.'

'Same calibre as this weapon?'

'Yep.'

'Find any of the loads?' Rebecca asked.

'All four,' the technician said. He pointed: 'Two in that wall, one in the door frame over there, and one right through the upholstery button on the back of that armchair.'

'So it looks as if he didn't hit whatever he was shooting at,' Rebecca said.

'Probably not. Four shell casings, four slugs. Everything's been neatly accounted for.'

Jack said, 'How could he have missed four times in such close quarters?'

'Damned if I know,' the technician said. He shrugged and went back to work.

The bedroom was even bloodier than the parlour. Two dead men shared it.

There were two living men, as well. A police photographer was snapping the bodies from every angle. As assistant medical examiner named Brendan Mulgrew, a tall thin man with a prominent Adam's apple, was studying the positions of both corpses.

One of the victims was on the king-size bed, his head at the foot of it, his bare feet pointed toward the headboard, one hand at his torn throat, the other hand at his side, the palm turned up, open. He was wearing a bathrobe and a suit of blood.

'Dominick Carramazza,' Jack said.

Looking at the ruined face, Rebecca said, 'How can you tell?'

'Just barely.'

The other dead man was on the floor, flat on his stomach, head turned to one side, face torn to ribbons. He was dressed like the one in the parlour: white shirt open at the neck, dark slacks, a shoulder holster.

Jack turned away from the gouged and oozing flesh. His stomach had gone sour; an acid burning etched its way up from his gut to a point under his heart. He fumbled in his coat pocket for a roll of Tums.

Both of the victims in the bedroom had been armed. But guns had been of no more help to them than to the man in the parlour.

The cadaver on the floor was still clutching a silencer-equipped pistol, which was as illegal as a howitzer at a presidential press conference. It was like the gun on the floor in the first room.

The man on the bed hadn't been able to hold on to his weapon. It was lying on the tangled sheets and blankets.

'Smith & Wesson .357 Magnum,' Jack said. 'Powerful enough to blow a hole as big as a fist right through anyone in its way.'

Being a revolver instead of a pistol, it wasn't fitted with a silencer, and Rebecca said, 'Fired indoors, it'd sound like a cannon. They'd have heard it from one end of this floor to the other.'

To Mulgrew, Jack said, 'Does it look as if both guns were fired?'

The ME nodded. 'Yeah. Judging from the expended shell casings, the magazine of the pistol is completely emptied. Ten rounds. The guy with the .357 Magnum managed to get off five shots.'

'And didn't hit his assailant,' Rebecca said.

'Apparently not,' Mulgrew said, 'although we're taking blood samples from all over the suite, hoping we'll come up with a type that doesn't belong to one of the three victims.'

They had to move to get out of the photographer's way.

Jack noticed two impressive holes in the wall to the left of the bed. 'Those from the .357?'

'Yes,' Mulgrew said. He swallowed hard; his Adam's apple bobbled. 'Both slugs went through the wall, into the next room.'

'Jesus. Anyone hurt over there?'

'No. But it was a close thing. The guy in the next room is mad as hell.'

'I don't blame him,' Jack said.

'Has anyone gotten his story yet?' Rebecca asked.

'He may have talked to the uniforms,' Mulgrew said, 'but I don't think any detectives have formally questioned him.'

Rebecca looked at Jack. 'Let's get to him while he's still fresh.'

'Okay. But just a second.' To Mulgrew, Jack said, 'These three victims . . . were they bitten to death?'

'Looks that way.'

'Rat bites?'

'I'd rather wait for lab results, the autopsy—'

'I'm only asking for an *unofficial* opinion,' Jack said.

'Well . . . unofficially . . . not rats.'

'Dogs? Cats?'

'Highly unlikely.'

'Find any droppings?'

Mulgrew was surprised. 'I thought of that, but it's funny you should. I looked everywhere. Couldn't find a single dropping.'

'Anything else strange?'

'You noticed the door, didn't you?'

'Besides that.'

'Isn't that enough?' Mulgrew said, astonished. 'Listen, the first two bulls on the scene had to break down the door to get in. The suite was locked up tight – from the inside. The windows are locked from the inside, too, and in addition to that, I think they're probably painted shut. So . . . no matter whether they were men or animals, how did the killers get away? You have a locked room mystery on your hands. I think that's pretty strange, don't you?'

Jack sighed. 'Actually, it's getting to be downright common.'

9

Ted Gernsby, a telephone company repairman, was working on a junction box in a storm drain not far from Wellton School. He was bracketed by work lights that he and Andy Carnes had brought down from the truck, and the lights were focused on the box; otherwise, the man-high drainage pipe was filled with cool, stagnant darkness.

The lights threw off a small measure of heat, and the air was naturally warmer underground than on the windswept street, although not *much* warmer. Ted shivered. Because the job involved delicate work, he had removed his gloves. Now his hands were growing stiff from the cold.

Although the storm drains weren't connected to the sewer system, and although the concrete conduits were relatively dry after weeks of no precipitation, Ted occasionally got a whiff of a dark, rotten odour that, depending on its intensity, sometimes made him grimace and sometimes made him gag. He wished Andy would hurry back with the circuit board that was needed to finish the repair job.

He put down a pair of needle-nose pliers, cupped his hands over his mouth, and blew warm air into them. He leaned past the work lights in order to see beyond the glare and into the unilluminated length of the tunnel.

A flashlight bobbled in the darkness, coming this way. It was Andy, at last.

But why was he running?

Andy Carnes came out of the gloom, breathing fast. He was in his early twenties, about twenty years younger than Ted; they had been working together only a week. Andy was a beachboy type with white-blond hair and a healthy complexion and freckles that were like waterspots on warm dry sand. He would have looked more at home in Miami or California; in New York, he seemed misplaced. Now, however, he was so pale that, by contrast, his freckles looked like dark holes in his face. His eyes were wild. He was trembling.

'What's wrong?' Ted asked.

'Back there,' Andy said shakily. 'In the branch tunnel. Just this side of the manhole.'

'Something there? What?'

Andy glanced back. 'They didn't follow me. Thank God. I was afraid they were after me.'

Ted Gernsby frowned. 'What're you talking about?'

Andy started to speak, hesitated, shook his head. Looking sheepish, yet still frightened, he said, 'You wouldn't believe it. Not in a million years. I don't believe it, and I'm the one who saw it!'

Impatient, Ted unclipped his own flashlight from the tool belt around his waist. He started back toward the branch drain.

'Wait!' Andy said. 'It might be . . . dangerous to go back there.'

'*Why?*' Ted demanded, exasperated with him.

'Eyes.' Andy shivered. 'That's what I saw first. A lot of eyes shining in the dark, there inside the mouth of the branch line.'

'Is that all? Listen, you saw a few rats. Nothing to worry about. When you've been on this job a while, you'll get used to them.'

'Not rats,' Andy said adamantly. 'Rats have red eyes, don't they? These were white. Or . . . sort of silvery. Silvery-white eyes. Very bright. It wasn't that they reflected my flashlight. No. I didn't even have the flash on them when I first spotted them. They *glowed.*

Glowing eyes, with their own light. I mean . . . Like jack-'o-lantern eyes. Little spots of fire, flickering. So then I turned the flash on them, and they were right there, no more than six feet from me, the most incredible damned things. Right there!'

'What?' Ted demanded. 'You still haven't told me what you saw.'

In a tremulous voice, Andy told him.

It was the craziest story Ted had ever heard, but he listened without comment, and although he was sure it couldn't be true, he felt a quiver of fear pass through him. Then, in spite of Andy's protests, he went back to the branch tunnel to have a look for himself. He didn't find anything at all, let alone the monsters he'd heard described. He even went into the tributary for a short distance, probing with the beam of his flashlight. Nothing.

He returned to the work site.

Andy was waiting in the pool of light cast by the big lamps. He eyed the surrounding darkness with suspicion. He was still pale.

'Nothing there,' Ted said.

'A minute ago, there was.'

Ted switched off his flashlight, snapped it onto his tool belt. He jammed his hands into the fur-lined pockets of his quilted jacket.

He said, 'This is the first time you've been sub-street with me.'

'So?'

'Ever been in a place like this before?'

Andy said, 'You mean in a sewer?'

'It's not a sewer. Storm drain. You ever been underground?'

'No. What's that got to do with it?'

'Ever been in a crowded theatre and suddenly felt . . . closed in?'

'I'm not claustrophobic,' Andy said defensively.

'Nothing to be ashamed of, you know. I've seen it

happen before. A guy is a little uncomfortable in small rooms, elevators, crowded places, though not so uncomfortable that you'd say he was claustrophobic. Then he comes down here on a repair job for the first time, and he starts feeling cramped up, starts to shake, gets short of breath, feels the walls closing in, starts hearing things, imagining things. If that's the case with you, don't worry about it. Doesn't mean you'll be fired or anything like that. Hell, no! They'll just make sure they don't give you another underground assignment; that's all.'

'I saw those things, Ted.'

'Nothing's there.'

'I *saw* them.'

10

Down the hall from the late Dominick Carramazza's hotel suite, the next room was large and pleasant, with a queen-size bed, a writing desk, bureau, chest of drawers, and two chairs. The colour scheme was coral with turquoise accents.

Burt Wicke, the occupant, was in his late forties. He was about six feet tall, and at one time he'd been solid and strong, but now all the hard meat of him was sheathed with fat. His shoulders were big but round, and his chest was big, and his gut overhung his belt, and as he sat on the edge of the bed, his slacks were stretched tight around his hammy thighs. Jack found it hard to tell if Wicke had ever been good looking. Too much rich food, too much booze, too many cigarettes, too much of everything had left him with a face that looked partly melted. His eyes protruded just a bit and were bloodshot. In that coral and turquoise room, Wicke looked like a toad on a birthday cake.

His voice was a surprise, higher pitched then Jack expected. He had figured Burt Wicke to be slow-moving, slow-talking, a weary and sedentary man, but Wicke spoke with considerable nervous energy. He couldn't sit still, either. He got up from the bed, paced the room, sat down in a chair, bolted up almost at once, paced, all the while talking, answering questions – and complaining. He was a non-stop complainer.

'This won't take long, will it? I've already had to cancel one business meeting. If this takes long, I'll have to cancel another.'

'It shouldn't take long,' Jack said.

'I had breakfast here in the room. Not a very good breakfast. The orange juice was too warm, and the coffee wasn't warm enough. I asked for my eggs over well, and they came sunny-side up. You'd think a hotel like this, a hotel with this reputation, a hotel this expensive, would be able to give you a decent room service breakfast. Anyway, I shaved and got dressed. I was standing in the bathroom, combing my hair when I heard somebody shouting. Then screaming. I stepped out of the bathroom and listened, and I was pretty sure it was all coming from next door there. More than one voice.'

'What were they shouting?' Rebecca asked.

'Sounded surprised, startled. Scared. Real scared.'

'No, what I mean is – do you remember any words they shouted?'

'No words.'

'Or maybe names.'

'They weren't shouting words or names; nothing like that.'

'What were they shouting?'

'Well, maybe it *was* words and names or both, but it didn't come through the wall all that distinctly. It was just noise. And I thought to myself: Christ, not something *else* gone wrong; this has been a rotten trip all the way.

Wicke wasn't only a complainer; he was a whiner. His voice had the power to set Jack's teeth on edge.

'Then what?' Rebecca asked.

'Well, the shouting part didn't last long. Almost right away, the shooting started.'

100

'Those two slugs came through the wall?' Jack asked, pointing to the holes.

'Not right then. Maybe a minute later. And what the hell is this joint made of, anyway, if the walls can't stop a bullet?'

'It was a .357 Magnum,' Jack said. 'Nothing'll stop that.'

'Walls like tissue paper,' Wicke said, not wanting to hear anything that might contribute to the hotel's exoneration. He went to the telephone that stood on a night-stand by the bed, and he put his hand on the receiver. 'As soon as the shooting started, I scrambled over here, dialled the hotel operator, told her to get the cops. They were a *very* long time coming. Are you always such a long time coming in this city when someone needs help?'

'We do our best,' Jack said.

'So I put the phone down and hesitated, not sure what to do, just stood listening to them screaming and shooting over there, and then I realized I might be in the line of fire, so I started toward the bathroom, figuring to hole up in there until it all blew over, and then all of a sudden, Jesus, I *was* in the line of fire. The first shot came through the wall and missed my face by maybe six inches. The second one was even closer. I dropped to the floor and hugged the carpet, but those were the last two shots – and just a few seconds later, there wasn't any more screaming, either.'

'Then what?' Jack asked.

'Then I waited for the cops.'

'You didn't go into the hall?'

'Why would I'

'To see what happened.'

'Are you crazy? How was I to know who might be out there in the hall? Maybe one of them with a gun was still out there.'

'So you didn't see anyone. Or hear anything important, like a name?'

'I already told you. No.'

Jack couldn't think of anything more to ask. He looked at Rebecca, and she seemed stymied, too. Another dead end.

They got up from their chairs, and Burt Wicke – still fidgety, still whining – said, 'This has been a rotten trip from the beginning, absolutely rotten. First, I have to make the entire flight from Chicago sitting next to a little old lady from Peoria who wouldn't shut up. Boring old bitch. And the plane hit turbulence like you wouldn't believe. Then yesterday, two deals fall through, and I find out my hotel has rats, an *expensive* hotel like this—'

'Rats?' Jack asked.

'Huh?'

'You said the hotel has rats.'

'Well, it does.'

'You've seen them?' Rebecca asked.

'It's a disgrace,' Wicke said. 'A place like this, with such an almighty reputation, but crawling with rats.'

'Have you seen them?' Rebecca repeated.

Wicke cocked his head, frowned. 'Why're you so interested in rats? That's got nothing to do with the murders.'

'Have you seen them?' Rebecca repeated in a harsher voice.

'Not exactly. But I heard them. In the walls.'

'You heard rats in the walls?'

'Well, in the heating system, actually. They sounded close, like they were right here in these walls, but you know how those hollow metal heating ducts can carry sound. The rats might've been on another floor, even in another wing, but they sure sounded close. I got up on the desk there and put my ear to the vent, and I swear they could've been inches away. Squeaking. A funny sort of squeaking. Chittering, twittering sounds. Maybe half a dozen rats, by the sound of it. I could hear their claws scraping on metal . . . a scratchy, rattly noise that gave me the creeps. I complained, but the management here doesn't bother attending to complaints. From the

102

way they treat their guests, you'd never know this was supposed to be one of the finest hotels in the city.'

Jack figured Burt Wicke had lodged an unreasonable number of vociferous, petty complaints prior to hearing the rats. By that time, the management had tagged him as either a hopeless neurotic or a grifter who was trying to establish excuses for not paying his bill.

Having paced to the window, Wicke looked up at the winter sky, down at the street far below. 'And now it's snowing. On top of everything else, the weather's got to turn rotten. It isn't fair.'

The man no longer reminded Jack of a toad. Now he seemed like a six-foot-tall, fat, hairy, stumpy-legged baby.

Rebecca said, 'When did you hear the rats?'

'This morning. Just after I finished breakfast, I called down to the front desk to tell them how terrible their room service food was. After a highly unsatisfactory conversation with the clerk on duty, I put the phone down – and that's the very moment when I heard the rats. After I'd listened to them a while and was positively sure they *were* rats, I called the manager himself to complain about *that,* again without satisfactory results. That's when I made up my mind to get a shower, dress, pack my suitcases, and find a new hotel before my first business appointment of the day.'

'Do you remember the exact time when you heard the rats?'

'Not to the minute. But it must've been around eight-thirty.'

Jack glanced at Rebecca. 'About one hour before the killing started next door.'

She looked troubled. She said, 'Weirder and weirder.'

11

In the death suite, the three ravaged bodies still lay where they had fallen.

The lab men hadn't finished their work. In the parlour,

103

one of them was vacuuming the carpet around the corpse. The sweepings would be analysed later.

Jack and Rebecca went to the nearest heating vent, a one-foot by eight-inch rectangular plate mounted on the wall, a few inches below the ceiling. Jack pulled a chair under it, stood on the chair, and examined the grille.

He said, 'The end of the duct has an inward-bent flange all the way round it. The screws go through the edges of the grille and through the flange.'

'From here,' Rebecca said, 'I see the head of two screws.'

'That's all there are. But anything trying to get out of the duct would have to remove at least one of those screws to loosen the grille.'

'And no rat is that smart.' she said.

'Even if it was a smart rat, like no other rat God ever put on this earth, a regular Albert Einstein of the rat kingdom, it still couldn't do the job. From inside the duct, it'd be dealing with the pointed, threaded end of the screw. It couldn't grip and turn the damned thing with only its paws.'

'Not with its teeth, either.'

'No. The job would require fingers.'

The duct, of course, was much too small for a man – or even a child – to crawl through it.

Rebecca said, 'Suppose a lot of rats, a few dozen of them, jammed up against one another in the duct, all struggling to get out through a ventilation grille. If a real horde of them put enough pressure on the other side of the grille, would they be able to pop the screws through the flange and then shove the grille into the room, out of their way?'

'Maybe,' Jack said with more than a little doubt. 'Even that sounds too smart for rats. But I guess if the holes in the flange were too much bigger than the screws that passed through them, the threads wouldn't bite on anything, and the grille could be forced off.'

He tested the vent plate that he had been examining.

It moved slightly back and forth, up and down, but not much.

He said, 'This one's pretty tightly fitted.'

'One of the others might be looser.'

Jack stepped down from the chair and put it back where he'd got it.

They went through the suite until they'd found all the vents from the heating system: two in the parlour, one in the bedroom, one in the bath. At each outlet, the grille was fixed firmly in place.

'Nothing got into the suite through the heating ducts,' Jack said. 'Maybe I can make myself believe that rats could crowd up against the back of the grille and force it off, but I'll never in a million years believe that they left through the same duct and somehow managed to replace the grille behind them. No rat – no animal of any kind you can name – could be that well trained, that dextrous.'

'No. Of course not. It's ridiculous.'

'So,' he said.

'So,' she said. She sighed. 'Then you think it's just an odd coincidence that the men here were apparently bitten to death shortly after Wicke heard rats in the walls.'

'I don't like coincidences,' he said.

'Neither do I.'

'They usually turn out not to *be* coincidences.'

'Exactly.'

'But it's still the most likely possibility. Coincidence, I mean. Unless . . .'

'Unless what?' she asked.

'Unless you want to consider voodoo, black magic—'

'No, thank you.'

'—demons creeping through the walls—'

'Jack, for God's sake!'

'—coming out to kill, melting back into the walls and just disappearing.'

'I won't listen to this.'

He smiled. 'I'm just teasing, Rebecca.'

'Like hell you are. Maybe you think you don't put any credence in that kind of baloney, but deep down inside, there's a part of you that's—'

'Excessively open-minded,' he finished.

'If you insist on making a joke of it—'

'I do. I insist.'

'But it's true, just the same.'

'I may be excessively open-minded, if that's even possible—'

'It is.'

'—but at least I'm not inflexible.'

'Neither am I.'

'Or rigid.'

'Neither am I.'

'Or frightened.'

'What's that supposed to mean?'

'You figure it.'

'You're saying I'm frightened?'

'Aren't you, Rebecca?'

'Of what?'

'Last night, for one thing.'

'Don't be absurd.'

'Then let's talk about it.'

'Not now.'

He looked at his watch. 'Twenty past eleven. We'll break for lunch at twelve. You promised to talk about it at lunch.'

'I said *if* we had time for lunch.'

'We'll have time.'

'I don't think so.'

'We'll have time.'

'There's a lot to be done here.'

'We can do it after lunch.'

'People to interrogate.'

'We can grill them after lunch.'

'You're impossible, Jack.'

'Indefatigable.'

'Stubborn.'

'Determined.'

'Damn it.'

'Charming, too,' he said.

She apparently didn't agree. She walked away from him. She seemed to prefer looking at one of the mutilated corpses.

Beyond the window, snow was falling heavily now. The sky was bleak. Although it wasn't noon yet, it looked like twilight out there.

12

Lavelle stepped out of the back door of the house. He went to the end of the porch, down three steps. He stood at the edge of the dead brown grass and looked up into the whirling chaos of snowflakes.

He had never seen snow before. Pictures, of course. But not the real thing. Until last spring, he had spent his entire life – thirty years – in Haiti, the Dominican Republic, Jamaica, and on several other Caribbean islands.

He had expected winter in New York to be uncomfortable, even arduous, for someone as unaccustomed to it as he was. However, much to his surprise, the experience had been exciting and positive, thus far. If it was only the novelty of winter that appealed to him, then he might feel differently when that novelty eventually wore off, but for the time being, he found the brisk winds and cold air invigorating.

Besides, in this great city he had discovered an enormous reservoir of the power on which he depended in order to do his work: the infinitely useful power of evil. Evil flourished everywhere, of course, in the countryside and in the suburbs, too, not merely within the boundaries of New York City. There was no shortage of evil in the Caribbean, where he had been a practising Bocor – a voodoo priest skilled in the uses of black magic – ever since he was twenty-two. But here, where so many people were crammed into such a relatively small piece of land, here where a score or two of murders were committed every week, here where assaults and rapes and robberies and burglaries numbered in the tens of thousands – even hundreds of thousands – every year, here where there were an army of hustlers looking for an advantage, legions of conmen searching for marks, psychos of every twisted sort, perverts, punks, wife-beaters, and thugs almost beyond counting – *this* was where the air was flooded with raw currents of evil that you could see and smell and feel – if, like Lavelle, you were sensitized to them. With each wicked deed, an effluvium of evil rose from the corrupted soul, contributing to the cracking currents in the air, making them stronger, potentially more destructive. Above and through the metropolis, vast tenebrous rivers of evil energy surged and churned. Ethereal rivers, yes. Of no substance. Yet the energy of which they were composed was real, lethal, the very stuff with which Lavelle could achieve virtually any result he wished. He could tap into those midnight tides and twilight pools of malevolent power; he could use them to cast even the most difficult and ambitious spells, curses, and charms.

The city was also crisscrossed by other, different currents of a benign nature, composed of the effluvium arising from good souls engaged in the performance of admirable deeds. These were rivers of hope, love, courage, charity, innocence, kindness, friendship, honesty, and dignity. This, too, was an extremely powerful energy, but it was of absolutely no use to Lavelle. A *Houngon*, a priest skilled at white magic, would be able to tap that benign energy for the purpose of healing, casting beneficial spells, and creating miracles. But Lavelle was a *Bocor*, not a *Houngon*. He had dedicated himself to the black arts, to the rites of *Congo* and *Pétro*, rather than to the various rites of *Rada*, white magic. And dedication to that dark sphere of sorcery also meant confinement to it.

Yet his long association with evil had not given him a bleak, mournful, or even sour aspect; he was a happy man. He smiled broadly as he stood there behind the house, at the edge of the dead brown grass, looking up into the whirling snow. He felt strong, relaxed, content, almost unbearably pleased with himself.

He was tall, six-three. He looked even taller in his narrow-legged black trousers and his long, well-fitted grey cashmere topcoat. He was unusually thin, yet powerful looking in spite of the lack of meat on his long frame. Not even the least observant could mistake him for a weakling, for he virtually radiated confidence and had eyes that made you want to get out of his way in a hurry. His hands were large, his wrists large and bony. His face was noble, not unlike that of the film actor, Sidney Poitier. His skin was exceptionally dark, very black, with an almost purple undertone, somewhat like the skin of a ripe eggplant. Snowflakes melted on his face and stuck in his eyebrows and frosted his wiry black hair.

The house out of which he had come was a three-storey brick affair, pseudo-Victorian, with a false tower, a slate-roof, and lots of gingerbread trim, but battered and weathered and grimy. It had been built in the early years of the century, had been part of a really fine residential neighbourhood at that time, had still been solidly middle-class by the end of World War Two (though declining in prestige), and had become distinctly lower middle-class by the late 70s. Most of the houses on the street had been converted to apartment buildings. This one had not, but it was in the same state of disrepair as all the others. It wasn't where Lavelle wanted to live; it was where he *had* to live until this little war was finished to his satisfaction; it was his hidey hole.

On both sides, other brick houses, exactly the same as this one, crowded close. Each overlooked its own fenced yard. Not much of a yard: a forty-by-twenty-foot plot of thin grass, now dormant under the harsh hand of winter. At the far end of the lawn was the garage and beyond the garage was a litter-strewn alley.

In one corner of Lavelle's property, up against the garage wall, stood a corrugated metal utility shed with a white enamel finish and a pair of green metal doors. He'd bought it at Sears, and their workmen had erected it a month ago. Now, when he'd had enough of looking up into the falling snow, he went to the shed, opened one of the doors, and stepped inside.

Heat assaulted him. Although the shed wasn't equipped with a heating system, and although the walls weren't even insulated, the small building – twelve foot by ten – was nevertheless extremely warm. Lavelle had no sooner entered and pulled the door shut behind him than he was obliged to strip out of his nine-hundred-dollar topcoat in order to breathe comfortably.

A peculiar, slightly sulphurous odour hung in the air. Most people would have found it unpleasant. But Lavelle sniffed, then breathed deeply, and smiled. He savoured the stench. To him, it was a sweet fragrance because it was the scent of revenge.

He had broken into a sweat.

He took off his shirt.

He was chanting in a strange tongue.

He took off his shoes, his trousers, his underwear.

Naked, he knelt on the dirt floor.

He began to sing softly. The melody was pure, compelling, and he carried it well. He sang in a low voice that could not have been heard by anyone beyond the boundaries of his own property.

Sweat streamed from him. His black body glistened.

He swayed gently back and forth as he sang. In a little while he was almost in a trance.

The lines he sang were lilting, rhythmic chains of words in an ungrammatical, convoluted, but mellifluous mixture of French, English, Swahili, and Bantu. It was partly a Haitian patois, partly a Jamaican patois, partly an African juju chant: the pattern-rich 'language' of voodoo.

He was singing about vengence. About death. About the blood of his enemies. He called for the destruction of the Carramazza family, one member at a time, according to a list he had made.

Finally he sang about the slaughter of that police detective's two children, which might become necessary at any moment.

The prospect of killing children did not disturb him. In fact, the possibility was exciting.

His eyes shone.

His long-fingered hands moved slowly up and down his lean body in a sensuous caress.

His breathing was laboured as he inhaled the heavy warm air and exhaled an even heavier, warmer vapour.

The beads of sweat on his ebony skin gleamed with reflected orange light.

Although he had not switched on the overhead light when he'd entered, the interior of the shed wasn't pitch black. The perimeter of the small, windowless room was shrouded in shadows, but a vague orange glow rose from the floor in the centre of the chamber. It came out of a hole about five feet in diameter. Lavelle had dug it while performing a complicated, six-hour ritual, during which he had spoken to many of the evil gods – Congo Savanna, Congo Maussai, Congo Moudongue – and the evil angels like the Zandor, the Ibos 'je rouge', the Petro Maman Pemba, and Ti Jean Pie Fin.

The excavation was shaped like a meteor crater, the walls sloping inward to form a basin. The centre of the basin was only three feet deep. However, if you stared into it long enough, it gradually began to appear much, much deeper than that. In some mysterious way, when you peered at the flickering light for a couple of minutes, when you tried hard to discern its source, your perspective abruptly and drastically changed, and you could see that the bottom of the hole was hundreds if not

111

thousands of feet below. It wasn't merely a hole in the dirt floor of the shed; not anymore; suddenly and magically, it was a doorway into the heart of the earth. But then, with a blink, it seemed only a shallow basin once more.

Now, still singing, Lavelle leaned forward.

He looked at the strange, pulsing orange light.

He looked into the hole.

Looked down.

Down . . .

Down into . . .

Down into the pit.

The Pit.

13

Shortly before noon, Nayva Rooney had finished cleaning the Dawson's apartment.

She had neither seen nor heard anything more of the rat – or whatever it had been – that she had pursued from room to room earlier in the morning. It had vanished.

She wrote a note to Jack Dawson, asking him to call her this evening. He had to be told about the rat, so that he could arrange to have the building superintendent hire an exterminator. She fixed the note to the refrigerator with a magnetic plastic butterfly that was usually used to hold a shopping list in place.

After she put on her rubber boots, coat, scarf, and gloves, she switched off the last light, the hall light. Now, the apartment was lit only by the thin, grey, useless daylight that seemed barely capable of penetrating the windows. The hall, windowless, was not lit at all. She stood perfectly still by the front door for more than a minute – listening.

The apartment remained tomb-silent.

At last, she let herself out and locked the door behind her.

A few minutes after Nayva Rooney had gone, there was movement in the apartment.

Something came out of Penny's and Davey's bedroom, into the gloomy hallway. It merged with the shadows. If Nayva had been there, she would have seen only its bright, glowing, fiery white eyes. It stood for a moment, just outside the door through which it had come, and then it moved down the hall toward the living room, its claws clicking on the wooden floor; it made a cold, angry, hissing noise as it went.

A second creature came out of the kid's room. It, too, was well hidden by the darkness in the apartment, just a shadow among shadows – except for its shining eyes.

A third small, dark, hissing beast appeared.

A fourth.

A fifth.

Another. And another . . .

Soon, they were all over the apartment: crouching in corners; perching on furniture or squirming under it; slinking along the base-board; climbing the walls with insectile skill; creeping behind the drapes; sniffing and hissing; scurrying restlessly from room to room and then back again; ceaselessly growling in what almost sounded like a guttural, foreign language; staying, for the most part, in the shadows, as if even the pale winter light coming through the windows was too harsh for them.

Then, suddenly, they all stopped moving and were motionless, as if a command had come to them. Gradually, they began to sway from side to side, their beaming eyes describing small arcs in the darkness. Their metronomic movement was in time with the song that Baba Lavelle sang in another, distant part of the city.

Eventually, they stopped swaying.

They did not become restless again.

They waited in the shadows, motionless, eyes shining.

Soon, they might be called upon to kill.

They were ready. They were eager.

CHAPTER THREE

1

Captain Walter Gresham, of Homicide, had a face like a shovel. Not that he was an ugly man; in fact, he was rather handsome in a sharp-edged sort of way. But his entire face sloped forward, all of his strong features pointing down and out, toward the tip of his chin, so that you were reminded of a garden spade.

He arrived at the hotel a few minutes before noon and met with Jack and Rebecca at the end of the elevator alcove on the sixteenth floor, by a window that looked down on Fifth Avenue.

'What we've got brewing here is a full-fledged gang war,' Gresham said. 'We haven't seen anything like this in my time. It's like something out of the roaring twenties, for God's sake! Even if it is just a bunch of hoods and scumbags killing one another, I don't like it. Absolutely won't tolerate it in my jurisdiction. I spoke with the commissioner before I came over here, and he's in full agreement with me: We can't go on treating this as if it were just an ordinary homicide investigation; we've got to put the pressure on. We're forming a special task force. We're converting two interrogation rooms into a task force headquarters, putting in special phone lines and everything.'

'Does that mean Jack and I are being pulled off the case?'

'No, no.' Gresham said. 'I'm putting you in charge of the task force. I want you to head back to the office, work up an attack plan, a strategy, figure out everything

114

you'll need. How many men – both uniforms and detectives? How much clerical support? How many vehicles? Establish emergency liaisons with city, state, and federal drug enforcement agencies, so we don't have to go through the bureaucracy every time we need information. Then meet me in my office at five o'clock.'

'We've still got work to do here,' Jack said.

'Others can handle that,' Gresham said. 'And by the way, we've gotten some answers to your queries about Lavelle.'

'The phone company?' Jack asked.

'That's one of them. They've no listed or unlisted number for anyone named Baba Lavelle. In the past year, they've had only two new customers named Lavelle. I sent a man around this morning to talk to both of them. Neither is black, like your Lavelle. Neither of them knows anyone named Baba. And neither of them made my man the least bit suspicious.'

Driven by a sudden hard wind, snow grated like sand across the window. Below, Fifth Avenue briefly vanished beneath whirling flakes.

'What about the power company?' Jack asked.

'Same situation,' Gresham said. 'No Baba Lavelle.'

'He might've used a friend's name for utility connections.'

Gresham shook his head. 'Also heard back from the Department of Immigration. No one named Lavelle – Baba or otherwise – applied for any residency permit, either short-term or long-term, in the past year.'

Jack frowned. 'So he's in the country illegally.'

'Or he's not here at all,' Rebecca said.

They looked at her, puzzled.

She elaborated: 'I'm not convinced there *is* a Baba Lavelle.'

'Of course there is,' Jack said.

But she said, 'We've *heard* a lot about him, and we've seen some smoke . . . But when it comes to getting hold

115

of physical evidence of his existence, we keep coming up empty-handed.'

Gresham was keenly interested, and his interest disheartened Jack. 'You think maybe Lavelle is just a red herring? Sort of a . . . paper man behind which the real killer or killers are hiding?'

'Could be,' Rebecca said.

'A bit of misdirection,' Gresham said, clearly intrigued. 'In reality, maybe it's one of the other mafia families making a move on the Carramazzas, trying to take the top rung of the ladder.'

'Lavelle exists,' Jack said.

Gresham said, 'You seem so certain of that. Why?'

'I don't know, really.' Jack looked out of the window at the snow-swept towers of Manhattan. 'I won't pretend I've got good reasons. It's just . . . instinct. I feel it in my bones. Lavelle is real. He's out there somewhere. He's out there . . . and I think he's the most vicious, dangerous son of a bitch any of us is ever going to run up against.'

2

At Wellton School, when classes on the third floor recessed for lunch, Penny Dawson wasn't hungry. She didn't even bother to go to her newly assigned locker and get her lunchbox. She stayed at her desk and kept her head down on her folded arms, eyes closed, pretending to nap. A sour, icy ball lay lead-heavy in the pit of her stomach. She was sick – not with any virus, but with fear.

She hadn't told anyone about the silver-eyed goblins in the basement. No one would believe she'd really seen them. And, for sure, no one would believe the goblins were eventually going to attempt to kill her.

But she knew what was coming. She didn't know why it was happening to her, of all people. She didn't know exactly how it would happen or when. She didn't know where the goblins came from. She didn't know if she had a chance of escaping them; maybe there was no way out. But she *did* know what they intended to do to her. Oh, yes.

It wasn't merely her own fate that worried her. She was scared for Davey, too. If the goblins wanted her, they might also want him.

She felt responsible for Davey, especially since their mother had died. After all, she was his big sister. A big sister had an obligation to watch over the little brother and protect him, even if he could be a pain in the neck sometimes.

Right now, Davey was down on the second floor with his classmates and teachers. For the time being, at least, he was safe. The goblins surely wouldn't show themselves when a lot of people were around; they seemed to be very secretive creatures.

But what about later? What would happen when school was out and it was time to go home?

She didn't see how she could protect herself or Davey.

Head down on her arms, eyes closed, pretending to nap, she said a silent prayer. But she didn't think it would do any good.

3

In the hotel lobby, Jack and Rebecca stopped at the public phones. He tried to call Nayva Rooney. Because of the task force assignment, he wouldn't be able to pick up the kids after school, as planned, and he hoped Nayva would be free to meet them and keep them at her place for a while. She didn't answer her phone, and he thought perhaps she was still at his apartment, cleaning, so he tried his own number, too, but he didn't have any luck.

Reluctantly, he called Faye Jamison, his sister-in-law, Linda's only sister. Faye had loved Linda almost as much as Jack, himself, had loved her. For that reason he had considerable affection for Faye – although she wasn't always an easy person to like. She was convinced that no one else's life could be well run without the benefit of her advice. She meant well. Her unsolicited counsel was based on a genuine concern for others, and she delivered her advice in a gentle, motherly voice even if the target of her kibitzing was twice her age. But she was nonetheless irritating for all of her good intentions, and there were times when her soft voice seemed, to Jack, as piercing as a police siren.

Like now, on the telephone, after he asked if she would pick up the kids at school this afternoon, she said, 'Of course, Jack I'll be glad to, but if they expect you to be there and then you don't show, they're going to be disappointed, and if this sort of thing happens too often, they're going to feel worse than just disappointed; they're going to feel abandoned.'

'Faye—'

'Psychologists say that when children have already lost one parent, they need—'

'Faye, I'm sorry, but I don't really have time right now to listen to what the psychologists say. I—'

'But you should *make* time for just that sort of thing, dear.'

He sighed. 'Perhaps I should.'

'Every modern parent ought to be well versed in child psychology.'

Jack glanced at Rebecca, who was waiting impatiently by the phones. He raised his eyebrows and shrugged as Faye rattled on:

'You're an old-fashioned, seat-of-the-pants parent, dear. You think you can handle everything with love and cookies. Now, of course, love and cookies are a part of it, but there's a whole lot more to the job than—'

'Faye, listen, nine times out of ten, I *am* there when I tell the kids I will be. But sometimes it isn't possible. This job doesn't have the most regular hours. A homicide detective can't walk away in the middle of pursuing a hot lead just because it's the end of his shift. Besides, there's a crisis here. A big one. Now, will you pick up the kids for me?'

'Of course, dear,' she said, sounding slightly hurt.

'I appreciate it, Faye.'

'It's nothing.'

'I'm sorry if I sounded . . . abrupt.'

'You didn't at all. Don't worry about it. Will Davey and Penny be staying for dinner?'

'If it's all right with you—'

'Of course it is. We love having them here, Jack. You know that. And will you be eating with us?'

'I'm not sure I'll be free by then.'

'Don't miss too many dinners with them, dear.'

'I don't plan to.'

'Dinnertime is an important ritual, an opportunity for the family to share the events of the day.'

'I know.'

'Children need that period of tranquillity, of togetherness, at the end of each day.'

'I know. I'll try my best to make it. I hardly ever miss.'

'Will they be sleeping over?'

'I'm sure I won't be that late. Listen, thanks a lot, Faye. I don't know what I'd do without you and Keith to lean on now and then, really, I don't. But I've got to run now. See you later.'

Before Faye could respond with more advice, Jack hung up, feeling both guilty and relieved.

A fierce and bitter wind was stored up in the west. It poured through the cold grey city in an unrelenting flood, harrying the snow before it.

Outside the hotel, Rebecca and Jack turned up their coat collars and tucked their chins down and cautiously negotiated the slippery, snow-skinned pavement.

Just as they reached their car, a stranger stepped up to them. He was tall, dark-complexioned, well dressed. 'Lieutenant Chandler? Lieutenant Dawson? My boss wants to talk to you.'

119

'Who's your boss?' Rebecca asked.

Instead of answering, the man pointed to a black Mercedes limousine that was parked farther along the hotel driveway. He started toward it, clearly expecting them to follow without further question.

After a brief hesitation, they actually did follow him, and when they reached the limousine, the heavily tinted rear window slid down. Jack instantly recognized the passenger, and he saw that Rebecca also knew who the man was: Don Gennaro Carramazza, patriarch of the most powerful mafia family in New York.

The tall man got in the front seat with the chauffeur, and Carramazza, alone in the back, opened his door and motioned for Jack and Rebecca to join him.

'What do you want?' Rebecca asked, making no move to get into the car.

'A little conversation,' Carramazza said, with just the vaguest trace of a Sicilian accent. He had a surprisingly cultured voice.

'So talk,' she said.

'Not like this. It's too cold,' Carramazza said. Snow blew past him, into the car. 'Let's be comfortable.'

'I am comfortable,' she said.

'Well, I'm not,' Carramazza said. He frowned. 'Listen, I have some extremely valuable information for you. I chose to deliver it myself. *Me*. Doesn't that tell you how important this is? But I'm not going to talk on the street, in public, for Christ's sake.'

Jack said, 'Get in, Rebecca.'

With an expression of distaste, she did as he said.

Jack got into the car after her. They sat in the two seats that flanked the built-in bar and television set, facing the rear of the limousine, where Carramazza sat facing forward.

Up front, Rudy touched a switch, and a thick Plexiglas partition rose between that part of the car and the passenger compartment.

Carramazza picked up an attaché case and put it on

120

his lap but didn't open it. He regarded Jack and Rebecca with sly contemplation.

The old man looked like a lizard. His eyes were hooded by heavy, pebbled lids. He was almost entirely bald. His face was wizened and leathery, with sharp features and a wide, thin-lipped mouth. He moved like a lizard, too: very still for long moments, then brief flurries of activity, quick dartings and swivellings of the head.

Jack wouldn't have been surprised if a long, forked tongue had flickered out from between Carramazza's dry lips.

Carramazza swivelled his head to Rebecca. 'There's no reason to be afraid of me, you know.'

She looked surprised. 'Afraid? But I'm not.'

'When you were reluctant to get into the car, I thought—'

'Oh, that wasn't fear,' she said icily. 'I was worried the dry cleaner might not be able to get the stink out of my clothes.'

Carramazza's hard little eyes narrowed.

Jack groaned inwardly.

The old man said, 'I see no reason why we can't be civil with one another, especially when it's in our mutual interest to cooperate.'

He didn't sound like a hoodlum. He sounded like a banker.

'Really?' Rebecca said. 'You really see no reason? Please allow me to explain.'

Jack said, 'Uh, Rebecca—'

She let Carramazza have it: 'You're a thug, a thief, a murderer, a dope pedlar, a pimp. Is that explanation enough?'

'Rebecca—'

'Don't worry, Jack. I haven't insulted him. You can't insult a pig merely by calling it a pig.'

'Remember,' Jack said, 'he's lost a nephew and a brother today.'

'Both of whom were dope pedlars, thugs, and murderers,' she said.

Carramazza was startled speechless by her ferocity.

Rebecca glared at him and said, 'You don't seem particularly grief-stricken by the loss of your brother. Does he look grief-stricken to you, Jack?'

Without a trace of anger or even any excitement in his voice, Carramazza said, 'In the *fratellanza*, Sicilian men don't weep.'

Coming from a withered old man, that macho declaration was outrageously foolish.

Still without apparent animosity, continuing to employ the soothing voice of a banker, Carramazza said, 'We do *feel*, however. And we do take our revenge.'

Rebecca studied him with obvious disgust.

The old man's reptilian hands remained perfectly still on top of the attaché case. He turned his cobra eyes on Jack.

'Lieutenant Dawson, perhaps I should deal with you in this matter. You don't seem to share Lieutenant Chandler's . . . prejudices.'

Jack shook his head. 'That's where you're wrong. I agree with everything she said. I just wouldn't have said it.'

He looked at Rebecca.

She smiled at him, pleased by his support.

Looking at her but speaking to Carramazza, Jack said, 'Sometimes, my partner's zeal and aggressiveness are excessive and counter-productive, a lesson she seems unable or willing to learn.'

Her smile faded fast.

With evident sarcasm, Carramazza said, 'What do I have here – a couple of self-righteous, holier-than-thou types? I suppose you've never accepted a bribe, not even back when you were a uniformed cop walking a beat and earning barely enough to pay the rent.'

Jack met the old man's hard, watchful eyes and said, 'Yeah. That's right. I never have.'

'Not even one gratuity—'

'No.'

'—like a free tumble in the hay with a hooker who was trying to stay out of jail or—'

'No.'

'—a little cocaine, maybe some grass, from a pusher who wanted you to look the other way.'

'No.'

'A bottle of liquor or a twenty-dollar bill at Christmas.'

'No.'

Carramazza regarded them in silence for a moment, while a cloud of snow swirled around the car and obscured the city. At last he said, 'So I've got to deal with a couple of freaks.' He spat out the word 'freaks' with such contempt that it was clear he was disgusted by the mere thought of an honest public official.

'No, you're wrong,' Jack said. 'There's nothing special about us. We're not freaks. Not all cops are corrupt. In fact, not even most of them are.'

'Most of them,' Carramazza disagreed.

'No,' Jack insisted. 'There're bad apples, sure, and weak sisters. But for the most part, I can be proud of the people I work with.'

'Most are on the take, one way or another,' Carramazza said.

'That's just not true.'

Rebecca said, 'No use arguing, Jack. He *has* to believe everyone else is corrupt. That's how he justifies the things he does.'

The old man sighed. He opened the attaché case on his lap, withdrew a manila envelope, handed it to Jack. 'This might help you.'

Jack took it with more than a little apprehension. 'What is it?'

'Relax,' Carramazza said, 'It isn't a bribe. It's information. Everything we've been able to learn about this man who calls himself Baba Lavelle. His last-known address. Restaurants he frequented before he started this war and went into hiding. The names and addresses of all the pushers who've distributed his merchandise over the past couple of months – though you won't be able to question some of them, any more.'

'Because you've had them killed?' Rebecca asked.

'Maybe they just left town.'

'Sure.'

'Anyway, it's all there,' Carramazza said. 'Maybe you already have all that information; maybe you don't; I think you don't.'

'Why're you giving it to us?' Jack asked.

'Isn't that obvious?' the old man asked, opening his hooded eyes a bit wider. 'I want Lavelle found. I want him stopped.'

Holding the nine-by-twelve envelope in one hand, tapping it against his knee, Jack said, 'I'd have thought you'd have a much better chance of finding him than we would. He's a drug dealer, after all. He's part of your world. You have all the sources, all the contacts—'

'The usual sources and contacts are of little or no use in this case,' the old man said. 'This Lavelle . . . he's a loner. Worse than that. It's as if . . . as if he's made of . . . smoke.'

'Are you sure he actually exists?' Rebecca asked. 'Maybe he's only a straw man. Maybe your *real* enemies created him in order to hide behind him.'

'He's real,' Carramazza said emphatically. 'He entered this country illegally last spring. Came here from Jamaica by way of Puerto Rico. There's a photograph of him in the envelope there.'

Jack hastily opened it, rummaged through the contents, and extracted an eight-by-ten glossy.

Carramazza said, 'It's an enlargement of a snapshot taken in a restaurant shortly after Lavelle began operating in what has been traditionally our territory.'

Traditionally our territory. Good God, Jack thought, he sounds as if he's some British duke complaining about poachers invading his fox-hunting fields!

The photo was a bit fuzzy, but Lavelle's face was sufficiently distinct so that, henceforth, Jack would be able to recognize him if he ever saw him on the street. The man was very black, handsome – indeed, striking – with a broad brow, deepest eyes, high cheekbones, and a wide mouth. In the picture he was smiling at someone who wasn't within the camera's field. He had an engaging smile.

Jack passed the picture to Rebecca.

Carramazza said, 'Lavelle wants to take away my business, destroy my reputation within the *fratellanza*, and make me look weak and helpless. *Me*. Me, the man who has controlled the organization with an iron hand for twenty-eight years! *Me!*'

Finally, emotion filled his voice: cold, hard anger. He went on, spitting out the words as if they tasted bad.

'But that isn't the worst of it. No. You see, he doesn't actually want the business. Once he's got it, he'll throw it away, let the other families move in and carve it up among themselves. He just doesn't want me or anyone named Carramazza to have it. This isn't merely a battle for the territory, not just a struggle for control. For Lavelle, this is strictly a matter of revenge. He wants to see me suffer in every way possible. He intends to isolate me and hopes to break my spirit by robbing me of my empire and by killing my nephews, my sons. Yes, all of them, one by one. He threatens to murder my best friends, as well, anyone who has ever meant anything to me. He promises to kill my five precious grandchildren. Can you believe such a thing? He threatens little babies! No vengeance, regardless of how justified it might be, should ever touch innocent children.'

'He's actually told you that he'll do all of those things?' Rebecca asked. 'When? When did he tell you?'

'Several times.'

'You've had face-to-face meetings?'

'No. He wouldn't survive a face-to-face meeting.'

The banker image had vanished. There was no veneer

125

of gentility now. The old man looked more reptilian than ever. Like a snake in a thousand-dollar suit. A very poisonous snake.

He said, 'This crudball Lavelle told me these things on the phone. My unlisted home number. I keep having the number changed, but the creep gets the new one every time, almost as soon as it's installed. He tells me . . . he says . . . after he has killed my friends, nephews, sons, grandkids, then . . . he says he's going to . . . he says he's going to . . .'

For a moment, recalling Lavelle's arrogant threats, Carramazza was unable to speak; anger locked his jaws; his teeth were clenched, and the muscles in his neck and cheeks were bulging. His dark eyes, always disturbing, now shone with a rage so intense, so inhuman that it communicated itself to Jack and sent a chill up his spine.

Eventually, Carramazza regained control of himself. When he spoke, however, his voice never rose above a fierce, frigid whisper. 'This scum, this nigger bastard, this piece of *shit* – he tells me he'll slaughter my wife, my Nina. *Slaughter* was the word he used. And when he's butchered her, he says, he'll then take my daughter from me, too.' The old man's voice softened when he spoke of his daughter. 'My Rosie. My beautiful Rosie, the light of my life. Twenty-seven, but she looks seventeen. And smart, too. A medical student. Going to be a doctor. Starts her internship this year. Skin like porcelain. The loveliest eyes you've ever seen.' He was quiet for a moment, seeing Rosie in his mind's eye, and then his whisper became harsh again: 'Lavelle says he'll rape my daughter and then cut her to pieces, dismember her . . . in front of my eyes. He has the balls to say such things to me!' With that last declaration, Carramazza sprayed spittle on Jack's overcoat. For a few seconds, the old man said nothing more; he just took deep, shuddering breaths. His talonlike fingers closed into fists, opened, closed, opened, closed. Then: 'I want the bastard stopped.'

'You've put all your people into the search for him?' Jack asked. 'Used all your sources?'

'Yes.'

'But you still can't find him.'

'*Nooo*,' Carramazza said, and in the drawing-out of that one word, he revealed a frustration almost as great as his rage. 'He's left his place in the Village, gone to ground, hiding out. That's why I'm bringing this information to you. You can put out an APB now that you've got his picture. Then every cop in the city will be looking for him, and that's a lot more men than I've got. You can even put it on the TV news, in the papers, and then virtually everyone in the whole damned city will have an eye out for him. If I can't get to him, then at least I want *you* to nail him and put him away. Once he's behind bars . . .'

'You'll have ways of reaching him in prison,' Rebecca said, finishing the thought to which Carramazza would not give voice. 'If we arrest him, he'll never stand trial. He'll be killed in jail.'

Carramazza wouldn't confirm what she had said, but they all knew it was true.

Jack said, 'You've told us Lavelle is motivated by revenge. But for what? What did you do to him that would make him want to exterminate your entire family, even your grandchildren?'

'I won't tell you that. I *can't* tell you because, if I did I might be compromising myself.'

'More likely *incriminating* yourself,' Rebecca said.

Jack slipped the photograph of Lavelle back into the envelope. 'I've been wondering about your brother Dominick.'

Gennaro Carramazza seemed to shrivel and age at the mention of his dead brother.

Jack said, 'I mean, he was apparently hiding out, in the hotel here, when Lavelle got to him. But if he knew he was targeted, why didn't he squirrel himself away at his own place or come to you for protection? Under the circumstances, no place in the city would be as safe as your house. With all this going down, surely you must have a fortress out there in Brooklyn Heights.'

'It is,' the old man said. 'My house is a fortress.' His eyes blinked once, twice, slow as lizard eyes. 'A fortress – but not safe. Lavelle has already struck inside my own house, in spite of the tight security.'

'You mean, he's killed in your house—'

'Yes.'

'Who?'

'Ginger and Pepper.'

'Who're they?'

'My doggies. A matched pair of papillons.'

'Ah.'

'Little dogs, you know.'

'I'm not really sure what they look like,' Jack said.

'Toy spaniels,' Rebecca said. 'Long, silky coats.'

'Yes, yes. Very playful,' Carramazza said. 'Always wrestling with each other, chasing. Always wanting to be held and petted.'

'And they were killed in your house.'

Carramazza looked up. 'Last night. Torn to pieces. Somehow – we *still* don't know how – Lavelle or one of his men got in, killed my sweet little dogs, and got out again without being spotted.' He slammed one bony hand down on his attaché case. 'Damnit, the whole thing's impossible! The house is sealed tight! Guarded by a small army!' He blinked more rapidly than he had done before, and his voice faltered. 'Ginger and Pepper were so gentle. They wouldn't bite anyone. Never. They hardly even barked. They didn't deserve to be treated so brutally. Two innocent little creatures.'

Jack was astounded. This murderer, this geriatric dope pedlar, this ancient racketeer, this supremely dangerous poisonous lizard of a man, who had been unable or

128

unwilling to weep for his dead brother, now seemed on the verge of tears over the slaying of his dogs.

Jack glanced at Rebecca. She was staring at Carramazza, half in wide-eyed wonder, half in the manner of someone watching a particularly loathesome creature as it crawled out from under a rock.

The old man said, 'After all, they weren't guard dogs. They weren't attack dogs. They posed no threat. Just a couple of adorable little toy spaniels . . .'

Not quite sure how to handle a maudlin mafia chieftan, Jack tried to get Carramazza off the subject of his dogs before the old man reached that pathetic and embarrassing state of mind on the edge of which he now teetered. He said, 'Word on the street is that Lavelle claims to be using voodoo against you.'

Carramazza nodded. 'That's what he says.'

'You believe it?'

'He seems serious.'

'But do you think there's anything to this voodoo business?'

Carramazza didn't answer. He gazed out the side window at the wind-whipped snow whirling past the parked limousine.

Although Jack was aware that Rebecca was scowling at him in disapproval, he pressed the point: 'You think there's anything to it?'

Carramazza turned his face away from the window. 'You mean, do I think it works? A month ago, anybody asked me the same thing, I'd have laughed, but now . . .'

Jack said, 'Now you're wondering if maybe . . .'

'Yeah. If maybe . . .'

Jack saw that the old man's eyes had changed. They were still hard, still cold, still watchful, but now there was something new in them. Fear. It was an emotion to which this vicious old bastard was long unaccustomed.

'Find him,' Carramazza said.

'We'll try,' Jack said.

'Because it's our job,' Rebecca said quickly, as if to dispel any notion that they were motivated by concern for Gennaro Carramazza and his bloodthirsty family.

'Stop him,' Carramazza said, and the tone of his voice was the closest he would ever come to saying 'please' to an officer of the law.

The Mercedes limousine pulled away from the kerb and down the hotel driveway, leaving tracks in the quarter-inch skin of snow that now covered the pavement.

For a moment, Jack and Rebecca stood on the sidewalk, watching the car.

The wind had abated. Snow was still falling, even more heavily than before, but it was no longer wind-driven; the lazy, swirling descent of the flakes made it seem, to Jack, as if he were standing inside one of those novelty paperweights that would produce a neatly contained snowstorm anytime you shook it.

Rebecca said, 'We better get back to headquarters.'

He took the photograph of Lavelle out of the envelope that Carramazza had given him, tucked it inside his coat.

'What're you doing?' Rebecca asked.

He handed her the envelope. 'I'll be at headquarters in an hour.'

'What are you talking about?'

'Two o'clock at the latest.'

'Where are you going?'

'There's something I want to look into.'

'Jack, we've got to set up the task force, prepare a—'

'You get it started.'

'There's too much work for one—'

'I'll be there by two, two-fifteen at the latest.'

'Damnit, Jack—'

'You can handle it on your own for a while.'

'You're going up to Harlem, aren't you?'

'Listen, Rebecca—'

'Up to that damned voodoo shop.'

He didn't say anything.

130

She said, 'I knew it. You're running up there to see Carver Hampton again. That charlatan. That fraud.'

'He's not a fraud. He believes in what he does. I said I'd get back to him today.'

'This is crazy.'

'Is it? Lavelle *does* exist. We have a photo now.'

'So he exists? That doesn't mean voodoo works!'

'I know that.'

'If you go up there, how am I supposed to get to the office?'

'You can take the car. I'll get a uniform to drive me.'

'Jack, damnit.'

'I have a hunch, Rebecca.'

'Hell.'

'I have a hunch that . . . somehow . . . the voodoo subculture – maybe not any real supernatural stuff – but at least the subculture itself is inextricably entwined with this. I have a strong hunch that's the way to approach the case.'

'Christ.'

'A smart cop plays his hunches.'

'And if you don't get back when you promise, if I'm stuck all afternoon, handling everything myself, and then if I have to go in and face Gresham with—'

'I'll be back by two-fifteen, two-thirty at the latest.'

'I'm not going to forgive you for this,' Jack.'

He met her eyes, hesitated, then said, 'Maybe I *could* postpone seeing Carver Hampton until tomorrow if . . .'

'If what?'

'If I knew you'd take just half an hour, just fifteen minutes, to sit down with me and talk about everything that happened between us last night. Where are we going from here?'

Her eyes slid away from his. 'We don't have *time* for that now.'

'Rebecca—'

'There's a lot of *work* to do, Jack!'

He nodded. 'You're right. You've got to get started

on the task force details, and I've got to see Carver Hampton.'

He walked away from her, toward the uniforms who were standing by the patrol cars.

She said, 'No later than two o'clock!'

'I'll make it as fast as I can,' he said.

The wind suddenly picked up again. It howled.

4

The new snow had brightened and softened the street. The neighbourhood was still seedy, grimy, litter-strewn, and mean, but it didn't look half as bad as it had yesterday, without snow.

Carver Hampton's shop was near the corner. It was flanked by a liquor store with iron bars permanently fixed over the display windows and by a shabby furniture store also huddled behind bars. Hampton's place was the only business on the block that looked prosperous, and there were no bars over its windows, either.

The sign above the door contained only a single word: *Rada*. Yesterday, Jack had asked Hampton what the shop's name signified, and he had learned that there were three great rites or spiritual divisions governing voodoo. Two of those were composed of evil gods and were called *Congo* and *Pétro*. The pantheon of benevolent gods was called the *Rada*. Since Hampton dealt only in substances, implements, and ceremonial clothing necessary for the practice of white (good) magic, that one word above the door was all he needed to attract exactly the clientele he was looking for – those people of the Caribbean and their descendants who, having been transplanted to New York City, had brought their religion with them.

Jack opened the door, and a bell announced his entrance, and he went inside, closing out the bitter December wind.

The shop was small, twenty feet wide and thirty deep.

In the centre were tables displaying knives, staffs, bells, bowls, other implements, and articles of clothing used in various rituals. To the right, low cabinets stood along the entire wall; Jack had no idea what was in them. On the other wall, to the left of the door, there were shelves nearly all the way to the ceiling, and these were crammed full of bottles of every imaginable size and shape, blue and yellow and green and red and orange and brown and clear bottles, each carefully labelled, each filled with a particular herb or exotic root or powdered flower or other substance used in the casting of spells and charms, the brewing of magical potions.

At the rear of the shop, in answer to the bell, Carver Hampton came out of the back room, through a green bead curtain. He looked surprised. 'Detective Dawson! How nice to see you again. But I didn't expect you'd come all the way back here, especially not in this foul weather. I thought you'd just call, see if I'd come up with anything for you.'

Jack went to the back of the shop, and they shook hands across the sales counter.

Carver Hampton was tall, with wide shoulders and a huge chest, about forty pounds overweight but very formidable; he looked like a pro football lineman who had been out of training for six months. He wasn't a handsome man. There was too much bone in his slablike forehead, and his face was too round for him ever to appear in the pages of *Gentleman's Quarterly;* besides, his nose, broken more than once, now had a distinctly squashlike appearance. But if he wasn't particularly good looking, he *was* very friendly looking, a gentle giant, a perfect black Santa Claus.

He said, 'I'm so sorry you came all this way for nothing.'

'Then you haven't turned up anything since yesterday?' Jack asked.

'Nothing much. I put the word out. I'm still asking here and there, poking around. So far, all I've been able

133

to find out is that there actually *is* someone around who calls himself Baba Lavelle and says he's a Bocor.'

'Bocor? That's a priest who practises witchcraft – right?'

'Right. Evil magic. That's all I've learned: that he's real, which you weren't sure of yesterday, so I suppose this is at least of some value to you. But if you'd telephoned—'

'Well, actually, I came to show you something that might be of help. A photograph of Baba Lavelle himself.'

'Truly?'

'Yes.'

'So you already know he's real. Let me see it, though. It ought to help if I can describe the man I'm asking around about.'

Jack withdrew the eight-by-ten glossy from inside his coat and handed it over.

Hampton's face changed the instant he saw Lavelle. If a black man could go pale, that was what Hampton did. It wasn't that the shade of his skin changed so much as that the gloss and vitality went out of it; suddenly it didn't seem like skin at all but like dark brown paper, dry and lifeless. His lips tightened. And his eyes were not the same as they had been a moment ago: haunted, now.

He said, 'This *man!*'

'What?' Jack asked.

The photograph quivered as Hampton quickly handed it back. He thrust it at Jack, as if desperate to be rid of it, as if he might somehow be contaminated merely by touching the photographic image of Lavelle. His big hands were shaking.

Jack said, 'What is it? What's the matter?'

'I know him,' Hampton said. 'I've . . . seen him. I just didn't know his name.'

'Where have you see him?'

'Here.'

'Right in the shop?'

134

'Yes.'

'When?'

'Last September.'

'Not since then?'

'No.'

'What was he doing here?'

'He came to purchase herbs, powdered flowers.'

'But I thought you dealt only in good magic. The *Rada*.'

'Many substances can be used by both the Bocor and the Houngon to obtain very different results, to work evil magic or good. These were herbs and powdered flowers that were extremely rare and that he hadn't been able to locate elsewhere in New York.'

'There are *other* shops like yours?'

'One shop somewhat like this, although not as large. And then there are two practising Houngons – not strong magicians, these two, little more than amateurs, neither of them powerful enough or knowledgeable enough to do well for themselves – who sell the stuff of magic out of their apartments. They have considerable lines of merchandise to offer to other practitioners. But none of those three have scruples. They will sell to either the Bocor or the Houngon. They even sell the instruments required for a blood sacrifice, the ceremonial hatchets, the razor-edged spoons used to scoop the living eye from the skull. Terrible people, peddling their wares to anyone, anyone at all, even to the most wicked and debased.'

'So Lavelle came here when he couldn't get everything he wanted from them.'

'Yes. He told me that he'd found most of what he needed, but he said my shop was the only one with a complete selection of even the most seldom-used ingredients for spells and incantations. Which is, of course, true. I pride myself on my selection and on the purity of my goods. But unlike the others, I won't sell to a Bocor – if I know what he is. Usually I can spot them.

135

I also won't sell to those amateurs with bad intentions, the ones who want to put a curse of death on a mother-in-law or cause sickness in some man who's a rival for a girl or a job. I'll have none of that. Anyway, this man, this one in the photograph—'

'Lavelle,' Jack said.

'But I didn't know his name then. As I was packaging the few things he'd selected, I discovered he was a Bocor, and I refused to conclude the sale. He thought I was like the other merchants, that I'd sell to just anyone, and he was furious when I wouldn't let him have what he wanted. I made him leave the shop, and I thought that was the end of it.'

'But it wasn't?' Jack asked.

'No.'

'He came back?'

'No.'

'Then what happened?'

Hampton came out from behind the sales counter. He went to the shelves where the hundreds upon hundreds of bottles were stored, and Jack followed him.

Hampton's voice was hushed, a note of fear in it: 'Two days after Lavelle was here, while I was alone in the shop, sitting at the counter back there, just reading – suddenly, every bottle on those shelves was flung off, to the floor. All in an instant. Such a crash! Half of them broke, and the contents mingled together, all ruined. I rushed over to see what had happened, what had caused it, and as I approached, some of the spilled herbs and powders and ground roots began to . . . well to *move*. . .to form together . . . and take on life. Out of the debris, composed of several substances, there arose . . . a black serpent, about eighteen inches in length. Yellow eyes. Fangs. A flickering tongue. As real as any serpent hatched from its mother's egg.'

Jack stared at the big man, not sure what to think of him or his story. Until this moment, he had thought that Carver Hampton was sincere in his religious beliefs

136

and a perfectly level-headed man, no less rational because his religion was voodoo rather than Catholicism or Judaism. However, it was one thing to believe in a religious doctrine and in the possibility of magic and miracles – and quite another thing altogether to claim to have *seen* a miracle. Those who swore they had seen miracles were hysterics, fanatics, or liars. Weren't they? On the other hand, if you were at all religious – and Jack was not a man without faith – then how could you believe in the possibility of miracles and the existence of the occult without also embracing the claims of at least some of those who said they had been witness to manifestations of the supernatural? Your faith could have no substance if you did not also accept the reality of its effects in this world. It was a thought that hadn't occurred to him before, and now he stared at Carver Hampton with mixed feelings, with both doubt and cautious acceptance.

Rebecca would say he was being excessively open-minded.

Staring at the bottles that now stood on the shelves, Hampton said, 'The serpent slithered toward me. I backed across the room. There was nowhere to go. I dropped to my knees. Recited prayers. They were the correct prayers for the situation, and they had their effect. Either that . . . or Lavelle didn't actually intend for the serpent to harm me. Perhaps he only meant it as a warning not to mess with him, a slap in the face for the way I had so unceremoniously ushered him out of my shop. At any rate, the serpent eventually dissolved back into the herbs and powders and ground roots of which it was composed.'

'How do you know it was Lavelle who did this thing?' Jack asked.

'The phone rang a moment after the snake . . . decomposed. It was this man, the one I had refused to serve. He told me that it was my prerogative, whether to serve him or not, and that he didn't hold it against me. But he said he wouldn't permit anyone to lay a hand on him as I'd done. So he had smashed my collection of herbs and had conjured up the serpent in retaliation. That's what he said. That's *all* he said. Then he hung up.'

'You didn't tell me that you'd actually, physically *thrown* him out of the shop,' Jack said.

'I didn't. I merely put a hand on his arm and . . . shall we say . . . *guided* him out. Firmly, yes, but without any real violence, without hurting him. Nevertheless, that was enough to make him angry, to make him seek revenge.'

'This was all back in September?'

'Yes.'

'And he's never returned?'

'No.'

'Never called?'

'No. And it took me almost three months to rebuild my inventory of rare herbs and powders. Many of these items are so very difficult to obtain. You can't imagine. I only recently completed restocking these shelves.'

'So you've got your own reasons for wanting to see this Lavelle brought down,' Jack said.

Hampton shook his head. 'On the contrary.'

'Huh?'

'I want nothing more to do with this.'

'But—'

'I can't help you any more, Lieutenant.'

'I don't understand.'

'It should be clear enough. If I help you, Lavelle will send something after me. Something worse than the serpent. And this time it won't be just a warning. No, this time, it'll surely be the death of me.'

Jack saw that Hampton was serious – and genuinely terrified. The man believed in the power of voodoo. He was trembling. Even Rebecca, seeing him now, wouldn't be able to claim that he was a charlatan. He *believed*.

Jack said, 'But you ought to want him behind bars as

much as I do. You ought to want to see him broken, after what he did to you.'

'You'll never put him in jail.'

'Oh, yes.'

'No matter what he does, you'll never be able to touch him.'

'We'll get him, all right.'

'He's an extremely powerful Bocor, Lieutenant. Not an amateur. Not your average spellcaster. He has the power of darkness, the ultimate darkness of death, the darkness of Hell, the darkness of the Other Side. It is a cosmic power, beyond human comprehension. He isn't merely in league with Satan, your Christian and Judaic king of demons. That would be bad enough. But you see, he is a servant, as well, of *all* the evil gods of the African religions, which go back into antiquity; he has that great, malevolent pantheon behind him. Some of those deities are far more powerful and immeasurably more vicious than Satan has ever been portrayed. A vast legion of evil entities are at Lavelle's beck and call, eager to let him use them because, in turn, *they* use *him* as a sort of doorway into this world. They are eager to cross over, to bring blood and pain and terror and misery to the living, for this world of ours is one into which they are usually denied passage by the power of the benevolent gods who watch over us.'

Hampton paused. He was hyperventilating. There was a faint sheen of perspiration on his forehead. He wiped his big hands over his face and took several slow deep breaths. He went on, then, trying to keep his voice calm and reasonable, but only half succeeding.

'Lavelle is a dangerous man, Lieutenant, infinitely more dangerous than you can ever comprehend. I also think he is very probably mad, insane; there was definitely a quality of insanity about him. That is a most formidable combination: evil beyond measure, madness, and the power of a masterfully skilled Bocor.'

'But you say you're a Houngon, a priest of white magic. Can't you use your power against him?'

'I'm a capable Houngon, better than many. But I'm not in this man's league. For instance, with great effort, I might be able to put a curse on his own supply of herbs and powders. I might be able to reach out and cause a few bottles to fall off the shelves in his study or wherever he keeps them – if I had seen the place first, of course. However, I wouldn't be able to cause so much destruction as he did. And I wouldn't be able to conjure up a serpent, as he did. I haven't that much power, that much finesse.'

'You could try.'

'No. Absolutely not. In any contest of powers, he would crush me. Like a bug.'

Hampton went to the door, opened it. The bell above it rang. Hampton stepped aside, holding the door wide open.

Jack pretended not to get the hint. 'Listen, if you'll just keep asking around—'

'No. I can't help you any more, Lieutenant. Can't you get that through your head?'

A frigid, blustery wind huffed and moaned and hissed and puffed at the open door, spraying snowflakes like flecks of spittle.

'Listen,' Jack said. 'Lavelle never has to know that you're asking about him. He—'

'He would find out!' Hampton said angrily, his eyes wide open as the door he was holding. 'He knows everything – or can find it out. Everything.'

'But—'

'Please go,' Hampton said.

'Hear me out. I—'

'Go.'

'But—'

'Go, get out, leave, now, damnit, now!' Hampton said in a tone of voice composed of one part anger, one part terror, and one part panic.

140

The big man's almost hysterical fear of Lavelle had begun to affect Jack. A chill rippled through him, and he found that his hands were suddenly clammy.

He sighed, nodded. 'All right, all right, Mr Hampton. But I sure wish—'

'Now, damnit, *now!*' Hampton shouted.

Jack got out of there.

5

The door to *Rada* slammed behind him.

In the snow-quieted street, the sound was like a rifle blast.

Jack turned and looked back, saw Carver Hampton drawing down the shade that covered the glass panel in the centre of the door. In bold white letters on the dark canvas, one word was printed: CLOSED.

A moment later the lights went out in the shop.

The snow on the sidewalk was now half an inch deep, twice what it had been when he had gone into Hampton's store. It was still coming down fast, too, out of a sky that was even more sombre and more claustrophobically close than it had been twenty minutes ago.

Cautiously negotiating the slippery pavement, Jack started toward the patrol car that was waiting for him at the kerb, white exhaust trail pluming up from it. He had taken only three steps when he was stopped by a sound that struck him as being out of place here on the wintry street: a ringing telephone. He looked right, left, and saw a pay phone near the corner, twenty feet behind the waiting black-and-white. In the uncitylike stillness that the muffling snow brought to the street, the ringing was so loud that it seemed to be issuing from the air immediately in front of him.

He stared at the phone. It wasn't in a booth. There weren't many real booths around these days, the kind with the folding door, like a small closet, that offered privacy; too expensive, Ma Bell said. This was a phone on a pole, with a scoop-shaped sound baffle bending around three sides of it. Over the years, he had passed a few other public telephones that had been ringing when there was no one waiting nearby to answer them; on those occasions, he had never given them a second glance, had never been the least bit tempted to lift the receiver and find out who was there; it had been none of his business. Just as *this* was none of his business. And yet . . . This time was somehow . . . different. The ringing snaked out like a lariat of sound, roping him, snaring him, holding him.

Ringing . . .
Ringing . . .
Insistent.
Beckoning.
Hypnotic.
Ringing . . .

A strange and disturbing transformation occurred in the Harlem neighbourhood around him. Only three things remained solid and real: the telephone, a narrow stretch of snow-covered pavement leading to the telephone, and Jack himself. The rest of the world seemed to recede into a mist that rose out of nowhere. The buildings appeared to fade away, dissolving as if this were a film in which one scene was fading out to be replaced by another. The few cars progressing hesitantly along the snowy street began to . . . evaporate; they were replaced by the creeping mist, a white-white mist that was like a movie theatre screen splashed with brilliant light but with no images. The pedestrians, heads bent, shoulders hunched, struggled against the wind and stinging snow; and gradually they receded and faded, as well. Only Jack was real. And the narrow pathway to the phone. And the telephone itself.

Ringing . . .
He was drawn.
Ringing . . .
Drawn toward the phone.
He tried to resist.

Ringing . . .

He suddenly realized he'd taken a step. Toward the phone.

And another.

A third.

He felt as if he were floating.

Ringing . . .

He was moving as if in a dream or a fever.

He took another step.

He tried to stop. Couldn't.

He tried to turn toward the patrol car. Couldn't.

His heart was hammering.

He was dizzy, disoriented.

In spite of the frigid air, he was sweating along the back of his neck.

The ringing of the telephone was analogous to the rhythmic, glittering, pendulum movement of a hypnotist's pocketwatch. The sound drew him relentlessly forward as surely as, in ancient times, the sirens' songs had pulled unwary sailors to their death upon the reefs.

He knew the call was for him. Knew it without understanding *how* he knew it.

He picked up the receiver. 'Hello?'

'Detective Dawson! I'm delighted to have this opportunity to speak with you. My good man, we are most definitely overdue for a chat.'

The voice was deep, although not a bass voice, and smooth and elegant, characterized by an educated British accent filtered through the lilting patterns of speech common to tropical zones, so that words like 'man' came out as 'mon'. Clearly a Caribbean accent.

Jack said, 'Lavelle?'

'Why, of course! Who else?'

'But how did you know—'

'That you were there? My dear fellow, in an off-handed sort of way, I am keeping tabs on you.'

'You're here, aren't you? Somewhere along the street, in one of the apartment buildings here.'

'Far from it. Harlem is not to my taste.'

'I'd like to talk to you,' Jack said.

'We are talking.'

'I mean, face-to-face.'

'Oh, I hardly think that's necessary.'

'I wouldn't arrest you.'

'You couldn't. No evidence.'

'Well, then—'

'But you'd detain me for a day or two on one excuse or another.'

'No.'

'And I don't wish to be detained. I've work to do.'

'I give you my word we'd only hold you a couple of hours, just for questioning.'

'Is that so?'

'You can trust my word when I give it. I don't give it lightly.'

'Oddly enough, I'm quite sure that's true.'

'Then why not come in, answer some questions, and clear the air, remove the suspicion from yourself?'

'Well, of course, I can't remove the suspicion because, in fact, I'm guilty,' Lavelle said. He laughed.

'You're telling me you're behind the murders?'

'Certainly. Isn't that what everyone's been telling you?'

'You've called me to confess?'

Lavelle laughed again. Then: 'I've called to give you some advice.'

'Yeah?'

'Handle this as the police in my native Haiti would handle it.'

'How's that?'

'They wouldn't interfere with a Bocor who possessed powers like mine.'

'Is that right?'

'They wouldn't dare.'

'This is New York, not Haiti. Superstitious fear isn't something they teach at the police academy.'

144

Jack kept his voice calm, unruffled. But his heart continued to bang against his rib cage.

Lavelle said, 'Besides, in Haiti, the police would not *want* to interfere if the Bocor's targets were such worthless filth as the Carramazza family. Don't think of me as a murderer, Lieutenant. Think of me as an exterminator, performing a valuable service for society. That's how they'd look at this in Haiti.'

'Our philosophy is different here.'

'I'm sorry to hear that.'

'We think murder is wrong regardless of who the victim is.'

'How unsophisticated.'

'We believe in the sanctity of human life.'

'How foolish. If the Carramazzas die, what will the world lose? Only thieves, murderers, pimps. Other thieves, murderers, and pimps will move in to take their place. Not me, you understand. You may think of me as their equal, as only a murderer, but I am not of their kind. I am a priest. I don't want to rule the drug trade in New York. I only want to take it away from Gennaro Carramazza as part of his punishment. I want to ruin him financially, leave him with no respect among his kind, and take his family and friends away from him, slaughter them, teach them how to grieve. When that is done, when he's isolated, lonely, afraid, when he has suffered for a while, when he's filled with blackest despair, I will at last dispose of him, too, but slowly and with much torture. Then I'll go away, back to the islands, and you won't ever be bothered with me again. I am merely an instrument of justice, Lieutenant Dawson.'

'Does justice really necessitate the murder of Carramazza's grandchildren?'

'Yes.'

'Innocent little children?'

'They aren't innocent. They carry his blood, his genes. That makes them as guilty as he is.'

Carver Hampton was right: Lavelle was insane.

'Now,' Lavelle said, 'I understand that you will be in trouble with your superiors if you fail to bring someone to trial for at least a few of these killings. The entire police department will take a beating at the hands of the press if something isn't done. I quite understand. So, if you wish, I will arrange to plant a wide variety of evidence incriminating members of one of the city's other mafia families. You can pin the murders of the Carramazzas on some other undesirables, you see, put them in prison, and be rid of yet another troublesome group of hoodlums. I'd be quite happy to let you off the hook that way.'

It wasn't only the circumstances of this conversation – the dreamlike quality of the street around the pay phone, the feeling of floating, the fever haze – that made it all seem so unreal; the conversation itself was so bizarre that it would have defied belief regardless of the circumstances in which it had taken place. Jack shook himself, but the world wasn't jarred to life like a stubborn wristwatch; reality didn't begin to tick again.

He said, 'You actually think I could take such an offer seriously?'

'The evidence I plant will be irrefutable. It will stand up in any court. You needn't fear you'd lose the case.'

'That's not what I mean,' Jack said. 'Do you really believe I'd conspire with you to frame innocent men?'

'They wouldn't be innocent. Hardly. I'm talking about framing other murderers, thieves, and pimps.'

'But they'd be innocent of *these* crimes.'

'A technicality.'

'Not in my book.'

Lavelle was silent for a moment. Then: 'You're an interesting man, Lieutenant. Naive. Foolish. But nevertheless interesting.'

'Gennaro Carramazza tells us that you're motivated by revenge.'

'Yes.'

'For what?'

'He didn't tell you that?'

'No. What's the story?'

Silence.

Jack waited, almost asked the question again.

Then Lavelle spoke, at last, and there was a new edge to his voice, a hardness, a ferocity. 'I had a younger brother. His name was Gregory. He didn't embrace the ancient arts of witchcraft, sorcery. He shunned them. He wouldn't have anything to do with the old religions of Africa. He had no time for voodoo, no interest in it. His was a very modern soul, a machine-age sensibility. He believed in science, not magic; he put his faith in progress and technology, not in the power of ancient gods. He didn't approve of my vocation, but he didn't believe I could really do harm to anyone – or do good either, for that matter. He thought of me as a harmless eccentric. Yet, for all this misunderstanding, I loved him and he loved me. We were brothers. *Brothers.* I would have done anything for him.'

'Gregory Lavelle . . . ,' Jack said thoughtfully. 'There's something familiar about the name.'

'Years ago, Gregory came here as a legal immigrant. He worked very hard, worked his way through college, received a scholarship. He always had writing talent, even as a boy, and he thought he knew what he ought to do with it. Here, he earned a degree in journalism from Columbia. He was first in his class. Went to work for the *New York Times.* For a year or so he didn't even do any writing; he just verified research in other reporters' pieces. Gradually, he promoted several writing assignments for himself. Small things. Of no consequence. What you would call 'human interest' stories. And then—'

'Gregory Lavelle,' Jack said. 'Of course. The crime reporter.'

'In time, my brother was assigned a few crime stories. Robberies. Dope busts. He did a very good job of covering them. Indeed, he started going after stories that hadn't been handed to him, bigger stories, stories that he'd dug up all by himself. Eventually he became the *Times'* resident expert on narcotics trafficking in the city. No one knew more about the subject, the involvement of the Carramazzas, the way the Carramazza organization had subverted so many vice squad detectives and city politicians; no one knew more than Gregory; no one. He published those articles—'

'I read them. Good work. Four pieces, I believe.'

'Yes. He intended to do more, at least half a dozen more articles. There was talk of a Pulitzer, just based on what he'd written so far. Already, he had dug up enough evidence to interest the police and to generate three indictments by the grand jury. He had the sources, you see: insiders in the police and in the Carramazza family, insiders who trusted him. He was convinced he could bring down Dominick Carramazza himself before it was all over. Poor, noble, foolish, brave little Gregory. He thought it was his duty to fight evil wherever he found it. The crusading reporter. He thought he could make a difference, all by himself. He didn't understand that the only way to deal with the powers of darkness is to make peace with them, accommodate yourself to them, as I have done. One night last March, he and his wife, Ona, were on their way to dinner . . .'

'The car bomb,' Jack said.

'They were both blown to bits. Ona was pregnant. It would have been their first child. So I owe Gennaro Carramazza for three lives – Gregory, Ona, and the baby.'

'The case was never solved,' Jack reminded him. 'There was no proof that Carramazza was behind it.'

'He was.'

'You can't be sure.'

'Yes, I can. I have my sources, too. Better even than Gregory's. I have the eyes and ears of the Underworld working for me.' He laughed. He had a musical, appealing laugh that Jack found unsettling. A madman should have a madman's laugh, not the warm chuckle of a favourite uncle. 'The Underworld, Lieutenant. But I don't mean the criminal underworld, the miserable *cosa nostra* with its Sicilian pride and empty code of honour. The Underworld of which I speak is a place much deeper than that which the mafia inhabits, deeper and darker. I have the eyes and ears of the ancient ones, the reports of demons and dark angels, the testimony of those entities who see all and know all.'

Madness, Jack thought. The man belongs in an institution.

But in addition to the madness, there was something else in Lavelle's voice that nudged and poked the cop's instincts in Jack. When Lavelle spoke of the supernatural, he did so with genuine awe and conviction; however, when he spoke of his brother, his voice became oily with phony sentiment and unconvincing grief. Jack sensed that revenge was not Lavelle's primary motivation and that, in fact, he might even have hated his straight-arrow brother, might even be glad (or at least relieved) that he was dead.

'Your brother wouldn't approve of this revenge you're taking,' Jack said.

'Perhaps he would. You didn't know him.'

'But I know enough about him to say with some confidence that he wasn't at all like you. He was a decent man. He wouldn't want all this slaughter. He would be repelled by it.'

Lavelle said nothing, but there was somehow a pouting quality to his silence, a smouldering anger.

Jack said, 'He wouldn't approve of the murder of anyone's grandchildren, revenge unto the third generation. He wasn't sick, like you. He wasn't crazy.'

'It doesn't matter whether he would approve,' Lavelle said impatiently.

'I suspect that's because it isn't really revenge that motivates you. Not deep down.'

Again, Lavelle was silent.

Pushing, probing for the truth, Jack said, 'So if your brother wouldn't approve of murder being done in his name, then why are you—'

'I'm not exterminating these vermin in my brother's name,' Lavelle said sharply, furiously. 'I'm doing it in my own name. Mine and no one else's. That must be understood. I never claimed otherwise. These deaths accrue to my credit, not to my brother's.'

'Credit? Since when is murder a credit, a character reference, a matter of pride? That's insane.'

'It isn't insane,' Lavelle said heatedly. The madness boiled up in him. 'It is the reasoning of the ancient ones, the gods of *Pétro* and *Congo*. No one can take the life of a Bocor's brother and go unpunished. The murder of my brother is an insult to me. It diminishes me. It mocks me. I cannot tolerate that. I will not! My power as a Bocor would be weakened forever if I were to forego revenge. The ancient ones would lose respect for me, turn away from me, withdraw their support and power.' He was ranting now, losing his cool. 'Blood must flow. The floodgates of death must be opened. Oceans of pain must sweep them away, all who mocked me by touching my brother. Even if I despised Gregory, he was of my family; no one can spill the blood of a Bocor's family and go unpunished. If I fail to take adequate revenge, the ancient ones will never permit me to call upon them again; they will not enforce my curses and spells any more. I must repay the murder of my brother with at least a score of murders of my own if I am to keep the respect and patronage of the gods of *Pétro* and *Congo*.'

Jack had probed to the roots of the man's true motivation, but he had gained nothing for his efforts. The true motivation made no sense to him; it seemed just one more aspect of Lavelle's madness.

'You really believe this, don't you?' Jack asked.

'It's the truth.'

'It's crazy.'

'Eventually, you will learn otherwise.'

'Crazy,' Jack repeated.

'One more piece of advice,' Lavelle said.

'You're the only suspect I've ever known to be so brimming over with advice. A regular Ann Landers.'

Ignoring him, Lavelle said, 'Remove yourself from this case.'

'You can't be serious.'

'Get out of it.'

'Impossible.'

'Ask to be relieved.'

'No.'

'You'll do it if you know what's good for you.'

'You're an arrogant bastard.'

'I know.'

'I'm a cop, for God's sake! You can't make me back down by threatening me. Threats just make me all the more interested in finding you. Cops in Haiti must be the same. It can't be *that* much different. Besides, what good would it do if I did ask to be relieved? Someone else would replace me. They'd still continue to look for you.'

'Yes, but whoever replaced you wouldn't be broad-minded enough to explore the possibility of voodoo's effectiveness. He'd stick to the usual police procedure, and I have no fear of that.'

Jack was startled. 'You mean my open-mindedness alone is a threat to you?'

Lavelle didn't answer the question. He said, 'All right. If you won't step out of the picture, then at least stop your research into voodoo. Handle this as Rebecca Chandler wants to handle it – as if it were an ordinary homicide investigation.'

'I don't believe your *gall*,' Jack said.

'Your mind is open, if only a narrow crack, to the possibility of a supernatural explanation. Don't pursue that line of inquiry. That's all I ask.'

151

'Oh, that's all, is it?'

'Satisfy yourself with fingerprint kits, lab technicians, your usual experts, the standard tools. Question all the witnesses you wish to question—'

'Thanks so much for the permission.'

'—I don't care about those things,' Lavelle continued, as if Jack hadn't interrupted. 'You'll never find me that way. I'll be finished with Carramazza and on my way back to the islands before you've got a single lead. Just forget about the voodoo angle.'

Astonished by the man's chutzpa, Jack said, 'And if I don't forget about it?'

The open telephone line hissed, and Jack was reminded of the black serpent of which Carver Hampton had spoken, and he wondered if Lavelle could somehow send a serpent over the telephone line, out of the earpiece, to bite him on the ear and head, or out of the mouthpiece, to bite him on the lips and on the nose and in the eyes . . . He held the receiver away from himself, looked at it warily, then felt foolish, and brought it back to his face.

Lavelle said, 'If you insist on learning more about voodoo, if you continue to pursue that avenue of investigation . . . then I will have your son and daughter torn to pieces.'

Finally, one of Lavelle's threats affected Jack. His stomach twisted, knotted.

Lavelle said, 'Do you remember what Dominick Carramazza and his bodyguards looked like—'

And then they were both talking at once, Jack shouting, Lavelle maintaining his cool and measured tone of voice:

'Listen, you creepy son of a bitch—'

'—back there in the hotel, old Dominick, all ripped up—'

'—you stay away from—'

'—eyes torn out, all bloody?'

'—my kids, or I'll—'

'When I'm finished with Davey and Penny—'

'—blow your fuckin' head off!'

'—they'll be nothing but dead meat—'

'I'm warning you—'

'—dog meat, garbage—'

'—I'll find you—'

'—and maybe I'll even rape the girl—'

'—you stinking scumbag!'

'—'cause she's really a tender, juicy little piece. I like them tender sometimes, very young and tender, innocent. The thrill is in the corruption, you see.'

'You threaten my kids, you asshole, you just threw away whatever chance you had. Who do you think you *are?* My God, *where* do you think you are? This is America, you dumb shit. You can't get away with that kind of stuff here, threatening my kids.'

'I'll give you the rest of the day to think it over. Then, if you don't back off, I'll take Davey and Penny. And I'll make it very painful for them.'

Lavelle hung up.

'Wait!' Jack shouted.

He rattled the disconnect lever, trying to re-establish contact, trying to bring Lavelle back. Of course, it didn't work.

He was gripping the receiver so hard that his hand ached and his muscles were bunched up all the way to the shoulder. He slammed the receiver down almost hard enough to crack the earpiece.

He was breathing like a bull that, for some time, had been taunted by the movement of a red cape. He was aware of his own pulse throbbing in his temples, and he could feel the heat in his flushed face. The knots in his stomach had drawn painfully tight.

After a moment, he turned away from the phone. He was shaking with rage. He stood in the falling snow, gradually getting a grip on himself.

Everything would be all right. Nothing to worry about. Penny and Davey were safe at school, where there were plenty of people to watch over them. It was a good reliable school, with first-rate security. And Faye would pick them up at three o'clock and take them to her place; Lavelle couldn't know about that. If he did decide to hurt the kids this evening, he'd expect to find them at the apartment; when he discovered they weren't at home, he wouldn't know where to look for them. In spite of what Carver Hampton had said, Lavelle couldn't know all and see all. Could he? Of course not. He wasn't God. He might be a Bocor, a priest with real power, a genuine sorcerer. But he wasn't God. So the kids would be safe with Faye and Keith. In fact, maybe it would be a good idea for them to stay at the Jamison apartment overnight. Or even for the next few days, until Lavelle was apprehended. Faye and Keith wouldn't mind; they'd welcome the visit, the opportunity to spoil their only niece and nephew. Might even be wise to keep Penny and Davey out of school until this was all over. And he'd talk to Captain Gresham about getting some protection for them, a uniformed officer to stay in the Jamison apartment when Jack wasn't able to be there. Not much chance Lavelle would track the kids down. Highly unlikely. But just in case . . . And if Gresham didn't take the threat seriously, if he thought an around-the-clock guard was an unjustified use of manpower, then something could be arranged with the guys, the other detectives; they'd help him, just as he'd help them if anything like this ever fell in their direction; each of them would give up a few hours of off-duty time, take a shift at the Jamisons'; anything for a buddy whose family was marked; it was part of the code. Okay. Fine. Everything would be all right.

The world, which had strangely receded when the telephone had begun to ring, now rushed back. Jack was aware of sound, first: a bleating automobile horn, laughter farther along the street, the clatter-clank of tyre chains on the snowy pavement, the howling wind. The buildings crowded in around him. A pedestrian scurried past, bent into the wind; and here came three black teenagers, laughing, throwing snowballs at one another as they ran. The mist was gone, and he didn't feel dizzy or disoriented any longer. He wondered if there actually had been any mist in the first place, and he decided the eerie fog had existed only in his mind, a figment of his imagination. What must have happened was . . . he must have had an attack of some kind; yeah, sure, nothing more than that.

But exactly what kind of attack? And why had he been stricken by it? What had brought it on? He wasn't an epileptic. He didn't have low blood pressure. No other physical maladies, as far as he was aware. He had never experienced a fainting spell in his life; nothing remotely like that. He was in perfect health. So why?

And how had he known the phone call was for him?

He stood there for a while, thinking about it, as thousands of snowflakes fluttered like moths around him.

Eventually he realized he ought to call Faye and explain the situation to her, warn her to be certain that she wasn't followed when she picked up the kids at Wellton School. He turned to the pay phone, paused. No. He wouldn't make the call here. Not on the very phone Lavelle had used. It seemed ridiculous to suppose that the man could have a tap on a public phone – but it also seemed foolish to test the possibility.

Calmer – still furious but less frightened than he had been – he headed back toward the patrol car that was waiting for him.

Three-quarters of an inch of snow lay on the ground. The storm was turning into a full-fledged blizzard.

The wind had icy teeth. It bit.

Lavelle returned to the corrugated metal shed at the rear of his property. Outside, winter raged; inside, fierce dry heat made sweat pop out of Lavelle's ebony skin and stream down his face, and shimmering orange light cast odd leaping shadows on the ribbed walls. From the pit in the centre of the floor, a sound arose, a chilling susurration, as of thousands of distant voices, angry whisperings.

He had brought two photographs with him: one of Davey Dawson, the other of Penny Dawson. He had taken both photographs himself, yesterday afternoon, on the street in front of Wellton School. He had been in his van, parked almost a block away, and he had used a 35mm Pentax with a telephoto lens. He processed the film in his own closet-size darkroom.

In order to put a curse on someone and be absolutely certain that it would bring about the desired calamity, a Bocor required an icon of the intended victim. Traditionally, the priest prepared a doll, sewed it together from scraps of cotton cloth and filled it with sawdust or sand, then did the best he could to make the doll's face resemble the face of the victim; that done, the ritual was performed with the doll as a surrogate for the real person.

But that was a tedious chore made even more difficult by the fact that the average Bocor – lacking the talent and skills of an artist – found it virtually impossible to make a cotton face look sufficiently like *anyone's* real countenance. Therefore, the need always arose to embellish the doll with a lock of hair or a nail clipping or a drop of blood from the victim. Obtaining any one of those items wasn't easy. You couldn't just hang around the victim's barbershop or beauty salon, week after week, waiting for him or her to come in and get a haircut. You couldn't very well ask him to save a few nail clippings for you the next time he gave himself a manicure. And about the only way to obtain a sample of the would-be victim's blood was to assault him and risk apprehension by the police, which was the very thing you were trying to avoid by striking at him with magic rather than with fists or a knife or a gun.

All of those difficulties could be circumvented by the use of a good photograph instead of a doll. As far as Lavelle knew, he was the only Bocor who had ever applied this bit of modern technology to the practice of voodoo. The first time he'd tried it, he hadn't expected it to work; however, six hours after the ritual was completed, the intended victim was dead, crushed under the wheels of a runaway truck. Since then, Lavelle had employed photographs in every ceremony that ordinarily would have called for a doll. Evidently, he possessed some of his brother Gregory's machine-age sensibility and faith in progress.

Now, kneeling on the earthen floor of the shed, beside the pit, he used a ballpoint pen to punch a hole in the top of each of the eight-by-ten glossies. Then he strung both photographs on a length of slender cord. Two wooden stakes had been driven into the dirt floor, near the brink of the pit, directly opposite each other, with the void between them. Lavelle tied one end of the cord to one of the wooden stakes, stretched it across the pit, and fastened the other end to the second stake. The pictures of the Dawson children dangled over the centre of the hole, bathed in the unearthly orange glow that shone up from the mysterious, shifting bottom of it.

Soon, he would have to kill the children. He was giving Jack Dawson a few hours yet, one last opportunity to back down, but he was fairly sure that Dawson would not relent.

He didn't mind killing children. He looked forward to it. There was a special exhilaration in the murder of the very young.

He licked his lips.

The sound issuing from the pit – the distant susurration that seemed to be composed of tens of thousands of hissing, whispering voices – grew slightly louder when the photographs were suspended where Lavelle wanted them. And there was a new, disquieting tone to the whispers, as well: not merely anger; not just a note of menace; it was an elusive quality that, somehow, spoke of monstrous needs, of a hideous voracity, of blood and perversion, the sound of a dark and insatiable *hunger*.

Lavelle stripped out of his clothes.

Fondling his genitals, he recited a short prayer.

He was ready to begin.

To the left of the shed door stood five large copper bowls. Each contained a different substance: white flour, corn meal, red brick powder, powdered charcoal, and powdered tannis root. Scooping up a handful of the red brick powder, allowing it to dribble in a measured flow from one end of his cupped hand, Lavelle began to draw an intricate design on the floor along the northern flank of the pit.

This design was called a *vèvè*, and it represented the figure and power of an astral force. There were hundreds of *vèvès* that a Houngon or a Bocor must know. Through the drawing of several appropriate *vèvès* prior to the start of a ritual, the priest was forcing the attention of the gods to the *Oumphor*, the temple, where the rites were to be conducted. The *vèvè* had to be drawn freehand, without assistance of a stencil and most certainly without the guidance of a preliminary sketch scratched in the earth; nevertheless, though done freehand, the *vèvè* had to be symmetrical and properly proportioned if it were to have any effect. The creation of the *vèvès* required much practice, a sensitive and agile hand, and a keen eye.

Lavelle scooped up a second handful of red brick powder and continued his work. In a few minutes he had drawn the *vèvè* that represented Simbi Y-An-Kitha, one of the dark gods of *Pétro*:

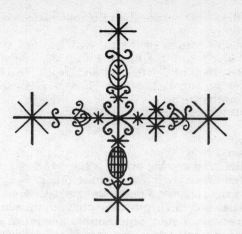

He scrubbed his hand on a clean dry towel, ridding himself of most of the brick dust. He scooped up a handful of flour and began to draw another *vèvè* along the southern flank of the pit. This pattern was much different from the first.

In all, he drew four intricate designs, one on each side of the pit. The third was rendered in charcoal powder. The fourth was done with powdered tannis root.

Then, careful not to disturb the *vèvès*, he crouched, naked, at the edge of the pit.

He stared down.

Down . . .

The floor of the pit shifted, boiled, changed, swirled, oozed, drew close, pulsed, receded. Lavelle had placed no fire or light of any kind inside the hole, yet it glowed and flickered. At first the floor of the pit was only three feet away, just as he had made it. But the longer he stared, the deeper it seemed to become. Now thirty feet instead of three. Now three hundred. Now three miles deep. Now as deep as the centre of the earth itself. And deeper, still deeper, deeper than the distance to the moon, the stars, deeper than the distance to the edge of the universe.

When the bottom of the pit had receded to infinity, Lavelle stood up. He broke into a five-note song, a repetitive chant of destruction and death, and he began the ritual by urinating on the photographs that he had strung on the cord.

7

In the squad car.

The hiss and crackle of the police-band radio.

Headed downtown. Toward the office.

Chain-rigged tyres singing on the pavement.

Snowflakes colliding soundlessly with the windshield. The wipers thumping with metronomic monotony.

Nick Iervolino, the uniformed officer behind the wheel, startled Jack out of a near-trance: 'You don't have to worry about my driving, Lieutenant.'

'I'm sure I don't,' Jack said.

'Been driving a patrol car for twelve years and never had an accident.'

'Is that right?'

'Never even put a scratch on one of my cars.'

'Congratulations.'

'Snow, rain, sleet – nothing bothers me. Never have the least little trouble handling a car. It's a sort of talent. Don't know where I get it from. My mother doesn't drive. My old man does, but he's one of the worst you've ever seen. Scares hell out of me to ride with him. But me – I have a knack for handling a car. So don't worry.'

'I'm not worried,' Jack assured him.

'You sure *seemed* worried.'

'How's that?'

'You were grinding the hell out of your teeth.'

'Was I?'

'I expected to hear your molars start cracking apart any second.'

'I wasn't aware of it. But believe me, I'm not worried about your driving.'

They were approaching an intersection where half a dozen cars were angled everywhichway, spinning their tyres in the snow, trying to get reoriented or at least out of the way. Nick Iervolino braked slowly, cautiously, until they were travelling at a crawl, then found a snaky route through the stranded cars.

On the other side of the intersection, he said, 'So if you aren't worried about my driving, what *is* eating at you?'

Jack hesitated, then told him about the call from Lavelle.

Nick listened, but without diverting his attention from the treacherous streets. When Jack finished, Nick said, 'Jesus Christ Almighty!'

'My sentiments exactly,' Jack said.

'You think he can do it? Put a curse on your kids? One that'll actually work?'

Jack turned the question back on him. 'What do you think?'

Nick pondered for a moment. Then: 'I don't know. It's a strange world we live in, you know. Flying saucers, Big Foot, the Bermuda Triangle, the Abominable Snowman, all sorts of weird things out there. I like to read about stuff like that. Fascinates me. There're millions of people out there who claim to've seen a lot of truly strange things. Not all of it can be bunk – can it? Maybe some of it. Maybe most of it. But not all of it. Right?'

'Probably not all of it,' Jack agreed.

'So maybe voodoo works.'

Jack nodded.

'Of course, for your sake, and for the kids, I hope to God it *doesn't* work,' Nick said.

They travelled half a block in silence.

Then Nick said, 'One thing bothers me about this Lavelle, about what he told you.'

'What's that?'

'Well, let's just say voodoo *does* work.'

'Okay.'

'I mean, let's just pretend.'

'I understand.'

'Well, if voodoo works, and if he wants you off the case, why would he use this magic power of his to kill your kids? Why wouldn't he just use it to kill you? That'd be a lot more direct.'

Jack frowned. 'You're right.'

'If he killed you, they'd assign another detective to the case, and it isn't too likely the new man would be as open-minded as you are about this voodoo angle. So the easiest way for Lavelle to get what he wants is to eliminate you with one of his curses. Now why doesn't he do that – supposing the magic works, I mean?'

'I don't know why.'

'Neither do I,' Nick said. 'Can't figure it. But I think maybe this is important, Lieutenant. Don't you?'

'How?'

'See, even if the guy's a lunatic, even if voodoo doesn't work and you're just dealing with a maniac, at least the rest of his story – all the weird stuff he told you – has its own kind of crazy logic. It's not filled with contradictions. Know what I mean?'

'Yes.'

'It hangs together, even if it is bullshit. It's strangely logical. Except for the threat against your kids. That doesn't fit. Illogical. It's too much trouble when he could just put a curse on *you*. So if he has the power, why doesn't he aim it at you if he's going to aim it at anyone?'

'Maybe it's just that he realizes he can't intimidate me by threatening my own life. Maybe he realizes the only way to intimidate me is through my kids.'

'But if he just destroyed you, had you chewed to pieces like all these others, then he wouldn't *have* to intimidate you. Intimidation is clumsy. Murder is cleaner. See what I mean?'

Jack watched the snow hitting the windshield, and he thought about what Nick had said. He had a hunch that it *was* important.

8

In the storage shed, Lavelle completed the ritual. He stood in orange light, breathing hard, dripping sweat. The beads of perspiration reflected the light and looked like droplets of orange paint. The whites of his eyes were stained by the same preternatural glow, and his well-buffed fingernails also gleamed orange.

Only one thing remained to be done in order to assure the deaths of the Dawson children. When the time came, when the deadline arrived for Jack Dawson and he didn't back off as Lavelle wanted, then Lavelle would only have to pick up two pair of ceremonial scissors and cut both ends of the slender cord from which the photographs hung. The pictures would fall into the pit and vanish in the furnacelike glow, and then the demonic powers would be set loose; the curse would be fulfilled. Penny and Davey Dawson wouldn't have a chance.

Lavelle closed his eyes and imagined he was standing over their bloody, lifeless bodies. That prospect thrilled him.

The murder of children was a dangerous undertaking, one which a Bocor did not contemplate unless he had no other choice. Before he placed a curse of death upon a child, he had better know how to shield himself from the wrath of the *Rada* gods, the gods of white magic, for they were infuriated by the victimization of children. If a Bocor killed an innocent child without knowing the charms and spells that would, subsequently, protect him from the power of the *Rada*, then he would suffer excruciating pain for many days and nights. And when the *Rada* finally snuffed him out, he wouldn't mind dying; indeed, he would be grateful for an end to his suffering.

Lavelle knew how to armour himself against the *Rada*. He had killed other children, before this, and had gotten

163

away with it every time, utterly unscathed. Nevertheless, he was tense and uneasy. There was always the
possibility of a mistake. In spite of his knowledge and
power, this was a dangerous scheme.

On the other hand, if a Bocor used his command of
supernatural machinery to kill a child, and if he got
away with it, then the gods of *Pétro* and *Congo* were so
pleased with him that they bestowed even greater power
upon him. If Lavelle could destroy Penny and Davey
Dawson and deflect the wrath of *Rada*, his mastery of
dark magic would be more awesome than ever before.

Behind his closed eyelids, he saw images of the dead,
torn, mutilated bodies of the Dawson children.

He laughed softly.

In the Dawson apartment, far across town from the
shed where Baba Lavelle was performing the ritual, two
dozen silver-eyed creatures swayed in the shadows, in
sympathy with the rhythm of the Bocor's chanting and
singing. His voice could not be heard in the apartment,
of course. Yet these things with demented eyes were
somehow aware of it. Swaying, they stood in the
kitchen, the living room – and in the dark hallway,
where they watched the door with panting anticipation.
When Lavelle reached the end of the ritual, all of the
small beasts stopped swaying at exactly the same time,
at the very instant Lavelle fell silent. They were rigid
now. Watchful. Alert. Ready.

In a storm drain beneath the Wellton School, other creatures rocked back and forth in the darkness, eyes
gleaming, keeping time with Lavelle's chants, though
he was much too far away to be heard. When he ceased
chanting, they stopped swaying and were as still, as
alert, as ready to attack as were the uninvited guests in
the Dawson apartment.

The traffic light turned red, and the crosswalk filled with a river of heavily bundled pedestrians, their faces hidden by scarves and coat collars. They shuffled and slipped and slid past the front of the patrol car.

Nick Iervolino said, 'I wonder . . .'

Jack said, 'What?'

'Well, just suppose voodoo *does* work.'

'We've already been supposing it.'

'Just for the sake of argument.'

'Yeah, yeah. We've been through this already. Go on.'

'Okay. So why does Lavelle threaten your kids? Why doesn't he just put a curse on you, bump you off, forget about them? That's the question.'

'That's the question,' Jack agreed.

'Well, maybe, for some reason, his magic won't work on you.'

'What reason?'

'I don't know.'

'If it works on other people – which is what we're supposing – then why wouldn't it work on me?'

'I don't know.'

'If it'll work on my kids, why wouldn't it work on me?'

'I don't know. Unless . . . well, maybe there's something different about you.'

'Different? Like what?'

'I don't know.'

'You sound like a broken record.'

'I know.'

Jack sighed. 'This isn't much of an explanation you've come up with.'

'Can you think of a better one?'

'No.'

The traffic light turned green. The last of the pedestrians had crossed. Nick pulled into the intersection and turned left.

After a while, Jack said, 'Different, huh?'

'Somehow.'

As they headed farther downtown, toward the office, they talked about it, trying to figure out what the difference might be.

10

At Wellton School, the last classes of the day were over at three o'clock. By 3:10, a tide of laughing, jabbering children spilled through the front doors, down the steps, onto the sidewalk, into the driving snow that transformed the grey urban landscape of New York into a dazzling fantasyland. Warmly dressed in knitted caps, earmuffs, scarves, sweaters, heavy coats, gloves, jeans, and high boots, they walked with a slight toddle, arms out at their sides because of all the layers of insulation they were wearing; they looked furry and cuddly and well padded and stumpy-legged, not unlike a bunch of magically animated teddy bears.

Some of them lived near enough and were old enough to be allowed to walk home, and ten of them piled into a minibus that their parents had bought. But most were met by a mother or father or grandparent in the family car or, because of the inclement weather, by one of those same relatives in a taxi.

Mrs Shepherd, one of the teachers, had the Dismissal Watch duty this week. She moved back and forth along the sidewalk, keeping an eye on everyone, making sure none of the younger kids tried to walk home, seeing that none of them got into a car with a stranger. Today, she had the added chore of stopping snowball battles before they could get started.

Penny and Davey had been told that their Aunt Faye would pick them up, instead of their father, but they couldn't see her anywhere when they came down the steps, so they moved off to one side, out of the way. They stood in front of the emerald-green, wooden gate that closed off the service passageway between the

Wellton School and the townhouse next door. The gate wasn't flush with the front walls of the two buildings, but recessed eight or ten inches. Trying to stay out of the sharp cold wind that cruelly pinched their cheeks and even penetrated their heavy coats, they pressed their backs to the gate, huddling in the shallow depression in front of it.

Davey said, 'Why isn't Dad coming?'

'I guess he had to work.'

'Why?'

'I guess he's on an important case.'

'What case?'

'I don't know.'

'It isn't dangerous, is it?'

'Probably not.'

'He won't get shot, will he?'

'Of course not.'

'How can you be sure?'

'I'm sure,' she said, although she wasn't sure at all.

'Cops get shot all the time.'

'Not that often.'

'What'll we do if Dad gets shot?'

Immediately after their mother's death, Davey had handled the loss quite well. Better than anyone had expected. Better than Penny had handled it, in fact. *He* hadn't needed to see a psychiatrist. He had cried, sure; he had cried a lot, for a few days, but then he had bounced back. Lately, however, a year and a half after the funeral, he had begun to develop an unnatural fear of losing his father, too. As far as Penny knew, she was the only one who noticed how terribly obsessed Davey was with the dangers – both real and imagined – of his father's occupation. She hadn't mentioned her brother's state of mind to her father or to anyone else, for that matter, because she thought she could straighten him out by herself. After all, she was his big sister; he was her responsibility; she had certain obligations to him. In the months right after their mother's death, Penny had failed Davey; at least that was how she felt. She had gone to pieces then. She hadn't been there when he'd needed her the most. Now, she intended to make it up to him.

'What'll we do if Dad gets shot?' he asked again.

'He isn't going to get shot.'

'But if he *does* get shot. What'll we do?'

'We'll be all right.'

'Will we have to go to an orphanage?'

'No, silly.'

'Where would we go then? Huh? Penny, where would we go?'

'We'd probably go to live with Aunt Faye and Uncle Keith.'

'Yuch.'

'They're all right.'

'I'd rather go live in the sewers.'

'That's ridiculous.'

'It'd be neat living in the sewers.'

'Neat is the last thing it'd be.'

'We could come out at night and steal our food.'

'From who – the winos asleep in the gutters?'

'We could have an alligator for a pet!'

'There aren't any alligators in the sewers.'

'Of course there are,' he said.

'That's a myth.'

'A what?'

'A myth. A made-up story. A fairytale.'

'You're nuts. Alligators live in sewers.'

'Davey—'

'Sure they do! Where *else* would alligators live?'

'Florida, for one place.'

'Florida? Boy, you're flako. Florida!'

'Yeah, Florida.'

'Only old retired coots and gold-digging bimbos live in Florida.'

Penny blinked. 'Where'd you hear *that*?'

'Aunt Faye's friend. Mrs Dumpy.'

'Dumphy.'

'Yeah. Mrs Dumpy was talking to Aunt Faye, see. Mrs Dumpy's husband wanted to retire to Florida, and he went down there by himself to scout around for a place to live, but he never came back 'cause what he did was he ran off with a gold-digging bimbo. Mrs Dumpy said only old coots and a lot of gold-digging bimbos live down there. And that's another good reason not to live with Aunt Faye. Her friends. They're all like Mrs Dumpy. Always whining, you know? Jeez. And Uncle Keith smokes.'

'A lot of people smoke.'

'His clothes stink from the smoke.'

'It's not that bad.'

'And his breath! Grody!'

'Your breath isn't always like flowers, you know.'

'Who'd want breath like flowers?'

'A bumblebee.'

'I'm no bumblebee.'

'You buzz a lot. You never shut up. Always buzz-buzz-buzz.'

'I do not.'

'*Buzzzzzzzzzz.*'

'Better watch it. I might sting, too.'

'Don't you dare.'

'I might sting real bad.'

'Davey, don't you dare.'

'Anyway, Aunt Faye drives me nuts.'

'She means well, Davey.'

'She . . . twitters.'

'Birds twitter, not people.'

'She twitters like a bird.'

It was true. But at the advanced age of almost-twelve, Penny had recently begun to feel the first stirrings of comradeship with adults. She wasn't nearly as comfortable ridiculing them as she had been just a few months ago.

Davey said, 'And she always nags Dad about whether we're being fed well.'

'She just worries about us.'

'Does she think Dad would *starve* us?'

'Of course not.'

'Then why's she always going on and on about it?'

'She's just . . . Aunt Faye.'

'Boy, you can say *that* again!'

An especially fierce gust of wind swept the street, found its way into the recess in front of the green gate. Penny and Davey shivered.

He said, 'Dad's got a good gun, doesn't he? They give cops really good guns, don't they? They wouldn't let a cop go out on the street with a half-ass gun, would they?'

'Don't say "half-ass."'

'Would they?'

'No. They give cops the best guns there are.'

'And Dad's a good shot, isn't he?'

'Yes.'

'How good?'

'Very good.'

'He's the best, isn't he?'

'Sure,' Penny said. 'Nobody's better with a gun than Daddy.'

'Then the only way he's going to get it is if somebody sneaks up on him and shoots him in the back.'

'That isn't going to happen,' she said firmly.

'It could.'

'You watch too much TV.'

They were silent for a moment.

Then he said, 'If somebody kills Dad, I want to get cancer and die, too.'

'Stop it, Davey.'

'Cancer or a heart attack or something.'

'You don't mean that.'

He nodded emphatically, vigorously: yes, yes, yes; he

170

did mean it; he absolutely, positively did. 'I asked God to make it happen that way if it has to happen.'

'What do you mean?' she asked, frowning at him.

'Each night. When I say my prayers. I always ask God not to let anything happen to Dad. And then I say, "Well, God, if you for some stupid reason just *have* to let him get shot, then please let me get cancer and die, too. Or let me get hit by a truck. Something."'

'That's morbid.'

He didn't say anything more.

He looked at the ground, at his gloved hands, at Mrs Shepherd walking her patrol – everywhere but at Penny. She took hold of his chin, turned his face to her. Tears shimmered in his eyes. He was trying hard to hold them back, squinting, blinking.

He was so small. Just seven years old and not big for his age. He looked fragile and helpless, and Penny wanted to grab hold of him and hug him, but she knew he wouldn't want her to do that when they might be seen by some of the other boys in his class.

She suddenly felt small and helpless herself. But that wasn't good. Not good at all. She had to be strong for Davey's sake.

Letting go of his chin, she said, 'Listen, Davey, we've got to sit down and talk. About Mom. About people dying, why it happens, you know, all that stuff, like what it means, how it's not the end for them but maybe only the beginning, up there in Heaven, and how we've got to just go on, no matter what. 'Cause we do. We've got to go on. Mom would be very disappointed in us if we didn't just go on. And if anything happened to Dad – which nothing *is* going to happen to him – but if by some wild chance it *did*, then he'd want us to go on, just the way Mom would want. He'd be very unhappy with us if we—'

'*Penny! Davey! Over here!*'

A yellow cab was at the kerb. The rear window was down, and Aunt Faye leaned out, waved at them.

Davey bolted across the sidewalk, suddenly so eager to be away from any talk of death that he was even glad to see his twittering old Aunt Faye.

Damn! I botched it, Penny thought. I was too blunt about it.

In that same instant, before she followed Davey to the taxi, before she even took one step, a sharp pain lanced through her left ankle. She twitched, yelped, looked down – and was immobilized by terror.

Between the bottom of the green gate and the pavement, there was a four-inch gap. A hand had reached through that gap, from the darkness in the covered serviceway beyond, and it had seized her ankle.

She couldn't scream. Her voice was gone.

It wasn't a human hand, either. Maybe twice the size of a cat's paw. But not a paw. It was a completely – although crudely – formed hand with fingers and a thumb.

She couldn't even whisper. Her throat was locked.

The hand wasn't skin-coloured. It was an ugly, mottled grey-green-yellow, like bruised and festering flesh. And it was sort of lumpy, a little ragged looking.

Breathing was no easier than screaming.

The small grey-green-yellow fingers were tapered and ended in sharp claws. Two of those claws had punctured her rubber boot.

She thought of the plastic baseball bat.

Last night. In her room. The thing under the bed.

She thought of the shining eyes in the school basement.

And now *this*.

Two of the small fingers had thrust inside her boot and were scraping at her, digging at her, tearing, gouging.

Abruptly, her breath came to her in a rush. She gasped, sucked in lungsful of frigid air, which snapped her out of the terror-induced trance that, thus far, had held her there by the gate. She jerked her foot away from the hand, tore loose, and was surprised that she was able to do so. She turned and ran to the taxi, plunged inside, and yanked the door shut.

She looked back toward the gate. There was nothing unusual in sight, no creature with small claw-tipped hands, no goblin capering in the snow.

The taxi pulled away from Wellton School.

Aunt Faye and Davey were talking excitedly about the snowstorm which, Faye said, was supposed to dump ten or twelve inches before it was done. Neither of them seemed to be aware that Penny was scared half to death.

While they chattered, Penny reached down and felt her boot. At the ankle, the rubber was torn. A flap of it hung loose.

She unzippered the boot, slipped her hand inside, under her sock, and felt the wound on her ankle. It burned a little. When she brought her hand out of the boot, there was some blood glistening on her fingertips.

Aunt Faye saw it. 'What's happened to you, dear?'

'It's okay,' Penny said.

'That's blood.'

'Just a scratch.'

Davey paled at the sight of the blood.

Penny tried to reassure him, although she was afraid that her voice was noticeably shaky and that her face would betray her anxiety: 'It's nothing, Davey. I'm all right.'

Aunt Faye insisted on changing places with Davey, so she would be next to Penny and could have a closer look at the injury. She made Penny take off the boot, and she peeled down the sock, revealing a puncture wound and several scratches on the ankle. It was bleeding but not very much; in a couple of minutes, even unattended, it would stop.

'How'd this happen?' Aunt Faye demanded.

Penny hesitated. More than anything, she wanted to tell Faye all about the creatures with shining eyes. She wanted help, protection. But she knew that she couldn't say a word. They wouldn't believe her. After all, she was The Girl Who Had Needed A Psychiatrist. If she started babbling about goblins with shining eyes, they'd think she was having a relapse; they would say she *still* hadn't adjusted to her mother's death, and they would make an appointment with a psychiatrist. While she was off seeing the shrink, there wouldn't be anyone around to keep the goblins away from Davey.

'Come on, come on,' Faye said. 'Fess up. What were you doing that you shouldn't have been doing?'

'Huh?'

'That's why you're hesitating. What were you doing that you knew you shouldn't be doing?'

'Nothing,' Penny said.

'Then how'd you get this cut?'

'I . . . I caught my boot on a nail.'

'Nail? Where?'

'On the gate.'

'What gate?'

'Back at the school, the gate where we were waiting for you. A nail was sticking out of it, and I got caught up on it.'

Faye scowled. Unlike her sister (Penny's mother), Faye was a redhead with sharp features and grey eyes that were almost colourless. In repose, hers was a pretty enough face; however, when she wanted to scowl, she could really do a first-rate job of it. Davey called it her 'witch look'.

She said, 'Was it rusty?'

Penny said, 'What?'

'The nail, of course. Was it rusty?'

'I don't know.'

'Well, you saw it, didn't you? Otherwise, how'd you know it was a nail?'

Penny nodded. 'Yeah. I guess it was rusty.'

'Have you had a tetanus shot?'

'Yeah.'

Aunt Faye peered at her with undisguised suspicion. 'Do you even know what a tetanus shot is?'

'Sure.'

'When did you get it?'

'First week of October.'

'I wouldn't have imagined that your father would think of things like tetanus shots.'

'They gave it to us at school,' Penny said.

'Is that right?' Faye said, still doubtful.

Davey spoke up: 'They make us take all *kinds* of shots at school. They have a nurse in, and all week we get shots. It's awful. Makes you feel like a pin cushion. Shots for mumps and measles. A flu shot. Other stuff. I *hate* it.'

Faye seemed to be satisfied. 'Okay. Just the same, when we get home, we'll wash that cut out really good, bathe it in alcohol, get some iodine on it, and a proper bandage.'

'It's only a scratch,' Penny said.

'We won't take chances. Now put your boot back on, dear.'

Just as Penny got her foot in the boot and pulled up the zipper, the taxi hit a pothole. They were all bounced up and thrown forward with such suddenness and force that they almost fell off the seat.

'Young man,' Faye said to the driver, even though he was at least forty years old, her own age, 'where on earth did you learn to drive a car?'

He glanced in the rearview mirror. 'Sorry, lady.'

'Don't you *know* the streets of this city are a mess?' Faye demanded. 'You've got to keep your eyes open.'

'I try to,' he said.

While Faye lectured the driver on the proper way to handle his cab, Penny leaned back against the seat, closed her eyes, and thought about the ugly little hand that had torn her boot and ankle. She tried to convince herself that it had been the hand of an ordinary animal of some kind; nothing strange; nothing out of the Twilight Zone. But most animals had paws, not hands. Monkeys had hands, of course. But this wasn't a monkey. No

175

way. Squirrels had hands of a sort, didn't they? And racoons. But this wasn't a squirrel or a racoon, either. It wasn't anything she had ever seen or read about.

Had it been trying to drag her down and kill her? Right there on the street?

No. In order to kill her, the creature – and others like it, others with the shining silver eyes – would have had to come out from behind the gate, into the open, where Mrs Shepherd and others would have seen them. And Penny was pretty sure the goblins didn't want to be seen by anyone but her. They were secretive. No, they definitely hadn't meant to kill her back there at the school; they had only meant to give her a good scare, to let her know they were still lurking around, waiting for the right opportunity . . .

But *why*?

Why did they want her and, presumably, Davey, instead of some other kids?

What made goblins angry? What did you have to do to make them come after you like this?

She couldn't think of anything she had done that would make anyone terribly angry with her; certainly not goblins.

Confused, miserable, frightened, she opened her eyes and looked out the window. Snow was piling up everywhere. In her heart, she felt as cold as the icy, wind-scoured street beyond the window.

PART TWO

Darkness devours every shining day.
Darkness demands and always has its way.
Darkness listens, watches, waits.
Darkness claims the day and celebrates.
Sometimes in silence darkness comes.
Sometimes with a gleeful banging of drums.
　　　　—The Book of Counted Sorrows

Who is more foolish—
the child afraid of the dark
or the man afraid of the light?
　　　　—Maurice Freehill

CHAPTER FOUR

1

At 5:30, Jack and Rebecca went into Captain Walter Gresham's office to present him with the manpower and equipment requirements of the task force, as well as to discuss strategy in the investigation.

During the afternoon, two more members of the Carramazza crime family had been murdered, along with their bodyguards. Already the press was calling it the bloodiest gang war since Prohibition. What the press still didn't know was that the victims (except for the first two) had not been stabbed or shot or garrotted or hung on meat hooks in traditional *cosa nostra* style. For the time being, the police had chosen not to reveal that all but the first two victims had been savagely bitten to death. When reporters uncovered that puzzling and grotesque fact, they would realize this was one of the biggest stories of the decade.

'That's when it'll get really bad,' Gresham said. 'They'll be all over us like fleas on a dog.'

The heat was on, about to get even hotter, and Gresham was as fidgety as a toad on a griddle. Jack and Rebecca remained seated in front of the captain's desk, but Gresham couldn't remain still behind it. As they conducted their business, the captain paced the room, went repeatedly to the windows, lit a cigarette, smoked less than a third of it, stubbed it out, realized what he had done, and lit another.

Finally the time came for Jack to tell Gresham about his latest visit to Carver Hampton's shop and about the telephone call from Baba Lavelle. He had never felt more awkward than he did while recounting those events under Gresham's sceptical gaze.

He would have felt better if Rebecca had been on his side, but again they were in adversary positions. She was angry with him because he hadn't gotten back to the office until ten minutes past three, and she'd had to do a lot of the task force preparations on her own. He explained that the snowy streets were choked with crawling traffic, but she was having none of it. She listened to his story, was as angry as he was about the threat to his kids, but was not the least bit convinced that he had experienced anything even remotely supernatural. In fact, she was frustrated by his insistence that a great deal about the incident at the pay phone was just plain uncanny.

When Jack finished recounting those events for Gresham, the captain turned to Rebecca and said, 'What do you make of it?'

She said, 'I think we can now safely assume that Lavelle is a raving lunatic, not just another hood who wants to make a bundle in the drug trade. This isn't just a battle for territory within the underworld, and we'd be making a big mistake if we tried to handle it the same way we'd handle an honest-to-God gang war.'

'What else?' Gresham asked.

'Well,' she said. 'I think we ought to dig into this Carver Hampton's background, see what we can turn up about him. Maybe he and Lavelle are in this together.'

'No.' Jack said. 'Hampton wasn't faking when he told me he was terrified of Lavelle.'

'How did Lavelle know precisely the right moment to call that pay phone?' Rebecca asked. 'How did he know *exactly* when you'd be passing by it? One answer is that he was in Hampton's shop the whole time you were there, in the back room, and he knew when you left.'

'He wasn't,' Jack said. 'Hampton's just not that good an actor.'

'He's a clever fraud,' she said. 'But even if he isn't tied to Lavelle, I think we ought to get men up to Harlem this evening and really scour the block with the pay phone . . . and the block across the intersection from it. If Lavelle wasn't in Hampton's shop, then he must have been watching it from one of the other buildings along that street. There's no other explanation.'

Unless maybe his voodoo really works, Jack thought.

Rebecca continued: 'Have detectives check the apartments along those two blocks, see if Lavelle is holed up in one. Distribute copies of the photograph of Lavelle. Maybe someone up there's seen him around.'

'Sounds good to me,' Gresham said. 'We'll do it.'

'And I believe the threat against Jack's kids ought to be taken seriously. Put a guard on them when Jack can't be there.'

'I agree,' Gresham said. 'We'll assign a man right now.'

'Thanks, Captain,' Jack said. 'But I think it can wait until morning. The kids are with my sister-in-law right now, and I don't think Lavelle could find them. I told her to make sure she wasn't being followed when she picked them up at school. Besides, Lavelle said he'd give me the rest of the day to make up my mind about backing off the voodoo angle, and I assume he meant this evening as well.'

Gresham sat on the edge of his desk. 'If you want, I can remove you from the case. No sweat.'

'Absolutely not,' Jack said.

'You take his threat seriously?'

'Yes. But I also take my work seriously. I'm on this one to the bitter end.'

Gresham lit another cigarette, drew deeply on it. 'Jack, do you actually think there could be anything to this voodoo stuff?'

Aware of Rebecca's penetrating stare, Jack said, 'It's

pretty wild to think maybe there could be something to it. But I just can't rule it out.'

'I can,' Rebecca said. 'Lavelle might believe in it, but that doesn't make it real.'

'What about the condition of the bodies?' Jack asked.

'Obviously,' she said, 'Lavelle's using trained animals.'

'That's almost as far-fetched as voodoo,' Gresham said.

'Anyway,' Jack said, 'we went through all of that earlier today. About the only small, vicious, trainable animal we could think of was the ferret. And we've all seen Pathology's report, the one that came in at four-thirty. The teeth impressions don't belong to ferrets. According to Pathology, they don't belong to any other animal Noah took aboard the ark, either.'

Rebecca said, 'Lavelle's from the Caribbean. Isn't it likely that he's using an animal indigenous to that part of the world, something our forensic experts wouldn't even think of, some species of exotic lizard or something like that?'

'Now you're grasping at straws,' Jack said.

'I agree,' Gresham said. 'But it's worth checking out, anyway. Okay. Anything else?'

'Yeah,' Jack said. 'Can you explain how I knew that call from Lavelle was for me? Why was I drawn to that pay phone?'

Wind stroked the windows.

Behind Gresham's desk, the ticking of the wall clock suddenly seemed much louder than it had been.

The captain shrugged. 'I guess neither of us has an answer for you, Jack.'

'Don't feel bad. I don't have an answer for me, either.'

Gresham got up from his desk. 'All right, if that's it, then I think the two of you ought to knock off, go home, get some rest. You've put in a long day already; the task force is functioning now, and it can get along without you until tomorrow. Jack, if you'll hang around just a couple of minutes, I'll show you a list of the available officers on every shift, and you can hand-pick the men you want to watch your kids.'

Rebecca was already at the door, pulling it open. Jack called to her. She glanced back.

He said, 'Wait for me downstairs, okay?'

Her expression was noncommittal. She walked out.

From the window, where he had gone to look down at the street, Walt Gresham said, 'It's like the arctic out there.'

2

The one thing Penny liked about the Jamisons' place was the kitchen, which was big by New York City apartment standards, almost twice as large as the kitchen Penny was accustomed to, and cozy. A green tile floor. White cabinets with leaded glass doors and brass hardware. Green ceramic-tile counters. Above the double sink, there was a beautiful out-thrusting greenhouse window with a four-foot-long, two-foot-wide planting bed in which a variety of herbs were grown all year long, even during the winter. (Aunt Faye liked to cook with fresh herbs whenever possible.) In one corner, jammed against the wall, was a small butcher's-block table, not so much a place to eat as a place to plan menus and prepare shopping lists; flanking the table, there was space for two chairs. This was the only room in the Jamisons' apartment in which Penny felt comfortable.

At twenty minutes past six, she was sitting at the butcher's-block table, pretending to read one of Faye's magazines; the words blurred together in front of her unfocused eyes. Actually, she was thinking about all sorts of things she didn't *want* to think about: goblins, death, and whether she'd ever be able to sleep again.

Uncle Keith had come home from work almost an hour ago. He was a partner in a successful stockbrokerage. Tall, lean, with a head as hairless as an egg, sporting a greying moustache and goatee, Uncle Keith always seemed distracted. You had the feeling he never gave you more than two-thirds of his attention when he was talking with you. Sometimes he would sit in his favourite chair for an hour or two, his hands folded in his lap, unmoving, staring at the wall, hardly even blinking, breaking his trance only two or three times an hour in order to pick up a brandy glass and take one tiny sip from it. Other times he would sit at a window, staring and chain-smoking. Secretly, Davey called Uncle Keith 'the moon man' because his mind always seemed to be somewhere on the moon. Since coming home today, he'd been in the living room, sipping slowly at a martini, puffing on one cigarette after another, watching TV news and reading the *Wall Street Journal* at the same time.

Aunt Faye was at the other end of the kitchen from the table where Penny sat. She had begun to prepare dinner, which was scheduled for seven-thirty: lemon chicken, rice, and stir-fried vegetables. The kitchen was the only place Aunt Faye was not too much like Aunt Faye. She enjoyed cooking, was very good at it, and seemed like a different person when she was in the kitchen; more relaxed, kinder than usual.

Davey was helping her prepare dinner. At least she was allowing him to think he was helping. As they worked they talked, not about anything important, this and that.

'Gosh, I'm hungry enough to eat a horse!' Davey said.

'That's not a polite thing to say,' Faye advised him. 'It brings to mind an unpleasant image. You should simply say, "I'm extremely hungry," or "I'm starved," or something like that.'

'Well, naturally, I meant a *dead* horse,' Davey said, completely misunderstanding Faye's little lesson in etiquette. 'And one that's been cooked, too. I wouldn't want to eat any *raw* horse, Aunt Faye. Yuch and double yuch. But, man-oh-man, I sure could eat a whole lot of just about anything you gimme right now.'

'My heavens, young man, you had cookies and milk when we got here this afternoon.'

'Only two cookies.'

'And you're famished already? You don't have a stomach; what *you* have is a bottomless pit!'

'Well, I hardly had any lunch,' Davey said. 'Mrs Shepherd – she's my teacher – she shared some of her lunch with me, but it was really dumb-awful stuff. All she had was yoghurt and tuna fish, and I *hate* both of 'em. So what I did, after she gave me a little of each, I nibbled at it, just to make her feel good, and then when she wasn't looking, I threw most of it away.'

'But doesn't your father pack a lunch for you?' Faye asked, her voice suddenly sharper than it had been.

'Oh, sure. Or when he doesn't have time, Penny packs it. But—'

Faye turned to Penny. 'Did he have a lunch to take to school today? Surely he doesn't have to beg for food!'

Penny looked up from her magazine. 'I made his lunch myself, this morning. He had an apple, a ham sandwich, and two big oatmeal cookies.'

'That sounds like a fine lunch to me,' Faye said, 'Why didn't you eat it, Davey?'

'Well, because of the rats, of course,' he said.

Penny twitched in surprise, sat up straight in her chair, and stared intently at Davey.

Faye said, 'Rats? What rats?'

'Holy-moly, I forgot to tell you!' Davey said. 'Rats must've got in my lunchbox during morning classes. Big old ugly rats with yellow teeth, come right up out of the sewers or somewhere. The food was all messed up, torn to pieces, and chewed on. *Grooooooooose,*' he said, drawing the word out with evident pleasure, not disgusted by the fact that rats had been at his lunch, actually excited about it, thrilled by it, as only a young boy could be. At his age, an incident like this was a real adventure.

Penny's mouth had gone as dry as ashes. 'Davey? Uh
. . . did you see the rats?'

'Nah,' he said, clearly disappointed. 'They were gone
by the time I went to get my lunchbox.'

'Where'd you have your lunchbox?' Penny asked.

'In my locker.'

'Did the rats chew on anything else in your locker?'

'Like what?'

'Like books or anything.'

'Why would they want to chew on books?'

'Then it was just the food?'

'Sure. What else?'

'Did you have your locker door shut?'

'I thought I did,' he said.

'Didn't you have it locked, too?'

'I thought I did.'

'And wasn't your lunchbox shut tight?'

'It *should* have been,' he said, scratching his head,
trying to remember.

Faye said, 'Well, obviously, it wasn't. Rats can't open
a lock, open a door, and pry the lid off a lunchbox. You
must have been very careless, Davey. I'm surprised at
you. I'll bet you ate one of those oatmeal cookies first
thing when you got to school, just couldn't wait, and
then forgot to put the lid back on the box.'

'But I didn't,' Davey protested.

'Your father's not teaching you to pick up after yourself,' Faye said. 'That's the kind of thing a mother
teaches, and your father's just neglecting it.'

Penny was going to tell them about how her own
locker had been trashed when she'd gone to school this
morning. She was even going to tell them about the
things in the basement because it seemed to her that
what had happened to Davey's lunch would somehow
substantiate her story.

But before Penny could speak, Aunt Faye spoke up
in her most morally indignant tone of voice: 'What *I*
want to know is what kind of school this is your father's

sent to you. What kind of dirty hole is this place, this Wellton?'

'It's a good school,' Penny said defensively.

'With *rats*?' Faye said. 'No good school would have rats. No halfway decent school would have rats. Why, what if they'd still been in the locker when Davey went for his lunch? He might've been bitten. Rats are filthy. They carry all kinds of diseases. They're disgusting. I simply can't imagine any school for young children being allowed to remain open if it has rats. The Board of Health has got to be told about this first thing tomorrow. Your father's going to have to do something about the situation immediately. I won't allow him to procrastinate. Not where your health is concerned. Why, your poor dear mother would be appalled by such a place, a school with rats in the walls. Rats! My God, rats carry everything from rabies to the plague!'

Faye droned on and on.

Penny tuned her out.

There wasn't any point in telling them about her own locker and the silver-eyed things in the school basement. Faye would insist they had been rats, too. When that woman got something in her head, there was no way of getting it out again, no way of changing her mind. Now, Faye was looking forward to confronting their father about the rats; she relished the thought of blaming him for putting them in a rat-infested school, and she wouldn't be the least receptive to anything Penny said, to any explanation or any conflicting facts that might put rats completely out of the picture and thereby spare their father from a scolding.

Even if I tell her about the hand, Penny thought, the little hand that came under the green gate, she'll stick to the idea that it's rats. She'll say I was scared and made a mistake about what I saw. She'll say it wasn't really a hand at all, but a rat, a slimy old rat biting at my boot. She'll turn it all around. She'll make it support the story she wants to believe, and it'll just be more

187

ammunition for her to use against Daddy. Damnit, Aunt Faye, why're you so stubborn?

Faye was chattering about the need for a parent to thoroughly investigate a school before sending children to it.

Penny wondered when her father would come to get them, and she prayed he wouldn't be too late. She wanted him to come before bedtime. She didn't want to be alone, just her and Davey, in a dark room, even if it was Aunt Faye's guest room, blocks and blocks away from their own apartment. She was pretty sure the goblins would find them, even here. She had decided to take her father aside and tell him everything. He wouldn't want to believe in goblins, at first. But now there was Davey's lunchbox to consider. And if she went back to their apartment with her father and showed him the holes in Davey's plastic baseball bat, she might be able to convince him. Daddy was a grownup, like Aunt Faye, sure, but he wasn't stubborn, and he *listened* to kids in a way that few grownups did.

Faye said, 'With all the money he got from your mother's insurance and from the settlement the hospital made, he could afford to send you to a top-of-the-line school. Absolutely top-of-the-line. I can't imagine why he settled on this Wellton joint.'

Penny bit her lip, said nothing.

She stared down at the magazine. The pictures and words swam in and out of focus.

The worst thing was that now she knew, beyond a doubt, that the goblins weren't just after her. They wanted Davey, too.

3

Rebecca had not waited for Jack, though he had asked her to. While he'd been with Captain Gresham, working out the details of the protection that would be provided for Penny and Davey, Rebecca apparently put on her coat and went home.

When Jack found that she had gone, he sighed and said softly, 'You sure aren't easy, baby.'

On his desk were two books about voodoo, which he had checked out of the library yesterday. He stared at them for a long moment, then decided he needed to learn more about Bocors and Houngons before tomorrow morning. He put on his coat and gloves, picked up the books, tucked them under one arm, and went down to the subterranean garage, beneath the building.

Because he and Rebecca were now in charge of the emergency task force, they were entitled to perquisites beyond the reach of ordinary homicide detectives, including the full-time use of an unmarked police sedan for each of them, not just during duty hours but around the clock. The car assigned to Jack was a one-year-old, sour-green Chevrolet that bore a few dents and more than a few scratches. It was the totally stripped-down model, without options or luxuries of any kind, just a get-around car, not a racer-and-chaser. The motor pool mechanics had even put the snow chains on the tyres. The heap was ready to roll.

He backed out of the parking space, drove up the ramp to the street exit. He stopped and waited while a city truck, equipped with a big snow-plough and a salt spreader and lots of flashing lights, passed by in the storm-thrashed darkness.

In addition to the truck, there were only two other vehicles on the street. The storm virtually had the night to itself. Yet, when the truck was gone and the way was clear, Jack still hesitated.

He switched on the windshield wipers.

To head toward Rebecca's apartment, he would have to turn left.

To go to the Jamisons' place, he ought to turn right.

The wipers flogged back and forth, back and forth, left, right, left, right.

He was eager to be with Penny and Davey, eager to hug them, to see them warm and alive and smiling.

Right, left, right.

Of course, they weren't in any real danger at the moment. Even if Lavelle was serious when he threatened them, he wouldn't make his move this soon, and he wouldn't know where to find them even if he *did* want to make his move.

Left, right, left.

They were perfectly safe with Faye and Keith. Besides, Jack had told Faye that he probably wouldn't make it for dinner; she was already expecting him to be late.

The wipers beat time to his indecision.

Finally he took his foot off the brake, pulled into the street, and turned left.

He needed to talk to Rebecca about what had happened between them last night. She had avoided the subject all day. He couldn't allow her to continue to dodge it. She would have to face up to the changes that last night had wrought in both their lives, major changes which he welcomed whole-heartedly but about which she seemed, at best, ambivalent.

Along the edges of the car roof, wind whistled hollowly through the metal beading, a cold and mournful sound.

Crouching in deep shadows by the garage exit, the thing watched Jack Dawson drive away in the unmarked sedan.

Its shining silver eyes did not blink even once.

Then, keeping to the shadows, it crept back into the deserted, silent garage.

It hissed. It muttered. It gabbled softly to itself in an eerie, raspy little voice.

Finding the protection of darkness and shadows wherever it wished to go – even where there didn't seem to have been shadows only a moment before – the thing slunk from car to car, beneath and around them, until it came to a drain in the garage floor. It descended into the midnight regions below.

4

Lavelle was nervous.

Without switching on any lamps, he stalked restlessly through his house, upstairs and down, back and forth, looking for nothing, simply unable to keep still, always moving in deep darkness but never bumping into furniture or doorways, pacing as swiftly and surely as if the rooms were all brightly lighted. He wasn't blind in darkness, never the least disoriented. Indeed, he was at home in shadows. Darkness, after all, was a part of him.

Usually, in either darkness or light, he was supremely confident and self-assured. But now, hour by hour, his self-assurance was steadily crumbling.

His nervousness had bred uneasiness. Uneasiness had given birth to fear. He was unaccustomed to fear. He didn't know quite how to handle it. So the fear made him even more nervous.

He was worried about Jack Dawson. Perhaps it had been a grave mistake to allow Dawson time to consider his options. A man like the detective might put that time to good use.

If he senses that I'm even slightly afraid of him, Lavelle thought, and if he learns more about voodoo, then he might eventually understand why I've got good reason to fear him.

If Dawson discovered the nature of his own special power, and if he learned to use that power, he would find and stop Lavelle. Dawson was one of those rare individuals, that one in ten thousand, who could do battle with even the most masterful Bocor and be reasonably certain of victory. If the detective uncovered the secret of himself, then he would come for Lavelle, well armoured and dangerous.

Lavelle paced through the dark house.

Maybe he should strike now. Destroy the Dawson

children this evening. Get it over with. Their deaths might send Dawson spiralling down into an emotional collapse. He loved his kids a great deal, and he was already a widower, already labouring under a heavy burden of grief; perhaps the slaughter of Penny and Davey would break him. If the loss of his kids didn't snap his mind, then it would most likely plunge him into a terrible depression that would cloud his thinking and interfere with his work for many weeks. At the very least, Dawson would have to take a few days off from the investigation, in order to arrange the funerals, and those few days would give Lavelle some breathing space.

On the other hand, what if Dawson was the kind of man who drew strength from adversity instead of buckling under the weight of it? What if the murder and mutilation of his children only solidified his determination to find and destroy Lavelle?

To Lavelle, that was an unnerving possibility.

Indecisive, the Bocor rambled through the lightless rooms as if he were a ghost come to haunt.

At last, he knew he must consult the ancient gods and humbly request the benefit of their wisdom.

He went to the kitchen and flicked on the overhead light.

From a cupboard, he withdrew a cannister filled with flour.

A radio stood on the counter. He moved it to the centre of the kitchen table.

Using the flour, he drew an elaborate *vèvè* on the table, all the way around the radio.

He switched on the radio.

An old Beatles song. *Eleanor Rigby*.

He turned the dial through a dozen stations that were playing every kind of music from pop to rock to country, classical, and jazz. He set the tuner at an unused frequency, where there was no spill-over whatsoever from the stations on both sides.

The soft crackle and hiss of the open airwaves filled the room and sounded like the sighing surf-roar of a far-off sea.

He scooped up one more handful of flour and carefully drew a small, simple *vèvè* on top of the radio itself.

At the sink he washed his hands, then went to the refrigerator and got a small bottle full of blood.

It was cat's blood, used in a variety of rituals. Once a week, always at a different pet store or animal pound, he bought a cat, brought it home, killed and drained it to maintain a fresh supply of blood.

He returned to the table now, sat down in front of the radio. Dipping his fingers in the cat's blood, he drew certain runes on the table and, last of all, on the plastic window over the radio dial.

He chanted for a while, waited, listened, chanted some more, until he heard an unmistakable yet indefinable change in the sound of the unused frequency. It had been dead just a moment ago. Dead air. Dead, random, meaningless sound. Now it was alive. It was still just the crackle-sputter-hiss of static, a silk-soft sound. But somehow different from what it had been a few seconds ago. *Something* was making use of the open frequency, reaching out from the Beyond.

Staring at the radio but not really seeing it, Lavelle said, 'Is someone there?'

No answer.

'Is someone there?'

It was a voice of dust and mummified remains: '*I wait.*' It was a voice of dry paper, of sand and splinters, a voice of infinite age, as bitterly cold as the night between the stars, jagged and whispery and evil.

It might be any one of a hundred thousand demons, or a full-fledged god of one of the ancient African religions, or the spirit of a dead man long ago condemned to Hell. There was no way of telling for sure which it was, and Lavelle wasn't empowered to make it speak

193

its name. Whatever it might be, it would be able to answer his questions.

'*I wait.*'

'You know of my business here?'

'*Yessss.*'

'The business involving the Carramazza family.'

'*Yessss.*'

If God had given snakes the power of speech, this was what they would have sounded like.

'You know the detective, this man Dawson?'

'*Yessss.*'

'Will he ask his superiors to remove him from the case?'

'*Never.*'

'Will he continue to do research into voodoo?'

'*Yessss.*'

'I've warned him to stop.'

'*He will not.*'

The kitchen had grown extremely cold in spite of the house's furnace, which was still operating and still spewing hot air out of the wall vents. The air seemed thick and oily, too.

'What can I do to keep Dawson at bay?'

'*You know.*'

'Tell me.'

'*You know.*'

Lavelle licked his lips, cleared his throat.

'*You know.*'

Lavelle said, 'Should I have his children murdered now, tonight, without further delay?'

5

Rebecca answered the door. She said, 'I sort of figured it would be you.'

He stood on the landing, shivering. 'We've got a raging blizzard out there.'

She was wearing a soft blue robe, slippers.

Her hair was honey-yellow. She was gorgeous.

She didn't say anything. She just looked at him.

He said, 'Yep, the storm of the century is what it is. Maybe even the start of a new ice age. The end of the world. I asked myself who I'd most like to be with if this actually was the end of the world—'

'And you decided on me.'

'Not exactly.'

'Oh?'

'I just didn't know where to find Jacqueline Bisset.'

'So I was second choice.'

'I didn't know Raquel Welch's address, either.'

'Third.'

'But out of four billion people on earth, third isn't bad.'

She almost smiled at him.

He said, 'Can I come in? I already took my boots off, see. I won't track up your carpet. And I've got very good manners. I never belch or scratch my ass in public – not intentionally, anyway.'

She stepped back.

He went in.

She closed the door and said, 'I was about to make something to eat. Are you hungry?'

'What've you got?'

'Drop-in guests can't afford to be choosy.'

They went into the kitchen, and he draped his coat over the back of a chair.

She said, 'Roast beef sandwiches and soup.'

'What flavour soup?'

'Minestrone.'

'Homemade?'

'Canned.'

'Good.'

'Good?'

'I hate homemade stuff.'

'Is that so?'

'Too many vitamins in homemade stuff.'

'Can there be too many?'

'Sure. Makes me all jumpy with excess energy.'

'Ah.'

'And there's too much taste in homemade,' he said.

'Overwhelms the palate.'

'You *do* understand! Give me canned any day.'

'Never too much taste in canned.'

'Nice and bland, easy to digest.'

'I'll set the table and get the soup started.'

'Good idea.'

'You slice the roast beef.'

'Sure.'

'It's in the refrigerator, in Saran Wrap. Second shelf, I think. Be careful.'

'Why, is it *alive*?'

'The refrigerator's packed pretty full. If you're not careful taking something out, you can start an avalanche.'

He opened the refrigerator. On each shelf, there were two or three layers of food, one atop the other. The storage spaces on the doors were crammed full of bottles, cans, and jars.

'You afraid the government's going to outlaw food?' he asked.

'I like to keep a lot of stuff on hand.'

'I noticed.'

'Just in case.'

'In case the entire New York Philharmonic drops in for a nosh?'

She didn't say anything.

He said, 'Most supermarkets don't have this much stock.'

She seemed embarrassed, and he dropped the subject.

But it was odd. Chaos reigned in the refrigerator, while every other inch of her apartment was neat, orderly, and even Spartan in its decor.

He found the roast beef behind a dish of pickled eggs, atop an apple pie in a bakery box, beneath a package of Swiss cheese, wedged in between two leftover casseroles on one side and a jar of pickles and a leftover chicken breast on the other side, in front of three jars of jelly.

For a while they worked in silence.

Once he had finally cornered her, he had thought it would be easy to talk about what had happened between them last night. But now he felt awkward. He couldn't decide how to begin, what to say first. The direct approach was best, of course. He ought to say, *Rebecca, where do we go from here*? Or maybe, *Rebecca, didn't it mean as much to you as it did to me*? Or maybe even, *Rebecca, I love you*. But everything he might have said sounded, in his own mind, either trite or too abrupt or just plain dumb.

The silence stretched.

She put placemats, dishes, and silverware on the table.

He sliced the beef, then a large tomato.

She opened two cans of soup.

From the refrigerator, he got pickles, mustard, mayonnaise, and two kinds of cheese. The bread was in the breadbox.

He turned to Rebecca to ask how she wanted her sandwich.

She was standing at the stove with her back to him, stirring the soup in the pot. Her hair shimmered softly against her dark blue robe.

Jack felt a tremour of desire. He marvelled at how very different she was now from the way she had been when he'd last seen her at the office, only an hour ago. No longer the ice maiden. No longer the Viking woman. She looked smaller, not particularly shorter but narrower of shoulder, slimmer of wrist, overall more slender, more fragile, more girlish than she had seemed earlier.

Before he realized what he was doing, he moved toward her, stepped up behind her, and put his hands on her shoulders.

She wasn't startled. She had sensed him coming. Perhaps she had even *willed* him to come to her.

At first her shoulders were stiff beneath his hands, her entire body rigid.

He pulled her hair aside and kissed her neck, made a chain of kisses along the smooth, sweet skin.

She relaxed, softened, leaned back against him.

He slid his hands down her sides, to the swell of her hips.

She sighed but said nothing.

He kissed her ear.

He slid one hand up, cupped her breast.

She switched off the gas burner on which the pot of minestrone was heating.

His arms were around her now, both hands on her flat belly.

He leaned over her shoulder, kissed the side of her throat. Through his lips, pressed to her supple flesh, he felt one of her arteries throb with her strong pulse; a rapid pulse; faster now and faster still.

She seemed to melt back into him.

No woman, except his lost wife, had ever felt this warm to him.

She pressed her bottom against him.

He was so hard he ached.

She murmured wordlessly, a feline sound.

His hands would not remain still but moved over her in gentle, lazy exploration.

She turned to him.

They kissed.

Her hot tongue was quick, but the kiss was long and slow.

When they broke, drawing back only inches, to take a much-needed breath, their eyes met, and hers were such a fiercely bright shade of green that they didn't seem real, yet he saw a very real longing in them.

Another kiss. This one was harder than the first, hungrier.

Then she pulled back from him. Took his hand in hers.

They walked out of the kitchen. Into the living room. The bedroom.

She switched on a small lamp with an amber glass shade. It wasn't bright. The shadows retreated slightly but didn't go away.

She took off her robe. She wasn't wearing anything else.

She looked as if she were made of honey and butter and cream.

She undressed him.

Many minutes later, on the bed, when he finally entered her, he said her name with a small gasp of wonder, and she said his. Those were the first words they had spoken since he had put his hands on her shoulders, out in the kitchen.

They found a soft, silken, satisfying rhythm and gave pleasure to each other on the cool, crisp sheets.

6

Lavelle sat at the kitchen table, staring at the radio.

Wind shook the old house,

To the unseen presence using the radio as a contact point with this world, Lavelle said, 'Should I have his children murdered now, tonight, without further delay?'

'*Yessss.*'

'But if I kill his children, isn't there a danger that Dawson will be more determined than ever to find me?'

'*Kill them.*'

'Do you mean killing them might break Dawson?'

'*Yessss.*'

'Contribute to an emotional or mental collapse?'

'*Yessss.*'

'Destroy him?'

'*Yessss.*'

'There is no doubt about that?'

'*He lovessss them very muchhhh.*'

'And there's no doubt what it would do to him?' Lavelle pressed.

'Kill them.'

'I want to be sure.'

'Kill them. Brutally. It musssst be esssspecccccially brutal.'

'I see. The brutality of it is the thing that will make Dawson snap. Is that it?'

'Yessss.'

'I'll do anything to get him out of my way, but I want to be absolutely sure it'll work the way I want it to work.'

'Kill them. Ssssmasssh them. Break their bonessss and tear out their eyessss. Rip out their tonguessss. Gut them assss if they were two pigssss for butchhhhering.'

7

Rebecca's bedroom.

Spicules of snow tapped softly on the window.

They lay on their backs, side by side on the bed, holding hands, in the butterscotch-coloured light.

Rebecca said, 'I didn't think it would happen again.'

'What?'

'This.'

'Oh.'

'I thought last night was an . . . aberration.'

'Really?'

'I was sure we'd never make love again.'

'But we did.'

'We sure did.'

'God, did we ever!'

She was silent.

He said, 'Are you sorry we did?'

'No.'

'You don't think *this* was the last time, do you?'

'No.'

'Can't be the last. Not as good as we are together.'

'So good together.'

'You can be so soft.'

'And you can be so hard.'

'Crude.'

'But true.'

A pause.

Then she said, 'What's happened to us?'

'Isn't that clear?'

'Not entirely.'

'We've fallen for each other.'

'But how could it happen so fast?'

'It wasn't fast.'

'All this time, just cops, just partners—'

'More than partners.'

'—then all of a sudden – *wham!*'

'It wasn't sudden. I've been falling a long time.'

'Have you?'

'For a couple of months, anyway.'

'I didn't realize it.'

'A long, long, slow fall.'

'Why didn't I realize?'

'You realized. Subconsciously.'

'Maybe.'

'What I wonder is why you resisted it so strenuously.'

She didn't reply.

He said, 'I thought maybe you found me repellent.'

'I find you irresistible.'

'Then why'd you resist?'

'It scares me.'

'What scares you?'

'This. Having someone. *Caring* about someone.'

'Why's that scare you?'

'The chance of losing it.'

'But that's silly.'

'It is not.'

'You've got to risk losing a thing—'

'I know.'

'—or else never have it in the first place.'

'Maybe that's best.'

'Not having it at all?'

'Yes.'

'That philosophy makes for a damned lonely life.'

'It still scares me.'

'We won't lose this, Rebecca.'

'Nothing lasts forever.'

'That's not what you'd call a good attitude.'

'Well, nothing does.'

'If you've been hurt by other guys—'

'It isn't that.'

'Then what is it?'

She dodged the question. 'Kiss me.'

He kissed her. Again and again.

They weren't passionate kisses. Tender. Sweet.

After a while he said, 'I love you.'

'Don't say that.'

'I'm not just saying it. I mean it.'

'Just don't say it.'

'I'm not a guy who says things he doesn't mean.'

'I know.'

'And I'm not saying it before I'm sure.'

She wouldn't look at him.

He said, 'I'm sure, Rebecca. I love you.'

'I asked you not to say that.'

'I'm not asking to hear it from you.'

She bit her lip.

'I'm not asking for a commitment,' he said.

'Jack—'

'Just say you don't hate me.'

'Will you stop—'

'Can't you please just say you don't hate me?'

She sighed. 'I don't hate you.'

He grinned. 'Just say you don't loathe me too much.'

'I don't loathe you too much.'

'Just say you like me a little bit.'

'I like you a little bit.'

'Maybe more than a little bit.'

'Maybe more than a little bit.'

'All right. I can live with that for now.'

'Good.'

'Meanwhile, I love you.'

'Damnit, Jack!'

She pulled away from him.

She drew the sheet over herself, all the way up to her chin.

'Don't be cold with me, Rebecca.'

'I'm not being cold.'

'Don't treat me like you treated me all day today.'

She met his eyes.

He said, 'I thought you were sorry last night ever happened.'

She shook her head: no.

'It hurt me, the way you were, today,' he said. 'I thought you were disgusted with me, with yourself, for what we'd done.'

'No. Never.'

'I know that now, but here you are drawing away again, keeping me at arm's length. What's *wrong*?'

She chewed on her thumb. Like a little girl.

'Rebecca?'

'I don't know how to say it. I don't know how to explain. I've never had to put it into words for anyone before.'

'I'm a good listener.'

'I need a little time to think.'

'So take your time.'

'Just a little time. A few minutes.'

'Take all the time you want.'

She stared at the ceiling, thinking.

He got under the sheet with her and pulled the blanket over both of them.

They lay in silence for a while.

Outside, the wind sang a two-note serenade.

She said, 'My father died when I was six.'

'I'm sorry. That's terrible. You never really had a chance to know him, then.'

'True. And yet, odd as it seems, I still sometimes miss

him so bad, you know, even after all these years – even a father I never really knew and can hardly remember. I miss him, anyway.'

Jack thought of his own little Davey, not even quite six when his mother had died.

He squeezed Rebecca's hand gently.

She said, 'But my father dying when I was six – in a way, that's not the worst of it. The worst of it is that I saw him die. I was there when it happened.'

'God. How . . . how did it happen?'

'Well . . . he and Mama owned a sandwich shop. A small place. Four little tables. Mostly take-out business. Sandwiches, potato salad, macaroni salad, a few desserts. It's hard to make a go of it in that business unless you have two things, right at the start: enough start-up capital to see you through a couple of lean years at the beginning, and a good location with lots of foot traffic passing by or office workers in the neighbourhood. But my folks were poor. They had very little capital. They couldn't pay the high rent in a good location, so they started in a bad one and kept moving whenever they could afford to, three times in three years, each time to a slightly better spot. They worked hard, so hard . . . My father held down another job, too, janitorial work, late at night, after the shop closed, until just before dawn. Then he'd come home, sleep four or five hours, and go open the shop for the lunch trade. Mama cooked a lot of the food that was served, and she worked behind the counter, too, but she also did some house cleaning for other people, to bring in a few extra dollars. Finally, the shop began to pay off. My dad was able to drop his janitorial job, and Mama gave up the house cleaning. In fact, business started getting so good that they were looking for their first employee; they couldn't handle the shop all by themselves any more. The future looked bright. And then . . . one afternoon . . . during the slack time between the lunch and dinner crowds, when Mama was out on an errand and

I was alone in the shop with my father . . . this guy came in . . . with a gun . . .'

'Oh, shit,' Jack said. He knew the rest of it. He'd seen it all before, many times. Dead storekeepers, sprawled in pools of their own blood, beside their emptied cash registers.

'There was something strange about this creep,' Rebecca said. 'Even though I was only six years old, I could tell there was something *wrong* with him the moment he came in, and I went to the kitchen and peeked out at him through the curtain. He was fidgety . . . pale . . . funny around the eyes . . .'

'A junkie?'

'That's the way it turned out, yeah. If I close my eyes now, I can still see his pale face, the way his mouth twitched. The awful thing is . . . I can see it clearer than I can see my own father's face. Those terrible eyes.'

She shuddered.

Jack said, 'You don't have to go on.'

'Yes. I do. I have to tell you. So you'll understand why . . . why I am like I am about certain things.'

'Okay. If you're sure—'

'I'm sure.'

'Then . . . did your father refuse to hand over the money to this son of a bitch – or what?'

'No. Dad gave him the money. All of it.'

'He offered no resistance at all?'

'None.'

'But cooperation didn't save him.'

'No. This junkie had a bad itch, a real bad need. The need was like something nasty crawling around in his head, I guess, and it made him irritable, mean, crazy-mad at the world. You know how they get. So I think maybe he wanted to kill somebody even more than he wanted the money. So . . . he just . . . pulled the trigger.'

Jack put an arm around her, drew her against him.

She said, 'Two shots. Then the bastard ran. Only one

of the slugs hit my father. But it . . . hit him . . . in the face.'

'Jesus,' Jack said softly, thinking of six-year-old Rebecca in the sandwich shop's kitchen, peering through the parted curtain, watching as her father's face exploded.

'It was a .45,' she said.

Jack winced, thinking of the power of the gun.

'Hollow-point bullets,' she said.

'Oh, Christ.'

'Dad didn't have a chance at point-blank range.'

'Don't torture yourself with—'

'Blew his head off,' she said.

'Don't think about it any more now,' Jack said.

'Brain tissue . . .'

'Put it out of your mind now.'

' . . . pieces of his skull . . .'

'It was a long time ago.'

' . . . blood all over the wall.'

'Hush now. Hush.'

'There's no more to tell.'

'You don't have to pour it out all at once.'

'I want you to understand.'

'Take your time. I'll be here. I'll wait. Take your time.'

8

In the corrugated metal shed, leaning over the pit, using two pair of ceremonial scissors with malachite handles, Lavelle snipped both ends of the cord simultaneously.

The photographs of Penny and Davey Dawson fell into the hole, vanished in the flickering orange light.

A shrill, unhuman cry came from the depths.

'Kill them,' Lavelle said.

9

Still in Rebecca's bed.

Still holding each other.

She said, 'The police only had my description to go on.'

'A six-year-old child doesn't make the best witness.'

'They worked hard, trying to get a lead on the creep who'd shot Daddy. They really worked hard.'

'They ever catch him?'

'Yes. But too late. Much too late.'

'What do you mean?'

'See, he got two hundred bucks when he robbed the shop.'

'So?'

'That was over twenty-two years ago.'

'Yeah?'

'Two hundred was a lot more money then. Not a fortune. But a lot more than it is now.'

'I still don't see what you're driving at.'

'It looked like an easy score to him.'

'Not too damned easy. He killed a man.'

'But he wouldn't have had to. He *wanted* to kill someone that day.'

'Okay. Right. So, twisted as he is, he figures it was easy.'

'Six months went by . . .'

'And the cops never got close to him?'

'No. So it looks easier and easier to the creep.'

A sickening dread filled Jack. His stomach turned over.

He said, 'You don't mean . . . ?'

'Yes.'

'He came back.'

'With a gun. The same gun.'

'But he'd have to've been nuts!'

'All junkies are nuts.'

Jack waited. He didn't want to hear the rest of it, but he knew she would tell him; had to tell him; was *compelled* to tell him.

She said, 'My mother was at the cash register.'

'No,' he said softly, as if a protest from him could somehow alter the tragic history of her family.

'He blew her away.'

'Rebecca . . .'

'Fired five shots into her.'

'You didn't . . . see this one?'

'No. I wasn't in the shop that day.'

'Thank God.'

'This time they caught him.'

'Too late for you.'

'Much too late. But it was after that when I knew what I wanted to be when I grew up. I wanted to be a cop, so I could stop people like that junkie, stop them from killing the mothers and fathers of other little girls and boys. There weren't women cops back then, you know, not real cops, just office workers in police stations, radio dispatchers, that sort of thing. I had no role models. But I knew I'd make it someday. I was determined. All the time I was growing up, there was never once when I thought about being anything else but a cop. I never even considered getting married, being a wife, having kids, being a mother, because I knew someone would only come along and shoot my husband or take my kids away from me or take me away from my kids. So what was the point in it? I would be a cop. Nothing else. A cop. And that's what I became. I think I felt guilty about my father's murder. I think I believed there must've been something I could have done that day to save him. And I *know* I felt guilty about my mother's death. I hated myself for not giving the police a better description of the man who shot my dad, hated myself for being numb and useless, because if I had been of more help to them, maybe they'd have gotten the guy before he killed Mama. Being a cop, stopping other creeps like that junkie, it was a way to atone for my guilt. Maybe that's amateur psychology. But not far off the mark. I'm sure it's part of what motivates me.'

'But you haven't any reason at all to feel guilty,' Jack

assured her. 'You did all you possibly could've done. You were only *six!*'

'I know. I understand that. But the guilt is there nevertheless. Still sharp, at times. I guess it'll always be there, fading year by year, but never fading away altogether.'

Jack was, at last, beginning to understand Rebecca Chandler – why she was the way she was. He even saw the reason for the overstocked refrigerator; after a childhood filled with so much bad news and unanticipated shocks and instability, keeping a well-supplied larder was one way to buy at least a small measure of security, a way to feel safe. Understanding increased his respect and already deep affection for her. She was a very special woman.

He had a feeling that this night was one of the most important of his life. The long loneliness after Linda's passing was finally drawing to an end. Here, with Rebecca, he was making a new beginning. A good beginning. Few men were fortunate enough to find two good women and be given two chances at happiness in their lives. He was very lucky, and he knew it, and that knowledge made him exuberant. In spite of a day filled with blood and mutilated bodies and threats of death, he sensed a golden future out there ahead of them. Everything was going to work out fine, after all. Nothing could go wrong. Nothing could go wrong now.

10

'Kill them, kill them,' Lavelle said.

His voice echoed down into the pit, echoed and echoed, as if it had been cast into a deep shaft.

The indistinct, pulsing, shifting, amorphous floor of the pit suddenly became more active. It bubbled, surged, churned. Out of that molten, lavalike substance – which might have been within arm's reach or, instead, miles below – something began to take shape.

Something monstrous.

11

'When your mother was killed, you were only—'

'Seven. Turned seven the month before she died.'

'Who raised you after that?'

My grandparents, my mother's folks.'

'Did that work out?'

'They loved me. So it worked for a while.'

'Only for a while?'

'My grandfather died.'

'*Another* death?'

'Always another one.'

'How?'

'Cancer. I'd seen sudden death already. It was time for me to learn about slow death.'

'How slow?'

'Two years from the time the cancer was diagnosed until he finally succumbed to it. He wasted away, lost sixty pounds before the end, lost all his hair from the radium treatments. He looked and acted like an entirely different person during those last few weeks. It was a ghastly thing to watch.'

'How old were you when you lost him?'

'Eleven and a half.'

'Then it was just you and your grandmother.'

'For a few years. Then she died when I was fifteen. Her heart. Not real sudden. Not real slow, either. After that, I was made a ward of the court. I spent the next three years, until I was eighteen, in a series of foster homes. Four of them, in all. I never got close to any of my foster parents; I never allowed myself to get close. I kept asking to be transferred, see. Because by then, even as young as I was, I realized that loving people, depending on them, *needing* them is just too dangerous. Love is just a way to set you up for a bad fall. It's the rug they pull out from under you at the very moment you finally decide that everything's going to be fine.

We're all so ephemeral. So fragile. And life's so unpredictable.'

'But that's no reason to insist on going it alone,' Jack said. 'In fact, don't you see – that's the reason we *must* find people to love, people to share our lives with, to open our hearts and minds to, people to depend on, cherish, people who'll depend on us when *they* need to know they're not alone. Caring for your friends and family, knowing they care for you – that's what keeps our minds off the void that waits for all of us. By loving and letting ourselves be loved, we give meaning and importance to our lives; it's what keeps us from being just another species of the animal kingdom, grubbing for survival. At least for a short while, through love, we can forget about the goddamned darkness at the end of everything.'

He was breathless when he finished – and astonished by what he had said, startled that such an understanding had been in him.

She slipped an arm across his chest. She held him fast.

She said, 'You're right. A part of me knows that what you've said is true.'

'Good.'

'But there's another part of me that's afraid of letting myself love or be loved, ever again. The part that can't bear losing it all again. The part that thinks loneliness is preferable to that kind of loss and pain.'

'But see, that's just it. Love given or love taken is *never* lost,' he said, holding her. 'Once you've loved someone, the love is always there, even after they're gone. Love is the only thing that endures. Mountains are torn down, built up, torn down again over millions and millions of years. Seas dry up. Deserts give way to new seas. Time crumbles every building man erects. Great ideas are proven wrong and collapse as surely as castles and temples. But love is a force, an energy, a power. At the risk of sounding like a Hallmark card, I think love is like a ray of sunlight, travelling for all eternity through space, deeper and deeper into infinity; like that ray of light, it never ceases to exist. Love endures. It's a binding force in the universe, like the energy within a molecule is a binding force, as surely as gravity is a binding force. Without the cohesive energy in a molecule, without gravity, without *love* – chaos. We exist to love and be loved, because love seems to me to be the only thing that brings order and meaning and light to existence. It must be true. Because if it isn't true, what purpose *do* we serve? Because if it isn't true – God help us.'

For minutes, they lay in silence, touching.

Jack was exhausted by the flood of words and feelings that had rushed from him, almost without his volition.

He desperately wanted Rebecca to be with him for the rest of his life. He dreaded losing her.

But he said no more. The decision was hers.

After a while she said, 'For the first time in ages, I'm not so afraid of loving and losing; I'm more afraid of not loving at all.'

Jack's heart lifted.

He said, 'Don't ever freeze me out again.'

'It won't be easy learning to open up.'

'You can do it.'

'I'm sure I'll backslide occasionally, withdraw from you a little bit, now and then. You'll have to be patient with me.'

'I can be patient.'

'God, don't I know it! You're the most infuriatingly patient man I've ever known.'

'Infuriatingly?'

'There've been times, at work, when I've been so incredibly bitchy, and I knew it, didn't want to be but couldn't seem to help myself. I wished, sometimes, you'd snap back at me, blow up at me. But when you finally responded, you were always so reasonable, so calm, so damned patient.'

'You make me sound too saintly.'

'Well, you're a good man, Jack Dawson. A nice man. A damned nice man.'

'Oh, I know, to you I seem perfect,' he said self-mockingly. 'But believe it or not, even I, paragon that I am, even *I* have a few faults.'

'No!' she said, pretending astonishment.

'It's true.'

'Name one.'

'I actually like to listen to Barry Manilow.'

'No!'

'Oh, I know his music's slick, too smooth, a little plastic. But it sounds good, anyway. I like it. And another thing. I *don't* like Alan Alda.'

'*Everyone* likes Alan Alda!'

'I think he's a phony.'

'You disgusting fiend!'

'And I like peanut butter and onion sandwiches.'

'Ach! *Alan Alda* wouldn't eat peanut butter and onion sandwiches.'

'But I have one great virtue that more than makes up for all of those terrible faults,' he said.

She grinned. 'What's that?'

'I love you.'

This time, she didn't ask him to refrain from saying it.

She kissed him.

Her hands moved over him.

She said, 'Make love to me again.'

12

Ordinarily, no matter how late Davey was allowed to stay up, Penny was permitted one more hour than he was. Being the last to bed was her just due, by virtue of her four-year age advantage over him. She always fought valiantly and tenaciously at the first sign of any attempt to deny her this precious and inalienable right. Tonight, however, at nine o'clock, when Aunt Faye suggested that Davey brush his teeth and hit the sack,

Penny feigned sleepiness and said that she, too, was ready to call it a night.

She couldn't leave Davey alone in a dark bedroom where the goblins might creep up on him. She would have to stay awake, watching over him, until their father arrived. Then she would tell Daddy all about the goblins and hope that he would at least hear her out before he sent for the men with the strait jackets.

She and Davey had come to the Jamison's without overnight bags, but they had no difficulty getting ready for bed. Because they occasionally stayed with Faye and Keith when their father had to work late, they kept spare toothbrushes and pyjamas here. And in the guest bedroom closet, there were fresh changes of clothes for them, so they wouldn't have to wear the same thing tomorrow that they'd worn today. In ten minutes, they were comfortably nestled in the twin beds, under the covers.

Aunt Faye wished them sweet dreams, turned out the light, and closed the door.

The darkness was thick, smothering.

Penny fought off an attack of claustrophobia.

Davey was silent a while. Then: 'Penny?'

'Huh?'

'You there?'

'Who do you think just said "huh?"'

'Where's Dad?'

'Working late.'

'I mean . . . really.'

'Really working late.'

'What if he's been hurt?'

'He hasn't.'

'What if he got shot?'

'He didn't. They'd have told us if he'd been shot. They'd probably even take us to the hospital to see him.'

'No, they wouldn't, either. They try to protect kids from bad news like that.'

'Will you stop worrying, for God's sake? Dad's all

214

right. If he'd been shot or anything, Aunt Faye and Uncle Keith would know all about it.'

'But maybe they *do* know.'

'We'd know if they knew.'

'How?'

'They'd show it, even if they were trying hard not to.'

'How would they show it?'

'They'd have treated us different. They'd have acted strange.'

'They *always* act strange.'

'I mean strange in a different sort of way. They'd have been especially nice to us. They'd have pampered us because they'd have felt sorry for us. And do you think Aunt Faye would have criticized Daddy all evening, the way she did, if she'd known he was shot and in a hospital somewhere?'

'Well . . . no. I guess you're right. Not even Aunt Faye would do that.'

They were silent.

Penny lay with her head propped up on the pillow, listening.

Nothing to be heard. Just the wind outside. Far off, the grumble of a snowplough.

She looked at the window, a rectangle of vague snowy luminosity.

Would the goblins come through the window?

The door?

Maybe they'd come out of a crack in the baseboard, come in the form of smoke and then solidify when they had completely seeped into the room. Vampires did that sort of thing. She'd seen it happen in an old Dracula movie.

Or maybe they'd come out of the closet.

She looked toward the darkest end of the room, where the closet was. She couldn't see it; only blackness.

Maybe there was a magical, invisible tunnel at the back of the closet, a tunnel that only goblins could see and use.

That was ridiculous. Or was it? The very idea of goblins was ridiculous, too; yet they were out there; she'd seen them.

Davey's breathing became deep and slow and rhythmic. He was asleep.

Penny envied him. She knew she'd never sleep again.

Time passed. Slowly.

Her gaze moved around and around the dark room. The window. The door. The closet. The window.

She didn't know where the goblins would come from, but she knew, without doubt, that they *would* come.

13

Lavelle sat in his dark bedroom.

The additional assassins had risen out of the pit and had crept off into the night, into the storm-lashed city. Soon, both of the Dawson children would be slaughtered, reduced to nothing more than bloody mounds of dead meat.

That thought pleased and excited Lavelle. It even gave him an erection.

The rituals had drained him. Not physically or mentally. He felt alert, fresh, strong. But his Bocor's power had been depleted, and it was time to replenish it. At the moment, he was a Bocor in name only; drained like this, he was really just a man – and he didn't like being just a man.

Embraced by the darkness, he reached upward with his mind, up through the ceiling, through the roof of the house, through the snow-filled air, up toward the rivers of evil energy that flowed across the great city. He carefully avoided those currents of benign energy that also surged through the night, for they were of no use whatsoever to him; indeed, they posed a danger to him. He tapped into the darkest, foulest of those ethereal waters and let them pour down into him, until his own reservoirs were full once more.

In minutes he was reborn. Now he was more than a

man. Less than a god, yes. But much, much more than just a man.

He had one more act of sorcery to perform this night, and he was happily anticipating it. He was going to humble Jack Dawson. At last he was going to make Dawson understand how awesome was the power of a masterful Bocor. Then, when Dawson's children were exterminated, the detective would understand how foolish he had been to put them at such risk, to defy a Bocor. He would see how easily he could have saved them – simply by swallowing his pride and walking away from the investigation. Then it would be clear to the detective that he, himself, had signed his own children's death warrants, and *that* terrible realization would shatter him.

14

Penny sat straight up in bed and almost shouted for Aunt Faye.

She had heard something. A strange, shrill cry. It wasn't human. Faint. Far away. Maybe in another apartment, several floors farther down in the building. The cry seemed to have come to her through the heating ducts.

She waited tensely. A minute. Two minutes. Three.

The cry wasn't repeated. There were no other unnatural sounds, either.

But she knew what she had heard and what it meant. They were coming for her and Davey. They were on their way now. Soon, they would be here.

15

This time, their love-making was slow, lazy, achingly tender, filled with much nuzzling and wordless murmuring and soft-soft stroking. A series of dreamy sensations: a feeling of floating, a feeling of being composed only of sunlight and other energy, an exhilaratingly weightless tumbling, tumbling. This time, it was not so much an act of sex as it was an act of emotional bonding, a spiritual pledge made with the flesh. And when, at last, Jack spurted deep within her velvet recesses, he felt as if he were fusing with her, melting into her, becoming one with her, and he sensed that she felt the same thing.

'That was wonderful.'

'Perfect.'

'Better than a peanut butter and onion sandwich?'

'Almost.'

'You bastard.'

'Hey, peanut butter and onion sandwiches are pretty darned terrific, you know!'

'I love you,' he said.

'I'm glad,' she said.

That was an improvement.

She still couldn't bring herself to say she loved him, too. But he wasn't particularly bothered about that. He knew she did.

He was sitting on the edge of the bed, dressing.

She was standing on the other side of the bed, slipping into her blue robe.

Both of them were startled by a sudden violent movement. A framed poster from a Jasper Johns art exhibition tore loose of its mountings and flew off the wall. It was a large poster, three and a half feet by two and a half feet, framed behind glass. It seemed to hang in the air for a moment, vibrating, and then it struck the floor at the foot of the bed with a tremendous crash.

'What the hell!' Jack said.

'What could've done that?' Rebecca said.

The sliding closet door flew open with a bang, slammed shut, flew open again.

The six-drawer highboy tipped away from the wall, toppled toward Jack, and he jumped out of the way, and the big piece of furniture hit the floor with the sound of a bomb explosion.

Rebecca backed against the wall and stood there, rigid wide-eyed, her hands fisted at her sides.

The air was cold. Wind whirled through the room. Not just a draft, but a wind almost as powerful as the one that whipped through the city streets, outside. Yet there was nowhere that a cold wind could have gained admission; the door and the window were closed tight.

And now, at the window, it seemed as if invisible hands grabbed the drapes and tore them loose of the rod from which they were hung. The drapes dropped in a heap, and then the rod itself was torn out of the wall and thrown aside.

Drawers slid all the way out of the nightstands and fell onto the floor, spilling their contents.

Several strips of wallpaper began to peel off the walls, starting at the top and going down.

Jack turned this way and that, frightened, confused, not sure what he should do.

The dresses mirror cracked in a spiderweb pattern.

The unseen presence stripped the blanket from the bed and pitched it onto the toppled highboy.

'Stop it!' Rebecca shouted at the empty air. '*Stop it!*'

The unseen intruder did not obey.

The top sheet was pulled from the bed. It whirled into the air, as if it had been granted life and the ability to fly; it floated off into a corner of the room, where it collapsed, lifeless again.

The fitted bottom sheet popped loose at two corners.

Jack grabbed it.

The other two corners came loose, as well.

Jack tried to hold on to the sheet. It was a feeble and pointless effort to resist whatever the power was wrecking the room, but it was the only thing he could think to do, and he simply *had* to do something. The sheet was quickly wrenched out of his hands with such force that he was thrown off balance. He stumbled and fell to his knees.

On a wheeled TV stand in the corner, the portable television set snapped on of its own accord, the volume booming. A fat woman was dancing the cha-cha with a cat, and a thunderous chorus was singing the praises of Purina Cat Chow.

Jack scrambled to his feet.

The mattress cover was skinned off the bed, lifted into the air, rolled into a ball, and thrown at Rebecca.

On the TV, George Plimpton was shouting like a baboon about the virtues of Intellivision.

The mattress was bare now. The quilted sheath dimpled; a rent appeared in it. The fabric tore right down the middle, from top to bottom, and stuffing erupted along with a few uncoiling springs that rose like cobras to an unheard music.

More wallpaper peeled down.

On the TV, a barker for the American Beef Council was shouting about the benefits of eating meat, while an unseen chef carved a bloody roast on camera.

The closet door slammed so hard that it jumped partially out of its track and rattled back and forth.

The TV screen imploded. Simultaneously with the sound of breaking glass, there was a brief flash of light within the guts of the set, and then a little smoke.

Silence.

Stillness.

Jack glanced at Rebecca.

She looked bewildered. And terrified.

The telephone rang.

The instant Jack heard it, he knew who was calling. He snatched up the receiver, held it to his ear, said nothing.

'You're panting like a dog, Detective Dawson,' Lavelle said. 'Excited? Evidently, my little demonstration thrilled you.'

Jack was shaking so badly and uncontrollably that he

didn't trust his voice. He didn't reply because he didn't want Lavelle to hear how scared he was.

Besides, Lavelle didn't seem interested in anything Jack might have to say; he didn't wait long enough to hear a reply even if one had been offered. The Bocor said, 'When you see your kids – dead, mangled, their eyes torn out, their lips eaten off, their fingers bitten to the bone – remember that you could have saved them. Remember that you're the one who signed their death warrants. You bear the responsibility for their death as surely as if you'd seen them walking in front of a train and didn't even bother to call out a warning to them. You threw away their lives as if they were nothing but garbage to you.'

A torrent of words spewed from Jack before he even realized he was going to speak: 'You fucking sleazy son of a bitch, you'd better not touch one hair on them! You'd better not—'

Lavelle had hung up.

Rebecca said, 'Who—'

'Lavelle.'

'You mean . . . all of this?'

'You believe in black magic now? Sorcery? Voodoo?'

'Oh, my God.'

'*I* sure as hell believe in it now.'

She looked around at the demolished room, shaking her head, trying without success to deny the evidence before her eyes.

Jack remembered his own scepticism when Carver Hampton had told him about the falling bottles and the black serpent. No scepticism now. Only terror now.

He thought of the bodies he had seen this morning and this afternoon, those hideously ravaged corpses.

His heart jackhammered. He was short of breath. He felt as if he might vomit.

He still had the phone in his hand. He punched out a number.

Rebecca said, 'Who're you calling?'

221

'Faye. She's got to get the kids out of there, fast.'

'But Lavelle can't know where they are.'

'He couldn't have known where *I* was, either. I didn't tell anyone I was coming to see you. I wasn't followed here; I'm sure I wasn't. He couldn't have known where to find me – and yet he *knew*. So he probably knows where to find the kids, too. Damnit, why isn't it ringing?'

He rattled the telephone buttons, got another dial tone, tried Faye's number again. This time he got a recording telling him that her phone was no longer in service. Not true, of course.

'Somehow, Lavelle's screwed up Faye's line,' he said, dropping the receiver. 'We've got to get over there right away, Jesus, we've got to get the kids out!'

Rebecca had stripped off her robe, had yanked a pair of jeans and a pull-over sweater from the closet. She was already half dressed.

'Don't worry,' she said. 'It'll be all right. We'll get to them before Lavelle does.'

But Jack had the sickening feeling that they were already too late.

CHAPTER FIVE

1

Again, sitting alone in his dark bedroom, with only the phosphoric light of the snowstorm piercing the windows, Lavelle reached up with his mind and tapped the psychic rivers of malignant energy that coursed through the night above the city.

His sorcerer's power was not only depleted this time but utterly exhausted. Calling forth a poltergeist and maintaining control over it – as he had done in order to arrange the demonstration for Jack Dawson a few minutes ago – was one of the most draining of all the rituals of black magic.

Unfortunately, it wasn't possible to use a poltergeist to destroy one's enemies. Poltergeists were merely mischievous – at worst, nasty – spirits; they were not evil. If a Bocor, having conjured up such an entity, attempted to employ it to murder someone, it would then be able to break free of his controlling spell and turn its energies upon him.

However, when used only as a tool to exhibit a Bocor's powers, a poltergeist produced impressive results. Sceptics were transformed into believers. The bold were made meek. After witnessing the work of a poltergeist, those who were already believers in voodoo and the supernatural were humbled, frightened, and reduced to obedient servants, pitifully eager to do whatever a Bocor demanded of them.

Lavelle's rocking chair creaked in the quiet room.

In the darkness, he smiled and smiled.

From the night sky, malignant energy poured down.

Lavelle, the vessel, was soon overflowing with power.

He sighed, for he was renewed.

Before long, the fun would begin.

The slaughter.

2

Penny sat on the edge of her bed, listening.

The sounds came again. Scraping, hissing. A soft thump, a faint clink, and again a thump. A far-off, rattling, shuffling noise.

Far off – but getting closer.

She snapped on the bedside lamp. The small pool of light was warm and welcome.

Davey remained asleep, undisturbed by the peculiar sounds. She decided to let him go on sleeping for the time being. She could wake him quickly if she had to, and one scream would bring Aunt Faye and Uncle Keith.

The raspy cry came again, faint, though perhaps not quite as faint as it had been before.

Penny got up from the bed, went to the dresser, which lay in shadows, beyond the fan of light from her nightstand lamp. In the wall above the dresser, approximately a foot below the ceiling, was a vent for the heating and air-conditioning systems. She cocked her head, trying to hear the distant and furtive noises, and she became convinced that they were being transmitted through the ducts in the walls.

She climbed onto the dresser, but the vent was still almost a foot above her head. She climbed down. She fetched her pillow from the bed and put it on the dresser. She took the thick seat cushions from the two chairs that flanked the window, and she piled those atop her bed pillow. She felt very clever and capable. Once on the dresser again, she stretched, rose up onto her toes, and was able to put her ear against the vent plate that covered the outlet from the ventilation system.

She had thought the goblins were in other apartment or common hallways, farther down in the buildings; she had thought the ducts were only carrying the sound of them. Now, with a jolt, she realized the ducts were carrying not merely the sound of the goblins but the goblins themselves. *This* was how they intended to get into the bedroom, not through the door or window, not through some imaginary tunnel in the back of the closet. They were in the ventilation network, making their way up through the building, twisting and turning, slithering and creeping, hurrying along the horizontal pipes, climbing laboriously through the vertical sections of the system, but steadily rising nearer and nearer as surely as the warm air was rising from the huge furnace below.

Trembling, teeth chattering, gripped by fear to which she *refused* to succumb, Penny put her face to the vent plate and peered through the slots, into the duct beyond.

The darkness in there was as deep and as black and as smooth as the darkness in a tomb.

Jack hunched over the wheel, squinting at the wintry street ahead.

The windshield was icing up. A thin, milky skin of ice had formed around the edges of the glass and was creeping inward. The wipers were caked with snow that was steadily compacting into lumps of ice.

'Is that damned defroster on full-blast?' he asked, even though he could feel the waves of heat washing up into his face.

Rebecca leaned forward and checked the heater controls 'Full-blast,' she affirmed.

'Temperature sure dropped once it got dark.'

'Must be ten degrees out there. Colder, if you figure in the wind-chill factor.'

Trains of snowploughs moved along the main avenues, but they were having difficulty getting the upper hand on the blizzard. Snow was falling in blinding sheets, so thick it obscured everything beyond the distance of one block. Worse, the fierce wind piled the snow in drifts that began to form again and reclaim the pavement only minutes after the ploughs had scraped it clean.

Jack had expected to make a fast trip to the Jamisons' apartment building. The streets held little or no traffic to get in his way. Furthermore, although his car was unmarked, it had a siren. And he had clamped the detachable red emergency beacon to the metal beading at the edge of the roof, thereby insuring right-of-way over what other traffic there was. He had expected to be holding Penny and Davey in his arms in ten minutes. Now, clearly, the trip was going to take twice that long.

Every time he tried to put on a little speed, the car started to slide, in spite of the snow chains on the tyres.

'We could *walk* faster than this!' Jack said ferociously.

'We'll get there in time,' Rebecca said.

'What if Lavelle is already there?'

'He's not. Of course he's not.'

And then a terrible thought rocked him, and he didn't want to put it into words, but he couldn't stop himself: 'What if he *called* from the Jamisons?'

'He didn't,' she said.

But Jack was abruptly obsessed with that horrendous possibility, and he could not control the morbid compulsion to say it aloud, even though the words brought hideous images to him:

'What if he killed all of them—'

(*Mangled bodies.*)

'—killed Penny and Davey—'

(*Eyeballs torn from sockets.*)

'—killed Faye and Keith—'

(*Throats chewed open.*)

'—and then called from right *there*—'

(*Fingertips bitten off.*)

'—called me from right there in the apartment, for Christ's sake—'

(*Lips torns, ears hanging loose.*)

'—while he was standing over their bodies!'

She had been trying to interrupt him. Now she shouted at him: 'Stop torturing yourself, Jack! We'll make it in time.'

'How the hell do you know we'll make it in time?' he demanded angrily, not sure why he was angry with her, just striking out at her because she was a convenient target, because he couldn't strike out at Lavelle or at the weather that was hindering him, and because he *had* to strike out at someone, something, or go absolutely crazy from the tension that was building in him like excess current flowing into an already overcharged battery. 'You can't *know!*'

'I know,' she insisted calmly. 'Just drive.'

'Goddamnit, stop patronizing me!'

'Jack—'

226

'He's got my kids!'

He accelerated too abruptly, and the car immediately began to slide toward the right-hand kerb.

He tried to correct their course by pulling on the steering wheel, instead of going along with the slide and turning into the direction of it, and even as he realized his mistake the car started to spin, and for a moment they were travelling sideways – and Jack had the gut-wrenching feeling that they were going to slam into the kerb at high speed, tip, and roll over – but even as they continued to slide they also continued to swing around on their axis until they were completely reversed from where they had been, a full 180 degrees, half the circumference of a circle, now sliding backwards along the street, looking out the icy windshield at where they had been instead of at where they were going and still they turned, turned like a carousel, until at last the car stopped just short of one entire revolution.

With a shudder engendered by a mental image of what might have happened to them, but aware that he couldn't waste time dwelling on their close escape, Jack started up again. He handled the wheel with even greater caution than before, and he pressed his foot lightly and slowly down on the accelerator.

Neither he nor Rebecca spoke during the wild spin, not even to cry out in surprise or fear, and neither of them spoke for the next block, either.

Then he said, 'I'm sorry.'

'Don't be.'

'I shouldn't have snapped at you like that.'

'I understand. You were crazy with worry.'

'Still am. No excuse. That was stupid of me. I won't be able to help the kids if I kill us before we ever get to Faye's place.'

'I understand what you're going through,' she said again, softer than before. 'It's all right. And everything'll be all right, too.'

He knew that she *did* understand all the complex

thoughts and emotions that were churning through him and nearly tearing him apart. She understood him better than just a friend could have understood, better than just a lover. They were more than merely compatible; in their thoughts and perceptions and feelings, they were in perfect sympathy, physically and psychologically synchronous. It had been a long time since he'd had anyone that close, that much a part of him. Eighteen months, in fact. Since Linda's death. Not so long, perhaps, considering he had never expected it to happen again. It was good not to be alone any more.

'Almost there, aren't we?' she asked.

'Two or three minutes,' he said, hunching over the wheel, peering ahead nervously at the slick, snowy street.

The windshield wipers, thickly crusted with ice, grated noisily back and forth, cleaning less and less of the glass with each swipe they took at it.

4

Lavelle got up from his rocking chair.

The time had come to establish psychic bonds with the small assassins that had come out of the pit and were now stalking the Dawson children.

Without turning on any lights, Lavelle went to the dresser, opened one of the top drawers, and withdrew a fistful of silk ribbons. He went to the bed, put the ribbons down, and stripped out of his clothes. Nude, he sat on the edge of the bed and tied a purple ribbon to his right ankle, a white one to his left ankle. Even in the dark, he had no difficulty discerning one colour from another. He tied a long scarlet ribbon around his chest, directly over his heart. Yellow around his forehead. Green around his right wrist; black around his left wrist. The ribbons were symbollic ties that would help to put him in intimate contact with the killers from the pit, as soon as he finished the ritual now begun.

It was not his intention to take control of those

demonic entities and direct their every move; he couldn't have done so, even if that *was* what he wanted. Once summoned from the pit and sent after their prey, the assassins followed their own whims and strategies until they had dealt with the intended victims; then, murder done, they were compelled to return to the pit. That was all the control he had over them.

The point of this ritual with the ribbons was merely to enable Lavelle to participate, first-hand, in the thrill of the slaughter. Psychically linked to the assassins, he would see through their eyes, hear with their ears, and feel with their golem bodies. When their razor-edged claws slashed at Davey Dawson, Lavelle would feel the boy's flesh rending in his own hands. When their teeth chewed open Penny's jugular, Lavelle would feel her warm throat against his own lips, too, and would taste the coppery sweetness of her blood.

The thought of it made him tremble with excitement.

And if Lavelle had timed it right, Jack Dawson would be there in the Jamison apartment when his children were torn to pieces. The detective ought to arrive just in time to see the horde descend on Penny and Davey. Although he would try to save them, he would discover that the small assassins couldn't be driven back or killed. He would be forced to stand there, powerless, while his children's precious blood spattered over him.

That was the best part.

Yes. Oh, yes.

Lavelle sighed.

He shivered with anticipation.

The small bottle of cat's blood was on the nightstand. He wet two fingertips in it, made a crimson spot on each cheek, wet his fingers again, annointed his lips. Then, still using blood, he drew a very simple *vèvè* on his bare chest.

He stretched out on the bed, on his back.

Staring at the ceiling, he began to chant quietly.

Soon, he was transported in mind and spirit. The

real psychic links, which the ribbons symbolized, were successfully achieved, and he was with the demonic entities in the ventilation system of the Jamisons' apartment building. The creatures were only two turns and perhaps twenty feet away from the end of the duct, where it terminated in the wall of the guest bedroom.

The children were near.

The girl was the nearer of the two.

Like the small assassins, Lavelle could sense her presence. Close. Very close. Only another bend in the pipe, then a straightaway, then a final bend.

Close.

The time had come.

5

Standing on the dresser, peering into the duct, Penny heard a voice calling out from within the wall, from another part of the ventilation system, but not far away now. It was a brittle, whispery, cold, hoarse voice that turned her blood to icy slush in her veins. It said, *'Penny? Penny?'*

She almost fell in her haste to get down from the dresser.

She ran to Davey, grabbed him, shook him. 'Wake up! Davey, wake up!'

He hadn't been asleep long, no more than fifteen minutes, but he was nevertheless groggy. 'Huh? Whaaa?'

'They're coming,' she said. 'They're coming. We've got to get dressed and get out of here. Fast. *They're coming!'*

She screamed for Aunt Faye.

6

The Jamisons' apartment was in a twelve-storey building on a cross street that hadn't yet been ploughed. The street was mantled with six inches of snow. Jack drove slowly forward and had no trouble for about twenty yards, but then the wheels sank into a hidden drift that had completely filled in a dip in the pavement. For a moment he thought they were stuck, but he threw the car into reverse and then forward and then reverse and then forward again, rocking it, until it broke free. Two-thirds of the way down the block, he tapped the brakes, and the car slid to a stop in front of the right building.

He flung open the door and scrambled out of the car. An arctic wind hit him with sledgehammer force. He put his head down and staggered around the front of the car, onto the sidewalk, barely able to see as the wind picked up crystals of snow from the ground and sprayed them in his face.

By the time Jack climbed the steps and pushed through the glass doors, into the lobby, Rebecca was already there. Flashing her badge and photo ID at the startled doorman, she said, 'Police.'

He was a stout man, about fifty, with hair as white as the snow outside. He was sitting at a Sheraton desk near the pair of elevators, drinking coffee and taking shelter from the storm. He must have been a day-shift man, filling in for the regular night-shift man (or perhaps new) because Jack had never seen him on the evenings when he'd come here to pick up the kids.

'What is it?' the doorman asked. 'What's wrong?'

This wasn't the kind of building where people were accustomed to anything being wrong; it was first-class all the way, and the mere prospect of trouble was sufficient to cause the doorman's face to turn nearly as pale as his hair.

Jack punched the elevator call button and said, 'We're going up to the Jamisons' apartment. Eleventh floor.'

'I know which floor they're on,' the doorman said, flustered, getting up so quickly that he bumped the desk and almost knocked over his coffee cup. 'But why—'

One set of elevator doors opened.

Jack and Rebecca stepped into the cab.

Jack shouted back to the doorman: 'Bring a passkey! I hope to God we don't need it.'

Because if we need it, he thought, that'll mean no one's left alive in the apartment to let us in.

The lift doors shut. The cab started up.

Jack reached inside his overcoat, drew his revolver.

Rebecca pulled her gun, too.

Above the doors, the panel of lighted numbers indicated that they had reached the third floor.

'Guns didn't help Dominick Carramazza,' Jack said shakily, staring at the Smith & Wesson in his hand.

Fourth floor.

'We won't need guns anyway,' Rebecca said. 'We've gotten here ahead of Lavelle. I know we have.'

But the conviction had gone out of her voice.

Jack knew why. The journey from her apartment had taken forever. It seemed less and less likely that they were going to be in time.

Sixth floor.

'Why're the elevators so goddamned slow in this building?' Jack demanded.

Seventh floor.

Eighth.

Ninth.

'*Move*, damnit!' he commanded the lift machinery, as if he thought it would actually speed up if he ordered it to do so.

Tenth floor.

Eleventh.

At last the doors slid open, and Jack stepped through them.

Rebecca followed close behind.

The eleventh floor was so quiet and looked so ordinary that Jack was tempted to hope.

Please, God, please.

There were seven apartments on this floor. The Jamisons had one of the two front units.

Jack went to their door and stood to one side of it.

His right arm was bent and tucked close against his side, and the revolver was in his right hand, held close to his face, the muzzle pointed straight up at the ceiling for the moment, but ready to be brought into play in an instant.

Rebecca stood on the other side, directly opposite him, in a similar posture.

Let them be alive. Please. Please.

His eyes met Rebecca's. She nodded. Ready.

Jack pounded on the door.

7

In the shadow-crowded room, on the bed, Lavelle breathed deeply and rapidly. In fact, he was panting like an animal.

His hands were curled at his sides, fingers hooked and rigid, as if they were talons. For the most part, his hands were still, but now and then they erupted in sudden violent movement, striking at the empty air or clawing frantically at the sheets.

He shivered almost continuously. Once in a while, he jerked and twitched as if an electric current had snapped through him; on these occasions, his entire body heaved up, off the bed, and slammed back down, making the mattress springs squeal in protest.

Deep in a trance, he was unaware of these spasms.

He stared straight up, eyes wide, seldom blinking, but he wasn't seeing the ceiling or anything else in the room. He was viewing other places, in another part of the city, where his vision was held captive by the eager pack of small assassins with which he had established psychic contact.

He hissed.

Groaned.

Gnashed his teeth.

He jerked, flopped, twisted.

Then lay silent, still.

Then clawed the sheets.

He hissed so forcefully that he sprayed spittle into the dark air around him.

His legs suddenly became possessed. He drummed his heels furiously upon the mattress.

He growled in the back of his throat.

He lay silent for a while.

Then he began to pant. He sniffed. Hissed again.

He smelled the girl. Penny Dawson. She had a wonderful scent. Sweet. Young. Fresh. Tender.

He wanted her.

8

Faye opened the door, saw Jack's revolver, gave him a startled look, and said, 'My God, what's that for? What're you doing? You know how I hate guns. Put that thing away.'

From Faye's demeanour as she stepped back to let them in, Jack knew the kids were all right, and he sagged a little with relief. But he said, 'Where's Penny? Where's Davey? Are they okay?'

Faye glanced at Rebecca and started to smile, then realized what Jack was saying, frowned at him, and said, 'Okay? Well, of course, they're okay. They're perfectly fine. I might not have kids of my own, but I know how to take care of them. You think I'd let anything happen to those two little monkeys? For heaven's sake, Jack, I don't—'

'Did anyone try to follow you back here from the school?' he asked urgently.

'And just what was all that nonsense about, anyway?' Faye demanded.

'It wasn't nonsense. I thought I made that clear. Did anyone try to follow you? You *did* look out for a tail, like I told you to – didn't you, Faye?'

'Sure, sure, sure. I looked. No one tried to follow us. And I don't think—'

They had moved out of the foyer, into the living room, while they had been talking. Jack looked around, didn't see the kids.

He said, 'Faye, where the hell are they?'

'Don't take that tone, for goodness sake. What are you—'

'Faye, damnit!'

She recoiled from him. 'They're in the guest room. With Keith,' she said quickly and irritably. 'They were put to bed at about a quarter past nine, just as they should have been, and we thought they were just about sound asleep when all of a sudden we heard Penny scream—'

'She screamed?'

'—and said there were rats in their room. Well, of course, we don't have any—'

Rats!

Jack bolted across the living room, hurried along the short hall, and burst into the guest room.

The bedside lamps, the standing lamp in the corner, and the ceiling lights were all blazing.

Penny and Davey were standing at the foot of one of the twin beds, still in their pyjamas. When they saw Jack, they cried out happily—'Daddy! Daddy!'—and ran to him, hugged him.

Jack was so overwhelmed at finding them alive and unhurt, so grateful, that for a moment he couldn't speak. He just grabbed hold of them and held them very tightly.

In spite of all the lights in the room, Keith Jamison was holding a flashlight. He was over by the dresser, holding the flash above his head, directing the beam into the darkness beyond the vent plate that covered the outlet in the heating duct. He turned to Jack, frowning, and said, 'Something odd's going on here. I—'

'Goblins!' Penny said, clutching Jack. 'They're coming, Daddy, they want me and Davey, don't let them, don't let them get us, oh please, I've been waiting for them, waiting and waiting, scared, and now they're almost here!' The words tumbled over one another, flooding out of her and then she sobbed.

'Whoa,' Jack said, holding her close and petting her, smoothing her hair. 'Easy now. Easy.'

Faye and Rebecca had followed him from the living room.

Rebecca was being her usual cool, efficient self. She was at the bedroom closet, getting the kids' clothes off hangers.

Faye said, 'First, Penny shouted that there were rats in her room, and then she started carrying on about goblins, nearly hysterical. I tried to tell her it was only a nightmare—'

'It *wasn't* a nightmare!' Penny shouted.

'Of course it was,' Faye said.

'They've been watching me all day,' Penny said. 'And there was one of them in our room last night, Daddy. And in the school basement today – a whole bunch of them. They chewed up Davey's lunch. And my books, too. I don't know what they want, but they're after us, and they're goblins, real goblins, I swear!'

'Okay,' Jack said. 'I want to hear all of this, every detail. But later. Now, we have to get out of here.'

Rebecca brought their clothes.

Jack said, 'Get dressed. Don't bother taking off your pyjamas. Just put your clothes on over them.'

Faye said, 'What on earth—'

'We've got to get the kids out of here,' Jack said. 'Fast.'

'But you act as if you actually believe this goblin talk,' Faye said, astonished.

Keith said, 'I sure don't believe in goblins, but I sure *do* believe we have some rats.'

'No, no, no,' Faye said, scandalized. 'We can't. Not in *this* building.'

'In the ventilation system,' Keith said. 'I heard them myself.' That's why I was trying to see in there with the flashlight when you came bursting in, Jack.'

'*Sssshhh,*' Rebecca said. 'Listen.'

236

The kids continued to get dressed, but no one spoke.

At first Jack heard nothing. Then . . . a peculiar hissing-muttering-growling.

That's no damned rat, he thought.

Inside the wall, something rattled. Then a scratching sound, a furious scrabbling. Industrious noises: clinking, tapping, scraping, thumping.

Faye said, 'My God.'

Jack took the flashlight from Keith, went to the dresser, pointed the light at the duct. The beam was bright and tightly focused, but it did little to dispel the blackness that pooled beyond the slots in the vent plate.

Another thump in the wall.

More hissing and muted growling.

Jack felt a prickling along the back of his neck.

Then, incredibly, a voice came out of the duct. It was a hoarse, crackling, utterly inhuman voice, thick with menace: *Penny? Davey? Penny?*

Faye cried out and stumbled back a couple of steps.

Even Keith, who was a big and rather formidable man, went pale and moved away from the vent. 'What the devil was *that*?'

To Faye, Jack said, 'Where're the kids' coats and boots? Their gloves?'

'Uh . . . in . . . in the kitchen. D-Drying out.'

'Get them.'

Faye nodded but didn't move.

Jack put a hand on her shoulder. 'Get their coats and boots and gloves, then meet us by the front door.'

She couldn't take her eyes off the vent.

He shook her. 'Faye! Hurry!'

She jumped as if he'd slapped her face, turned, and ran out of the bedroom.

Penny was almost dressed, and she was holding up remarkably well, scared but in control. Davey was sitting on the edge of the bed, trying not to cry, crying anyway, wiping at the tears on his face, glancing apologetically at Penny and biting his lip and trying very hard to follow her example; his legs were dangling over the side of the bed, and Rebecca was hastily tying his shoes for him.

From the vent: *'Davey? Penny?'*

'Jack, for Christ's sake, what's going on here?' Keith asked.

Not bothering to respond, having no time or patience for questions and answers just now, Jack pointed the flashlight at the vent again and glimpsed movement in the duct. Something silvery lay in there; it glowed and flickered like a white-hot fire – then blinked and was gone. In its place, something dark appeared, shifted, pushed against the vent plate for a moment, as if trying to dislodge it, then withdrew when the plate held. Jack couldn't see enough of the creature to get a clear idea of its general appearance.

Keith said, 'Jack. The vent screw.'

Jack had already seen it. The screw was revolving, slowly coming out of the edge of the vent plate. The creature inside the duct was turning the screw, unfastening it from the other side of the flange to which the plate was attached. The thing was muttering, hissing, and grumbling softly while it worked.

'Let's go,' Jack said, striving to keep his voice calm. 'Come on, come on. Let's get out of here right now.'

The screws popped loose. The vent plate swung down, away from the ventilation outlet, hanging from the one remaining screw.

Rebecca hustled the kids toward the door.

A nightmare crawled out of the duct. It hung there on the wall, with utter disregard for gravity, as if there were suction pads on its feet, although it didn't seem equipped with anything of that sort.

'Jesus,' Keith said, stunned.

Jack shuddered at the thought of this repulsive little beast touching Davey or Penny.

The creature was the size of a rat. In shape, at least, its body was rather like that of a rat, too: low-slung, long in the flanks, with shoulders and haunches that were large and muscular for an animal of its size. But there the resemblance to a rat ended, and the nightmare began. This thing was hairless. Its slippery skin was darkly mottled grey-green-yellow and looked more like a slimy fungus than like flesh. The tail was not at all similar to a rat's tail; it was eight or ten inches long, an inch wide at the base, segmented in the manner of a scorpion's tail, tapering and curling up into the air above the beast's hindquarters, like that of a scorpion, although it wasn't equipped with a stinger. The feet were far different from a rat's feet: They were oversized by comparison to the animal itself; the long toes were triple-jointed, gnarly; the curving claws were much too big for the feet to which they were fitted; a razor-sharp, multiply barbed spur curved out from each heel. The head was even more deadly in appearance and design than were the feet; it was formed over a flattish skull that had many unnaturally sharp angles, unnecessary convexities and concavities, as if it had been moulded by an inexpert sculptor. The snout was long and pointed, a bizarre cross between the muzzle of a wolf and that of a crocodile. The small monster opened its mouth and hissed, revealing too many pointed teeth that were angled in various directions along its jaws. A surprisingly long black tongue slithered out of the mouth, glistening, like a strip of raw liver; the end of it was forked, and it fluttered continuously.

But the thing's eyes were what frightened Jack the most. They appeared not to be eyes at all; they had no pupils or irises, no solid tissue that he could discern. There were just empty sockets in the creature's malformed skull, crude holes from which radiated a harsh, cold, brilliant light. The intense glow seemed to come from a fire within the beast's own mutant cranium. Which simply could not *be*. Yet was. And the thing wasn't blind, either, as it should have been; there wasn't any question about its ability to see, for it fixed those fire-filled 'eyes' on Jack, and he could feel its demonic gaze as surely as he would have felt a knife rammed into his gut. That was the other thing that disturbed him, the very worst aspect of those mad eyes: the death-cold, hate-hot, soul-withering feeling they imparted when you dared to meet them. Looking into the thing's eyes, Jack felt both physically and spiritually ill.

With insectile disregard for gravity, the beast slowly crept head-first down the wall, away from the duct.

A second creature appeared at the opening in the ventilation system. This one wasn't anything like the first. It was in the form of a small man, perhaps ten inches high, crouching up there in the mouth of the duct. Although it possessed the crude form of a man, it was in no other way humanlike. Its hands and feet resembled those of the first beast, with dangerous claws and barbed spurs. The flesh was funguslike, slippery looking, though less green, more yellow and grey. There were black circles around the eyes and patches of corrupt-looking black flesh fanning out from the nostrils. Its head was misshapen, with a toothy mouth that went from ear to ear. And it had those same hellish eyes, although they were smaller than the eyes in the ratlike thing.

Jack saw that the man-form beast was holding a weapon. It looked like a miniature spear. The point was well-honed; it caught the light and glinted along its cutting edge.

Jack remembered the first two victims of Lavelle's crusade against the Carramazza family. They had both been stabbed hundreds of times with a weapon no bigger than a penknife – yet not a penknife. The medical examiner had been perplexed; the lab technicians had been baffled. But, of course, it wouldn't have occurred to them to explore the possibilities that those homicides were the work of ten-inch voodoo devils and that the murder weapons were miniature spears.

Voodoo devils? Goblins? Gremlins? What exactly were those things?

Did Lavelle mould them from clay and then somehow invest them with life and malevolent purpose?

Or were they conjured up with the help of pentagrams and sacrifices and arcane chants, the way demons were supposedly called forth by Satanists? *Were* they demons?

Where did they come from?

The man-form thing didn't creep down the wall behind the first beast. Instead, it leapt out of the duct, dropping to the top of the dresser, landing on its feet, agile and quick.

It looked past Jack and Keith, and it said, *'Penny? Davey?'*

Jack pushed Keith across the threshold, into the hall, then followed him and pulled the door shut behind them.

An instant later, one of the creatures – probably the manlike beast – crashed against the other side of the door and began to claw frantically at it.

The kids were already out of the hall, in the living room.

Jack and Keith hurried after them.

Faye shouted, 'Jack! Quick! They're coming through the vent out here!'

'Trying to cut us off,' Jack said.

Jesus, we're not going to make it, they're everywhere, the damned building's infested with them, they're all around us—

In his mind, Jack quickly slammed the door on those bleak thoughts, closed it tight and locked it and told himself that their worst enemies were their own pessimism and fear, which could enervate and immobilize them.

Just this side of the foyer, in the living room, Faye and Rebecca were helping the kids put on coats and boots.

Snarling, hissing, and eager wordless jabbering issued from the vent plate in the wall above the long sofa. Beyond the slots in that grille, silver eyes blazed in the

241

darkness. One of the screws was being worked loose from inside.

Davey had only one boot on, but time had run out.

Jack picked up the boy and said, 'Faye, bring his other boot, and let's get moving.'

Keith was already in the foyer. He'd been to the closet and had got coats for himself and Faye. Without pausing to put them on, he grabbed Faye by the arm and hurried her out of the apartment.

Penny screamed.

Jack turned toward the living room, instinctively crouching slightly and holding Davey even tighter.

The vent plate was off the duct above the sofa. Something was starting to come out of the darkness there.

But that wasn't why Penny had screamed. Another hideous intruder had come out of the kitchen, and that was what had seized her attention. It was two-thirds of the way through the dining room, scurrying toward the living room archway, coming straight at them. Its coloration was different from that of the other beasts, although no less disgusting; it was a sickly yellow-white with cancerous-looking green-black pockmarks all over it, and like the other beasts Lavelle had sent, this one appeared to be slick, slimy. It was also a lot bigger than any of the others, almost three times the size of the ratlike creature in the bedroom. Somewhat resembling an iguana, although more slender through its body than an iguana, this spawn of nightmares was three to four feet in length, had a lizard's tail, a lizard's head and face. Unlike an iguana, however, the small monster had eyes of fire, six legs, and a body so slinky that it appeared capable of tying itself in knots; it was the very slinkiness and flexibility that made it possible for a creature of this size to slither through the ventilation pipes. Furthermore, it had a pair of batlike wings which were atrophied and surely useless but which unfurled and flapped and fluttered with frightening effect.

The thing charged into the living room, tail whipping

242

back and forth behind it. Its mouth cracked wide, emitting a cold shriek of triumph as it bore down on them.

Rebecca dropped to one knee and fired her revolver. She was at point-blank range; she couldn't miss; she didn't. The slug smashed squarely into its target. The shot lifted the beast off the floor and flung it backwards as if it were a bundle of rags. It landed hard, clear back at the archway to the dining room.

It should have been blown to pieces. It wasn't.

The floor and walls should have been splashed with blood – or with whatever fluid pumped through these creature's veins. But there was no mess whatsoever.

The thing flopped and writhed on its back for a few seconds, then rolled over and got onto its feet, wobbled sideways. It was disorientated and sluggish, but unharmed. It scuttled around in a circle, chasing its own tail.

Meanwhile, Jack's eyes were drawn to the repulsive thing that had come out of the duct above the sofa. It hung on the wall, mewling, approximately the size of a rat but otherwise unlike a rodent. More than anything else, it resembled a featherless bird. It had an egg-shaped head perched atop a long, thin neck that might have been that of a baby ostrich, and it had a wickedly pointed beak which it kept slashing at the air. However, its flickering, fiery eyes were not like those of any bird, and no bird on earth possessed stubby tentacles, like these, instead of legs. The beast was an abomination, a mutant horror; just looking at it made Jack queasy. And now, behind it, another similar though not identical creature crept out of the duct.

'Guns aren't any damn use against these things,' Jack said.

The iguana-form monstrosity was becoming less disorientated. In a moment it would regain its senses and charge at them again.

Two more creatures appeared at the far end of the dining room, crawling out of the kitchen, coming fast.

A screech drew Jack's attention to the far end of the living room, where the hallway led back to the bedrooms and baths. The man-shaped thing was standing there, squealing, holding the spear above its head. It ran toward them, crossing the carpet with shocking speed.

Behind it came a horde of small but deadly creatures, reptilian-serpentine-canine-insectile-rodentlike-arachnoid grotesqueries. In that instant Jack realized that they were, indeed, the Hellborn; they were demonic entities summoned from the depths of Hell by Lavelle's sorcery. That must be the answer, insane as it seemed, for there was no place else from which such gruesome horrors *could* have come. Hissing and chattering and snarling, they flopped and rolled over one another in their eagerness to reach Penny and Davey. Each of them was quite different from the one before it, although all of them shared at least two features: the eyes of silver-white fire, like windows in a furnace – and murderously sharp little teeth. It was as if the gates of Hell had been flung open.

Jack rushed Penny into the foyer. Carrying Davey, he followed his daughter out of the front door, into the eleventh-floor corridor, and hurried toward Keith and Faye, who stood with the white-haired doorman at one of the elevators, keeping the lift open.

Behind Jack, Rebecca fired three shots.

Jack stopped, turned. He wanted to go back for her, but he wasn't sure how he could do that and still protect Davey.

'Daddy! Hurry!' Penny screamed from where she stood half in and half out of the elevator.

'Daddy, let's go, let's go,' Davey said, clinging to him.

Much to Jack's relief, Rebecca came out of the apartment, unharmed. She fired one shot into the Jamisons' foyer, then pulled the door shut.

By the time Jack reached the elevators, Rebecca was right behind him. Gasping for breath, he put Davey down, and all seven of them, including the doorman, crowded into the cab, and Keith hit the button that was marked LOBBY.

The doors didn't immediately slide shut.

'They're gonna get in, they're gonna get in,' Davey cried, voicing the fear that had just flashed into everyone's mind.

Keith pushed the LOBBY button again, kept his thumb on it this time.

Finally the doors slid shut.

But Jack didn't feel any safer.

Now that he was closed up tight in the cramped cab, he wondered if they would have been wiser to take the stairs. What if the demons could put the lift out of commission, stop it between floors? What if they crept into the elevator shaft and descended onto the stranded cab? What if that monstrous horde found a way to get inside? God in heaven, what if . . . ?

The elevator started down.

Jack looked up at the ceiling of the cab. There was an emergency escape hatch. A way out. And a way *in*. This side of the hatch was featureless: no hinges, no handles. Apparently, it could be pushed up and out – or pulled up and out by rescue workers on the other side. There would be a handle out there on the roof of the cab, which would make it easy for the demons, if they came. But since there wasn't a handle on the inside, the hatch couldn't be held down; the forced entrance of those vicious creatures couldn't be resisted – if they came.

God, please, don't let them come.

The elevator crawled down its long cables as slowly as it had pulled itself up. Tenth floor . . . ninth . . .

Penny had taken Davey's boot from Faye. She was helping her little brother get his foot into it.

Eighth floor.

In a haunted voice that cracked more than once, but still with her familiar imperious tone, Faye said, 'What were they, Jack? What were those things in the vents?'

'Voodoo,' Jack said, keeping his eyes on the lighted floor indicator above the doors.

Seventh floor.

'Is this some sort of joke?' the doorman asked.

'Voodoo devils, I think,' Jack told Faye, 'but don't ask me to explain how they got here or anything about them.'

Shaken as she was, and in spite of what she'd heard and seen in the apartment, Faye said, 'Are you out of your mind?'

'Almost wish I was.'

Sixth floor.

'There aren't such things as voodoo devils,' Faye said. 'There aren't any—'

'Shut up,' Keith told her. 'You didn't see them. You left the guest room before they came out of the vent in there.'

Fifth floor.

Penny said, 'And you'd gotten out of the apartment before they started coming through the living room vent, Aunt Faye. You just didn't see them – or you'd believe.'

Fourth floor.

The doorman said, 'Mrs Jamison, how well do you know these people? Are they—'

Ignoring and interrupting him, Rebecca spoke to Faye and Keith: 'Jack and I have been on a weird case. Psychopathic killer. Claims to waste his victims with voodoo curses.'

Third floor.

Maybe we're going to make it, Jack thought. Maybe we won't be stopped between floors. Maybe we'll get out of here alive.

And maybe not.

To Rebecca, Faye said, 'Surely *you* don't believe in voodoo.'

'I didn't,' Rebecca said. 'But now . . . yeah.'

With a nasty shock, Jack realized the lobby might be teeming with small, vicious creatures. When the elevator doors opened, the nightmare horde might come rushing in, clawing and biting.

'If it's a joke, I don't get it,' the doorman said.

Second floor.

Suddenly Jack didn't want to reach the lobby, didn't want the lift doors to open. Suddenly he just wanted to go on descending in peace, hour after hour, on into eternity.

The lobby.

Please, no!

The doors opened.

The lobby was deserted.

They poured out of the elevator, and Faye said, 'Where are we going?'

Jack said, 'Rebecca and I have a car—'

'In this weather—'

'Snow chains,' Jack said, cutting her off sharply. 'We're taking the car and getting the kids out of here, keep moving around, until I can figure out what to do.'

'We'll go with you,' Keith said.

'No,' Jack said, ushering the kids toward the lobby doors. 'Being with us is probably dangerous.'

'We can't go back upstairs,' Keith said. 'Not with those . . . those demons or devils or whatever the hell they are.'

'Rats,' Faye said, apparently having decided that she could deal with the uncouth more easily than she could deal with the unnatural. 'Only some rats. Of course, we'll go back. Sooner or later, we'll *have* to go back, set traps, exterminate them. The sooner the better, in fact.'

Paying no attention to Faye, talking over her head to Keith, Jack said, 'I don't think the damned things will hurt you and Faye. Not unless you were to stand between them and the kids. They'll probably kill anyone who tries to protect the kids. That's why I'm getting them away from you. Still, I wouldn't go back there tonight. A few of them might wait around.'

'You couldn't drag me back there tonight,' Keith assured him.

'Nonsense,' Faye said. 'Just a few rats—'

'Damnit, woman,' Keith said, 'it wasn't a rat that called for Davey and Penny from inside that duct!'

Faye was already pale. When Keith reminded her of the voice in the ventilation system, she went pure white.

They all paused at the doors, and Rebecca said, 'Keith, is there someone you can stay with?'

'Sure,' Keith said. 'One of my business partners, Anson Dorset, lives on this same block. On the other side of the street. Up near the avenue. We can spend the night there, with Anson and Francine.'

Jack pushed the door open. The wind tried to slam it shut again, almost succeeded, and snow exploded into the lobby. Fighting the wind, turning his face away from the stinging crystals, Jack held the door open for the others and motioned them ahead of him. Rebecca went first, then Penny and Davey, then Faye and Keith.

The doorman was the only one left. He was scratching his white-haired head and frowning at Jack. 'Hey, wait. What about me?'

'What about you? You're not in any danger,' Jack said, starting through the door, in the wake of the others.

'But what about all the gunfire upstairs?'

Turning to the man again, Jack said, 'Don't worry about it. You saw our ID when we came in here, right? We're cops.'

'Yeah, but who got shot?'

'Nobody,' Jack said.

'Then who were you shooting at?'

'Nobody.'

Jack went out into the storm, letting the door blow shut behind him.

The doorman stood in the lobby, face pressed to the glass door, peering out at them, as if he were a fat and unpopular schoolboy who was being excluded from a game.

The wind was a hammer. The spicules of snow were nails. The storm was busily engaged on its carpentry work, building drifts in the street.

By the time Jack reached the bottom of the steps in front of the apartment building, Keith and Faye were already angling across the street, heading up toward the avenue, toward the building where their friends lived. Step by step, they were gradually disappearing beyond the phosphorescent curtains of wind-blown snow.

Rebecca and the kids were standing at the car.

Raising his voice above the huffing and moaning of the wind, Jack said, 'Come on, come on. Get in. Let's get out of here.'

Then he realized something was wrong.

Rebecca had one hand on the door handle, but she wasn't opening the door. She was staring into the car, transfixed.

Jack moved up beside her and looked through the window and saw what she saw. Two of the creatures. Both on the back seat. They were wrapped in shadows, and it was impossible to see exactly what they looked like, but their glowing silver eyes left no doubt that they were kin to the murderous things that had come out of the heating ducts. If Rebecca had opened the door without looking inside, if she hadn't noticed that the beasts were waiting in there, she might have been attacked and overwhelmed. Her throat could have been torn open, her eyes gouged out, her life taken before Jack was even aware of the danger, before he had a chance to go to her assistance.

'Back off,' he said.

The four of them moved away from the car, huddled on the sidewalk, wary of the night around them.

They were the only people on the wintry street, now. Faye and Keith were out of sight. There were no ploughs, no cars, no pedestrians. Even the doorman was no longer watching them.

It's strange, Jack thought, to feel this isolated and this alone in the heart of Manhattan.

'What now?' Rebecca asked urgently, her eyes fixed on the car, one hand on Davey, one hand inside her coat where she was probably gripping her revolver.

'We keep moving,' Jack said, too surprised and too scared to think of anything better.

Don't Panic.

'Where?' Rebecca asked.

'Toward the avenue,' he said.

Calm. Easy. Panic will finish us.

'The way Keith went?' Rebecca asked.

'No. The other avenue. Third Avenue. It's closer.'

'I hope there're people out there,' she said.

'Maybe even a patrol car.'

And Penny said, 'I think we're a whole lot safer around people, out in the open.'

'I think so too, sweetheart,' Jack said. 'So let's go now. And stay close together.'

Penny took hold of Davey's hand.

The attack came suddenly. The thing rushed out from beneath their car. Squealing. Hissing. Eyes beaming silvery light. Dark against the snow. Swift and sinuous. Too damned swift. Lizardlike. Jack saw that much in the storm-diluted glow of the streetlamps, reached for his revolver, remembered that bullets couldn't kill these things, also realized that they were in too close quarters to risk using a gun anyway, and by then the thing was among them, snarling and spitting – all of this in but a single second, one *tick* of time, perhaps even less. Davey shouted. And tried to get out of the thing's way. He couldn't avoid it. The beast pounced on the boy's boot. Davey kicked. It clung to him. Jack lifted-pushed Penny out of the way. Put her against the wall of the apartment building. She crouched there. Gasping. Meanwhile, the lizard had started climbing Davey's legs. The boy flailed

250

at it. Stumbled. Staggered backwards. Shrieking for help. Slipped. Fell. All of this in only one more second, maybe two – *tick, tick* – and Jack felt as if he were in a fever dream, with time distorted as it could be only in a dream. He went after the boy, but he seemed to be moving through the air as thick as syrup. The lizard was on the front of Davey's chest now, its tail whipping back and forth, its clawed feet digging at the heavy coat, trying to tear the coat to shreds so that it could then rip open the boy's belly, and its mouth was wide, its muzzle almost at the boy's face – *no!* – and Rebecca got there ahead of Jack. *Tick.* She tore the disgusting thing off Davey's chest. It wailed. It bit her hand. She cried out in pain. Threw the lizard down. Penny was screaming: 'Davey, Davey, Davey!' *Tick.* Davey had regained his feet. The lizard went after him again. This time, Jack got hold of the thing. In his bare hands. On the way up to the Jamisons' apartment, he'd removed his gloves in order to be able to use his gun more easily. Now, shuddering at the feel of the thing, he ripped it off the boy. Heard the coat shredding in its claws. Held it at arm's length. *Tick.* The creature felt repulsively cold and oily in Jack's hand, although for some reason he had expected it to be hot, maybe because of the fire inside its skull, the silvery blaze that now flickered at him through the gaping sockets where the demon's eyes should have been. The beast squirmed. *Tick.* It tried to wrench free of him, and it was strong, but he was stronger. *Tick.* It kicked the air with its wickedly clawed feet. *Tick. Tick. Tick, tick, tick . . .*

Rebecca said, 'Why isn't it trying to bite you?'

'I don't know,' he said breathlessly.

'What's different about you?'

'I don't know.'

But he remembered the conversation he'd had with Nick Iervolino in the patrol car, earlier today, on the way downtown from Carver Hampton's shop in Harlem. And he wondered . . .

251

The lizard-thing had a second mouth, this one in its stomach, complete with sharp little teeth. The aperture gaped at Jack, opened and closed, but this second mouth was no more eager to bite him than was the mouth in the lizard's head.

'Davey, are you all right?' Jack asked.

'Kill it, Daddy,' the boy said. He sounded terrified but unharmed. 'Please kill it. Please.'

'I only wish I could,' Jack said.

The small monster twisted, flopped, wriggled, did its best to slither out of Jack's hands. The feel of it revolted him, but he gripped it even tighter than before, harder, dug his fingers into the cold oily flesh.

'Rebecca, what about your hand?'

'Just a nip,' she said.

'Penny?'

'I . . . I'm okay.'

'Then the three of you get out of here. Go to the avenue.'

'What about you?' Rebecca asked.

'I'll hold on to this thing, give you a head start.' The lizard thrashed. 'Then I'll throw it as far as I can before I follow you.'

'We can't leave you alone,' Penny said desperately.

'Only for a minute or two,' Jack said. 'I'll catch up. I can run faster than the three of you. I'll catch up easy. Now go on. Get out of here before another one of these damned things charges out from somewhere. *Go!*'

They ran, the kids ahead of Rebecca, kicking up plumes of snow as they went.

The lizard-thing hissed at Jack.

He looked into those eyes of fire.

Inside the lizard's malformed skull, flames writhed, fluttered, flickered, but never wavered, burned bright and intense, all shades of white and silver, but somehow it didn't seem like a *hot* fire; it looked cool, instead.

Jack wondered what would happen if he poked a finger through one of those sockets, into the fire beyond.

Would he actually find fire in there? Or was it an illusion? If there really was fire in the skull, would he burn himself? Or would he discover that the flames were as lacking in heat as they appeared to be?

White flames. Sputtering.

Cold flames. Hissing.

The lizard's two mouths chewed at the night air.

Jack wanted to see more deeply into that strange fire.

He held the creature closer to his face.

He stared into the empty sockets.

Whirling flames.

Leaping flames.

He had the feeling there was something beyond the fire, something amazing and important, something awesome that he could almost glimpse between those scintillating, tightly contained pyrotechnics.

He brought the lizard even closer.

Now his face was only inches from its muzzle.

He could feel the light of its eyes washing over him.

It was a bitterly cold light.

Incandescent.

Fascinating.

He peered intently into the skull fire.

The flames almost parted, almost permitted him to see what lay beyond them.

He squinted, trying harder to see.

He wanted to understand the great mystery.

The mystery beyond the fiery veil.

Wanted, needed, *had* to understand it.

White flames.

Flames of snow, of ice.

Flames that held a shattering secret.

Flames that beckoned . . .

Beckoned...

He almost didn't hear the car door opening behind him. The 'eyes' of the lizard-thing had seized him and half mesmerized him. His awareness of the snow-swept street around him had grown fuzzy. In a few more seconds, he would have been lost. But they misjudged; they opened the car door one moment too soon, and he heard it. He turned, threw the lizard-thing as far as he could into the stormy darkness.

He didn't wait to see where it fell, didn't look to see what was coming out of the unmarked sedan.

He just ran.

Ahead of him, Rebecca and the kids had reached the avenue. They turned left at the corner, moving out of sight.

Jack pounded through the snow, which was almost over the tops of his boots in some places, and his heart triphammered, and his breath spurted from him in white clouds, and he slipped, almost fell, regained his balance, ran, ran, and it seemed to him that he wasn't running along a real street, that this was only a street in a dream, a nightmare place from which there was no escape.

10

In the elevator, on the way up to the fourteenth floor, where Anson and Francine Dorset had an apartment, Faye said, 'Not a word about voodoo or any of that nonsense. You hear me? They'll think you're crazy.'

Keith said, 'Well, I don't know about voodoo. But I sure as hell saw something strange.'

'Don't you *dare* go raving about it to Anson and Francine. He's your business partner, for heaven's sake. You've got to go on working with the man. That's going to be hard to do if he thinks you're some sort of superstitious nut. A broker's got to have an image of stability. A banker's image. Bankers and brokers. People want to see stable, conservative men at a brokerage firm before they trust it with their investments. You can't afford the damage to your reputation. Besides, they were only rats.'

'They weren't rats,' he said. 'I saw—'

'Nothing but rats.'

'I know what I saw.'

'Rats,' she insisted. 'But we're not going to tell Anson and Francine we have rats. What would they think of us? I won't have them knowing we live in a building with rats. Why, Francine already looks down at me; she looks down at everyone; she thinks she's such a blue blood, that family she comes from. I won't give her the slightest advantage. I swear I won't. Not a word about rats. What we'll tell them is that there's a gas leak. They can't see our building from their apartment, and they won't be going out on a night like this, so we'll tell them we've been evacuated because of a gas leak.'

'Faye—'

'And tomorrow morning,' she said determinedly, 'I'll start looking for a new place for us.'

'But—'

'I won't live in a building with rats. I simply won't do it, and you can't expect me to. You should want out of there yourself, just as fast as it can be arranged.'

'But they weren't—'

'We'll sell the apartment. And maybe it's even time we got out of this damned dirty city altogether. I've been half wanting to get out for years. You know that. Maybe it's time we start looking for a place in Connecticut. I know you won't be happy about commuting, but the train isn't so bad, and think of all the advantages. Fresh air. A bigger place for the same money. Our own pool. Wouldn't *that* be nice? Maybe Penny and Davey could come and stay with us for the entire summer. They shouldn't spend their entire childhood in the city. It isn't healthy. Yes, definitely, I'll start looking into it tomorrow.'

'Faye, for one thing, everything'll be shut up tight on account of the blizzard—'

'That won't stop me. You'll see. First thing tomorrow.'

The elevator doors opened.

In the fourteenth-floor corridor, Keith said, 'Aren't you worried about Penny and Davey? I mean, we left them—'

255

'They'll be fine,' she said, and she even seemed to believe it. 'It was only rats. You don't think rats are going to follow them out of the building? They're in no danger from a few rats. What I'm most worried about is that father of theirs, telling them its voodoo, scaring them like that, stuffing their heads full of such nonsense. What's gotten into that man? Maybe he does have a psychotic killer to track down, but voodoo has nothing to do with it. He doesn't sound rational. I just can't understand him; no matter how hard I try, I just can't.'

They had reached the door to the Dorset apartment. Keith rang the bell.

Faye said, 'Remember, not a word!'

Anson Dorset must have been waiting with his hand on the doorknob ever since they phoned up from downstairs, for he opened up at once, just as Faye issued that warning to Keith. He said, 'Not a word about what?'

'Rats,' Keith said. 'All of a sudden, it seems as if our building is infested with rats.'

Faye cast a murderous look at him.

He didn't care. He wasn't going to spin an elaborate story about a gas leak. They could be caught too easily in a lie like that, and then they'd look like fools. So he told Anson and Francine about a plague of vermin, but he didn't mention voodoo or say anything about the weird creatures that had come out of the guest room vent. He conceded that much to Faye because she was absolutely right on that score: A stock broker had to maintain a conservative, stable, level-headed image at all times – or risk ruin.

But he wondered how long it would be before he could forget what he had seen.

A long time.

A long, long, time.

Maybe never.

11

Sliding a little, then stomping through a drift that put

snow inside his boots, Jack turned the corner, onto the avenue. He didn't look back because he was afraid he'd discover the goblins – as Penny called them – close at his heels.

Rebecca and the kids were only a hundred feet ahead. He hurried after them.

Much to his dismay, he saw that they were the only people on the broad avenue. There were only a few cars, all deserted and abandoned after becoming stuck in the snow. Nobody out walking. And who, in his right mind, *would* be out walking in gale-force winds, in the middle of a blinding snowstorm? Nearly two blocks away, red taillights and revolving red emergency beacons gleamed and winked, barely visible in the sheeting snow. It was a train of ploughs, but they were headed the other way.

He caught up with Rebecca and the kids. It wasn't difficult to close the gap. They were no longer moving very fast. Already, Davey and Penny were flagging. Running in deep snow was like running with lead weights on the feet; the constant resistance was quickly wearing them down.

Jack glanced back the way they had come. No sign of the goblins. But those lantern-eyed creatures would show up, and soon. He couldn't believe they had given up this easily.

When they *did* come, they would find easy prey. The kids would have slowed to a weary, shambling walk in another minute.

Jack didn't feel particularly spry himself. His heart was pounding so hard and fast that it seemed as if it would tear loose of its moorings. His face hurt from the cold, biting wind, which also stung his eyes and brought tears to them. His hands hurt and were somewhat numb, too, because he hadn't had time to put on his gloves again. He was breathing hard, and the arctic air cracked his throat, made his chest ache. His feet were freezing because of all the snow that had gotten into his boots. He wasn't in any condition to provide much protection to the kids, and that realization made him angry and fearful, for he and Rebecca were the only people standing between the kids and death.

As if excited by the prospect of their slaughter, the wind howled louder, almost gleefully.

The wind-bare trees, rising from cut-out planting beds in the wide sidewalk, rattled their stripped limbs in the wind. It was the sound of animated skeletons.

Jack looked around for a place to hide. Just ahead, five brownstone apartment houses, each four storeys tall, were sandwiched between somewhat higher and more modern (though less attractive) structures. To Rebecca, he said, 'We've got to get out of sight,' and he hurried all of them off the sidewalk, up the snow-covered steps, through the glass-panelled front doors, into the security foyer of the first brownstone.

The foyer wasn't well heated; however, by comparison with the night outside, it seemed wonderfully tropical. It was also clean and rather elegant, with brass mailboxes and a vaulted wooden ceiling, although there was no doorman. The complex mosaic-tile floor – which depicted a twining vine, green leaves, and faded yellow flowers against an ivory background – was highly polished, and not one piece of tile was missing.

But, even as pleasant as it was, they couldn't stay here. The foyer was also brightly lighted. They would be spotted easily from the street.

The inner door was also glass panelled. Beyond it lay the first-floor hall, the elevator and stairs. But the door was locked and could be opened only with a key or with a lock-release button in one of the apartments.

There were sixteen apartments in all, four on each floor. Jack stepped to the brass mailboxes and pushed the call button for a Mr and Mrs Evans on the fourth floor.

A woman's voice issued tinnily from the speaker at the top of the mailbox. 'Who is it?'

'Is this the Grofeld apartment?' Jack asked, knowing full well that it wasn't.

'No,' the unseen woman said. 'You've pressed the wrong button. The Grofelds' mailbox is next to ours.'

'Sorry,' he said as Mrs Evans broke the connection.

He glanced toward the front door, at the street beyond.

Snow. Naked, blackened trees shaking in the wind. The ghostly glow of storm-shrouded streetlamps.

But nothing worse than that. Nothing with silvery eyes. Nothing with lots of pointed little teeth.

Not yet.

He pressed the Grofelds' button, asked if this were the Santini apartment, and was curtly told that the Santinis' mailbox was the next one.

He rang the Santinis and was prepared to ask if theirs was the Porterfield apartment. But the Santinis apparently expected someone and were considerably less cautious than their neighbours, for they buzzed him through the inner door without asking who he was.

Rebecca ushered the kids inside, and Jack quickly followed, closing the foyer door behind them.

He could have used his police ID to get past the foyer, but it would have taken too long. With the crime rate spiralling upward, most people were more suspicious these days than they'd once been. If he had been straightforward with Mrs Evans, right there at the start, she wouldn't have accepted his word that he was a cop. She would have wanted to come down – and rightly so – to examine his badge through the glass panel in the inner door. By that time, one of Lavelle's demonic assassins might have passed by the building and spotted them.

Besides, Jack was reluctant to involve other people, for to do so would be to put their lives at risk if the goblins should suddenly arrive and attack.

Apparently, Rebecca shared his concern about dragging strangers into it, for she warned the kids to be especially quiet as she escorted them into a shadowy recess under the stairs, to the right of the main entrance.

Jack crowded into the nook with them, away from the door. They couldn't be seen from the street or from the stairs above, not even if someone leaned out over the railing and looked down.

After less than a minute had passed, a door opened a few floors overhead. Footsteps. Then someone, apparently Mr Santini, said, 'Alex? Is that you?'

Under the stairs, they remained silent, unmoving.

Mr Santini waited.

Outside, the wind roared.

Mr Santini descended a few steps. 'Is anyone there?'

Go away, Jack thought. You haven't any idea what you might be walking into. *Go away.*

As if he were telepathic and had received Jack's warning, the man returned to his apartment and closed the door.

Jack sighed.

Eventually, speaking in a tremulous whisper, Penny said, 'How will we know when it's safe to go outside again?'

'We'll just give it a little time, and then when it seems right . . . I'll slip out there and take a peek,' Jack said softly.

Davey was shaking as if it were colder in here than it was outside. He wiped his runny nose with the sleeve of his coat and said, 'How much time will we wait?'

'Five minutes,' Rebecca told him, also whispering. 'Ten at most. They'll be gone by then.'

'They will?'

'Sure. They might already be gone.'

'You really think so?' Davey asked. 'Already?'

'Sure,' Rebecca said. 'There's a good chance they didn't follow us. But even if they did come after us, they won't hang around this area all night.'

'Won't they?' Penny asked doubtfully.

'No, no, no,' Rebecca said. 'Of course they won't. Even goblins get bored, you know.'

'Is that what they are?' Davey asked. 'Goblins? Really?'

'Well, it's hard to know exactly what we ought to call them,' Rebecca said.

'Goblins was the only word I could think of when I saw them,' Penny said. 'It just popped into my mind.'

'And it's a pretty darned good word,' Rebecca assured her. 'You couldn't have thought of anything better, so far as I'm concerned. And, you know, if you think back to all the fairytales you ever heard, goblins were always more bark than bite. About all they ever really did to anyone was scare them. So if we're patient and careful, really careful, then everything will be all right.'

Jack admired and appreciated the way Rebecca was handling the children, alleviating their anxiety. Her voice had a soothing quality. She touched them continually as she spoke to them, squeezed and stroked them, gentled them down.

Jack pulled up his sleeve and looked at his watch.

10:14.

They huddled together in the shadows under the stairs, waiting. Waiting.

CHAPTER SIX

1

For a while Lavelle lay on the floor of the dark bedroom, stunned, breathing only with difficulty, numb with pain. When Rebecca Chandler shot a few of those small assassins in the Jamisons' apartment, Lavelle had been in psychic contact with them, and he'd felt the impact of the bullets on their golem bodies. He hadn't been injured, not any more than the demonic entities themselves had been injured. His skin wasn't broken. He wasn't bleeding. In the morning, there would be no bruises, no tenderness of flesh. But the impact of those slugs had been agonizingly real and had rendered him briefly unconscious.

He wasn't unconscious now. Just disoriented. When the pain began to subside a little, he crawled around the room on his belly, not certain what he was searching for, not even certain where he was. Gradually he regained his senses. He crept back to the bed, levered himself onto the mattress, and flopped on his back, groaning.

Darkness touched him.

Darkness healed him.

Snow tapped the windows.

Darkness breathed over him.

Roof rafters creaked in the wind.

Darkness whispered to him.

Darkness.

Eventually, the pain was gone.

But the darkness remained. It embraced and caressed him. He suckled on it. Nothing else soothed as completely and as deeply as the darkness.

In spite of his unsettling and painful experience, he was eager to re-establish the psychic link with the creatures that were in pursuit of the Dawsons. The ribbons were still tied to his ankles, wrists, chest, and head. The spots of cat's blood were still on his cheeks. His lips were still annointed with blood. And the blood *vèvè* was still on his chest. All he had to do was repeat the proper chants, which he did, staring at the tenebrous ceiling. Slowly, the bedroom faded around him, and he was once again with the silver-eyed horde, relentlessly stalking the Dawson children.

10:15.

10:16.

While they huddled under the stairs, Jack looked at the bite on Rebecca's left hand. Three puncture marks were distributed over an area as large as a nickel, on the meatiest part of her palm, and there was a small tear in the skin, as well, but the lizard-thing hadn't bitten deeply. The flesh was only slightly puffy. The wound no longer wept; there was only dried blood.

'How does it feel?'

'Burns a bit,' she said.

'That's all?'

'It'll be fine. I'll put my glove on; that ought to help prevent it from breaking open and bleeding again.'

'Keep a watch on it, okay? If there's any discoloration, any more swelling, anything at all odd about it, maybe we ought to get you to a hospital.'

'And when I talk to the doctor, what shall I say?'

'Tell him you were bitten by a goblin. What else?'

'Might be worth it just to see his expression.'

10:17.

Jack examined Davey's coat, at which the lizard had clawed in a murderous frenzy. The garment was heavy and well made; the fabric was sturdy. Nevertheless, the creature's claws had sliced all the way through in at least three places – and through the quilted lining, too.

It was a miracle that Davey was unharmed. Although the claws had pierced the coat as if it were so much cheesecloth, they hadn't torn the boy's sweater or shirt; they hadn't left even one shallow scratch on his skin.

Jack thought about how close he had come to losing both Davey and Penny, and he was acutely aware that he might still lose them before this case was closed. He put one hand to his son's fragile face. An icy premonition of dreadful loss began to blossom within him, spreading frozen petals of terror and despair. His throat clenched. He struggled to hold back tears. He must not cry. The kids would come apart if he cried. Besides, if he gave in to despair now, he would be surrendering – in some small but significant way – to Lavelle. Lavelle was evil, not just another criminal, not merely corrupted, but *evil*, the very essence and embodiment of it, and evil thrived on despair. The best weapons against evil were hope, optimism, determination, and faith. Their chances of survival depended on their ability to keep hoping, to believe that life (not death) was their destiny, to believe that good could triumph over evil, simply to *believe*. He would not lose his kids. He would not allow Lavelle to have them.

'Well,' he said to Davey, 'it's too well ventilated for a winter coat, but I think we can fix that.' He took off his long neckscarf, wound it overtop the boy's damaged coat, twice around his small chest, and knotted it securely at his waist. 'There. That ought to keep the gaps closed. You okay, skipper?'

Davey nodded and tried very hard to look brave. He said, 'Dad, do you think maybe what you need here is a magic sword?'

'A magic sword?' Jack said.

'Well, isn't that what you've got to have if you're going to kill a bunch of goblins?' the boy asked earnestly. 'In all the stories, they usually have a magic sword or a magic staff, see, or maybe just some magic powder, and that's what always does in the goblins or the witches or ogres or whatever it is that has to be done in. Oh, and sometimes, what it is they have . . . it's a magic jewel, you know, or a sorcerer's ring. So, since you and Rebecca are detectives, maybe this time it's a goblin gun. Do you know if the police department has anything like that? A goblin gun?'

'I don't really know,' Jack said solemnly, wanting to hug the boy very close and very tight. 'But it's a darned good suggestion, son. I'll look into it.'

'And if they don't have one,' Davey said, 'then maybe

264

you could just ask a priest to sort of bless your own gun, the one you already have, and then you could load it up with lots and lots of silver bullets. That's what they do with werewolves, you know.'

'I know. And that's a good suggestion, too. I'm real glad to see you're thinking about ways to beat these things. I'm glad you aren't giving up. That's what's important – not giving up.'

'Sure,' Davey said, sticking his chin out. 'I know *that*.'

Penny was watching her father over Davey's shoulder. She smiled and winked.

Jack winked back at her.

10:20.

With every minute that passed uneventfully, Jack felt safer.

Not *safe*. Just safer.

Penny gave him a very abbreviated account of her encounters with the goblins.

When the girl finished, Rebecca looked at Jack and said, 'He's been keeping a watch on them. So he'd always know exactly where to find them when the time came.'

To Penny, Jack said, 'My God, baby, why didn't you wake me last night when the thing was in your room?'

'I didn't really see it—'

'But you heard it.'

'That's all.'

'And the baseball bat—'

'Anyway,' Penny said with a sudden odd shyness, unable to meet his eyes, 'I was afraid you'd think I'd gone . . . crazy . . . again.'

'Huh? Again?' Jack blinked at her. 'What on earth do you mean – *again*?'

'Well . . . you know . . . like after Mama died, the way I was then . . . when I had my . . . trouble.'

'But you weren't crazy,' Jack said. 'You just needed a little counselling; that's all, honey.'

'That's what you called him,' the girl said, barely audible. 'A counsellor.'

'Yeah. Dr Hannaby.'

'Aunt Faye, Uncle Keith, everyone called him a counsellor. Or sometimes a doctor.'

'That's what he was. He was there to counsel you, to show you how to deal with your grief over your mom's death.'

The girl shook her head: no. 'One day, when I was in his office, waiting for him . . . and he didn't come in to start the session right away . . . I started to read the college degrees on his wall.'

'And?'

With evident embarrassment, Penny said, 'I found out he was a psychiatrist. Psychiatrists treat crazy people. That's when I knew I was a little bit . . . crazy.'

Surprised and dismayed that such a misconception could have gone uncorrected for so long, Jack said, 'No, no, no. Sweetheart, you've got it all wrong.'

Rebecca said, 'Penny, for the most part, psychiatrists treat ordinary people with ordinary problems. Problems that we all have at one time or another in our lives. Emotional problems, mostly. That's what yours were. *Emotional* problems.'

Penny looked at her shyly. She frowned. Clearly, she wanted to believe.

'They treat some mental problems, too, of course,' Rebecca said. But in their offices, among their regular patients, they hardly ever see anyone who's really, really insane. Truly crazy people are hospitalized or kept in institutions.'

'Sure,' Jack said. He reached for Penny's hands, held them. They were small, delicate hands. The fragility of her hands, the vulnerability of an eleven-year-old who liked to think of herself as grown up – it made his heart ache. 'Honey, you were never crazy. Never even close to crazy. What a terrible thing to've been worrying about all this time.'

The girl looked from Jack to Rebecca to Jack again. 'You really mean it? You really mean lots of ordinary, everyday people go to psychiatrists?'

'Absolutely,' he said. 'Honey, life threw you a pretty bad curve, what with your mom dying so young, and I was so broken up myself that I wasn't much good at helping you handle it. I guess . . . I should have made an extra-special effort. But I was feeling so bad, so lost, so helpless, so darned sorry for myself that I just wasn't able to heal both of us, you and me. That's why I sent you to Dr Hannaby when you started having your problems. Not because you were crazy. Because you needed to talk to someone who wouldn't start crying about your mom as soon as *you* started crying about your mom. Understand?'

'Yeah,' Penny said softly, tears shining in her eyes, brightly suspended but unspilled.

'Positive?'

'Yeah. I really do, Daddy. I understand now.'

'So you should have come to me last night, when the thing was in your room. Certainly after it poked holes in that plastic baseball bat. I wouldn't have thought you were crazy.'

'Neither would I,' Davey said. 'I never-ever thought you were crazy, Penny. You're probably the least craziest person I know.'

Penny giggled, and Jack and Rebecca couldn't help grinning, but Davey didn't know what was so funny.

Jack hugged his daughter very tight. He kissed her face and her hair. He said, 'I love you, peanut.'

Then he hugged Davey and told him he loved him, too.

And then, reluctantly, he looked at his wristwatch. 10:24.

Ten minutes had elapsed since they had come into the brownstone and had taken shelter in the space under the big staircase.

'Looks like they didn't follow us,' Rebecca said.

'Let's not be too hasty,' he said. 'Give it another couple of minutes.'

10:25.

10:26.

He didn't relish going outside and having a look around. He waited one more minute.

10:27.

Finally he could delay no longer. He eased out from the staircase. He took two steps, put his hand on the brass knob of the foyer door – and froze.

They were here. The goblins.

One of them was clinging to the glass panel in the centre of the door. It was a two-foot-long, wormlike thing with a segmented body and perhaps two dozen legs. Its mouth resembled that of a fish: oval, with the teeth set far back from the writhing, sucking lips. Its fiery eyes fixed on Jack.

He abruptly looked away from that white-hot gaze, for he recalled how the eyes of the lizard had nearly hypnotized him.

Beyond the worm-thing, the security foyer was crawling with other, different devils, all of them small, but all of them so incredibly vicious and grotesque in appearance that Jack began to shake and felt his bowels turn to jelly. There were lizard-things in various sizes and shapes. Spider-things. Rat-things. Two of the man-form beasts, one of them with a tail, the other with a sort of cock's comb on its head and along its back. Dog things. Crablike, feline, snakelike, beetle-form, scorpionlike, dragonish, clawed and fanged, spiked and spurred and sharply horned *things*. Perhaps twenty of them. No. More then twenty. At least thirty. They slithered and skittered across the mosaic-tile floor, and they crept tenaciously up the walls, their foul tongues darting and fluttering ceaselessly, teeth gnashing and grinding, eyes shining.

Shocked and repelled, Jack snatched his hand away from the brass doorknob. He turned to Rebecca and the kids. 'They've found us. They're here. Come on. Got to get out. Hurry. Before it's too late.'

They came away from the stairs. They saw the worm-thing on the door and the horde in the foyer beyond. Rebecca and Penny stared at that Hellborn pack without speaking, both of them driven beyond the need – and perhaps beyond the ability – to scream. Davey was the only one who cried out. He clutched at Jack's arm.

'They must be inside the building by now,' Rebecca said. 'In the walls.'

They all looked toward the hallway's heating vents.

'How do we get out?' Penny asked.

How, indeed?

For a moment no one spoke. ·

In the foyer other creatures had joined the worm-thing on the glass of the inner door.

'Is there a rear entrance?' Rebecca wondered.

'Probably,' Jack said. 'But if there is, then these things will be waiting there, too.'

Another pause.

The silence was oppressive and terrifying – like the unspent energy in the raised blade of a cocked guillotine.

'Then we're trapped,' Penny said.

Jack felt his own heart beating. It shook him.

Think.

'Daddy, don't let them get me, please don't let them,' Davey said miserably.

Jack glanced at the elevator, which was opposite the stairs. He wondered if the devils were already in the elevator shaft. Would the doors of the lift suddenly open, spilling out a wave of hissing, snarling, snapping death?

Think!

He grabbed Davey's hand and headed toward the foot of the stairs.

Following with Penny, Rebecca said, 'Where are you going?'

'This way.'

They climbed the steps toward the second floor.

Penny said, 'But if they're in the walls, they'll be all through the building.'

'Hurry,' was Jack's only answer. He led them up the steps as fast as they could go.

3

In Carver Hampton's apartment above his shop in Harlem, all the lights were on. Ceiling lights, reading lamps, table lamps, and floor lamps blazed; no room was left in shadow. In those few corners where the lamplight didn't reach, candles had been lit; clusters of them stood in dishes and pie pans and cake tins.

Carver sat at the small kitchen table, by the window, his strong brown hands clamped around a glass of Chivas Regal. He stared out at the falling snow, and once in a while he took a sip of the Scotch.

Fluorescent bulbs glowed in the kitchen ceiling. The stove light was on. And the light above the sink, too. On the table, within easy reach, were packs of matches, three boxes of candles, and two flashlights – just in case the storm caused a power failure.

This was not a night for darkness.

Monstrous things were loose in the city.

They *fed* on darkness.

Although the night-stalkers had not been sent to get Carver, he could sense them out there in the stormy streets, prowling, hungry; they radiated a palpable evil, the pure and ultimate evil of the Ancient Ones. The creatures now loose in the storm were foul and unspeakable presences that couldn't go unnoticed by a man of Carver Hampton's powers. For one who was gifted with the ability to detect the intrusion of other-worldly forces into this world, their mere existence was an intolerable abrasion of the nerves, the soul. He assumed they were Lavelle's hellish emissaries, bent on the brutal destruction of the Carramazza family, for to the best of his knowledge there was no other Bocor in New York who could have summoned such creatures from the Underworld.

He sipped his Scotch. He wanted to get roaring drunk. But he wasn't much of a drinking man. Besides, this night of all nights, he must remain alert, totally in control of himself. Therefore, he allowed himself only small sips of whisky.

The Gates had been opened. The very Gates of Hell. Just a crack. The latch had barely been slipped. And through the application of his formidable powers as a Bocor, Lavelle was holding the Gates against the crush of demonic entities that sought to push forth from the other side. Carver could sense all of those things in the currents of the ether, in the invisible and soundless tides of benign and malevolent energies that ebbed and flowed over the great metropolis.

Opening the Gates was a wildly dangerous step to have taken. Few Bocors were even capable of doing it. And of those few, fewer still would have dared such a thing. Because Lavelle evidently was one of the most powerful Bocors who had ever drawn a *vèvè*, there was good reason to believe that he would be able to maintain control of the Gates and that, in time, when the Carramazzas were disposed of, he would be able to cast back the creatures that he had permitted out of Hell. But if he lost control for even a moment . . .

Then God help us, Carver thought.

If He *will* help us.

If He *can* help us.

A hurricane-force gust of wind slammed into the building and whined through the eaves.

The window rattled in front of Carver, as if something more than the wind was out there and wanted to get in at him.

A whirling mass of snow pressed to the glass. Incredibly, those hundreds upon hundreds of quivering, suspended flakes seemed to form a leering face that glared at Hampton. Although the wind huffed and hammered and whirled and shifted directions and then shifted back again, that impossible face did not dissolve and drift away on the changing air currents; it hung there, just beyond the pane, unmoving, as if it were painted on canvas.

Carver lowered his eyes.

In time the wind subsided a bit.

When the howling of it had quieted to a moan, he looked up once more. The snow-formed face was gone.

He sipped his Scotch. The whisky didn't warm him. Nothing could warm him this night.

Guilt was one reason he wished he could get drunk. He was eaten by guilt because he had refused to give Lieutenant Dawson any more help. That had been wrong. The situation was too dire for him to think only about himself. The Gates were open, after all. The world stood at the brink of Armageddon – all because one Bocor, driven by ego and pride and an unslakeable thirst for blood, was willing to take any risk, no matter how foolish, to settle a personal grudge. At a time like this, a Houngon had certain responsibilities. Now was an hour for courage. Guilt gnawed at him because he kept remembering the midnight-black serpent that Lavelle had sent, and with that memory tormenting him, he couldn't find the courage he required for the task that called.

Even if he dared get drunk, he would still have to carry that burden of guilt. It was far too heavy – immense – to be lifted by booze alone.

Therefore, he was now drinking in hope of finding courage. It was a peculiarity of whisky that, in moderation, it could sometimes make heroes of the very same men of whom it had made buffoons on other occasions.

He must find the courage to call Detective Dawson and say, *I want to help.*

More likely than not, Lavelle would destroy him for becoming involved. And whatever death Lavelle chose to administer, it would not be an easy one.

He sipped his Scotch.

He looked across the room at the wall phone.

Call Dawson, he told himself.

He didn't move.

He looked at the blizzard-swept night outside.

He shuddered.

4

Breathless, Jack and Rebecca and the kids reached the fourth-floor landing in the brownstone apartment house.

Jack looked down the stairs they'd just climbed. So far, nothing was after them.

Of course, something could pop out of one of the walls at any moment. The whole damned world had become a carnival funhouse.

Four apartments opened off the hall. Jack led the others past all four of them without knocking, without ringing any doorbells.

There was no help to be found here. These people could do nothing for them. They were on their own.

At the end of the hall was an unmarked door. Jack hoped to God it was what he thought it was. He tried the knob. From this side, the door was unlocked. He opened it hesitantly, afraid that the goblins might be waiting on the other side. Darkness. Nothing rushed at him. He felt for a light switch, half expecting to put his hand on something hideous. But he didn't. No goblins. Just the switch. *Click.* And, yes, it was what he hoped: a final flight of steps, considerably steeper and narrower than the eight flights they had already conquered, leading up to a barred door.

'Come on,' he said.

Following him without question, Davey and Penny and Rebecca clumped noisily up the stairs, weary but still too driven by fear to slacken their pace.

At the top of the steps, the door was equipped with two deadbolt locks, and it was braced by an iron bar. No burglar was going to get into this place by way of the roof. Jack snapped open both deadbolts and lifted the bar out of its braces, stood it to one side.

The wind tried to hold the door shut. Jack shouldered it open, and then the wind caught it and pulled on it instead of pushing, tore it away from him, flung it outward with such tremendous force that it banged against the outside wall. He stepped across the threshold, onto the flat roof.

Up here, the storm was a living thing. With a lion's ferocity, it leapt out of the night, across the parapet, roaring and sniffing and snorting. It tugged at Jack's coat. It stood his hair on end, then plastered it to his head, then stood it on end again. It expelled its frigid breath in his face and slipped cold fingers under the collar of his coat.

He crossed to that edge of the roof which was nearest the next brownstone. The crenellated parapet was waist-high. He leaned against it, looked out and down. As he had expected, the gap between the buildings was only about four feet wide.

Rebecca and the kids joined him, and Jack said, 'We'll cross over.'

'How do we bridge it?' Rebecca asked.

'Must be something around that'll do the job.'

He turned and surveyed the roof, which wasn't entirely cast in darkness; in fact, it possessed a moon-pale luminescence, thanks to the sparkling blanket of snow that covered it. As far as he could see, there were no loose pieces of lumber or anything else that could be used to make a bridge between the two buildings. He ran to the elevator housing and looked on the other side of it, and he looked on the far side of the exit box that contained the door at the head of the stairs, but he found nothing. Perhaps something useful lay underneath the snow, but there was no way he could locate it without first shovelling off the entire roof.

He returned to Rebecca and the kids. Penny and Davey remained hunkered down by the parapet, sheltering against it, keeping out of the biting wind, but Rebecca rose to meet him.

He said, 'We'll have to jump.'

'What?'

'Across. We'll have to jump across.'

'We can't,' she said.

'It's less than four feet.'

'But we can't get a running start.'

'Don't need it. Just a small gap.'

'We'll have to stand on this wall,' she said, touching the parapet, 'and jump from there.'

'Yeah.'

'In this wind, at least one of us is sure as hell going to lose his balance even before he makes the jump – get hit by a hard gust of wind and just fall right off the wall.'

'We'll make it,' Jack said, trying to pump up his own enthusiasm for the venture.

She shook her head. Her hair blew in her face. She pushed it out of her eyes. She said, 'Maybe, with luck, both you and I could do it. Maybe. But not the kids.'

'Okay. So one of us will jump on the other roof, and one of us will stay here, and between us we'll hand the kids across, from here to there.'

'Pass them over the gap?'

'Yeah.'

'Over a fifty-foot drop?'

'There's really not much danger,' he said, wishing he believed it. 'From these two roofs, we could reach across and hold hands.'

'Holding hands is one thing. But transferring something as heavy as a child—'

'I'll make sure you have a good grip on each of them before I let go. And as you haul them in, you can brace yourself against the parapet over there. No sweat.'

'Penny's getting to be a pretty big girl.'

'Not that big. We can handle her.'

'But—'

'Rebecca, those *things* are in this building, right under our feet, looking for us right this very minute.'

She nodded. 'Who goes first?'

'You.'

'Gee, thanks.'

He said, 'I can help you get up on top of the wall, and I can hold you until just a split second before you jump. That way, there's hardly any chance you could lose your balance and fall.'

'But after I'm over there and after we've passed the kids across, who's going to help *you* get on top of the wall and keep your balance up there?'

'Let me worry about that when the time comes,' he said.

Wind like a freight train whistled across the roof.

5

Snow didn't cling to the corrugated metal storage shed at the rear of Lavelle's property. The falling flakes melted when they touched the roof and walls of that small structure. Wisps of steam were actually rising from the leeward slope of the roof; those pale snakes of vapour writhed up until they came within range of the wind's brisk broom; then they were swept away.

Inside, the shed was stifling hot.

Nothing moved except the shadows. Rising out of the hole in the floor, the irregularly pulsing orange light was slightly brighter than it had been earlier. The flickering of it caused the shadows to shiver, giving an illusion of movement to every inanimate object in the dirt-floored room.

The cold night air wasn't the only thing that failed to penetrate these metal walls. Even the shrieking and soughing of the storm wind was inaudible herein. The atmosphere within the shed was unnatural, uncanny, disquieting, as if the room had been lifted out of the ordinary flow of time and space, and was now suspended in a void.

The only sound was that which came from deep within the pit. It was a distant hissing-murmuring-whispering-growling, like ten thousand voices in a far-off place, the distance-muffled roar of a crowd. An angry crowd.

Suddenly, the sound grew louder. Not a great deal louder. Just a little.

At the same moment, the orange light beamed brighter than ever before. Not a lot brighter. Just a little. It was as if a furnace door, already ajar, had been pushed open another inch.

The interior of the shed grew slightly warmer, too.

The vaguely sulphurous odour became stronger.

And something strange happened to the hole in the floor. All the way around the perimeter, bits of earth broke loose and fell inward, away from the rim, vanishing into the mysterious light at the bottom. Like the increase in the brilliance of that light, this alteration in the rim of the hole wasn't major; only an incremental change. The diameter was increased by less than one inch. The dirt stopped falling away. The perimeter stabilized. Once more, everything in the shed was perfectly still.

But now the pit was bigger.

6

The top of the parapet was ten inches wide. To Rebecca it seemed no wider than a tightrope.

At least it wasn't icy. The wind scoured the snow off the narrow surface, kept it clean and dry.

With Jack's help, Rebecca balanced on the wall, in a half crouch. The wind buffeted her, and she was sure that she would have been toppled by it if Jack hadn't been there.

She tried to ignore the wind and the stinging snow that pricked her exposed face, ignored the chasm in front of her, and focused both her eyes and her mind on the roof of the next building. She had to jump far enough to clear the parapet over there and land on the roof. If she came down a bit short, on top of that waist-high wall, on that meagre strip of stone, she would be unbalanced for a moment, even if she landed flat on both feet. In that instant of supreme vulnerability, the wind would snatch at her, and she might fall, either forward onto the roof, or backward into the empty air between the buildings. She didn't dare let herself think about *that* possibility, and she didn't look down.

She tensed her muscles, tucked her arms in against her sides, and said, 'Now,' and Jack let go of her, and she jumped into the night and the wind and the driving snow.

Airborne, she knew at once that she hadn't put enough power into the jump, knew she was not going to make it to the other roof, knew she would crash into the parapet, knew she would fall backwards, knew that she was going to die.

But what she *knew* would happen *didn't* happen. She cleared the parapet, landed on the roof, and her feet slipped out from under her, and she went down on her backside, hard enough to hurt but not hard enough to break any bones.

As she got to her feet, she saw the dilapidated pigeon coop. Pigeon-keeping was neither a common nor an unusual hobby in this city; in fact, this coop was smaller than some, only six feet long. At a glance she was able to tell that it hadn't been used for years. It was so weathered and in such disrepair that it would soon cease to be a coop and would become just a pile of junk.

She shouted to Jack, who was watching from the other building: 'I think maybe I've found our bridge!'

Aware of how fast time was running out, she brushed some of the snow from the roof of the coop and saw that it appeared to be formed by a single six-foot sheet of one-inch plywood. That was even better than she had hoped; now they wouldn't have to deal with two or three loose planks. The plywood had been painted many times over the years, and the paint had protected it from rot once the coop was abandoned and maintenance discontinued; it seemed sturdy enough to support the kids and even Jack. It was loose along one entire side, which was a great help to her. Once she brushed the rest of the snow off the coop roof, she gripped it by the loose end, pulled it up and back. Some of the nails popped out, and some snapped off because they were rusted clear through. In a few seconds she had wrenched the plywood free.

She dragged it to the parapet. If she tried to lever it onto the wall and shove it out toward Jack, the strong wind would get under it, treat it like a sail, lift it, tear it out of her hands, and send it kiting off into the storm. She had to wait for a lull. One came fairly soon, and she quickly heaved the plywood up, balanced it on top of the parapet, slid it out toward Jack's reaching hands. In a moment, as the wind whipped up once more, they had the bridge in place. Now, with the two of them holding it, they would be able to keep it down even if a fierce wind got under it.

Penny made the short journey first, to show Davey how easily it could be done. She wriggled across on her belly, gripping the edges of the board with her hands, pulling herself along. Convinced it could be done, Davey followed safely after her.

Jack came last. As soon as he was on the bridge, there was, of course, no one holding the far end of it. However, his weight held it in place, and he didn't scramble completely off until there was another lull in the wind. Then he helped Rebecca drag the plywood back onto the roof.

'Now what?' she asked.

'One building's not enough,' he said. 'We've got to put more distance between us and them.'

Using the plywood, they crossed the gulf between the second and third apartment houses, went from the third roof to the fourth, then from the fourth to the fifth. The next building was ten or twelve stories higher than this one. Their roof-hopping had come to an end, which was just as well, since their arms were beginning to ache from dragging and lifting the heavy sheet of plywood.

At the rear of the fourth brownstone, Rebecca leaned over the parapet and looked down into the alley, four stories below. There was some light down there: a street-lamp at each end of the block, another in the middle, plus the glow that came from all the windows of the first-floor apartments. She couldn't see any goblins in the alley, or any other living creatures for that matter – just snow in blankets and mounds, snow twirling in small and short-lived tornadoes, snow in vaguely phosphorescent sheets like the gowns of ghosts racing in front of the wind. Maybe there were goblins crouching in the shadows somewhere, but she didn't really think so because she couldn't see any glowing white eyes.

A black, iron, switchback fire escape descended to the alley in a zig-zag path along the rear face of the building. Jack went down first, stopping at each landing to wait for Penny and Davey; he was prepared to break their fall if they slipped on the cold, snow-covered, and occasionally ice-sheathed steps.

Rebecca was the last off the roof. At each landing on the fire escape, she paused to look down at the alley, and each time she expected to see strange, threatening creatures loping through the snow toward the foot of the iron steps. But each time, she saw nothing.

When they were all in the alley, they turned right, away from the row of brownstones, and ran as fast as they could toward the cross street. When they reached the street, already slowing from a run to a fast walk, they turned away from Third Avenue and headed back toward the centre of the city.

Nothing followed them.

Nothing came out of the dark doorways they passed.

For the moment they seemed safe. But more than that . . . they seemed to have the entire metropolis to themselves, as if they were the only four survivors of doomsday.

Rebecca had never seen it snow this hard. This was a rampaging, lashing, hammering storm more suitable to the savage polar ice fields. Her face was numb, and her eyes were watering, and she ached in every joint and muscle from the constant struggle required to resist the insistent wind.

Two thirds of the way to Lexington Avenue, Davey stumbled and fell and simply couldn't find the energy to continue on his own. Jack carried him.

From the look of her, Penny was rapidly using up the last of her reserves, as well. Soon, Rebecca would have to take Davey, so Jack could then carry Penny.

And how far and how fast could they expect to travel under those circumstances? Not far. Not very damned fast. They needed to find transportation within the next few minutes.

They reached the avenue, and Jack led them to a large steel grate which was set in the pavement and from which issued clouds of steam. It was a vent from one sort of underground tunnel or another, most likely from the subway system. Jack put Davey down, and the boy was able to stand on his own feet. But it was obvious that he would still have to be carried when they started out again. He looked terrible; his small face was drawn, pinched, and very pale except for enormous dark circles around his eyes. Rebecca's heart went out to him, and she wished there was something she could do to make him feel better, but she didn't feel so terrific herself.

The night was too cold and the heated air rising out of the street wasn't heated enough to warm Rebecca as she stood at the edge of the grate and allowed the wind to blow the foul-smelling steam in her face; however, there was an illusion of warmth, if not the real thing, and at the moment the mere illusion was sufficiently spirit-lifting to forestall everyone's complaints.

To Penny, Rebecca said, 'How're you doing, honey?'

'I'm okay,' the girl said, although she looked haggard. 'I'm just worried about Davey.'

Rebecca was amazed by the girl's resilience and spunk.

Jack said, 'We've got to get a car. I'll only feel safe when we're in a car, rolling, moving; they can't get at us when we're moving.'

'And it'll b-b-be warm in a c-car,' Davey said.

But the only cars on the street were those that were parked at the kerb, unreachable beyond a wall of snow thrown up by the ploughs and not yet hauled away. If any cars had been abandoned in the middle of the avenue, they had already been towed away by the snow emergency crews.

None of those workmen were in sight now. No ploughs, either.

'Even if we could find a car along here that wasn't ploughed in,' Rebecca said, 'it isn't likely there'd be keys in it – or snow chains on the tyres.'

'I wasn't thinking of these cars,' Jack said. 'But if we can find a pay phone, put in a call to headquarters, we could have them send out a department car for us.'

'Isn't that a phone over there?' Penny asked, pointing across the broad avenue.

'Snow's so thick, I can't be sure,' Jack said, squinting at the object that had drawn Penny's attention. 'It *might* be a phone.'

'Let's go have a look,' Rebecca said.

Even as she spoke, a small but sharply clawed hand came out of the grating, from the space between two of the steel bars.

Davey saw it first, cried out, stumbled back, away from the rising steam.

A goblin's hand.

And another one, scrabbling at the toe of Rebecca's boot. She stomped on it, saw shining silver-white eyes in the darkness under the grate, and jumped back.

A third hand appeared, and a fourth, and Penny and

Jack got out of the way, and suddenly the entire steel grating rattled in its circular niche, tilted up at one end, slammed back into place, but immediately tilted up again, a little farther than an inch this time, but fell back, rattled, bounced. The horde below was trying to push out of the tunnel.

Although the grating was large and immensely heavy, Rebecca was sure the creatures below would dislodge it and come boiling out of the darkness and steam. Jack must have been equally convinced, for he snatched up Davey and ran. Rebecca grabbed Penny's hand, and they followed Jack, fleeing down the blizzard-pounded avenue, not moving as fast as they should, not moving very fast at all. None of them dared to look back.

Ahead, on the far side of the divided thoroughfare, a Jeep station wagon turned the corner, tyres churning effortlessly through the snow. It bore the insignia of the city department of streets.

Jack and Rebecca and the kids were headed downtown, but the Jeep was headed uptown. Jack angled across the avenue, toward the centre divider and the other lanes beyond it, trying to get in front of the Jeep and cut it off before it was past them.

Rebecca and Penny followed.

If the driver of the Jeep saw them, he didn't give any indication of it. He didn't slow down.

Rebecca was waving frantically as she ran, and Penny was shouting, and Rebecca started shouting, too, and so did Jack, shouting their fool heads off because the Jeep was their only hope of escape.

7

At the table in the brightly lighted kitchen above *Rada*, Carver Hampton played a few hands of solitaire. He hoped the game would take his mind off the evil that was loose in the winter night, and he hoped it would help him overcome his feelings of guilt and shame, which plagued him because he hadn't done anything to stop that evil from having its way in the world. But the cards couldn't distract him. He kept looking out the window beside the table, sensing something unspeakable out there in the dark. His guilt grew stronger instead of weaker; it chewed on his conscience.

He was a Houngon.

He had certain responsibilities.

He could not condone such monstrous evil as this.

Damn.

He tried watching television. *Quincy*. Jack Klugman was shouting at his stupid superiors, crusading for Justice, exhibiting a sense of social compassion greater than Mother Teresa's, and otherwise comporting himself more like Superman than like a real medical examiner. On *Dynasty*, a bunch of rich people were carrying on in the most licentious, vicious, Machiavellian manner, and Carver asked himself the same question he always asked himself when he was unfortunate enough to catch a few minutes of *Dynasty* or *Dallas* or one of their clones: If *real* rich people in the *real* world were this obsessed with sex, revenge, back-stabbing, and petty jealousies, how could any of them ever have had the time and intelligence to make any money in the first place? He switched off the TV.

He was a Houngon.

He had certain responsibilities.

He chose a book from the living room shelf, the new Elmore Leonard novel, and although he was a big fan of Leonard's, and although no one wrote stories that moved faster than Leonard's stories, he couldn't concentrate on this one. He read two pages, couldn't remember a thing he'd read, and returned the book to the shelf.

He was a Houngon.

He returned to the kitchen, went to the telephone. He hesitated with his hand on it.

He glanced at the window. He shuddered because the vast night itself seemed to be demoniacally alive.

He picked up the phone. He listened to the dial tone for a while.

Detective Dawson's office and home numbers were on a piece of notepaper beside the telephone. He stared at the home number for a while. Then, at last, he dialled it.

It rang several times, and he was about to give up, when the receiver was lifted at the other end. But no one spoke.

He waited a couple of seconds, then said, 'Hello?'

No answer.

'Is someone there?'

No response.

At first he thought he hadn't actually reached the Dawson number, that there was a problem with the connection, that he was listening to dead air. But as he was about to hang up, a new and frightening perception seized him. He sensed an evil presence at the other end, a supremely malevolent entity whose malignant energy poured back across the telephone line.

He broke out in a sweat. He felt soiled. His heart raced. His stomach turned sour, sick.

He slammed the phone down. He wiped his damp hands on his pants. They still felt unclean, merely from holding the telephone that had temporarily connected him with the beast in the Dawson apartment. He went to the sink and washed his hands thoroughly.

The thing at the Dawsons' place was surely one of the entities that Lavelle had summoned to do his dirty work for him. But what was it doing there? What did this mean? Was Lavelle crazy enough to turn loose the powers of darkness not only on the Carramazzas but on the police who were investigating those murders?

If anything happens to Lieutenant Dawson, Hampton thought, I'm responsible because I refused to help him.

Using a paper towel to blot the cold sweat from his face and neck, he considered his options and tried to decide what he should do next.

There were only two men in the street department's Jeep station wagon, which left plenty of room for Penny, Davey, Rebecca, and Jack.

The driver was a merry-looking, ruddy-faced man with a squashed nose and big ears; he said his name was Burt. He looked closely at Jack's police ID and, satisfied that it was genuine, was happy to put himself at their disposal, swing the Jeep around, and run them back to headquarters, where they could get another car.

The Jeep was wonderfully warm and dry.

Jack was relieved when the doors were all safely shut and the Jeep began to pull out.

But just as they were making a U-turn in the middle of the deserted avenue, Burt's partner, a freckle-faced young man named Leo, saw something moving through the snow, coming toward them from across the street.

'Hey, Burt, hold on a sec. Isn't that a cat out there?'

'So what if it is?' Burt asked.

'He shouldn't be out in weather like this.'

'Cats go where they want,' Burt said. 'You're the cat fancier; you should know how independent they are.'

'But it'll freeze to death out there,' Leo said.

As the Jeep completed the turn, and as Burt slowed down a bit to consider Leo's statement, Jack squinted through the side window at the dark shape loping across the snow; it moved with feline grace. Farther back in the storm, beyond several veils of falling snow, there might have been other things coming this way; perhaps it was even the entire nightmare pack moving in for the kill, but it was hard to tell for sure. However, the first of the goblins, the catlike thing that had caught Leo's eye was undeniably out there, only thirty or forty feet away and closing fast.

'Stop just a sec,' Leo said. 'Let me get out and scoop up the poor little fella.'

'No!' Jack said. 'Get the hell out of here. That's no damned cat out there.'

Startled, Burt looked over his shoulder at Jack.

Penny began to shout the same thing again and again, and Davey took up her chant: 'Don't let them in, don't let them in here, don't let them in!'

Face pressed to the window in his door, Leo said, 'Jesus, you're right. It isn't any cat.'

'*Move!*' Jack shouted.

The thing leaped and struck the side window in front of Leo's face. The glass cracked but held.

Leo yelped, jumped, scooted backwards across the front seat, crowding Burt.

Burt tramped down on the accelerator, and the tyres spun for a moment.

The hideous cat-thing clung to the cracked glass.

Penny and Davey were screaming. Rebecca tried to shield them from the sight of the goblin.

It probed at them with eyes of fire.

Jack could almost feel the heat of that inhuman gaze. He wanted to empty his revolver at the thing, put half a dozen slugs into it, though he knew he couldn't kill it.

The tyres stopped spinning, and the Jeep took off with a lurch and a shudder.

Burt held the steering wheel with one hand and used the other hand to try to push Leo out of the way, but Leo wasn't going to move even an inch closer to the fractured window where the cat-thing had attached itself.

The goblin licked the glass with its black tongue.

The Jeep careened toward the divider in the centre of the avenue, and it started to slide.

Jack said, 'Damnit, don't lose control!'

'I can't steer with him on my lap,' Burt said.

He rammed an elbow into Leo's side, hard enough to accomplish what all the pushing and shoving and shouting hadn't managed to do; Leo moved – although not much.

The cat-thing grinned at them. Double rows of sharp and pointed teeth gleamed.

Burt stopped the sliding Jeep just before it would have hit the centre divider. In control again, he accelerated.

The engine roared.

Snow flew up around them.

Leo was making odd gibbering sounds, and the kids were crying, and for some reason Burt began blowing the horn, as if he thought the sound would frighten the thing and make it let go.

Jack's eyes met Rebecca's. He wondered if his own gaze was as bleak as hers.

Finally, the goblin lost its grip, fell off, tumbled away into the snowy street.

Leo said, 'Thank God,' and collapsed back into his own corner of the front seat.

Jack turned and looked out the rear window. Other dark beasts were coming out of the whiteness of the storm. They loped after the Jeep, but they couldn't keep up with it. They quickly dwindled.

Disappeared.

But they were still out there. Somewhere.

Everywhere.

9

The shed.

The hot, dry air.

The stench of Hell.

Again, the orange light abruptly grew brighter than it had been, not a lot brighter, just a little, and at the same time the air became slightly hotter, and the noises coming out of the pit grew somewhat louder and angrier, although they were still more of a whisper than a shout.

Again, around the perimeter of the hole, the earth loosened of its own accord, dropped away from the rim, tumbled to the bottom and vanished in the pulsing orange glow. The diameter had increased by more than two inches before the earth became stable once more.

And the pit was bigger.

PART THREE

WEDNESDAY 11:20 P.M. – THURSDAY 2:30 A.M.

You know, Tolstoy, like myself, wasn't taken in by superstitions – like science and medicine.
—George Bernard Shaw

There is superstition in avoiding superstition.
—Francis Bacon

CHAPTER SEVEN

1

At headquarters, the underground garage was lighted but not very brightly lighted. Shadows crouched in corners; they spread like a dark fungus on the walls; they lay in wait between the rows of cars and other vehicles; they clung to the concrete ceilings and watched all that went on beneath them.

Tonight, Jack was scared of the garage. Tonight, the omnipresent shadows themselves seemed to be alive and, worse, seemed to be creeping closer with great cleverness and stealth.

Rebecca and the kids evidently felt the same way about the place. They stayed close together, and they looked around worriedly, their faces and bodies tense.

It's all right, Jack told himself. The goblins can't have known where we were going. For the time being, they've lost track of us. For the moment, at least, we're safe.

But he didn't *feel* safe.

The night man in charge of the garage was Ernie Tewkes. His thick black hair was combed straight back from his forehead, and he wore a pencil-thin moustache that looked odd on his wide upper lip.

'But each of you already signed out a car,' Ernie said, tapping the requisition sheet on his clipboard.

'Well, we need two more,' Jack said.

'That's against regulations, and I—'

'To hell with the regulations,' Rebecca said. 'Just give us the cars. *Now.*'

'Where're the two you already got?' Ernie asked. 'You didn't wrack them up, did you?'

'Of course not,' Jack said. 'They're bogged down.'

'Mechanical trouble?'

'No. Stuck in snow drifts,' Jack lied.

They had ruled out going back for the car at Rebecca's apartment, and they had also decided they didn't dare return to Faye's and Keith's place. They were sure the devil-things would be waiting at both locations.

'Drifts?' Ernie said. 'Is that all? We'll just send a tow truck out, get you loose, and put you on the road again.'

'We don't have time for that,' Jack said impatiently, letting his gaze roam over the darker portions of the cavernous garage. 'We need two cars right now.'

'Regulations say—'

'Listen,' Rebecca said, 'weren't a number of cars assigned to the Carramazza task force?'

'Sure,' Ernie said. 'But—'

'And aren't some of those cars still here in the garage, right now, unused?'

'Well, at the moment, nobody's using them,' Ernie admitted. 'But maybe—'

'And who's in charge of the task force?' Rebecca demanded.

'Well . . . you are. The two of you.'

'This is an emergency related to the Carramazza case, and we need those cars.'

'But you've already got cars checked out, and regulations say you've got to fill out breakdown or loss reports on them before you can get—'

'Forget the bullshit bureaucracy,' Rebecca said angrily. 'Get us new wheels now, this minute, or so help me God I'll rip that funny little moustache out of your face, take the keys off your pegboard there, and get the cars myself.'

Ernie stared wide-eyed at her, evidently stunned by

both the threat and the vehemence with which it was delivered.

In this particular instance, Jack was delighted to see Rebecca revert to a nail-eating, hard-nosed Amazon.

'Move!' she said, taking one step toward Ernie.

Ernie moved. Fast.

While they waited by the dispatcher's booth for the first car to be brought around, Penny kept looking from one shadowy area to another. Again and again, she thought she saw things moving in the gloom: darkness slithering through darkness; a ripple in the shadows between two patrol cars; a throbbing in the pool of blackness that lay behind a police riot wagon; a shifting, malevolent shape in the pocket of darkness in that corner over there; a watchful, hungry shadow hiding among the ordinary shadows in that other corner; movement just beyond the stairway and more movement on the other side of the elevators and something scuttling stealthily across the dark ceiling and—

Stop it!

Imagination, she told herself. If the place was crawling with goblins, they'd have attacked us already.

The garage man returned with a slightly battered blue Chevrolet that had no police department insignia on the doors, though it did have a big antenna because of its police radio. Then he hurried away to get the second car.

Jack and Rebecca checked under the seats of the first one, to be sure no goblins were hiding there.

Penny didn't want to be separated from her father, even though she knew separation was part of the plan, even though she had heard all the good reasons why it was essential for them to split up, and even though the time to leave had now come. She and Davey would go with Rebecca and spend the next few hours driving slowly up and down the main avenues, where the snowploughs were working the hardest and where there was the least danger of getting stuck; they didn't dare get stuck because they were vulnerable when they stayed in one place too long, safe only while they were on wheels and moving, where the goblins couldn't get a fix on them. In the meantime her father would go up to Harlem to see a man named Carver Hampton, who would probably be able to help him find Lavelle. Then he was going after that witch-doctor. He was sure he wouldn't be in terrible danger. He said that, for some reason he really didn't understand, Lavelle's magic had no effect on him. He said putting the cuffs on Lavelle wouldn't be any more difficult or dangerous than putting them on any other criminal. He meant it, too. And Penny wanted to believe that he was absolutely right. But deep in her heart, she was certain she would never see him again.

Nevertheless, she didn't cry too much, and she didn't hang on him too much, and she got into the car with Davey and Rebecca. As they drove out of the garage, up the exit ramp, she looked back. Daddy was waving at them. Then they reached the street and turned right, and he was out of sight. From that moment, it seemed to Penny that he was already as good as dead.

2

A few minutes after midnight, in Harlem, Jack parked in front of *Rada*. He knew Hampton lived above the store, and he figured there must be a private entrance to the apartment, so he went around to the side of the building, where he found a door with a street number.

There were a lot of lights on the second floor. Every window glowed brightly.

Standing with his back to the pummelling wind, Jack pushed the buzzer beside the door but wasn't satisfied with just a short ring; he held his thumb there, pressing down so hard that it hurt a little. Even through the closed door, the sound of the buzzer swiftly became irritating. Inside, it must be five or six times louder. If

Hampton looked out through the fisheye security lens in the door and saw who was waiting and decided not to open up, then he'd better have a damned good pair of earplugs. In five minutes the buzzer would give him a headache. In ten minutes it would be like an icepick probing in his ears. If that didn't work, however, Jack intended to escalate the battle; he'd look around for a pile of loose bricks or several empty bottles or other hefty pieces of rubbish to throw through Hampton's windows. He didn't care about being charged with reckless use of authority; he didn't care about getting in trouble and maybe losing his badge. He was past the point of polite requests and civilized debate.

To his surprise, in less than half a minute the door opened, and there was Carver Hampton, looking bigger and more formidable than Jack remembered him, not frowning as expected but smiling, not angry but delighted.

Before Jack could speak, Hampton said, 'You're all right! Thank God for that. Thank God. Come in. You don't know how glad I am to see you. Come in, come in.' There was a small foyer beyond the door, then a set of stairs, and Jack went in, and Hampton closed the door but didn't stop talking. 'My God, man, I've been worried half to death. Are you all right? You look all right. Will you please, for God's sake, tell me you're all right?'

'I'm okay,' Jack said. 'Almost wasn't. But there's so much I have to do, so much I—'

'Come upstairs,' Hampton said, leading the way. 'You've got to tell me what's happened, all of it, every detail. It's been an eventful and momentous night; I know it; I sense it.'

Pulling off his snow-encrusted boots, following Hampton up the narrow stairs, Jack said, 'I should warn you – I've come here to demand your help, and by God you're going to give it to me, one way or the other.'

'Gladly,' Hampton said, further surprising him. 'I'll do whatever I possibly can; anything.'

At the top of the stairs, they came into a comfortable-looking, well-furnished living room with a great many books on shelves along one wall, an oriental tapestry on the wall opposite the books, and a beautiful oriental carpet, predominantly beige and blue, occupying most of the floor space. Four blown-glass table lamps in striking blues and greens and yellows were placed with such skill that you were drawn by their beauty no matter which way you were facing. There were also two reading lamps, more functional in design, one by each of the big armchairs. Both of those and all four of the blown-glass lamps were on. However, their light didn't fully illuminate every last corner of the room, and in those areas where there otherwise might have been a few thin shadows, there were clusters of burning candles, at least fifty of them in all.

Hampton evidently saw that he was puzzled by the candles, for the big man said. 'Tonight there are two kinds of darkness in this city, Lieutenant. First, there's that darkness which is merely the absence of light. And then there's that darkness which is the physical presence – the very manifestation – of the ultimate, Satanic evil. That second and malignant form of darkness feeds upon and cloaks itself in the first and more ordinary kind of darkness, cleverly disguises itself. *But it's out there!* Therefore, I don't wish to have shadows close to me this night, if I can avoid it, for one never knows when an innocent patch of shade might be something more than it appears.'

Before this investigation, even as excessively open-minded as Jack had always been, he wouldn't have taken Carver Hampton's warning seriously. At best, he would have thought the man eccentric; at worst, a bit mad. Now, he didn't for a moment doubt the sincerity or the accuracy of the Houngon's statements. Unlike Hampton, Jack wasn't afraid that the shadows themselves would suddenly leap at him and clutch him with insubstantial yet somehow deadly hands of darkness; however, after the things he had seen tonight, he couldn't rule out even that bizarre possibility. Anyway, because of what might be hiding within the shadows, he, too, preferred bright light.

'You look frozen,' Hampton said. 'Give me your coat. I'll hang it over the radiator to dry. Your gloves, too. Then sit down, and I'll bring you some brandy.'

'I don't have time for brandy,' Jack said, leaving his coat buttoned and his gloves on. 'I've got to find Lavelle. I—'

'To find and stop Lavelle,' Hampton said, 'you've got to be properly prepared. That's going to take time. Only a fool would go rushing back out into that storm with only a half-baked idea of what to do and where to go. And you're no fool, Lieutenant. So give me your coat. I can help you, but it's going to take longer than two minutes.'

Jack sighed, struggled out of his heavy coat, and gave it to the Houngon.

Minutes later, Jack was ensconced in one of the armchairs, holding a glass of Remy Martin in his cupped hands. He had taken off his shoes and socks and had put them by the radiator, too, for they had got thoroughly soaked by the snow that had got in over the tops of his boots as he'd waded through the drifts. For the first time all night, his feet began to feel warm.

Hampton opened the gas jets in the fireplace, poked a long-stemmed match in among the ceramic logs, and flames *whooshed* up. He turned the gas high. 'Not for the heat, so much as to chase the darkness from the flue,' he said. He shook out the match, dropped it into a copper scuttle that stood on the hearth. He sat down in the other armchair, facing Jack across a coffee table on which were displayed two pieces of Lalique crystal – a clear bowl with green lizards for handles, and a tall frosted vase with a graceful neck. 'If I'm to know how to proceed, you'll have to tell me everything that—'

'First, I've got some questions,' Jack said.

'All right.'

'Why wouldn't you help me earlier today?'

'I told you. I was scared.'

'Aren't you scared now?'

'More than ever.'

'Then why're you willing to help me now?'

'Guilt. I was ashamed of myself.'

'It's more than that.'

'Well, yes. As a Houngon, you see, I routinely call upon the gods of *Rada* to perform feats for me, to fulfil blessings I bestow on my clients and on others I wish to help. And, of course, it's the gods who make my magic potions work as intended. In return, it is incumbent upon me to resist evil, to strike against the agents of *Congo* and *Pétro* wherever I encounter them. Instead, for a while, I tried to hide from my responsibilities.'

'If you had refused again to help me . . . would these benevolent gods of *Rada* continue to perform their feats for you and fulfil the blessings you bestow? Or would they abandon you and leave you without power?'

'It's highly unlikely they would abandon me.'

'But possible?'

'Remotely, yes.'

'So, at least in some small degree, you're also motivated by self-interest. Good. I like that. I'm comfortable with that.'

Hampton lowered his eyes, stared into his brandy for a moment, then looked at Jack again and said, 'There's another reason that I must help. The stakes are higher than I first thought when I threw you out of the shop this afternoon. You see, in order to crush the Carramazzas, Lavelle has opened the Gates of Hell and has let out a host of demonic entities to do his killing for him. It was an insane, foolish, terribly prideful, stupid thing for him to have done, even if he is perhaps the most masterful

Bocor in the world. He could have conjured up the spiritual essence of a demon and could have sent *that* after the Carramazzas; then there would have been no need to open the Gates at all, no need to bring those hateful creatures to this plane of existence in *physical* form. Insanity! Now, the Gates are open only a crack, and at the moment Lavelle is in control. I can sense that much through the cautious application of my own power. But Lavelle is a madman and, in some lunatic fit, might decide to fling the Gates wide, just for the fun of it. Or perhaps he'll grow weary and weaken; and if he weakens enough, the forces on the other side will surely burst the Gates against Lavelle's will. In either case, vast multitudes of monstrous creatures will come forth to slaughter the innocent, the meek, the good, and the just. Only the wicked will survive, but they'll find themselves living in Hell on Earth.'

3

Rebecca drove up the Avenue of the Americas, almost to Central Park, then made an illegal U-turn in the middle of the deserted intersection and headed downtown once more, with no cause to worry about other drivers. There actually was some traffic – snow removal vehicles, an ambulance, even two or three radio cabs – but for the most part the streets were bare of everything but snow. Twelve or fourteen inches had fallen, and it was still coming down fast. No one could see the lane markings through the snow; even where the ploughs scraped, they didn't make it all the way down to bare pavement. And no one was paying any attention to one-way signs or to traffic signals, most of which were on the blink because of the storm.

Davey's exhaustion had eventually proved greater than his fear. He was sound asleep on the back seat.

Penny was still awake, although her eyes were blood-shot and watery looking. She was clinging resolutely to consciousness because she seemed to have a compulsive need to talk, as if continual conversation would somehow keep the goblins away. She was also staying awake because, in a round-about fashion, she seemed to be leading up to some important question.

Rebecca wasn't sure what was on the girl's mind, and when, at last, Penny got to it, Rebecca was surprised by the kid's perspicacity.

'Do you like my father?'

'Of course,' Rebecca said. 'We're partners.'

'I mean, do you like him more than just as a partner?'

'We're friends. I like him very much.'

'More than just friends?'

Rebecca glanced away from the snowy street, and the girl met her eyes. 'Why do you ask?'

'I just wondered,' Penny said.

Not quite sure what to say, Rebecca returned her attention to the street ahead.

Penny said, 'Well? Are you? More than just friends?'

'Would it upset you if we were?'

'Gosh, no!'

'Really?'

'You mean, maybe I might be upset because I'd think you were trying to take my mother's place?'

'Well, that's sometimes a problem.'

'Not with me, it isn't. I loved my Mom, and I'll never forget her, but I know she'd want me and Davey to be happy, and one thing that'll make us real happy is if we could have another mom before we're too old to enjoy her.'

Rebecca almost laughed in delight at the sweet, inno-cent, and yet curiously sophisticated manner in which the girl expressed herself. But she bit her tongue and remained straight-faced because she was afraid that Penny might misinterpret her laughter. The girl was so *serious*.

Penny said, 'I think it would be terrific – you and Daddy. He needs someone. You know . . . someone . . . to love.'

'He loves you and Davey very much. I've never known a father who loved his children – who *cherished* them – as much as Jack loves and cherishes the two of you.'

'Oh, I know that. But he needs more than us.' The girl was silent for a moment, obviously deep in thought. Then: 'See, there're basically three types of people. First, you've got your givers, people who just give and give and give and never expect to take anything in return. There aren't many of those. I guess that's the kind of person who sometimes ends up being made a saint a hundred years after he dies. Then there're your givers-and-takers, which is what most people are; that's what I am, I guess. And way down at the bottom, you've got your takers, the scuzzy types who just take and take and never-ever give anything to anyone. Now, I'm not saying Daddy's a complete giver. I know he isn't a saint. But he's not exactly a giver-and-taker, either. He's somewhere inbetween. He gives a whole lot more than he takes. You know? He enjoys giving more than he enjoys getting. He needs more than just Davey and me to love . . . because he's got a lot more love in him than just that.' She sighed and shook her head in evident frustration. 'Am I making any sense at all?'

'A lot of sense,' Rebecca said. 'I know exactly what you mean, but I'm amazed to be hearing it from an eleven-year-old girl.'

'Almost twelve.'

'Very grown up for your age.'

'Thank you,' Penny said gravely.

Ahead, at a cross street, a roaring river of wind moved from east to west and swept up so much snow that it almost looked as if the Avenue of the Americas terminated there, in a solid white wall. Rebecca slowed down, switched the headlights to high beam, drove through the wall and out the other side.

'I love your father,' she told Penny, and she realized she hadn't yet told Jack. In fact, this was the first time in twenty years, the first time since the death of her grandfather, that she had admitted loving anyone. Saying those words was easier than she had thought it would be. 'I love him, and he loves me.'

'That's fabulous,' Penny said, grinning.

Rebecca smiled. 'It is rather fabulous, isn't it?'

'Will you get married?'

'I suspect we will.'

'Double fabulous.'

'Triple.'

'After the wedding, I'll call you Mom instead of Rebecca – if that's all right.'

Rebecca was surprised by the tears that suddenly rose in her eyes, and she swallowed the lump in her throat and said, 'I'd like that.'

Penny sighed and slumped down in her seat. 'I was worried about Daddy. I was afraid that witch-doctor would kill him. But now that I know about you and him . . . well, that's one more thing he has to live for. I think it'll help. I think it's real important that he's got not just me and Davey but you to come home to. I'm still afraid for him, but I'm not so afraid as I was.'

'He'll be all right,' Rebecca said. 'You'll see. He'll be just fine. We'll all come through this just fine.'

A moment later, when she glanced at Penny, she saw that the girl was asleep.

She drove on through the whirling snow.

Softly, she said, 'Come home to me, Jack. By God, you'd better come home to me.'

4

Jack told Carver Hampton everything, beginning with the call from Lavelle on the pay phone in front of *Rada*, and concluding with the rescue by Burt and Leo in their Jeep, the trip to the garage for new cars, and the decision to split up and keep the kids safely on the move.

Hampton was visibly shocked and distressed. He sat very still and rigid throughout the story, not even once

304

moving to sip his brandy. Then, when Jack finished, Hampton blinked and shuddered and downed his entire glassful of Remy Martin in one long swallow.

'And so you see,' Jack said, 'when you said these things came from Hell, maybe some people might've laughed at you, but not me. I don't have any trouble believing you, even though I'm not too sure how they made the trip.'

After sitting rigidly for long minutes, Hampton suddenly couldn't keep still. He got up and paced. 'I know something of the ritual he must have used. It would only work for a master, a Bocor of the first rank. The ancient gods wouldn't have answered a less powerful sorcerer. To do this thing, the Bocor must first dig a pit in the earth. It's shaped somewhat like a meteor crater, sloping to a depth of two or three feet. The Bocor recites certain chants . . . uses certain herbs . . . And he pours three types of blood into the hole – cat, rat, and human. As he sings a final and very long incantation, the bottom of the pit is miraculously transformed. In a sense . . . in a way that is impossible to explain or understand, the pit becomes far deeper than two or three feet; it interfaces with the Gates of Hell and becomes a sort of highway between this world and the Underworld. Heat rises from the pit, as does the stench of Hell, and the bottom of it appears to become molten. When the Bocor finally summons the entities he wants, they pass out through the Gates and then up through the bottom of the pit. On their way, these spiritual beings acquire physical bodies, golem bodies composed of the earth through which they pass; clay bodies that are nevertheless flexible and fully animated and *alive*. From your vivid descriptions of the creatures you've seen tonight, I'd say they were the incarnations of minor demons and of evil men, once mortal, who were condemned to Hell and are its lowest residents. Major demons and the ancient evil gods themselves would be considerably larger, more vicious, more powerful, and infinitely more hideous in appearance.'

'Oh, these damned things were plenty hideous enough,' Jack assured him.

'But, supposedly, there are many Ancient Ones whose physical forms are so repulsive that the mere act of looking at them results in instant death for he who sees,' Hampton said, pacing.

Jack sipped his brandy. He needed it.

'Furthermore,' Hampton said, 'the small size of these beasts would seem to support my belief that the Gates are currently open only a crack. The gap is too narrow to allow the major demons and the dark gods to slip out.'

'Thank God for that.'

'Yes,' Carver Hampton agreed. 'Thank *all* the benevolent gods for that.'

5

Penny and Davey were still asleep. The night was lonely without their company.

The windshield wipers flogged the snow off the glass.

The wind was so fierce that it rocked the sedan and forced Rebecca to grip the steering wheel more firmly than she had done before.

Then something made a noise beneath the car. *Thump, thump.* It knocked against the undercarriage hard enough to startle her, though not loud enough to wake the kids.

And again. *Thump, thump.*

She glanced in the rearview mirror, trying to see if she'd run over anything. But the car's back window was partially frosted, limiting her view, and the tyres churned up plumes of snow so thick that they cast everything behind the car into obscurity.

She nervously scanned the lighted instrument panel in the dashboard, but she couldn't see any indication of trouble. Oil, fuel, alternator, battery – all seemed in good shape; no warning lights, no plunging needles on the gauges. The car continued to purr along through the blizzard. Apparently, the disconcerting noise hadn't been related to a mechanical problem.

She drove half a block without a recurrence of the sound, then an entire block, then another one. She began to relax.

Okay, okay, she told herself. Don't be so damned jumpy. Stay calm and be cool. That's what the situation calls for. Nothing's wrong now, and nothing's going to *go* wrong, either. I'm fine. The kids are fine. The car's fine.

Thump-thump-thump.

6

The gas flames licked the ceramic logs.

The blown-glass lamps glowed softly, and the candles flickered, and the special darkness of the night pressed against the windows.

'Why wouldn't those creatures bite me? Why can't Lavelle's sorcery harm me?'

'There can be only one answer,' Hampton said. 'A Bocor has no power whatsoever to harm a righteous man. The righteous are well-armoured.'

'What's that supposed to mean?'

'Just what I said. You're righteous, virtuous. You're a man whose soul bears the stains of only the most minor sins.'

'You've got to be kidding.'

'No. By the manner in which you've led your life, you've earned immunity to the dark powers, immunity to the curses and charms and spells of sorcerers like Lavelle. You cannot be touched.'

'That's just plain ridiculous,' Jack said, feeling uncomfortable in the role of a righteous man.

'Otherwise, Lavelle would have had you murdered by now.'

'I'm no angel.'

'I didn't say you were. Not a saint, either. Just a righteous man. That's good enough.'

'Nonsense. I'm not righteous or—'

'If you thought of yourself as righteous, that would be a sin – the sin of *self*-righteousness. Smugness, an unshakeable conviction of your own moral superiority, a self-satisfied blindness to your own faults – none of those qualities is descriptive of you.'

'You're beginning to embarrass me,' Jack said.

'You see? You aren't even guilty of the sin of excessive pride.'

Jack held up his brandy. 'What about this? I drink.'

'To excess?'

'No. But I swear and curse. I sure do my own share of that. I take the Lord's name in vain.'

'A very minor sin.'

'I don't attend church.'

'Church-going has nothing to do with righteousness. The only thing that really counts is how you treat your fellow human beings. Listen, let's pin this down; let's be absolutely sure this is why Lavelle can't touch you. Have you ever stolen from anyone?'

'No.'

'Have you ever cheated someone in a financial transaction?'

'I've always looked out for my own interests, been aggressive in that regard, but I don't believe I've ever cheated anyone.'

'In your official capacity, have you ever accepted a bribe?'

'No. You can't be a good cop if you've got your hand out.'

'Are you a gossip, a slanderer?'

'No. But forget about that small stuff.' He leaned forward in his armchair and locked eyes with Hampton and said, 'What about murder? I've killed two men. Can I kill two men and still be righteous? I don't think so. That strains your thesis more than a little bit.'

Hampton looked stunned but only for a moment. He blinked and said, 'Oh. I see. You mean that you killed them in the line of duty.'

'Duty is a cheap excuse, isn't it? Murder is murder. Right?'

'What crimes were these men guilty of?'

'The first was a murderer himself. He robbed a series of liquor stores and always shot the clerks. The second was a rapist. Twenty-two rapes in six months.'

'When you killed these men, was it necessary? Could you have apprehended them without resorting to a gun?'

'In both cases they started shooting first.'

Hampton smiled, and the hard lines of his battered face softened. 'Self-defence isn't a sin, Lieutenant.'

'Yeah? Then why'd I feel so dirty after I pulled the trigger? Both times. I felt soiled. Sick. Once in a while, I still have a nightmare about those men, bodies torn apart by bullets from my own revolver . . .'

'Only a righteous man, a very virtuous man, would feel remorse over the killing of two vicious animals like the men you shot down.'

Jack shook his head. He shifted in his chair, uncomfortable with this new vision of himself. 'I've always seen myself as a fairly average, ordinary guy. No worse and no better than most people. I figure I'm just about as open to temptation, just about as corrupt as the next joe. And in spite of everything you've said, I *still* see myself that way.'

'And you always will.' Hampton said. 'Humility is part of being a righteous man. But the point is, to deal with Lavelle, you don't have to *believe* you're really a righteous man; you just have to *be* one.'

'Fornication,' Jack said in desperation. 'That's a sin.'

'Fornication is a sin only if it is obsessive, adulterous, or an act of rape. An obsession is sinful because it violates the moral precept "All things in moderation". Are you obsessed with sex?'

'I like it a lot.'

'Obsessed?'

'No.'

'Adultery is a sin because it is a violation of the marriage vows, a betrayal of trust, and a conscious cruelty,' Hampton said. 'When your wife was alive, did you ever cheat on her?'

'Of course not. I was in love with Linda.'

'Before your marriage or after your wife's death, did you ever go to bed with somebody else's wife? No? Then you aren't guilty of either form of adultery, and I know you're incapable of rape.'

'I just can't buy this righteousness stuff, this idea that I'm one of the chosen or something. It makes me queasy. Look, I didn't cheat on Linda, but while we were married I saw other women who turned me on, and I fantasized, and I *wanted* them, even if I didn't do anything about it. My *thoughts* weren't pure.'

'Sin isn't in the thought but in the deed.'

'I am *not* a saintly character,' Jack said adamantly.

'As I told you, in order to find and stop Lavelle, you don't need to *believe* – you only need to *be*.'

7

Rebecca listened to the car with growing dread. Now, there were other sounds coming from the undercarriage, not just the odd thumping, but rattling and clanking and grating noises, as well. Nothing loud. But worrisome.

We're only safe as long as we keep moving.

She held her breath, expecting the engine to go dead at any moment.

Instead, the noises stopped again. She drove four blocks with only the normal sounds of the car and the overlaid moan and hiss of the storm wind.

But she didn't relax. She knew something was wrong, and she was sure it would start acting up again. Indeed, the silence, the anticipation, was almost worse than the strange noises.

Still psychically linked with the murderous creatures he had summoned from the pit, Lavelle drummed his heels on the mattress and clawed at the dark air. He was pouring sweat; the sheets were soaked; but he was not aware of that.

He could smell the Dawson children. They were very close. The time had almost come. Just minutes now. A short wait. And then the slaughter.

9

Jack finished his brandy, put the glass on the coffee table, and said, 'There's a big hole in your explanation.'

'And what's that?' Hampton asked.

'If Lavelle can't harm me because I'm a righteous man, then why can he hurt my kids? They're not wicked, for God's sake. They're not sinful little wretches. They're damned good kids.'

'In the view of the gods, children can't be considered righteous; they're simply innocent. Righteousness isn't something we're born with; it's a state of grace we achieve only through years of virtuous living. We become righteous people by consciously choosing good over evil in thousands of situations in our day-to-day lives.'

'Are you telling me that God – or all the benevolent gods, if you'd rather put it that way – protects the righteous but not the innocent?'

'Yes.'

'Innocent little children are vulnerable to Lavelle, but I'm not? That's outrageous, unfair, just plain wrong.'

'You have an overly keen sense of injustice, both real and imagined. That's because you're a righteous man.'

Now it was Jack who could no longer sit still. While Hampton slumped contentedly in an armchair, Jack paced in his bare feet.

'Arguing with you is goddamned frustrating!'

311

'This is my field, not yours. I'm a theologist, not legitimized by a degree from any university, but not merely an amateur, either. My mother and father were devout Roman Catholics. In finding my own beliefs I studied every religion, major and minor, before becoming convinced of the truth and efficacy of voodoo. It's the only creed that has always accommodated itself to other faiths; in fact, voodoo absorbs and uses elements from every religion with which it comes into contact. It is a synthesis of many doctrines that usually war against one another—everything from Christianity and Judaism to sun-worship and pantheism. I am a man of religion, Lieutenant, so it's to be expected that I'll tie you in knots on this subject.'

'But what about Rebecca, my partner? She was bitten by one of these creatures, but she's not, by God, a wicked or corrupt person.'

'There are degrees of goodness, of purity. One can be a good person and not yet truly righteous, just as one can be righteous and not yet be a saint. I've met Miss Chandler only once, yesterday. But from what I saw of her, I suspect she keeps her distance from people, that she has, to some degree, withdrawn from life.'

'She had a traumatic childhood. For a long time, she's been afraid to let herself love anyone or form any strong attachments.'

'There you have it,' Hampton said. 'One can't earn the favour of the *Rada* and be granted immunity to the powers of darkness if one withdraws from life and avoids a lot of those situations that call for a choice between good and evil, right and wrong. It is the making of those choices that enables you to achieve a state of grace.'

Jack was standing at the hearth, warming himself in the heat of the gas fire – until the leaping flames suddenly reminded him of the goblins' eye sockets. He turned away from the blaze. 'Just supposing I *am* a righteous man, how does that help me find Lavelle?'

312

'We must recite certain prayers,' Hampton said. 'And there's a purification ritual you must undergo. When you've done those things, the gods of *Rada* will show you the way to Lavelle.'

'Then let's not waste any more time. Come on. Let's get started.'

Hampton rose from his chair, a mountain of a man. 'Don't be too eager or too fearless. It's best to proceed with caution.'

Jack thought of Rebecca and the kids in the car, staying on the move to avoid being trapped by the goblins, and he said, 'Does it matter whether I'm cautious or reckless? I mean, Lavelle can't harm me.'

'It's true that the gods have provided you with protection from sorcery, from all the powers of darkness. Lavelle's skill as a Bocor won't be of any use to him. But that doesn't mean you're immortal. It doesn't mean you're immune to the dangers of *this* world. If Lavelle is willing to risk being caught for the crime, willing to risk standing trial, then he could still pick up a gun and blow your head off.'

10

Rebecca was on Fifth Avenue when the thumping and rattling in the car's undercarriage began again. It was louder this time, loud enough to wake the kids, And it wasn't just beneath them, any more; now, it was also coming from the front of the car, under the hood.

Davey stood up in back, holding on to the front seat, and Penny sat up straight and blinked the sleep out of her eyes and said, 'Hey, what's that noise?'

'I guess we're having some sort of mechanical trouble,' Rebecca said, although the car was running well enough.

'It's the goblins,' Davey said in a voice that was half filled with terror and half with despair.

'It can't be them,' Rebecca said.

Penny said, 'They're under the hood.'

'No,' Rebecca said. 'We've been moving around

steadily since we left the garage. There's no way they could have gotten into the car. No way.'

'Then they were there even in the garage,' Penny said.

'No. They'd have attacked us right there.'

'Unless,' Penny said, 'maybe they were afraid of Daddy.'

'Afraid he could stop them,' Davey said.

'Like he stopped the one that jumped on you,' Penny said to her brother, 'the one outside Aunt Faye's place.'

'Yeah. So maybe the goblins figured to hang under the car and just wait till we were alone.'

'Till Daddy wasn't here to protect us.'

Rebecca knew they were right. She didn't want to admit it, but she *knew*.

The clattering in the undercarriage and the thumping-rattling under the hood increased, became almost frantic.

'They're tearing things apart,' Penny said.

'They're gonna stop the car!' Davey said.

'They'll get in,' Penny said, 'They'll get in at us, and there's no way to stop them.'

'Stop it!' Rebecca said. 'We'll come out all right. They won't get us.'

On the dashboard, a red warning light came on. In the middle of it was the word OIL.

The car had ceased to be a sanctuary.

Now it was a trap.

'They won't get us. I swear they won't,' Rebecca said again, but she said it as much to convince herself as to reassure the children.

Their prospects for survival suddenly looked as bleak as the winter night around them.

Ahead, through the sheeting snow, less than a block away, St Patrick's Cathedral rose out of the raging storm, like some great ship on a cold night sea. It was a massive structure, covering one entire city block.

Rebecca wondered if voodoo devils would dare enter a church. Or were they like vampires in all the novels and movies? Did they shy away in terror and pain from the mere sight of a crucifix?

Another red warning light came on. The engine was overheating.

In spite of the two gleaming indicators on the instrument panel, she tramped on the accelerator, and the car surged forward. She angled across the lanes, toward the front of St. Patrick's.

The engine sputtered.

The cathedral offered small hope. Perhaps false hope. But it was the only hope they had.

11

The ritual of purification required total immersion in water prepared by the Houngon.

In Hampton's bathroom, Jack undressed. He was more than a little surprised by his own new-found faith in these bizarre voodoo practices. He expected to feel ridiculous as the ceremony began, but he didn't feel anything of the sort because he had *seen* those Hellborn creatures.

The bathtub was unusually long and deep. It occupied more than half the bathroom. Hampton said he'd had it installed expressly for ceremonial baths.

Chanting in an eerily breathless voice that sounded too delicate to be coming from a man of his size, reciting prayers and petitions in a patois of French and English and various African tribal languages, Hampton used a bar of green soap – Jack thought it was Irish Spring – to draw *vèvès* all over the inside of the tub. Then he filled it with hot water. To the water, he added a number of substances and items that he had brought upstairs from his shop: dried rose petals; three bunches of parsley; seven vine leaves; one ounce of orgeat, which is a syrup made from almonds, sugar, and orange blossoms; powdered orchid petals; seven drops of perfume; seven polished stones in seven colours, each from the shore of a different body of water in Africa; three coins; seven

315

ounces of sea water taken from within the territorial limits of Haiti; a pinch of gunpowder; a spoonful of salt; lemon oil; and several other materials.

When Hampton told him that the time had come, Jack stepped into the pleasantly scented bath. The water was almost too hot to bear, but he bore it. With steam rising around him, he sat down, pushed the coins and stones and other hard objects out of his way, then slid onto his tailbone, until only his head remained above the waterline.

Hampton chanted for a few seconds, then said, 'Totally immerse yourself and count to thirty before coming up for air.'

Jack closed his eyes, took a deep breath, and slid flat on his back, so that his entire body was submerged. He had counted only to ten when he began to feel a strange tingling from head to foot. Second by second, he felt somehow . . . *cleaner* . . . not just in body but in mind and spirit, as well. Bad thoughts, fear, tension, anger, despair – all were leeched out of him by the specially treated water.

He was getting ready to confront Lavelle.

12

The engine died.

A snowbank loomed.

Rebecca pumped the brakes, They were extremely soft, but they still worked, The car slid nose-first into the mounded snow, hitting with a *thunk* and a crunch, harder than she would have liked, but not hard enough to hurt anyone.

Silence.

They were in front of the main entrance to St. Patrick's.

Davey said, 'Something's inside the seat! It's coming through!'

'What?' Rebecca asked, baffled by his statement, turning to look at him.

He was standing behind Penny's seat, pressed up against it, but facing the other way, looking at the backrest of the rear seat where he had been sitting just a short while ago. Rebecca squinted past him and saw movement under the upholstery. She heard an angry, muffled snarling, too.

One of the goblins must have gotten into the trunk, It was chewing and clawing through the seat, burrowing toward the interior of the car.

'Quick,' Rebecca said. 'Come up here with us, Davey. We'll all go out through Penny's door, one after the other, real quick, and then straight into the church. Hurry.'

Making desperate wordless sounds, Davey climbed into the front seat, between Rebecca and Penny.

At the same moment, Rebecca felt something pushing at the floor boards under her feet. A second goblin was tearing its way into the car from that direction.

If there were only two of the beasts, and if both of them were busily engaged in boring holes into the car, they might not immediately realize that their prey was making a run for the cathedral. It was at least something to hope for; not much, but something.

At a signal from Rebecca, Penny flung open the door and went out, into the storm.

Heart hammering, gasping in shock when the bitterly cold wind hit her, Penny scrambled out of the car, slipped on the snowy pavement, almost fell, windmilled her arms, and somehow kept her balance. She expected a goblin to rush out from beneath the car, expected to feel teeth sinking through one of her boots and into her ankle, but nothing like that happened. The streetlamps, shrouded and dimmed by the storm, cast an eerie light like that in a nightmare. Penny's distorted shadow preceded her as she clambered up the ridge of snow that had been formed by passing ploughs. She struggled all the way to the top, panting, using her hands and knees and feet, getting snow in her face and under her gloves and inside her boots, and then she jumped down to the sidewalk, which was buried under a smooth blanket of virgin snow, and she headed toward the cathedral, never looking back, never, afraid of what she might see behind her, pursued (at least in her imagination) by all the monsters she had seen in the foyer of that brownstone apartment house earlier tonight. The cathedral steps were hidden under deep snow, but Penny grabbed the brass handrail and used it as a guide, stomped all the way up the steps, suddenly wondering if the doors would be unlocked at this late hour. Wasn't a cathedral always open? If it was locked now, they were dead. She went to the centre-most portal, gripped the handle, pulled, thought for a moment that it *was* locked, then realized it was just a very heavy door, seized the handle with both hands, pulled harder than before, opened the door, held it wide, turned and finally looked back the way she'd come.

Davey was two-thirds of the way up the steps, his breath puffing out of him in jets of frost-white steam. He looked so small and fragile. But he was going to make it.

Rebecca came down off the ridge of snow at the kerb, onto the sidewalk, stumbled, fell to her knees.

Behind her, two goblins reached the top of the piled-up snow.

Penny screamed. 'They're coming! Hurry!'

When Rebecca fell to her knees, she heard Penny scream, and she got up at once, but she took only one step before the two goblins dashed past her, Jesus, as fast as the wind, a lizard-thing and a cat-thing, both of them screeching. They didn't attack her, didn't nip at her or hiss, didn't even pause. They weren't interested in her at all; they just wanted the kids.

Davey was at the cathedral door now, standing with Penny, and both of them were shouting at Rebecca.

The goblins reached the steps and climbed half of them in what seemed like a fraction of a second, but then they abruptly slowed down, as if they had realized they were rushing toward a holy place, although that realization didn't stop them altogether. They crept slowly and cautiously from step to step, sinking half out of sight in the snow.

Rebecca yelled at Penny – 'Get in the church and close the door!' – but Penny hesitated, apparently hoping that Rebecca would somehow make it past the goblins and get to safety herself (if the cathedral actually *was* safe), but even at their slower pace the goblins were almost to the top of the steps. Rebecca yelled again. And again Penny hesitated. Now, moving slower by the second, the goblins were within one step of the top, only a few feet away from Penny and Davey . . . and now they *were* at the top, and Rebecca was shouting frantically, and at last Penny pushed Davey into the cathedral. She followed her brother and stood just inside the door for a moment, holding it open, peering out. Moving slower still, but still moving, the goblins headed for the door. Rebecca wondered if maybe these creatures *could* enter a church when the door was held open for them, just as (according to legend) a vampire could enter a house only if invited or if someone held the door for him. It was probably crazy to think the same rules that supposedly governed mythical vampires would apply to these very *real* voodoo devils.

Nevertheless, with new panic in her voice, Rebecca shouted at Penny again, and she ran halfway up the steps because she thought maybe the girl couldn't hear her above the wind, and she screamed at the top of her voice, 'Don't worry about me! Close the door! Close the door!' And finally Penny closed it, although reluctantly, just as the goblins arrived at the threshold.

The lizard-thing threw itself at the door, rebounded from it, and rolled onto its feet again.

The cat-thing wailed angrily.

Both creatures scratched at the portal, but neither of them showed any determination, as if they knew that, for them, this was too great a task. Opening a cathedral door – opening the door to *any* holy place – required far greater power than they possessed.

Frustrated, they turned away from the door. Looked at Rebecca. Their fiery eyes seemed brighter than the eyes of the other creatures she had seen at the Jamisons' and in the foyer of that brownstone apartment house.

She backed down one step.

The goblins started toward her.

She descended all the other steps, stopping only when she reached the sidewalk.

The lizard-thing and the cat-thing stood at the top of the steps, glaring at her.

Torrents of wind and snow raced along Fifth Avenue, and the snow was falling so heavily that it almost seemed she would drown in it as surely as she would have drowned in an onrushing flood.

The goblins descended one step.

Rebecca backed up until she encountered the ridge of snow at the kerb.

The goblins descended a second step, a third.

CHAPTER EIGHT

1

The bath of purification lasted only two minutes. Jack dried himself on three small, soft, highly absorbent towels which had strange runes embroidered in the corners they were of a material not quite like anything he had ever seen before.

When he had dressed, he followed Carver Hampton into the living room and, at the Houngon's direction, stood in the centre of the room, where the light was brightest.

Hampton began a long chant, holding an *asson* over Jack's head, then slowly moving it down the front of him, then around behind him and up along his spine to the top of his head, once more.

Hampton had explained that the *asson* – a gourd rattle made from a calabash plucked from a liana of a *calebassier courant* tree – was the symbol of office of the Houngon. The gourd's natural shape provided a convenient handle. Once hollowed out, the bulbous end was filled with eight stones in eight colours because that number represented the concept of eternity and life everlasting. The vertebrae of snakes were included with the stones, for they were symbolic of the bones of ancient ancestors who, now in the spirit world, might be called upon for help. The *asson* was also ringed with brightly coloured porcelain beads. The beads, stones, and snake vertebrae produced an unusual but not unpleasant sound.

Hampton shook the rattle over Jack's head, then in front of his face. For almost a minute, singing hypnotically in some long-dead African language, he shook the *asson* over Jack's heart. He used it to draw figures in the air over each of Jack's hands and over each of his feet.

Gradually, Jack became aware of numerous appealing odours. First, he detected the scent of lemons. Then crysanthemums. Magnolia blossoms. Each fragrance commanded his attention for a few seconds, until the air currents brought him a new odour. Oranges. Roses. Cinnamon. The scents grew more intense by the second. They blended together in a wonderfully harmonious fashion. Strawberries. Chocolate. Hampton hadn't lit any sticks of incense; he hadn't opened any bottles of perfume or essences. The fragrances seemed to occur spontaneously, without source, without reason. Black walnuts. Lilacs.

When Hampton finished chanting, when he put down the *asson*, Jack said, 'Those terrific smells – where are they coming from?'

'They're the olfactory equivalents of visual apparitions,' Hampton said.

Jack blinked at him, not sure he understood. 'Apparitions? You mean . . . *ghosts*?'

'Yes. Spirits. Benign spirits.'

'But I don't see them.'

'You're not meant to see them. As I told you, they haven't materialized visually. They've manifested themselves as fragrances, which isn't an unheard of phenomenon.'

Mint.

Nutmeg.

'Benign spirits,' Hampton repeated, smiling. 'The room is filled with them, and that's a very good sign. They're messengers of the *Rada*. Their arrival here, at this time, indicates that the benevolent gods support you in your battle against Lavelle.'

'Then I'll find Lavelle and stop him?' Jack asked. 'Is that what this means – that I'll win out in the end? Is it all predetermined?'

'No, no,' Hampton said. 'Not at all. This means only that you've got the support of the *Rada*. But Lavelle has the support of the dark gods. The two of you are instruments of higher forces. One will win, and one will lose; that's all that's predetermined.'

In the corners of the room, the candle flames shrank until they were only tiny sparks at the tips of the wicks. Shadows sprang up and writhed as if they were alive. The windows vibrated, and the building shook in the grip of a sudden, tremendous wind. A score of books flew off the shelves and crashed to the floor.

'We have evil spirits with us, as well,' Hampton said.

In addition to the pleasant fragrances that filled the

room, a new odour assaulted Jack. It was the stench of corruption, rot, decay, death.

2

The goblins had descended all but the last two of the cathedral steps. They were within only a dozen feet of Rebecca.

She turned and bolted away from them.

They shrieked with what might have been anger or glee or both – or neither. A cold, alien cry.

Without looking back, she knew they were coming after her.

She ran along the sidewalk, the cathedral at her right side, heading toward the corner, as if she intended to flee to the next block, but that was only a ruse. After she'd gone ten yards, she made a sharp right turn, toward the cathedral, and mounted the steps in a snow-kicking frenzy.

The goblins squealed.

She was halfway up the steps when the lizard-thing snared her left leg and sank claws through her jeans, into her right calf. The pain was excruciating.

She screamed, stumbled, fell on the steps. But she continued upward, crawling on her belly, with the lizard hanging on her leg.

The cat-thing leaped onto her back. Clawed at her heavy coat. Moved quickly to her neck. Tried to nip her throat. It got only a mouthful of coat collar and knitted scarf.

She was at the top of the steps.

Whimpering, she grabbed the cat-thing and tore it loose.

It bit her hand.

She pitched it away.

The lizard was still on her leg. It bit her thigh a couple of inches above her knee.

She reached down, clutched it, was bitten on the other

323

hand. But she ripped the lizard loose and pitched it down the steps.

Eyes shining silver-white, the cat-form goblin was already coming back at her, squalling, a windmill of teeth and claws.

Energized by desperation, Rebecca gripped the brass handrail and lurched to her feet in time to kick out at the cat. Fortunately, the kick connected solidly, and the goblin tumbled end over end through the snow.

The lizard rushed toward her again.

There was no end to it. She couldn't possibly keep both of them at bay. She was tired, weak, dizzy, and wracked with pain from her wounds.

She turned and, trying hard to ignore the pain that flashed like an electric current through her leg, she flung herself toward the door through which Penny and Davey had entered the cathedral.

The lizard-thing caught the bottom of her coat, climbed up, around her side, onto the front of the coat, clearly intending to go for her face this time.

The catlike goblin was back, too, grabbing at her foot, squirming up her leg.

She reached the door, put her back to it.

She was at the end of her resources, heaving each breath in and out as if it were an iron ingot.

This close to the cathedral, right up against the wall of it, the goblins became sluggish, as she had hoped they would, just as they had done when pursuing Penny and Davey. The lizard, its claws hooked in the front of her coat, let go with one deformed hand and swiped at her face. But the creature was no longer too fast for her. She jerked her head back in time and felt the claws trace only light scratches on the underside of her chin. She was able to pull the lizard off without being bitten; she threw it as hard as she could, out toward the street. She pried the cat-thing off her leg, too, and pitched it away from her.

Turning quickly, she yanked open the door, slipped

inside St Patrick's Cathedral, and pushed the door shut after her.

The goblins thumped against the other side of it, once, and then were silent.

She was safe. Amazingly, thankfully safe.

She limped away from the door, out of the dimly lighted vestibule in which she found herself, past the marble holy water fonts, into the vast, vaulted, massively-columned nave with its rows and rows of polished pews. The towering stained-glass windows were dark and sombre with only night beyond them, except in a few places where an errant beam from a streetlamp outside managed to find and pierce a cobalt blue or brilliant red piece of glass. Everything here was big and solid-looking – the huge pipe organ with its thousands of brass pipes soaring up like the spires of a smaller cathedral, the great choir loft above the front portals, the stone steps leading up to the high pulpit and the brass canopy above it – and that massiveness contributed to the feeling of safety and peace that settled over Rebecca.

Penny and Davey were in the nave, a third of the way down the centre aisle, talking excitedly to a young and baffled priest. Penny saw Rebecca first, shouted, and ran toward her. Davey followed, crying with relief and happiness at the sight of her, and the cassocked priest came, too.

They were the only four in the immense chamber, but that was all right. They didn't need an army. The cathedral was an inviolable fortress. Nothing could harm them there. Nothing. The cathedral was safe. It *had* to be safe, for it was their last refuge.

3

In the car in front of Carver Hampton's shop, Jack pumped the accelerator and raced the engine, warming it.

325

He looked sideways at Hampton and said, 'You sure you really want to come along?'

'It's the last thing I want to do,' the big man said. 'I don't share your immunity to Lavelle's powers. I'd much rather stay up there in the apartment, with all the lights on and the candles burning.'

'Then stay. I don't believe you're hiding anything from me. I really believe you've done everything you can. You don't owe me anything more.'

'I owe *me*. Going with you, helping you if I can – that's the right thing to do. I owe it to myself not to make another wrong choice.'

'All right then.' Jack put the car in gear but kept his foot on the brake pedal. 'I'm still not sure I understand how I'm going to find Lavelle.'

'You'll simply *know* what streets to follow, what turns to make,' Hampton said. 'Because of the purification bath and the other rituals we performed, you're now being guided by a higher power.'

'Sounds better than a Three-A map, I guess. Only . . . I sure don't feel anything guiding me.'

'You will, Lieutenant. But first, we've got to stop at a Catholic church and fill these jars' – he held up two small, empty jars that would hold about eight ounces each —'with holy water. There's a church straight ahead, about five blocks from here.'

'Fine,' Jack said. 'But one thing.'

'What's that?'

'Will you drop the formality, stop calling me Lieutenant? My name's Jack.'

'You can call me Carver, if you like.'

'I'd like.'

They smiled at each other, and Jack took his foot off the brake, switched on the windshield wipers, and pulled out into the street.

They entered the church together.

The vestibule was dark. In the deserted nave there

were a few dim lights burning, plus three or four votive candles flickering in a wrought iron rack that stood on this side of the communion railing and to the left of the chancel. The place smelled of incense and furniture polish that had evidently been used recently on the well-worn pews. Above the altar, a large crucifix rose high into the shadows.

Carver genuflected and crossed himself. Although Jack wasn't a practising Catholic, he felt a sudden strong compulsion to follow the black man's example, and he realized that, as a representative of the *Rada* on this special night, it was incumbent upon him to pay obeisance to all the gods of good and light, whether it was the Jewish god of the old testament, Christ, Buddha, Mohammed, or any other deity. Perhaps this was the first indication of the 'guidance' of which Carver had spoken.

The marble font, just this side of the narthex, contained only a small puddle of holy water.

'We won't even be able to fill one jar,' Jack said.

'Don't be so sure,' Carver said, unscrewing the lid from one of the containers. He handed the open jar to Jack. 'Try it.'

Jack dipped the jar into the font, scraped it along the marble, scooped up some water, didn't think he'd gotten more than two ounces, and blinked in surprise when he held the jar up and saw that it was full. He was even more surprised to see just as much water left in the font as had been there before he'd filled the jar.

He looked at Carver.

The black man smiled and winked. He screwed the lid on the jar and put it in his coat pocket. He opened the second jar and handed it to Jack.

Again, Jack was able to fill the container, and again the small puddle of water in the font appeared untouched.

4

Lavelle stood by the window, looking out at the storm.

He was no longer in psychic contact with the small assassins. Given more time, time to marshal their forces, they might yet be able to kill the Dawson children, and if they did he would be sorry he'd missed it. But time was running out.

Jack Dawson was coming, and no sorcery, regardless of how powerful it might be, would stop him.

Lavelle wasn't sure how everything had gone wrong so quickly, so completely. Perhaps it had been a mistake to target the children. The *Rada* was always incensed at a Bocor who used his power against children, and they always tried to destroy him if they could. Once committed to such a course, you had to be extremely careful. But, damnit, he *had* been careful. He couldn't think of a single mistake he might have made, He was well armoured; he was protected by all the power of the dark gods.

Yet Dawson was coming.

Lavelle turned away from the window.

He crossed the dark room to the dresser.

He took a .32 automatic out of the top drawer.

Dawson was coming. Fine. Let him come.

5

Rebecca sat down in the aisle of the cathedral and pulled up the right leg of her jeans, above her knee. The claw and fang wounds were bleeding freely, but she was in no danger of bleeding to death. The jeans had provided some protection. The bites were deep but not too deep. No major veins or arteries had been severed.

The young priest, Father Walotsky, crouched beside her, appalled by her injuries. 'How did this happen? What did this to you?'

Both Penny and Davey said, '*Goblins*', as if they were getting tired of trying to make him understand.

Rebecca pulled off her gloves. On her right hand was a fresh, bleeding bite mark, but no flesh was torn away; it was just four small puncture wounds. The gloves, like her jeans, had provided at least some protection. Her left hand bore two bite marks; one was bleeding and seemed no more serious than the wound on her right hand, painful but not mortal, while the other was the old bite she'd received in front of Faye's apartment building.

Father Walotsky said, 'What's all that blood on your neck?' He put a hand to her face, gently pressed her head back, so he could see the scratches under her chin.

'Those're minor,' she said. 'They sting, but they're not serious.' 'I think we'd better get you some medical attention,' he said. 'Come on.'

She pulled down the leg of her jeans.

He helped her to her feet. 'I think it would be all right if I took you to the rectory.'

'No,' she said.

'It's not far.'

'We're staying here,' she said.

'But those look like animal bites. You've got to have them attended to. Infection, rabies . . . Look, its not far to the rectory. We don't have to go out in the storm, either. There's an underground passage between the cathedral and—'

'No,' Rebecca said firmly. 'We're staying here, in the cathedral, where we're protected.'

She motioned for Penny and Davey to come close to her, and they did, eagerly, one on each side of her.

The priest looked at each of them, studied their faces, met their eyes, and his face darkened, 'What *are* you afraid of?'

'Didn't the kids tell you some of it?' Rebecca asked.

'They were babbling about goblins, but—'

'It wasn't just babble,' Rebecca said, finding it odd to be the one professing and defending a belief in the supernatural, she who had always been anything *but* excessively open-minded on the subject. She hesitated. Then, as succinctly as possible, she told him about Lavelle, the slaughter of the Carramazzas, and the voodoo devils that were now after Jack Dawson's children.

When she finished, the priest said nothing and couldn't meet her eyes. He stared at the floor for long seconds.

She said, 'Of course, you don't believe me.'

He looked up and appeared to be embarrassed. 'Oh, I don't think you're lying to me . . . exactly. I'm sure *you* believe everything you've told me. But, to me, voodoo is a sham, a set of primitive superstitions. I'm a priest of the Holy Roman Church, and I believe in only one Truth, the Truth that Our Saviour—'

'You believe in Heaven, don't you? And Hell?'

'Of course. That's part of Catholic—'

'These things have come straight up from Hell, Father. If I'd told you that it was a *Satanist* who had summoned these demons, if I'd never mentioned the word voodoo, then maybe you still wouldn't have believed me, but you wouldn't have dismissed the possibility so fast, either, because your religion encompasses Satan and Satanists.'

'I think you should—'

Davey screamed.

Penny said, 'They're here!'

Rebecca turned, breath caught in her throat, heart hanging in mid-beat.

Beyond the archway through which the centre aisle of the nave entered the vestibule, there were shadows, and in those shadows were silver-white eyes glowing brightly. Eyes of fire. Lots of them.

6

Jack drove the snow-packed streets, and as he approached each intersection, he somehow sensed when a right turn was required, when he should go left instead, and when he should just speed straight through. He didn't know *how* he sensed those things; each time, a feeling came over him, a feeling he couldn't put into words, and he gave himself to it, followed the guidance that was being given to him. It was certainly unorthodox procedure for a cop accustomed to employing less exotic techniques in the search for a suspect. It was also creepy, and he didn't like it. But he wasn't about to complain, for he desperately wanted to find Lavelle.

Thirty-five minutes after they collected the two small jars of holy water, Jack made a left turn into a street of pseudo-Victorian houses. He stopped in front of the fifth one. It was a three-storey brick house with lots of gingerbread trim. It was in need of repairs and painting, as were all the houses in the block, a fact that even the snow and darkness couldn't hide. There were no lights in the house; not one. The windows were perfectly black.

'We're here,' Jack told Carver.

He cut the engine, switched off the headlights.

7

Four goblins crept out of the vestibule, into the centre aisle, into the light that, while not bright, revealed their grotesque forms in more stomach-churning detail than Rebecca would have liked.

At the head of the pack was a foot-tall, man-form creature with four fire-filled eyes, two in its forehead. Its head was the size of an apple, and in spite of the four eyes, most of the misshapen skull was given over to a mouth crammed full and bristling with teeth. It also had four arms and was carrying a crude spear in one spike-fingered hand.

It raised the spear above its head in a gesture of challenge and defiance.

Perhaps because of the spear, Rebecca was suddenly possessed of a strange but unshakeable conviction that the man-form beast had once been – in very ancient times – a proud and bloodthirsty African Warrior who had been condemned to Hell for his crimes and who was now forced to endure the agony and humiliation of having his soul embedded within a small, deformed body.

The man-form goblin, the three even more hideous creatures behind it, and the other beasts moving through the dark vestibule (and now seen only as pairs of shining eyes) all moved slowly, as if the very air inside this house of worship was, for them, an immensely heavy burden that made every step a painful labour. None of them hissed or snarled or shrieked, either. They just approached silently, sluggishly, but implacably.

Beyond the goblins, the doors to the street still appeared to be closed. They had entered the cathedral by some other route, through a vent or a drain that was unscreened and offered them an easy entrance, a virtual invitation, the equivalent of the 'open door' that they, like vampires, probably needed in order to come where evil wasn't welcome.

Father Walotsky, briefly mesmerized by his first glimpse of the goblins, was the first to break the silence. He fumbled in a pocket of his black cassock, withdrew a rosary, and began to pray.

The man-form devil and the three things immediately behind it moved steadily closer, along the main aisle, and other monstrous beings crept and slithered out of the dark vestibule, while new pairs of glowing eyes appeared in the darkness there. They still moved too slowly to be dangerous.

But how long will that last? Rebecca wondered. Perhaps they'll somehow become conditioned to the atmosphere in the cathedral. Perhaps they'll gradually become bolder and begin to move faster. What then?

Pulling the kids with her, Rebecca began to back up the aisle, toward the altar. Father Walotsky came with them, the rosary beads clicking in his hands.

8

They slogged through the snow to the foot of the steps that led up to Lavelle's front door.

Jack's revolver was already in his hand. To Carver Hampton, he said, 'I wish you'd wait in the car.'

'No.'

'This is police business.'

'It's more than that. You know it's more than that.'

Jack sighed and nodded.

They climbed the steps.

Obtaining an arrest warrant, pounding on the door, announcing his status as an officer of the law – none of that usual procedure seemed necessary or sensible to Jack. Not in this bizarre situation. Still, he wasn't comfortable or happy about just barging into a private residence.

Carver tried the doorknob, twisted it back and forth several times. 'Locked.'

Jack could see that it was locked, but something told him to try it for himself. The knob turned under his hand, and the latch clicked softly, and the door opened a crack.

'Locked for me,' Carver said, 'but not for you.'

They stepped aside, out of the line of fire.

Jack reached out, pushed the door open hard, and snatched his hand back.

But Lavelle didn't shoot.

They waited ten or fifteen seconds, and the snow blew in through the open door. Finally, crouching, Jack moved into the doorway and crossed the threshold, his gun thrust out in front of him.

The house was exceptionally dark. Darkness would work to Lavelle's advantage, for he was familiar with the place, while it was all strange territory to Jack.

He fumbled for the light switch and found it.

He was in a broad entrance hall. To the left were in-laid oak stairs with an ornate railing. Directly ahead, beyond the stairs, the hall narrowed and led all the way to the rear of the house. A couple of feet ahead and to the right, there was an archway, beyond which lay more darkness.

333

Jack edged to the brink of the arch. A little light spilled in from the hall, but it showed him only a section of bare floor. He supposed it was a living room.

He reached awkwardly around the corner, trying to present a slim profile, feeling for another light switch, found and flipped it. The switch operated a ceiling fixture; light filled the room. But that was just about the only thing in it – light. No furniture. No drapes. A film of grey dust, a few balls of dust in the corners, a lot of light, and four bare walls.

Carver moved up beside Jack and whispered. 'Are you sure this is the right place?'

As Jack opened his mouth to answer, he felt something whiz past his face and, a fraction of a second later, he heard two loud shots, fired from behind him. He dropped to the floor, rolled out of the hall, into the living room.

Carver dropped and rolled, too. But he had been hit. His face was contorted by pain. He was clutching his left thigh, and there was blood on his trousers.

'He's on the stairs,' Carver said raggedly 'I got a glimpse.'

'Must've been upstairs, then came down behind us.'

'Yeah.'

Jack scuttled to the wall beside the archway, crouched there. 'You hit bad?'

'Bad enough,' Carver said. 'Won't kill me, though. You just worry about getting him.'

Jack leaned around the archway and squeezed off a shot right away, at the staircase, without bothering to look or aim first.

Lavelle was there. He was halfway down the final flight of stairs, hunkered behind the railing.

Jack's shot tore a chunk out of the bannister two feet from the Bocor's head.

Lavelle returned the fire, and Jack ducked back, and shattered plaster exploded from the edge of the archway.

Another shot.

Then silence.

Jack leaned out into the archway again and pulled off three shots in rapid succession, aiming at where Lavelle had been, but Lavelle was already on his way upstairs, and all three shots missed him, and then he was out of sight.

Pausing to reload his revolver with the loose bullets he carried in one coat pocket, Jack glanced at Carver and said, 'Can you make it out to the car on your own?'

'No. Can't walk with this leg. But I'll be all right here. He only winged me. You just go get him.'

'We should call an ambulance for you.'

'*Just get him!*' Carver said.

Jack nodded, stepped through the archway, and went cautiously to the foot of the stairs.

9

Penny, Davey, Rebecca and Father Walotsky took refuge in the chancel, behind the altar railing. In fact, they climbed up onto the altar platform, directly beneath the crucifix.

The goblins stopped on the other side of the railing. Some of them peered between the ornate supporting posts. Others climbed onto the communion rail itself, perched there, eyes flickering hungrily, black tongues licking slowly back and forth across their sharp teeth.

There were fifty or sixty of them now, and more were still coming out of the vestibule, far back at the end of the main aisle.

'They w-won't come up here, w-w-will they?' Penny asked. 'Not this c-close to the crucifix. *Will they?*'

Rebecca hugged the girl and Davey, held them tight and close. She said, 'You can see they've stopped. It's all right. It's all right now. They're afraid of the altar. They've stopped.'

But for how long? she wondered.

Jack climbed the stairs with his back flat against the wall, moving sideways, trying to be utterly silent, nearly succeeding. He held his revolver in his left hand, with his arm rigidly extended, aiming at the top of the steps, his aim never wavering as he ascended, so he'd be ready to pull the trigger the instant Lavelle appeared. He reached the landing without being shot at, climbed three steps of the second flight, and then Lavelle leaned out around the corner above, and both of them fired – Lavelle twice, Jack once.

Lavelle pulled the trigger without pausing to take aim, without even knowing exactly where Jack was. He just took a chance that two rounds, placed down the centre of the stairwell, would do the job. Both missed.

On the other hand, Jack's gun was aimed along the wall, and Lavelle leaned right into its line of fire. The slug smashed into his arm at the same moment he finished pulling the trigger of his own gun. He screamed, and the pistol flew out of his hand, and he stumbled back into the upstairs hall where he'd been hiding.

Jack took the stairs two at a time, jumping over Lavelle's pistol as it came tumbling down. He reached the second-floor hallway in time to see Lavelle enter a room and slam the door behind him.

Downstairs, Carver lay on the dust-filmed floor, eyes closed. He was too weary to keep his eyes open. He was growing wearier by the second.

He didn't feel like he was lying on a hard floor. He felt as if he were floating in a warm pool of water, somewhere in the tropics. He remembered being shot, remembered falling; he knew the floor really was there, under him, but he just couldn't feel it.

He figured he was bleeding to death. The wound didn't *seem* that bad, but maybe it was worse than he thought. Or maybe it was just the shock that made him feel this way. Yeah, that must be it, shock, just shock, not bleeding to death after all, just suffering from shock, but of course shock could kill, too.

Whatever the reasons, he floated, oblivious of his own pain, just bobbing up and down, drifting on the hard floor that wasn't hard at all, drifting on some far-away tropical tide . . . until, from upstairs, there was the sound of gunfire and a shrill scream that snapped his eyes open. He had an out-of-focus, floor-level view of the empty room. He blinked his eyes rapidly and squinted until his clouded vision cleared, and then he wished it *hadn't* cleared because he saw that he was no longer alone.

One of the denizens of the pit was with him, its eyes aglow.

Upstairs, Jack tried the door that Lavelle had slammed. It was locked, but the lock probably didn't amount to much, just a privacy set, flimsy as they could be made, because people didn't want to put heavy and expensive locks *inside* a house.

'Lavelle?' he shouted.

No answer.

'Open up. No use trying to hide in there.'

From inside the room came the sound of a shattering window.

'Shit,' Jack said.

He stepped back and kicked at the door, but there was more to the lock than he'd expected, and he had to kick it four times, as hard as he could, before he finally smashed it open.

He switched on the light. An ordinary bedroom. No sign of Lavelle.

The window in the opposite wall was broken out. Drapes billowed on the in-rushing wind.

Jack checked the closet first, just to be sure that this wasn't a bit of misdirection to enable Lavelle to get behind his back. But no one waited in the closet.

He went to the window. In the light that spilled past him, he saw footprints in the snow that covered the porch roof. They led out to the edge. Lavelle had jumped down to the yard below.

Jack squeezed through the window, briefly snagging his coat on a shard of glass, and went out onto the roof.

In the cathedral, approximately seventy or eighty goblins had come out of the vestibule. They were lined up on the communion rail and between the supporting posts under the rail. Behind them, other beasts slouched up the long aisle.

Father Walotsky was on his knees, praying, but he didn't seem to be doing any good, so far as Rebecca could see.

In fact, there were some bad signs. The goblins weren't as sluggish as they had been. Tails lashed. Mutant heads whipped back and forth. Tongues flickered faster than before.

Rebecca wondered if they could, through shear numbers, overcome the benign power that held sway within the cathedral and that had, so far, prevented them from attacking. As each of the demonic creatures entered, it brought its own measure of malignant energy. If the balance of power tipped in the other direction . . .

One of the goblins hissed. They had been perfectly silent since entering the cathedral, but now one of them hissed, and then another, and then three more, and in seconds all of them were hissing angrily.

Another bad sign.

Carver Hampton.

When he saw the demonic entity in the hallway, the floor suddenly seemed a bit more solid to him. His heart began to pound, and the real world came swimming back to him out of the tropical hallucination – although

338

this part of the real world contained, at this time, something from a nightmare.

The thing in the hall skittered toward the open arch and the living room. From Carver's perspective, it looked enormous, at least his own size, but he realized it wasn't really as large as it seemed from his peculiar floor-level point of view. But big enough. Oh, yes. Its head was the size of his fist. Its sinous, segmented, wormlike body was half again as long as his arm. Its crablike legs ticked against the wooden floor. The only features on its misshapen head were an ugly suckerlike mouth full of teeth and those haunting eyes of which Jack Dawson had spoken, those eyes of silver-white fire.

Carver found the strength to move. He hitched himself backwards across the floor, gasping in exhaustion and wincing with rediscovered pain, leaving a trail of blood in his wake. He came up against the wall almost at once, startling himself; he'd thought the room was bigger than that.

With a thin, high-pitched keening, the worm-thing came through the archway and scurried toward him.

When Lavelle jumped off the porch roof, he didn't land on his feet. He slipped in the snow and crashed onto his wounded arm. The explosion of pain almost blew him into unconsciousness.

He couldn't understand why everything had gone so wrong. He was confused and angry. He felt naked, powerless; that was a new feeling for him. He didn't like it.

He crawled a few feet through the snow before he could find the strength to stand, and when he stood he heard Dawson shouting at him from the edge of the porch roof. He didn't stop, didn't wait passively to be captured, not Baba Lavelle the great Bocor. He headed across the rear lawn toward the storage shed.

His source of power lay beyond the pit, with the dark

gods on the other side. He would demand to know why they were failing him. He would demand their aid.

Dawson fired one shot, but it must have been just a warning because it didn't come anywhere close to Lavelle.

The wind battered him and threw snow in his face, and with blood pouring out of his shattered arm he wasn't easily able to resist the storm, but he stayed on his feet and reached the shed and pulled open the door – and cried out in shock when he saw that the pit had grown. It now occupied the entire small building, from one corrugated wall to the other, and the light coming from it wasn't orange any longer but blood-red and so bright it hurt his eyes.

Now he knew why his malevolent benefactors were letting him go down to defeat. They had allowed him to use them only as long as they could use him, in turn. He had been their conduit to this world, a means by which they could reach out and claw at the living. But now they had something better than a conduit; now they had a doorway to this plane of existence, a *real* doorway that would permit them to leave the Underworld. And it was thanks to him that they'd been given it. He had opened the Gates just a crack, confident that he could hold them to that narrow and insignificant breach, but he had lost control without knowing it, and now the Gates were surging wide. The Ancient Ones were coming. They were on their way. They were almost here. When they arrived, Hell would have relocated to the surface of the earth.

In front of his feet, the rim of the pit was continuing to crumble inward, faster and faster.

Lavelle stared in horror at the beating heart of hate-light within the pit. He saw something dark at the bottom of that intense red glow. It rippled. It was huge. And it was rising toward him.

Jack jumped from the roof, landed on both feet in the

snow, and started after Lavelle. He was halfway across the lawn when Lavelle opened the door to the corrugated metal shed. The brilliant and eerie crimson light that poured forth was sufficient to stop Jack in his tracks.

It was the pit, of course, just as Carver had described it. But it surely wasn't as small as it was supposed to be, and the light wasn't soft and orange. Carver's worst fear was coming true: the Gates of Hell were swinging open all the way.

As that mad thought struck Jack, the pit suddenly grew larger than the shed that had once contained it. The corrugated metal walls fell away into the void. Now there was only a hole in the ground. Like a giant searchlight, the red beams from the pit speared up into the dark and storm-churned sky.

Lavelle staggered back a few steps, but he was evidently too terrified to be able to turn and run.

The earth trembled.

Within the pit, something roared. It had a voice that shook the night.

The air stank of sulphur.

Something snaked up from the depths. It was like a tentacle but not exactly a tentacle, like a chitinous insect leg but not exactly an insect leg, sharply jointed in several places and yet as sinuous as a serpent. It soared up to a height of fifteen feet. The tip of the thing was equipped with long whiplike appendages that writhed around a loose, drooling, toothless mouth large enough to swallow a man whole. Worse, it was in some ways exceedingly clear that this was only a minor feature of the huge beast rising from the Gates; it was as small, proportionately, as a human finger compared to an entire human body. Perhaps this was the only thing that the escaping Lovecraftian entity has thus far been able to estrude between the opening Gates – this one finger.

The giant, insectile, tentacular limb bent toward Lavelle. The whiplike appendages at the tip lashed out, snared him, and lifted him off the ground, into the blood-red light. He screamed and flailed, but he could do nothing to prevent himself from being drawn into that obscene, drooling mouth. And then he was gone.

In the cathedral, the last of the goblins had reached the communion railing. At least a hundred of them turned blazing eyes on Rebecca, Penny, Davey and Father Walotsky.

Their hissing was now augmented with an occasional snarl.

Suddenly the four-eyed, four-armed manlike demon leaped off the rail, into the chancel. It took a few tentative steps forward and looked from side to side; there was an air of wariness about it. Then it raised its tiny spear, shook it, and shrieked.

Immediately, all of the other goblins shrieked, too.

Another one dared to enter the chancel.

Then a third. Then four more.

Rebecca glanced sideways, toward the sacristy door. But it was no use running in there. The goblins would only follow. The end had come at last.

The worm-thing reached Carver Hampton where he sat on the floor, his back pressed to the wall. It reared up, until half its disgusting body was off the floor.

He looked into those bottomless, fiery eyes and knew that he was too weak a Houngon to protect himself.

Then, out behind the house, something roared; it sounded enormous and very much alive.

The earth quaked, and the house rocked, and the worm-demon seemed to lose interest in Carver. It turned half away from him and moved its head from side to side, began to sway to some music that Carver could not hear.

With a sinking heart, he realized what had temporarily enthralled the thing: the sound of other Hell-trapped souls screeching toward a long-desired freedom, the

342

triumphant ululation of the Ancient Ones at last breaking their bonds.

The end had come.

Jack advanced to the edge of the pit. The rim was dissolving, and the hole was growing larger by the second. He was careful not to stand at the very brink.

The fierce red glow made the snowflakes look like whirling embers. But now there were shafts of bright white light mixed in with the red, the same silvery-white as the goblins' eyes, and Jack was sure this meant the Gates were opening dangerously far.

The monstrous appendage, half insectile and half like a tentacle, swayed above him threateningly, but he knew it couldn't touch him. Not yet, anyway. Not until the Gates were all the way open. For now, the benevolent gods of *Rada* still possessed some power over the earth, and he was protected by them.

He took the jar of holy water from his coat pocket. He wished he had Carver's jar, as well, but this would have to do. He unscrewed the lid and threw it aside.

Another menacing shape was rising from the depths. He could see it, a vague dark presence rushing up through the nearly blinding light, howling like a thousand dogs.

He had accepted the reality of Lavelle's black magic and of Carver's white magic, but now he suddenly was able to do more than accept it; he was able to understand it in concrete terms, and he knew he now understood it better than Lavelle or Carver ever had or ever would. He looked into the pit and he *knew*. Hell was not a mythical place, and there was nothing supernatural about demons and gods, nothing holy or unholy about them. Hell – and consequently Heaven – were as real as the earth; they were merely other dimensions, other planes of physical existence. Normally, it was impossible for a living man or woman to cross over from one plane to the other. But religion was the crude and clumsy science that had theorized ways in which to bring the planes together, if only temporarily, and magic was the tool of that science.

After absorbing that realization, it seemed as easy to believe in voodoo or Christianity or any other religion as it was to believe in the existence of the atom.

He threw the holy water, jar and all, into the pit.

The goblins surged through the communion rail and up the steps toward the altar platform.

The kids screamed, and Father Walotsky held his rosary out in front of him as if certain it would render him impervious to the assault. Rebecca drew her gun, though she knew it was useless, took careful aim on the first of the pack.

And all one hundred of the goblins turned to clumps of earth which cascaded harmlessly down the altar steps.

The worm-thing swung its hateful head back toward Carver and hissed and struck at him.

He screamed.

Then gasped in surprise as nothing more than dirt showered over him.

The holy water disappeared into the pit.

The jubilant squeals, the roars of hatred, the triumphant screams all ceased as abruptly as if someone had pulled the plug on a stereo. The silence lasted only a second, and then the night was filled with cries of anger, rage, frustration and anguish.

The earth shook more violently than before.

Jack was knocked off his feet, but he fell backwards, away from the pit.

He saw that the rim had stopped dissolving. The hole wasn't getting any larger.

The mammoth appendage that towered over him, like some massive fairytale serpent, did not take a swipe at him as he had been afraid it might. Instead, its disgus-

344

ting mouth sucking ceaselessly at the night, it collapsed back into the pit.

Jack got to his feet again. His overcoat was caked with snow.

The earth continued to shake. He felt as if he were standing on an egg from which something deadly was about to hatch. Cracks radiated out from the pit, half a dozen of them – four, six, even eight inches wide and as much as ten feet long. Jack found himself between the two largest gaps, on an unstable island of rocking, heaving earth. The snow melted into the cracks, and light shone up from the strange depths, and heat rose in waves as if from an open furnace door, and for one ghastly moment it seemed as if the entire world would shatter underfoot. Then quickly, mercifully, the cracks closed up again, sealed tight, as if they had never been.

The light began to fade within the pit, changing from red to orange around the edges.

The hellish voices were fading, too.

The gates were easing shut.

With a flush of triumph, Jack inched closer to the rim, squinting into the hole, trying to see more of the monstrous and fantastic shapes that writhed and raged beyond the glare.

The light suddenly pulsed, grew brighter, startling him. The screaming and bellowing became louder.

He stepped back.

The light dimmed once more, then grew brighter again, dimmed, grew brighter. The immortal entities beyond the Gates were struggling to keep them open, to force them wide.

The rim of the pit began to dissolve again. Earth crumbled away in small clods. Then stopped. Then started. In spurts, the pit was still growing.

Jack's heart seemed to beat in concert with the crumbling of the pit's perimeter. Each time the dirt began to fall away, his heart seemed to stop; each time the perimeter stabilized, his heart began to beat again.

Maybe Carver Hampton had been wrong. Maybe holy water and the good intentions of a righteous man had not been sufficient to put an end to it. Perhaps it had gone too far. Perhaps nothing could prevent Armageddon now.

Two glossy black, segmented, whiplike appendages, each an inch in diameter, lashed up from the pit, snapped in front of Jack, snaked around him. One wound around his left leg from ankle to crotch. The other looped around his chest, spiralled down his left arm, curled around his wrist, snatched at his fingers. His leg was jerked out from under him. He fell, thrashing, flailing desperately at the attacker but to no avail; it had a steel grip; he couldn't free himself, couldn't pry it loose. The beast from which the tentacles sprouted was hidden far down in the pit, and now it tugged at him, dragged him toward the brink, a demonic fisherman reeling in its catch. A serrated spine ran the length of each tentacle, and the serrations were sharp; they didn't immediately cut through his clothes, but where they crossed the bare skin of his wrist and hand, they sliced open his flesh, cut deep.

He had never known such pain.

He was suddenly scared that he would never see Davey, Penny or Rebecca again.

He began to scream.

In St Patrick's Cathedral, Rebecca took two steps toward the piles of now-ordinary earth that had, only a moment ago, been living creatures, but she stopped short when the scattered dirt trembled with a current of impossible, perverse life. The stuff wasn't dead after all. The grains and clots and clumps of soil seemed to draw moisture from the air; the stuff became damp; the separate pieces in each loose pile began to quiver and strain and draw laboriously toward the others. This evilly enchanted earth was apparently trying to regain its forms, struggling to reconstitute the goblins. One small lump, lying apart from all the others, began to shape itself into a tiny, wickedly clawed foot.

'Die, damnit,' Rebecca said. '*Die!*'

Sprawled on the rim of the pit, certain that he was going to be pulled into it, his attention split between the void in front of him and the pain blazing in his savaged hand, Jack screamed—

—and at that same instant the tentacle around his arm and torso abruptly whipped free of him. The second demonic appendage slithered away from his left leg a moment later.

The hell-light dimmed.

Now, the beast below was wailing in pain and torment of its own. Its tentacles lashed erratically at the night above the pit.

In that moment of chaos and crisis, the gods of *Rada* must have visited a revelation upon Jack, for he knew – without understanding *how* he knew – that it was his blood that had made the beast recoil from him. In a confrontation with evil, perhaps the blood of a righteous man was (much like holy water) a substance with powerful magical qualities. And perhaps his blood could accomplish what holy water alone could not.

The rim of the pit began to crumble again. The hole grew wider. The Gates were again rolling open. The light rising out of the earth turned from orange to crimson once more.

Jack pushed up from his prone position and knelt at the brink. He could feel the earth slowly – and then not so slowly – coming apart beneath his knees. Blood was streaming off his torn hand, dripping from all five finger-tips. He leaned out precariously, over the pit, and shook his hand, flinging scarlet droplets into the centre of the seething light.

Below, the shrieking and keening swelled to an even more ear-splitting pitch than it had when he'd tossed the holy water into the breach. The light from the devil's furnace dimmed and flickered, and the perimeter of the pit stabilized.

He cast more of his blood into the chasm, and the tortured cries of the damned faded but only slightly. He blinked and squinted at the pulsing, shifting, mysteriously indefinable bottom of the hole, leaned out even farther to get a better look—

—and with a *whoosh* of blisteringly hot air, a huge face rose up toward him, ballooning out of the shimmering light, a face as big as a truck, filling most of the pit. It was the leering face of all evil. It was composed of slime and mould and rotting carcasses, a pebbled and cracked and lumpy and pock-marked face, dark and mottled, riddled with pustules, maggot-rich, with vile brown foam dripping from its ragged and decaying nostrils. Worms wriggled in its night-black eyes, and yet it could see, for Jack could feel the terrible weight of its hateful gaze. Its mouth broke open – a vicious, jagged slash large enough to swallow a man whole – and bile-green fluid drooled out. Its tongue was long and black and prickled with needle-sharp thorns that punctured and tore its own lips as it licked them.

Dizzied, dispirited, and weakened by the unbearable stench of death that rose from the gaping mouth, Jack shook his wounded hand above the apparition, and a rain of blood fell away from his weeping stigmata. 'Go away,' he told the thing, choking on the tomb-foul air. 'Leave. Go. *Now.*'

The face receded into the furnace glow as his blood fell upon it. In a moment it vanished into the bottom of the pit.

He heard a pathetic whimpering. He realized he was listening to himself.

And it wasn't over yet. Below, the multitude of voices became louder again, and the light grew brighter, and dirt began to fall away from the perimeter of the hole once more.

Sweating, gasping, squeezing his sphincter muscles

to keep his bowels from loosening in terror, Jack wanted to run away from the pit. He wanted to flee into the night, into the storm and the sheltering city. But he knew that was no solution. If he didn't stop it now, the pit would widen until it grew large enough to swallow him no matter where he hid.

With his uninjured right hand, he pulled and squeezed and clawed at the wounds in his left hand until they had opened farther, until his blood was flowing much faster. Fear had anaesthetized him; he no longer felt any pain. Like a Catholic priest swinging a sacred vessel to cast holy water or incense in a ritual of sanctification, he sprayed his blood into the yawning mouth of Hell.

The light dimmed somewhat but pulsed and struggled to maintain itself. Jack prayed for it to be extinguished, for if this did not do the trick, there was only one other course of action: He would have to sacrifice himself entirely; he would have to go down into the pit. And if he went down there . . . he knew he would never come back.

The last evil energy seemed to have drained out of the clumps of soil on the altar steps. The dirt had been still for a minute or more. With each passing second, it was increasingly difficult to believe that the stuff had ever really been alive.

At last Father Walotsky picked up a clod of earth and broke it between his fingers.

Penny and Davey stared in fascination. Then the girl turned to Rebecca and said, 'What happened?'

'I'm not sure,' she said. 'But I think your daddy accomplished what he set out to do. I think Lavelle is dead.' She looked out across the immense cathedral, as if Jack might come strolling in from the vestibule, and she said softly, 'I love you, Jack.'

The light faded from orange to yellow to blue.

Jack watched tensely, not quite daring to believe that it was finally finished.

A grating-creaking came out of the earth, as if enormous gates were swinging shut on rusted hinges. The faint cries rising from the pit had changed from expressions of rage and hatred and triumph to pitiful moans of despair.

Then the light was extinguished altogether.

The grating and creaking ceased.

The air no longer had a sulphurous stench.

No sounds at all came from the pit.

It wasn't a doorway any longer. Now, it was just a hole in the ground.

The night was still bitterly cold, but the storm seemed to be passing.

Jack cupped his wounded hand and packed it full of snow to slow the bleeding down now that he no longer *needed* blood. He was still too high on adrenalin to feel any pain.

The wind was barely blowing now, but to his surprise it brought a voice to him. Rebecca's voice. Unmistakable. And four words that he much wanted to hear: 'I love you, Jack.'

He turned, bewildered.

She was nowhere in sight, yet her voice seemed to have been at his ear.

He said, 'I love you, too,' and he knew that, wherever she was, she heard him as clearly as he had heard her.

The snow had slackened off. The flakes were no longer small and hard but big and fluffy, as they had been at the beginning of the storm. They fell lazily now, in wide, swooping spirals.

Jack turned away from the pit and went back into the house to call an ambulance for Carver Hampton.

We can embrace love; it's not too late.
Why do we sleep, instead, with hate?
Belief requires no suspension
to see that Hell is our invention.
We make Hell real; we stoke its fires.
And in its flames our hope expires.
Heaven, too, is merely our creation.
We can grant ourselves our own salvation.
All that's required is imagination.

—The Book of Counted Sorrows